THE
SNOW
GRAVES

BOOKS BY ROGER STELLJES

ROGER STELLJES

THE SNOW GRAVES

bookouture

Published by Bookouture in 2023

An imprint of Storyfire Ltd.
Carmelite House
50 Victoria Embankment
London EC4Y 0DZ

www.bookouture.com

ISBN: 978-1-83790-153-1
eBook ISBN: 978-1-83790-152-4

To Roger and Mary. I don't say it nearly often enough, but thank you for everything. My success is yours.

PROLOGUE

Wait here! Nico signed to his little sister Alisha.

He tiptoed his way in his stocking feet to the top of the basement steps. In the reflection of the windowpanes of the French doors to the dining room, he saw the black-leather panted legs and combat boots slowly making their way up the steps to the second floor. He took two soft steps into the kitchen and gently slipped the truck key fob from the hook and then soft-shoed back down the steps. At the bottom, he knelt to his nine-year-old sister, zipping up her worn light-pink coat. He signed: *We have to run to the truck.*

She nodded.

Nico opened the door, took Alisha's hand, and ran with her into the frigid morning.

Bap! Bap! Bap!

Nico's head snapped to look up. The shots were just above them. Rudick's bedroom.

He kept running, dragging Alisha through the backyard toward the left side of the garage.

Bap! Bap! Bap!

That was Tripp's room.

The shooter would be looking for him. Nico ran around the side of the garage, unlocking the truck. He hefted Alisha into the backseat. "Buckle up!"

He ran around and jumped in, spun the wheels in the gravel and raced away.

Bap! Bap! Bap! Bap! Bap! Bap!

Shots pelted the truck. He ducked as glass shattered behind him.

Looking back, he saw Alisha's eyes wide in fear. The cab's rear window was gone. Cold air flooded in, but Alisha wasn't hit.

He raced down the winding rutted gravel road, flying around the turns, fishtailing, struggling to stay on the road and then taking big air over a sudden drop. His body hurled forward and his forehead banged on the steering wheel.

He checked the rearview mirror. Clear.

Jolting over one last deep rut, the truck burst out of the dense woods and onto the H-4 highway.

Nico turned hard right, fishtailing across the road, falling in behind two cars, running side-by-side heading south toward Manchester Bay. He slammed the accelerator, passing the car in the left lane on the shoulder, coming within inches of it on his right side before zooming in front and then jerking back into the left lane, both cars' horns blaring behind him.

He turned to Alisha. "Hang on!"

A black blur coming around a bend behind them. An SUV, a half-mile back, coming fast.

He sped up, swerving through traffic as he passed the sign listing the three Manchester Bay exits. He looked back. The black SUV was coming, weaving its way through traffic, closing in on him.

Nico turned forward.

"Shit!"

He jammed the brakes with both feet, fishtailing again on

the road, slowing rapidly before he hit the back of another car. Now he was boxed in on the right by two vehicles, one a large pickup truck. The black SUV was almost to him now.

He pulled left onto the gravel shoulder again, shooting the narrow gap between the car and the guardrail, his left side scraping and rattling against the rails. He swerved back into the left lane and zoomed ahead. Looking back, the black SUV pulled the same move.

Nico jerked the wheel right, cutting horizontally across the lane in front of another car that jammed on its brakes. He drove down the steep embankment careening onto the exit lane, turning hard left and powering ahead. He looked back, the SUV doing the same.

At the bottom of the ramp, the stoplight turned red. He charged through it, turning hard left and zooming back under the highway. He looked back and saw the SUV stopped but that was momentary.

He drove up the hill to the university.

At the top there were people walking about, the campus starting to stir for the day. His heart still pounding and Alisha silent in the backseat, he turned left and then worked his way around the northside of the campus, along a quiet street, residential homes and apartments to the left, the campus to the right. He spotted a park bench along the sidewalk just south of the mall.

He quick parked, then ran around and hefted Alisha out and carried her to the bench, wiping the dirt and muck away before sitting her down.

He looked her in the eye, signing: *I need you to stay here.*

No! Alisha replied, shaking her head, her eyes filled with tears.

Stay here, he signed firmly before leaning in and giving her a hug. "I'll come back. I promise."

ONE

"WE SHOULDN'T BE HERE."

Three weeks earlier

"You need to play ball here, Reardon," Gresh pleaded. "Come on, man. This is serious. I was hoping inviting you here, we could work this out." He looked nervously to Waltripp, Nico and Gill, all there to help convey the message. But his friend Reardon Banz wasn't listening.

"I'm done with this deal, Ron. It's bullshit. I make half of what I was. Why would I continue? No offense, *boys*," Banz said acerbically, "but I can get my supply from the Twin Cities for the same price and make double what I am now."

"Come on," Gresh pleaded.

"Shit, Ron, what happened to competition?"

"You made a deal with us," Waltripp retorted, tightening the gloves on his hands.

"We deliver," Gill said. "You sell. That's the deal."

"Yeah, because that fat fuck, whatever his name was, stuck a gun in my face. You gonna shoot me in here?"

Waltripp snapped a quick heavy punch into Banz's jaw,

staggering him. "No, I'm not going to shoot you," he said, punching him in the stomach and then lifting his knee into his chin, sending him dazed to floor. "I'm just going to get rid of you."

"No!" Gresh cried. "Not in here."

Waltripp shoved the dazed man to the floor and jumped on top of him and grabbed Banz's windpipe in his gloved hands, squeezing.

Nico joined in, holding Banz's arms down. Gill grabbed his ankles while Waltripp continued to squeeze, pressing his thumbs, putting all his weight into it, strangling Banz, his eyes bulging, unable to fight back, held down by the three men. His eyes shifted to Gresh, as if to say help me. Gresh stood by, his eyes wide in their own fear, helpless to intervene.

Waltripp grunted as he tightened his hold on the man's throat, his arms trembling as he pressed. He felt the fight in Banz's body dissipate and then go still beneath him. He rolled off him.

"You had to do that here!" Gresh yelled.

"Shut up," Waltripp growled in a low voice. He looked to Gill, who went to the apartment door, peering out the eyehole. "Anything?"

"No."

"Damn, Tripp," Nico moaned. "Now what do we do?"

Buzz! Buzz! Buzz!

"Who is that?" Waltripp demanded.

"Shhh," Gresh said as he shuffled down the hallway to his bedroom where the lights were off. He snuck a peek around the side of the window shade. "You gotta be kidding me."

"Who is it?" Gill asked.

"Her," he replied, pointing to a picture on the wall.

* * *

"I'm nervous," Grace said.

"Don't be," Cam said confidently to his girlfriend as he parked his Jeep in the visitor slot at the back of the old red-and-brown brick three-story apartment building a half-mile north of campus. "I'm with you."

"Ron is—"

"Not going to be a problem," he replied confidently. "Ron is a would-be tough guy, not an actual tough guy."

"But the drugs."

"True, he might be high, which is all the more reason to get your stuff and be done with it."

"Still," Grace said, biting her bottom lip. "These things really aren't all that important."

"The Ansel Adams print? You told me you paid a couple hundred dollars for that."

"I know, but—"

"Come on," Cam said as he pushed open his truck door. He walked around the other side and opened Grace's door. They walked over to the building vestibule and Grace hit the button for unit 204.

There was no answer.

She hit the buzzer again but still no response. She stepped back and looked out from the vestibule up to the second-floor apartment. The curtains were pulled for the large picture window, but they could tell lights were on inside. Cam hit the buzzer again. There was no response.

"Huh."

"I don't think he's there."

"The light is on," he said.

"Yeah, but he could be down the hall."

"Or high out of his mind," Cam said derisively as he checked his watch. "We could wait here a few minutes, see if anyone comes in or leaves and we could get in."

"I don't know about that," Grace said. "Ron did that to me."

"So, turnabout is—"

"I'm not stooping to his level."

Cam smiled. "That's one of the things I like about you."

"What?"

"There's a right way and a wrong way," he said and checked his watch. "It's just after seven thirty. Let's go to the coffee shop for a bit. We can study and then we'll come back and try again later."

* * *

Ron peeked ever so slightly around the far edge of the shade. Grace and Cam got back into his black Jeep Cherokee. He hated that guy, although he didn't dare challenge him. He had several inches and pounds on him. "They're gone. Now what?"

"We wait. Transport is being arranged," Tripp said and looked to the floor. "We need your area rug."

* * *

"Your spring trip is to where again?" Grace asked. Spring break was two weeks away and they both had trips planned.

"Destin, in the Florida Panhandle," Cam said. "My room-mate's uncle is letting us rent his condo for the week. It's a couple of blocks from the ocean but he has a small swimming pool. Not as swanky as the place you're going. South Beach? Pretty nice."

"You need better friends," Grace said with a seductive smile, letting Cam massage her legs that were comfortably draped over his muscular thighs. She had mostly been on her phone while he worked through his Calculus II homework. She liked that he worked hard at school and was dedicated. "You could always come down and visit us."

"That's a *really* long drive," he said as he closed his laptop and then stuffed it in his backpack. "It would take like eight hours."

"But then you'd be able to see me in my swimsuit, the light blue one I bought." She pulled him down to her. "Then you could untie it," she said, before kissing him. "Besides, it would keep your eyes off any other girls in the greater Destin area."

They had been dating for a little over four months. She'd known him for about a year and they'd slowly become friends, living in the same apartment complex. After she broke up with Ron, she'd been rattled and wary. Cam came along as a safe friend, the two of them just hanging out and studying more frequently together and getting comfortable with one another. And then it was as if one day she was planning her schedule around his, had texted him several times and it dawned on her, I have a new boyfriend. *How did that happen?*

That had led her to the thought that if we're doing that, we might as well do the other fun stuff that comes with having a boyfriend. She made the first move in kissing him and then inviting him to spend the night.

Cam was serious about where he was going, yet easygoing and kind with a little fun rambunctiousness to him that came out at parties. She'd dated enough to know that they were still in the early love haze but at the same time, she really liked him. This time things felt different. And she sensed that he felt the same way. This was serious.

A barista came by their table. "We'll be closing in ten minutes."

They slowly packed up their things, finishing the last of their coffees. "Let's go try again," Cam suggested.

Grace sighed in reluctance. "Okay."

The drive took five minutes but as they pulled into the parking lot, there was a black van parked in the visitor space.

"There looks to be a space further down," Grace said, pointing to the left.

Cam pulled in and parked. He undid his seatbelt and looked back as he reached for the door handle and then halted. "Hold on," he said, reaching for her left arm. "Look."

They both looked back to see Ron holding open the back door. Two men came out carrying a large bulky roll, dashing quickly from the lighted vestibule to the van.

"That looks like a rug," Grace said. "He had an area rug in his bedroom."

"Is it really thick?" Cam asked, looking back to her.

"No, not really. Why?"

"Because that one looks awfully thick," Cam said as the two men shoved the roll into the back of the black van. The two men who'd carried the rug in turn got into the front of the van and quickly drove away. "This is... odd."

"I don't like this," Grace said. "We shouldn't be here."

"Duck down," Cam said, lowering himself in the seat, watching the van pass behind him in the rearview mirror. After the van passed, he looked to his left and saw Ron step back outside the vestibule. A black Cadillac Escalade pulled up in front of the rear door. He could see the driver and another man in the front seat and... still another man was in the backseat, although obscured.

Cam grabbed his phone.

"What are you doing? Don't take a photo."

"I'm taking a Note."

* * *

Ron slipped back inside the vestibule and watched as the Escalade pulled away. As he turned to go up the steps he stopped and looked back out into the parking lot.

Shit!

He rushed up the steps to his apartment and went to the picture window and peeked around the side of the curtain. The

black Jeep Cherokee backed out of the parking space and raced
away.

TWO

"THE QUESTION IS WHO ELSE YOU GOT."

Maggie Duncan stood behind her best friend Cathy, a black comb in her left hand and scissors in her right, working through the layers of her long black hair. "How was the date Saturday night?"

"It was... good."

Maggie stepped around. "It went well? You liked him?"

Cathy nodded and then let a sly smile out. "It went *very* well. I had a really nice time."

"Did you... you know?"

"No. No, no, no," Cathy replied with a hand wave. "I did... kiss him a little though."

"And how was that?"

"Oh God, I was so nervous, Mags. I mean I hadn't kissed anyone but Nate for twenty years. But... it was nice."

Maggie smiled. "I guess that means you'll be going out again?"

"Tomorrow night."

"Oh, it was *that* good? I'm so happy for you."

Cathy had just finalized her divorce. Living next door, Maggie had been there for her to lean on to get through first

Nate's affair, then the divorce, support and custody battle and finally the process of healing and building the confidence to restart life again. She was so proud that her friend was putting herself out there. Nobody deserved some good in her life more than Cathy.

"How is the job search coming?"

"I have an interview next Monday. Mannion Companies."

"Doing what?"

"Office assistant in operations."

"That sounds promising."

"It will feel odd to go back to work after all these years but I'm ready for it."

"Dating and working," Maggie said. "You're back living, my friend."

An hour later Maggie had finished styling Cathy's hair, organizing, and fluffing it with her fingers. "What do you think?"

"I think I'm going to look *awesome* tomorrow night."

"I'll tell you what. When you get ready, if you want any help, call me over. I'll give it a little extra flair for ya."

"I will."

A few minutes later, Maggie held the salon door open for Cathy. "Watch your step. I put out some salt earlier but there could still be some ice on the sidewalk."

"I will be. Gosh, I'm so looking forward to spring."

"It's been a long, really long, winter," Maggie replied, looking up at the dreary gray overcast sky, the temperature in the mid-twenties. The temps were starting to warm, but the snowpack, while beginning to thin, remained.

"Are you going to the state basketball tournament this weekend in Minneapolis?"

"Oh, I haven't decided yet. Some years I go, some I don't." Her husband Rob was a social studies teacher at Holmstrand High School and an assistant coach for the basketball team.

Her stepson Brian played on the team with Leo, Cathy's son. Rob and Brian were going down Friday to stay in a hotel and watch all the games. Maggie was on the fence. "Are you going?"

"Not this year. Leo is going down with another family."

"That leaves free time for going on a date then, doesn't it?"

"Stop it," Cathy said, with a dismissive wave, and smile.

Maggie closed the door, walked through her salon and into the kitchen and made herself a cup of tea. She took a sip of the Earl Grey and peered out the front picture window of their two-story Tudor-style brick and stucco house, glancing to see Cathy walking back up her own driveway next door in the fading daylight. It was nearly 4:30 p.m. The sun would only remain in the sky for another ninety minutes or so. She took another drink of her tea when her next appointment, Jenny Christiansen, came walking down the street. Maggie walked back through the house and to the salon.

"Hey there," Maggie greeted cheerily, letting Jenny in.

"Maggie, how are you?"

"I'm terrific."

"Business sure must be. It took me two weeks to get an appointment and I have a big in with the owner."

Maggie smiled. "It has sure been good lately. I'm as busy as I want to be anyway."

"Good for you, girl."

"Come on in and take a seat," Maggie said, guiding her to the beauty chair and then turning her to the mirror. "So, what have you got for me, Jen?"

"I brought this." It was a page cut out of a magazine.

Maggie examined the page. She'd cut Jenny's long, straight light-blonde Norwegian hair for years. This would not be the normal trim off two inches and color for her. She wanted to go from long straight blonde hair to a short pixie style. "You want to go this short?"

"Yes," Jenny said, smiling. "I've had this style for so long. It's tired. It's time for a change, something spicy and cute."

"This will be that, for sure." Maggie pulled on a black Maggie's Salon smock around Jenny and then stood behind her, the two of them looking in the mirror, soft rock music playing quietly through the overhead speakers. "I'll be taking off—" she put her hands two inches below Jenny's ears "—this much."

"Yes," she said, flashing an eager smile. "That's what I want. That and a color. My roots are... eek, graying, Mag. I'm going gray."

"Jen, that happens to the best of us."

* * *

"I lost them," Gill said, leaning forward, peering ahead after they came around the bend and into downtown Holmstrand. They'd been tracking the pair since sunup, but this was the first time all day they were away from the campus and crowds. "It's dark. Hard to see."

"I see it," Nico said. "He's four vehicles ahead. Close up on him. It's dark, I don't want to lose them in this neighborhood."

"Got it," Gill said.

Nico looked to the backseat. "You good to go?"

"Just need a look."

"He's turning right." Gill sped up and took the same turn, now only a block behind as they drove into a residential neighborhood. The Cherokee took a left and then a quick right, pulling into a driveway.

"It's dark. I don't see anybody outside," Gill said.

Nico looked to the backseat. "What do you think?"

* * *

"Leo," Cam greeted his cousin with a wave as he came along the front sidewalk.

"Cam, Gracie," Leo greeted as he stepped onto the front stoop. "Right on time. Dinner is ready. Mom made spaghetti."

"Excellent!" Cam exclaimed.

"Sounds great," Grace said.

* * *

They pulled down their ski masks. Gill lowered the rear passenger window.

"Go!" Nico said. "Now!"

* * *

"How does that look?" Maggie asked, standing behind Jenny, having turned the chair around to the mirror.

"Oh, Maggie, I like it. I love how it—"

Boom! Boom! Boom! Boom! Boom! Boom!

"Get down!" Maggie said, grabbing Jenny from the barber chair to the floor, the shots continuing.

"Were those—"

"Gunshots. Yeah," Maggie said as she crawled over to the back door, the shots having stopped.

A vehicle roared away.

Then an eerie, still silence.

Maggie closed her eyes and waited for it.

"*Nooooo!*"

* * *

"Get us out of here! Go! Go!" Nico yelled.

Gill raced past the houses and turned hard left. They were heading back to the main street of town.

"Turn right," Nico ordered and then looked to the back. "Did you get them both?"

"Oh yeah."

"The question is who else you got. I saw two others."

"Don't care nothin' bout that."

* * *

Maggie grabbed a stack of light-blue towels off the counter. "Come on," she said as she opened the door.

"Maggie?" Jenny said warily.

"The shooting is done."

A voice outside bellowed: "*Oh my God, Leo! LEO!*"

"That's Cathy!" Jenny exclaimed, catching up.

Maggie skip-shuffled quickly along the walkway on the side of her house until she could see the front of Cathy's house. Jenny was right behind her. There were two bodies lying on the sidewalk. Another body looked to be on the top step. "Oh God, no," Maggie exclaimed as she high kneed with her long legs through the snow-covered yard. "Come on! Come on!"

Neighbors were warily coming out onto their front steps.

"Call 911!" Maggie yelled repeatedly as she rushed through the yard.

On the front sidewalk to Cathy's house, her nephew Cameron lay motionless, his eyes wide open. She crouched and quick checked for a pulse, but he was already gone. A girl was lying face down against the bottom of the steps. On the top step, Cathy's son Leo was lying sideways in the entryway, propped up against the front door frame, his chest bloodied.

Maggie rolled the girl over. She was conscious, barely. She was wounded in two places, blood oozing out of her chest, her breathing labored, her eyes slits. She pressed a towel to one wound to her left chest and then another to her abdomen. "Jenny, press on these, hard! Talk to her. Keep her conscious."

"O-o-okay." Jenny pressed on the towels as other neighbors were running to the scene now. "It's going to be okay. It's going to be okay."

Maggie jumped up to the top step. Leo was hit twice that she could see, once in the upper left chest and then once on the inside of his right thigh, just above his knee. His body was trembling, and his left leg was twitching uncontrollably. He gasped for air, his eyes wide, looking to his mother.

"Maggie?" Cathy wailed.

"Leo! Leo!" Maggie called to him as she examined the wounds. "Stay with me, Leo."

Leo groaned, his body trembling.

A siren was audible in the distance.

She put the last towel on the wound to Leo's upper chest. "Cathy? *Cathy!* Hold this towel on the wound. Apply pressure. Hold it tight. *Tight!*"

"O-o-okay," Cathy said, tears streaking down her face.

Maggie examined the thigh wound again. It was bleeding profusely, maybe the femoral artery. She undid Leo's belt and yanked it from his pant loops. She wrapped it around his leg above the wound. Then she took off her apron, wrapped that around the leg too and with the belt, made a tourniquet. She looked up to see Cathy applying pressure to the chest wound.

"Keep talking to him, Cath. Talk to him."

"Leo. Hey, honey, it's going to be okay..."

* * *

How?

That was the singular thought that ran through Maggie's mind as she held a now lukewarm cup of tea in both her hands and stared blankly out the front window of her home. Her hands and clothes were caked in dried blood.

The police and then paramedics arrived at Cathy's, but it

was too late. Despite her efforts to stem the bleeding, Leo Randall died on his front stoop in his mother's arms.

Cameron Jensen lay dead on the sidewalk along with his girlfriend, Grace, despite Jenny's best efforts to help.

Rob stood solemnly behind her, his long wiry arms wrapped gently around her waist, her head resting just under his chin. The cool night air of the normally sleepy neighborhood now illuminated with the bright blue, yellow and reds of flashing police lights.

For Rob, a teacher, coach, and a man of faith, it was horrific and impossible to believe. *How could this happen here? In our little neighborhood and town where nothing bad ever happened?*

Maggie closed her eyes and let out a small sigh. For her, it had been a long time, but the scene and sounds of it were all too familiar.

THREE

"THAT'S WHEN IT GOT WEIRD."

"A drive-by shooting? In Holmstrand? I can't... fathom it," Tori murmured as Braddock drove into the southern edge of Holmstrand, lights and siren blaring. "When I was a kid, nothing bad ever happened here. It defines sleepy small town."

"'The times they are a-changin'," Braddock said, quoting Minnesota's own, Bob Dylan. "And not for the better."

Holmstrand was eight miles north of Manchester Bay up the H-4, perched on the far northeast end of the Northern Pine lakes chain. A small, quiet but growing town of just over 4,000 residents, it was historically known for its kitschy shopping district and Nordic architecture. In the summer there were the Wednesday afternoon turtle races that drew little kids from all over lakes county. In the last decade, as Manchester Bay grew rapidly, some of it had spilled over to Holmstrand. Now the quaint shops were intermixed with restaurants and local breweries. It was becoming a trendy place to go to dinner for the locals in Manchester Bay, let alone the cabin goers that flooded the area all summer long.

"Did you talk to Boe?" Tori asked.

Janette Boe, the new Shepard County Sheriff, had been on the job two months.

"Just for a minute. She's at a fundraiser up in Crosslake," Braddock said. "She's making her way over."

"Fundraiser?"

"This job is a stepping stone," Braddock said. "She has higher aspirations for higher office."

Braddock turned off the main street three blocks east and then was waved through by a Holmstrand police patrol officer. He parked. Tori swept her shoulder length hair behind her ears, before pulling on a black-wool stocking cap and zipping up her black puffer coat over her white hoodie. Braddock pulled on his thick winter gloves.

"I left New York City to get away from this shit," he murmured.

"That's not why you left," Tori said, reaching for the door handle. "Nor why I left."

"Yeah, yeah, yeah," he replied. "But I sure as hell never expected I'd have to deal with this here. Did you?"

Tori closed her eyes and sighed. "No."

The house was a quaint gray two-story with white shutters set back twenty yards from the street. They slowly walked up the cement driveway, taking in the sad scene as a frigid northwest wind drifted in.

The entire area around the house and into the street had been cordoned off. One body lay on the sidewalk just left of the front steps, another at the bottom of the front steps and a third just inside the entryway to the house, all covered by black sheets. Forensic scientists bustled about, taking photographs, and marking evidence.

Steak approached.

"What's the story?" Braddock asked.

"Three dead." Steak turned and gestured to the sidewalk. "Under the sheet on the sidewalk is Cameron Jensen, aged twenty-one. Student at Central Minnesota State University. At the base of the steps is his girlfriend, Grace Horn, also a student at the university, same age. The third lying in the entryway is Leo Randall, age seventeen, a junior at Holmstrand High School. This is his home. From what I've learned, Cameron Jensen is his cousin. Grace the cousin's girlfriend. They were here for dinner."

"Any witnesses?" Braddock said, crouching and lifting the sheet over Jensen to take a look.

"Leo's mother, Cathy Randall. She witnessed it. She's at a neighbor's house down the street now."

"She saw her son shot and killed?"

Steak nodded.

"Brutal," Tori moaned. "Husband?"

"They're divorced," Steak said. "The father was out of town on a sales trip. He's making his way back."

"Has anyone talked to Cathy Randall?" Braddock asked as he moved to examine Grace Horn.

"A patrol officer did, briefly. He didn't get much. She was distraught."

"What did he get?" Tori asked as she crouched on the front step in front of Leo Randall.

"Just after six thirty or so, Jensen and Horn get here. Leo is in the doorway, greeting them both. Horn is at the base of the steps, Jensen on the sidewalk. A vehicle, maybe a gray or bluish SUV, rolls by the house and opens fire. We don't have a handle yet on how many shots were fired but at least eleven that we can visually account for. Jensen was hit three times, Randall and Horn twice each and I see two holes in the house's siding to the left of the front door and two more in the sheetrock in the entryway."

"Anyone else see what happened?"

"No. Only the mother. She... saw it. The next-door neighbor, Maggie Duncan, and her salon customer heard it."

"Salon? Beauty salon?"

"Yeah, the neighbor runs it out of the back of the house," Steak explained. "Duncan and her customer named—" he checked his notebook "—Jenny Christiansen, heard the gunshots, an engine roar away and then they heard Cathy Randall scream. They both rushed over and tried to give aid but to no avail. All three were dead when the paramedics got here."

Braddock and Tori stopped at the neighbor's house. Maggie Duncan was still in her bloody clothes, sitting at the table in her kitchen with her husband, Rob. She grasped a wet kitchen rag in her hand, trying to scrub away the blood.

"I was in the back, in the salon with Jenny, finishing up her hair when I heard the gunshots," Maggie recalled, her voice not wavering. "I'm not sure how many shots, but they were in rapid succession. Jenny and I waited a moment and then we ran over and tried to help but all of them were hit so badly."

"Have you seen anyone around your neighborhood the last few days that raised any suspicion?" Braddock asked. "The odd vehicle loitering around?"

"No. Not that I noticed anyway. You, Rob?"

"No. I mean, this is a tight-knit neighborhood," Rob Duncan said. "We're all friends. We have an active text string amongst all the neighbors, and if anyone sees anything unusual, it gets sent out, but nobody has shared anything lately."

"Are you close with Cathy Randall?"

"Maggie is," Rob said. "She and Cathy are best friends really."

Maggie let out a long sigh. "Cath has been through so much the last couple of years with her divorce and all. Now to lose Leo..." She shook her head.

"Are you aware of any issues that Leo Randall might have been having?" Braddock asked.

"No, my gosh, he couldn't be a nicer boy," Maggie said. "He's... he was..." She wiped away a tear. "He was good friends with our kids."

"I teach and coach at the high school," Rob Duncan said. "I coached Leo in basketball. It's a small school. If he had a problem of this magnitude, I'd have known."

"Did you know Cameron Jensen at all?"

"No, not really. I mean, we've both seen him come to the house, but I didn't know him," Maggie said. "I just can't... what Cathy is going to be going through... What is wrong with people! A drive-by shooting? Here?"

Braddock and Tori walked down the street to the Christiansen house. A Holmstrand patrol officer Braddock knew greeted them at the front steps.

"How is it in there?" Braddock asked.

The officer shook his head. "She saw her only child gunned down in front of her, along with her nephew. How good will she ever be? How do you ever unsee that?"

"You don't," Tori said.

"You have your ear to the street. Has there been anything percolating around here?" Braddock asked the officer.

"That led to something like this?" the officer asked. "Hell no. I can't believe this. Will, you know our town, you too, Tori. Our biggest issue now is thieves getting into cabins closed for the season or stealing boats. Not this... shit."

They found Cathy Randall in the back of the house, sitting catatonic on a couch with her friend Jenny.

Braddock let Tori take the lead. She took a chair to the side of the couch and made the introductions. "I'm so sorry for your loss. We all are."

Cathy nodded.

"I know... this is difficult," Tori started. "Can you tell me what you saw?"

Cathy sniffled and wiped her nose with a tissue. "Leo and I were getting dinner ready. Cam is my nephew and he and Grace were coming up for dinner. They arrived and Leo went to greet them. I was in the hallway between the kitchen and front door. Leo opened the door and stepped outside. Next thing shots rattled all around. Leo went down and I saw a SUV race away. I went to Leo and then saw Grace and Cam..." Her voice drifted off and her friend Jenny put her arm around her.

Tori gave her a moment to recompose herself. "Can you describe the SUV?"

"Um..." She sniffed. "It was gray or light blue, I think."

"Did you notice the make or model?"

"No."

"Did you see the shooter or shooters?"

"No. It was dark. I just saw it race away. I just couldn't... believe... what had happened."

Tori nodded. "Can you think of why anyone would want to shoot your son or Cam or Grace?"

Cathy shook her head. "No."

"Did Leo have any issues at school you're aware of?"

"No. None."

"And how long had he been home tonight?"

"Since school ended. He was home at four thirty when I got back from having my hair done at Maggie's. I did send him to the market for milk."

"And that was when?"

"Four forty-five, five o'clock, somewhere in there. He was gone like fifteen minutes and back. It was an hour or so later that Cam and Grace arrived."

Tori pulled out their business cards and wrote her and Braddock's cell phone numbers on the back. "Call if you think of anything," Tori said and then reached for Cathy Randall's hand. "Or call just if you need to talk."

The two of them made a beeline back to the Randall house. "This isn't about Leo, is it?" Braddock said.

"I'd bet my pension it's not."

Steak saw them walking purposefully.

"This isn't about Leo Randall. He was home for hours before the shooting," Braddock said.

"Whereas Jensen and Horn drove up here from the university," Tori continued. "They parked in the driveway, take the long sidewalk up to the house."

Braddock picked up the thread. "The shooter or shooters tailed them up here and when they're walking up the sidewalk, they saw their chance."

Tori looked out to the street and visualized it. "They come around the corner, roll by the front of the house, slow down and—"

"Boom," Steak said, seeing it now.

"Jensen and Horn are the targets and Leo was just… unlucky. He was lined up with them in this five-foot wide shooting box," Tori said, standing in the doorway now. "The shooter or shooters come by and let it rip. These three lined up almost in a row. With a steady enough hand, they couldn't help but hit them all."

"This was a hit," Braddock said as Tori carefully stepped up onto the front landing.

"What the hell did these kids do?" Steak muttered.

Tori gestured at the doorbell. "Steak, this is one of those video doorbells. These things record right?"

"Yeah, most do but only when they're triggered."

"And they're triggered by motion. Like someone walking up the sidewalk, right?"

"Yes."

"Let's see what it recorded."

Twenty minutes later, after running back down to Cathy Randall and accessing the doorbell app, they transferred the video to a laptop computer. Steak pressed play.

The video started with the glow of a bright light off to the right.

"The headlights for the Jeep I imagine," Braddock mused quietly. "The driveway is to that side."

A few moments later, Grace Horn came into view from the right, followed by Cameron Jensen. Then the back right side of Leo Randall was visible as he stepped out onto the stoop.

A vehicle zoomed into the background, a light-colored SUV with its headlights turned off.

Rapid muzzle flashes filled the screen.

"Whoa!" Steak muttered.

"My God," Tori murmured.

Horn, Jensen and then Randall immediately collapsed to the ground. The SUV raced away in an instant.

"Run it again," Braddock ordered.

"There it comes," Steak gestured, freezing the frame at the first muzzle flash. "Shooter is in the backseat."

"So at least a driver," Braddock said. "And I bet a spotter in the front seat too. Three people."

"Can we make out anything about that SUV?" Tori asked.

"It's... a light color, maybe gray if Cathy Randall's recall is on the mark. But I can't tell the model." They ran the video back several times but the three of them couldn't tell what kind of SUV it was. They could only really see the bottom half and couldn't see the shooter, only the muzzle flashes.

Steak ran it back one more time. Braddock froze the screen. "There! You can kind of see our shooter." It was a side view. "He turns his head right there. He's wearing a light-colored hoodie."

"That doesn't tell us much," Steak muttered. "We can't see his face. We can't put an alert out for someone in a light-colored hoodie."

"Maybe the forensics people can wash this, lighten it and get more out of it," Tori suggested. "What next?" she asked Braddock.

"We need to go see Cameron Jensen's parents."

Braddock drove north from Holmstrand to Pequot Lakes, the next town north on the H-4. Cathy Randall had called her sister after the shooting, which had triggered Steak to call the chief of police in Pequot Lakes with the request to keep the Jensen's at home rather than coming to the scene. The chief met them outside before leading them inside to find the Jensen's surrounded by friends and neighbors. Braddock introduced himself.

"I'm Tori Hunter," Tori said as she took a chair next to Mrs. Jensen. "I'm an investigator with the sheriff's department."

"I've heard of you," Karin Jensen said.

Tori nodded and leaned forward, solemn. "I'm just so sorry for your loss. Just so sorry."

"What happened to our son?"

"It's very early in the investigation, but here is what we think we know so far."

For the second time tonight, Braddock watched in both appreciation and quiet admiration as Tori took the lead in speaking with a grieving family. At the police academy they teach you those five key words: "I'm sorry for your loss." He'd observed veteran officers and partners convey those very words and thought he'd developed a way of communicating such terrible news with a measure of sympathy and grace.

Then when he watched Tori do it for the first time many months ago, he quickly realized that while he'd learned how to communicate, he hadn't learned to relate. That's what Tori could do, better than anyone he'd ever seen. In those worst moments for a family, she had such a gracious and compassionate way of speaking and connecting. He knew it was born of her own tragic experiences. She understood what families were going through. He'd seen distraught families come to understand that Tori was with them, find comfort in her words and trust that she would do all she could to seek answers for them.

For ten minutes, Tori didn't so much ask questions as converse with the Jensens, about Cameron and how proud his parents were of him. It was devastating yet also cathartic for them to speak about him that way, in the past tense, but with the pride only a parent could have. And he knew from that Tori would glean not only information, but motivation as well.

"What was Cam's life like these days? He went to the university?"

"He loved it over there. He was living just off campus with friends. He was just a normal college student," Karin explained.

The Jensen's were unaware of any issues Cam had with anyone, despite Tori's probing of the topic. "He wasn't the kind to go looking for trouble, yet he seemed more than capable of handling any trouble that came along," David Jensen said.

"What do you mean by that?" Tori asked.

"Oh, just that he could handle himself. He was solidly built yet had a good head on his shoulders. Cam was studying to be an engineer. He was analytical and not prone to rash decisions. And he was happy about Grace. I could tell he really liked her, and she liked him. Things were—" David Jensen's lip started to tremble "—really... coming together for him."

"I liked Grace too," Karin said, dabbing at her eyes before looking to Tori. "But I know she had issues with an old boyfriend. He was bad news. Cam told me about it."

"Issues?"

"Cam told me one time that he was threatening her. She

had told Cam that the boy got into drugs. That's why she broke up with him. She was afraid of him, although Cam said he knew this guy and didn't seem to think he was that much of a danger."

"Do you have a name?"

"No, I can't... remember it. I'm sure Cam or Grace's roommates would know it. Or her parents."

Grace Horn had lived in an apartment building a block off the campus for Central Minnesota State University. It was apparent that word of the shooting had quickly spread through campus. Tori, who taught classes at the university, had received calls and texts from professors looking for information.

Horn's roommate Kristy let them inside their apartment. It was crowded with other classmates who were there in support. After Tori and Braddock introduced themselves, they asked some basic questions, getting background on Grace.

Tori took a seat next to Kristy and asked, "Before Grace started dating Cam Jensen, did she have an old boyfriend?"

"Yes."

"What was his name?"

"Ron, Ron Gresh. They dated last year and through the summer but then she broke up with him at the start of fall semester. Did he do this?"

Kristy went there quick.

"Why would you say that?" Tori asked neutrally. "Did Ron cause her some trouble?"

Kristy nodded. "Yes."

"What kind?"

"He started doing and then dealing drugs."

"What kind of drugs?"

"Pot at first last year, but lots of people do that. That was no big deal, but then he turned darker. One night he came to our apartment when school started, and he had a gun and heroin and meth with him. He tried to get Grace to do it with him. She said no and then broke it off right then and there. She kicked him out."

"How did he take that?"

"Not well," Kristy said. "For a while he wouldn't take no for an answer. He kept showing up here, but she wouldn't buzz him in. One time, he slipped in when someone left the building and was up here pounding on our door. He called her constantly. One night he accosted her in our parking lot and had her pinned up against his car until others saw him and he fled."

"Did she report him to the police or campus security?"

"To campus security, yes, but by that point he'd withdrawn from the university. After that incident he didn't show up here again. It was a tough couple of months but then Cam came along."

"And that was going well?"

"Yes," Kristy said. "She really liked him. He was stable and focused on school. And he was... a bigger guy. He used to play football. I think he made her feel safe."

"You asked if Ron did this. Do you think he would have been capable of something like this?" Tori asked.

Kristy thought for a moment. "He scared her, but Cam wasn't fazed, which I think made Grace feel a bit better about things. Cam thought Ron was a wannabe thug going through a phase. Grace had some things at Ron's apartment across town. She was afraid to go and get them from him, but Cam was like, let's go and get it over with."

"Do you know, did they ever do that?" Braddock asked.

"Yes," Kristy said. "Last night."

"Last night?" Tori replied, letting her eyes slide to Braddock.

"And what happened?" he asked.

"Grace was kind of spooked about it," Kristy said.

"Why?"

"All she would say is she and Cam saw something... odd."

"What?"

"They went there earlier in the night and said they walked right up and hit the buzzer for his apartment but there was no answer. It was odd, though."

"Odd how?" Tori asked.

"Grace said the light was on in the apartment, but nobody responded. They went to a coffee shop for a few hours and then went back later, after the coffee shop closed. And that's when it got weird."

"How so?"

"Grace said they parked and were going to get out of the car when they saw Ron and some others haul a carpet out the back door of the apartment building and put it into a van that immediately drove away. After that, an SUV drove up and Ron talked to someone in it for a minute before he went back inside."

"After they saw this, did they then go see Ron? Get Grace's things?" Tori asked.

"No. They left without seeing him. I think they were both spooked by it. Like they saw something maybe they weren't supposed to."

"And you said a... carpet?" Braddock asked, his eyes shifting to Tori.

"Yeah, like an area rug, but it was... bulky, Grace said."

"Bulky, how?" Tori pressed. "Did she say more?"

"No, but she was kind of freaked out about it."

"What you're describing, Kristy," Braddock stated. "Sounds like maybe they thought a body might be rolled up in that rug."

Kristy nodded. "They both said... something like that. Grace was worried it might have been Brandon."

"Who's Brandon?"

"Ron's roommate. He's a really good guy but Grace said he was having problems with Ron and what he was doing. He was just trying to make it through the school year because they had leased the apartment together. But then Grace texted me earlier today that she'd seen Brandon on campus." Kristy pulled out her phone and showed them the text, which read: *Saw Brandon. TG.*

"Did Grace, or Cam talk about going to the police?"

Kristy sighed. "I told them they should."

"But?"

"Grace was reluctant. She didn't want to cause Ron any trouble." She looked to Tori. "They should have gone to you, shouldn't they?"

FOUR

"WHY BE SO CAREFUL AND THEN TAKE SUCH A RISK?"

Janette Boe fussed with the tie for her sheriff's uniform when Tori and Braddock walked in.

Tall and angular with short straight blonde hair, high cheekbones and icy blue eyes, she and her husband had returned to Manchester Bay a year ago after both retired from the U.S. Marshals Service. While her husband took a position overseeing security at the Mannion Companies, she'd been contemplating a run for the state legislature when she was asked to complete the remaining two years of her predecessor Cal Lund's term as sheriff.

Thus far, she'd made a reasonably good impression on Braddock. She had a law enforcement background and was smart enough to realize when to let good people do their jobs. She also had political aspirations. So, while Braddock liked her, he was wary that any decision of import she made was run through the prism of what impact would this have on her political future. As he'd mentioned to Tori more than once, "If you're so focused on the next job, you forget to do the one you have."

"What do we know so far?" Boe asked.

"We have a possible suspect," Braddock replied, explaining

Ron Gresh. "The roommate went there without any prompting from us. Said he was using and dealing drugs and had something of a violent streak to him."

"Using and dealing?" Boe asked, eyebrows raised.

"Yeah. Grace Horn broke it off with Gresh when he escalated his use from marijuana to heroin, had a gun and started dealing, at least according to the roommate. That was at the very beginning of the school year over at the university. He did not take the breakup lying down." He gave her the background on Gresh's stalking of Grace, getting inside the apartment and the parking lot confrontation. "A few months later she started dating Jensen."

"She moved on," Boe said. "He didn't?"

"Maybe not. Fast forward to last night. Horn still had some things at Gresh's apartment that she wanted back but had been afraid to go get them from him. Jensen wasn't so afraid and said he'd go with her. The roommate says that Jensen and Horn went to his apartment last night to retrieve the items but instead, saw something odd."

"Odd?"

"A body wrapped in a rug," Tori blurted. "I'm jumping to conclusions, but that's what it sounds like." She provided a fuller description. "It could have just been a rug, but... then there was tonight."

"Assume it was a body, do we have any idea *who* that could have been?" Boe said.

"No, not yet," Braddock said. "Grace's roommate said they were worried it was Gresh's roommate, but they saw him on campus today, so he was safe. We don't know if it was a body or not but... like Tori said, tonight happened. So, it could be that it was a body, and that's the issue, or it could be Gresh saw her with Jensen and snapped. Either way, we need to find him."

"Interesting," Boe said and then looked to Braddock. "You

mentioned drugs. If it was a body, any chance it's tied into what you've already been digging in on?"

For the better part of five months, he and Steak had off and on been investigating the disappearance of local drug dealers. No dead bodies had been found, but three drug dealers had disappeared with no evidence that they had done so voluntarily, according to friends and family members. They had vanished.

Steak and the narcotics unit's theory was that someone was making a move on the local drug trade, but the who remained elusive. They had few leads. Steak was working his local sources but was coming up empty. Nevertheless, Boe had suggested something that had been percolating in Braddock's own mind throughout the night.

"That thought popped into my head briefly earlier, but what gives me pause is these three kids don't seem to have been involved in that world at all."

"Horn was," Tori said. "At least tangentially because of Gresh."

"Is Gresh part of that drug circuit you're investigating? Could the body in the carpet be another dealer?" Boe hypothesized. "And Gresh and whoever else those two kids saw last night are part of all that? Hardly a leap of logic to suggest a drive-by shooting has a connection to the drug trade."

Braddock looked to Tori who shrugged as if to say anything is possible.

"You'd have to ask yourself, under that theory, why you'd be so careful as to make these other dealers disappear without a trace but tonight you engage in a very public drive-by shooting," Tori said. "Why be so careful and then take such a risk?"

"It's incongruous," Boe said. "But—"

"It's not the worst thought I've heard tonight," Braddock said. "If Horn and Jensen saw something last night they weren't supposed to, then they had to be dealt with quickly before they talked."

"That's one way to make sense of it all," Tori said.

"I'm speaking with the media shortly," Boe said as she checked her uniform again in the mirror. She didn't say it with glee, but she didn't sound disappointed either. "What's next?"

"Gresh's apartment. It's being watched now. We're not going in tame."

FIVE

"ILLINOIS."

Braddock and Tori were parked two blocks from the apartment building when Steak and Eggleston pulled up.

"Who the hell is this guy?" Steak asked.

"An angry ex-boyfriend," Tori quipped as she pulled on her Kevlar vest.

"Seriously?" Eggleston asked.

"Could be," Braddock replied and gave them the quick rundown. "He's worth a good look. Gear up. If he is our guy, he mowed down three people tonight and he won't hesitate to throw down on us."

Two Manchester Bay patrol officers were awaiting their arrival, along with the landlord. Gresh's apartment was in a long unit situated along the north backside of the property. Braddock, Tori and one officer entered from the front, Steak, Eggs and the other uniformed officer from the rear and they all made their way up to the second floor and stacked up. His back against the wall left of the door, Braddock pounded on the door. "Police! Open up!"

They heard the deadlock flip open. A young man in sweatpants with fatigued hair—not Ron Gresh—opened the door and his eyes immediately widened and he jumped back. "Whoa!"

Braddock yanked the man into the hallway, spun him around and pushed him against the wall and quickly frisked him.

"What the heck?" the man said, while Tori stared him down. "What is thi—"

Braddock finished and spun him around. "Stand."

"Yes, sir."

The patrol officers, followed by Steak and Eggleston had rushed inside. From the hallway they heard a series of, "Clears!"

"Nobody else here," Steak said, peeking around the corner. "We'll start poking around."

Other apartment tenants peered out into the hallway.

"Go back inside," Tori ordered. "Nothing to worry about."

Braddock stepped to the man they'd pulled into the hallway. "Your name?"

"Brandon Olson."

"Where is Ron Gresh?"

"I-I-I don't know."

"Have you seen him tonight?"

"No," Brandon replied, nervously shaking his head.

"You know where he is, Brandon?"

"No, sir. I-I-I go out of my way not to know what he's up to these days. Why?"

"Because Grace Horn and Cam Jensen were two of the three people murdered in a drive-by shooting tonight up in Holmstrand."

Brandon's jaw dropped. "Ah, man. No, no, no, not Gracie."

"Call him, right now," Braddock ordered and followed Brandon into the apartment.

"O-o-okay," Brandon replied, his hands shaking. "I'll give it a try."

While Braddock tended to Brandon, Tori explored. Down the hallway, the first bedroom on the right was Brandon's. His laptop was powered up, a textbook open and a small desk lamp on. The small room itself was relatively clean and organized, other than the overflowing pile of clothes preventing the closet door from shutting.

Gresh's room was at the end of the hall and was a far more instructive mess. The room smelled faintly of marijuana, and amongst the empty energy drink and soda cans on the cluttered nightstand, she found a neon glass bong and the two smaller one hitter pipes. But that wasn't what drew her attention.

"Braddock!"

Braddock padded down the hallway. "Yeah?" He walked in the room. "Oh... hey, now that's a little on the creepy side."

On the wall to the left of the bed was a mass of photos, a veritable picture shrine to Grace Horn. There were rings of small photos massed around a larger one. There were a few photos of her with Gresh, some intimate photos where she was wearing little to nothing, others of her in various locations.

"It appears reports of his fixation with her are accurate," Tori murmured as she examined the array. "Look at these photos." She gestured to four on the left side. "She wasn't posing for those. He took them from a distance, probably when he was stalking her."

"Brandon called. He isn't answering," Braddock said and then left the room, dragging Brandon back. "How long has this shit been on his wall?"

"Uh... I don't know," he replied.

"I ain't buying that."

"Hey, his room is his room. My room is my room. I don't step foot in here. Especially these days."

"Bullshit," Braddock said, leaning in.

Brandon cowered a little but answered. "Dude's changed, sir. I'm telling you. I was on the same dorm floor with him freshman year two years ago and rented this place with him last year and he was cool. Fun to hang and party with, although he started to hit the pot a little too much, but lots of people do that. He stayed up here all last summer while I went home to Sioux Falls. When I got back in the fall, he wasn't the same guy. And it got worse through the fall semester."

"Worse how?"

"More drugs. His appearance was changing. He was... dark, his eyes, his demeanor. When I came back from winter break, he was even worse. I started getting nervous being around him, so did my girlfriend. One night he pulled a switchblade."

"On you?"

"No. Just to make a show of cutting an apple but still..." Brandon said. "At first, I thought it was posturing. Like he wanted me to see him as some tough guy. But then I sensed he was into some things I wanted nothing to do with. I've spent as many nights at my girlfriend's apartment as I can because it's not a good scene around him."

"Drugs?"

"Yeah."

"Is he dealing?" Braddock asked.

Brandon nodded.

"Just that or more?"

"It seemed like more with the people he brought around. He was running with a different crowd."

"Different how?"

"They weren't students. They were older, rougher, carrying guns. Ron had a gun up in here about a month ago and I said no eff'n way. I wanted nothing to do with it. Neither did Grace. She bailed on his ass right quick when she saw him in the fall. And he didn't finish the fall semester in school. Told me he was unsure about school and wanted to work."

"Who is he working for?"

"I don't know, he never said, and I never asked, but whoever it is, I don't think they pay by check and issue a W-2."

Tori tugged open a desk drawer with her gloved right hand and found two rolls of cash bound with rubber bands. She picked out the rolls and held them up.

"My point. He pays me cash and I pay the rent and utilities. Other than that, we aren't talking these days. I'm just trying to get through to the end of the year."

"When did you last see him?"

"It's been since Friday."

"Were you here last night?"

"No. Tonight's the first night I've been here since Friday. I've been at my girlfriend's."

"And you didn't know anything about this... shrine here?" Tori asked.

"No. But when Grace dumped him, he didn't take it well. He was angry."

"Angry enough to shoot three people?"

"I don't know," Brandon said, shaking his head. "I don't know. I don't know if he has that... in him."

"Would you be shocked if he did?"

"At this point—" Brandon shook his head again "—probably not."

She shifted her gaze to Braddock with a raised eyebrow. Her way of asking, what do you think?

His read was that Brandon was a good kid in a dire situation, then he noticed something else. Gresh's clothes were shoved against the wall and under the bed, but in the center of the room the old wood floor was clear. He turned to Brandon. "Did your roommate have a rug on the floor in here?"

Brandon looked down and nodded. "Yeah. Area rug, kind of an Afghan look to it."

"Do you know where it went?"

"No. Like I said, sir. I've stayed out of his stuff."

Braddock nodded while Tori examined the floor before looking up to him. "It would probably be big enough given the square footage here."

"Big enough? For what?" Brandon asked.

"Never mind that," Braddock said. "Do you have a phone number for Gresh's parents?"

"Yes, sir," Brandon said and scrolled through his contacts. "Here. That's his mom's phone number. 319 area code is for Cedar Rapids, Iowa."

Braddock jotted the number down.

"You said you've been staying at your girlfriend's place?" Tori asked.

"Yeah."

"Go there and stay there for a few days until the dust settles. For now, this is a crime scene. Understand?"

"And if you hear from him," Braddock said, "your next move five seconds later is to call me. Do I make myself clear?"

"Yes, sir."

It was after 1:00 a.m. when the four of them went back to the government center. Braddock called down to the Cedar Rapids police department. An officer was dispatched to Gresh's mother's home and soon called Braddock with an update.

"And?" Tori asked when Braddock came into the conference room.

"Gresh's mom claims she hasn't heard from her son in a couple of weeks. She last saw him at Christmas. He came home for a few days, but then left."

"What did she say of her son?"

"She acknowledged the changes in him," Braddock said as he screwed the cap off a bottle of water and took a long drink. "He didn't look good when he was home for the holidays. Didn't communicate much."

Tori nodded. "He was there out of obligation."

"Right. Left the moment he could," Braddock said. "She was worried about him but when she started asking questions, he got defensive. She tried calling him while the officer was there with her, but he didn't answer. She said she would call if she heard from him."

"You believe all that?" Steak asked.

"Yeah, I do. The patrol cop's read was she was concerned about him. He has two older sisters, but the mom says they're not close. But just the same, the police in Cedar Rapids will be paying her a second visit tomorrow and tracking down the sisters as well," Braddock said.

"It feels like he's our guy," Steak said. "Especially after seeing that wall in the bedroom."

"It was a little... creepy," Tori said.

"Way creepy!" Eggleston agreed. "He was obsessed with Grace and killed her and the boy she left him for. Plus, he's in the wind. Unreachable."

"Nobody is unreachable these days unless they want to be," Tori said. "Let's say I can get there on Gresh, what about the other two in the SUV with him? What's their motivation? They want a murder charge just so he can knock off his ex-girl-friend?" She crinkled her nose and shook her head. "I don't think this is about Grace per se. It's more likely about what she and Jensen saw last night."

"If he is our guy, he won't have his cell phone with him for fear we'll track it," Braddock said. "We'll still get a warrant for it. We have an alert out for him. Every LEO within two hundred miles has eyes out for Gresh, as well as in Cedar Rapids in case he decides to try and hide down there." He switched topics. "What about up in Holmstrand? After we left, did you learn anything else on the scene?"

"We'll need to hit the area anew tomorrow, but between me, Eggs, and the Holmstrand cops, we hit every house in a two-block radius. There are no eyewitnesses beyond Cathy Randall," Steak said, flipping open his notebook. "Plenty of people heard the shots but nobody saw the shooter or the SUV. The next-door neighbor, the one with the salon, Maggie Duncan, did have an old security camera for her business mounted under the eaves of her garage angled to the street."

"And?"

"We looked at it. It's so dark you can barely see it but there is a vehicle that zooms by. You can tell it's an SUV, but that's it. It's a dark grainy side view from a hundred feet away. The BCA has it for analysis. I don't expect much will come of it."

"As for anyone else, people didn't rush to the windows when they heard the shots, they ducked for cover," Eggleston added. "Jennison's forensics team is working the scene to see if they can turn anything up. They'll also work that doorbell video to see if we can identify more."

* * *

Paul Marrone was driven along the winding dirt road as it weaved its way through the woods until they arrived at the two-story house on the left side.

"Looks like a full house," Marrone's driver Stevie muttered. They parked and walked to the house. Rudick answered the door, holding a beer as he let the two men inside.

"Who else is here now?" Marrone asked Rudick.

"Tripp, Gill, and Nico. Our guys."

"What the hell happened out there?" Marrone demanded.

"We did what you wanted," Tripp said, sitting back, taking a long drink of his beer, nonplussed. Given the collection in front of him, it clearly wasn't his first, second or third of the night.

"Really. Tonight, is what we wanted?"

"You wanted it cleaned up. We cleaned it up. We followed

them all day looking for our shot. They went several different places through the afternoon around campus, but they were in crowds. They finally left the campus and drove up to Holmstrand. That's when we made our move. The street was quiet, dark and nobody was outside. There was no traffic or surveillance cameras. Horn and Jensen were right there. We weren't going to get a better look than that."

"What about this other kid?" Marrone asked.

"I don't know who he was. We saw him at the last second. It was too late. Not his night."

Marrone grimaced at the thought of the stray person killed. "You got away clean at least?"

"Yes. It was dark, the streets were tree-lined. Nobody else was outside. We were out of the town in less than thirty seconds and made a long loop around the eastern half of the county, watching our back the entire way. Nobody was ever behind us. We were back here an hour after it all went down."

"So where's Gresh?"

"Out at the trailer," Gill said.

"Keep him out there. And out of sight," Marrone said. Everyone's eyes looked past him. He turned around to see a little girl in pink pajamas holding a light-blue blanket at the top of the basement steps.

"Oh crap," Nico said, pushing himself up from the table, gesturing frantically to the girl. She gestured back. "Sorry," he said to the group and then to the girl. "What are you doing up here?" He took her hand and led her back downstairs.

Marrone turned to Rudick. "Who the hell is that?"

"Nico's little sister Alisha. She's nine," Tripp replied. "She's sleeping downstairs."

"This is no damn place for a child," Marrone growled, looking at Tripp and Rudick. "We can't have that shit."

"I know, I know," Tripp said, holding up his hands. "Nico's a good worker for us. His mom had a stroke a week ago, a bad one. She's in the ICU in St. Cloud, just barely hanging on, is probably going to die. Alisha doesn't have anybody else. Plus, you saw, she's deaf. She has to be with somebody who can sign, and Nico can."

"I don't care," Marrone warned. "She can't stay here. Get her out first thing. Tell him now."

"Okay," Tripp said and slowly went down the steps.

He turned to Rudick. "And keep Gresh out of sight until we see which way this all blows. Three people were shot tonight. The sheriff's department is all over the scene in Holmstrand. Braddock and his team are on this. If they focus on Gresh—"

"We'll handle it," Rudick replied.

* * *

Maggie's mind whirred, the whole event replaying on an endless loop.

The gunshots. The rapid rat-a-tat-tat.

She hadn't heard it or felt it in so long it had shocked her. Much of the aftermath was a blur on the sidewalk and steps until Cathy's rasped wail when Leo's expression faded, his eyes went blank, and he slumped lifelessly against the iron railing for the steps. Cathy had held him in her arms, embracing him, trying to feel, absorb his last bits of life, begging him to stay with her.

Rolling onto her back, she opened her eyes. Rob was lying softly to her right, his back to her, sound asleep and gently snoring. The snoring had become more consistent, a newer development the last year or so, along with a few gray hairs at his temples, all part of moving into his mid-forties. She only found him more handsome as a result.

She reached for her phone. It was 3:42 a.m. The phone came alive and was still on the text from Jenny. After the shooting, Cathy had gone down to her house. Jenny texted that all

Cathy saw was a light-colored SUV racing away in the dark. At that time of night, in the dark, would anyone else have seen anything?

An engine started outside. She lifted off the comforter and slipped out of bed and pulled on her thick bathrobe. She tweezed open the curtains with her fingers to see a police patrol car pull away, leaving two units behind to maintain watch over the scene, the yellow crime-scene tape streamed around the front of the property, fluttering in the light night wind.

Stepping into her fuzzy slippers she tiptoed out of the bedroom and downstairs to the kitchen. She poured herself a small glass of milk and then found herself wandering back into her salon.

When she and Rob first moved to Holmstrand, she worked at a salon in Manchester Bay and quickly built a loyal clientele. After a year, the owner decided to sell the salon but to someone that Maggie didn't gel with. There was a small porch off the back of the garage of their house that they rarely used. Rob suggested she convert it to a salon and, "Work for yourself. Set your own hours and schedule." It was a small space but more than adequate for a one-person operation.

During the days when Rob was at school, she oversaw construction. When the contractor was building the cabinetry, she had him construct a built-in desk. Underneath the desk, on the left side, she had him put in a hidden compartment. She'd told him it was so she could store cash on site. She opened it via a latch under the lip of one of the desk drawers. Pulling the latch, the compartment door released. Inside was a locked emergency cash box, an old 9mm Beretta, two spare magazines, a screw-on suppressor, two old flip phones and a smartphone. She retrieved the smartphone and closed the cabinet.

She kept a small safe on the floor behind her desk for the business and therefore had a security camera installed over the side door to the salon as well as one situated under the eaves at

the corner of the garage, directed to the street. They were intentionally visible to anyone who bothered to look.

What couldn't be seen were the other four small wireless
cameras hidden around the house's perimeter. Two in the backyard, one covering the front yard and one in a small bird house
mounted on the tree in the front yard facing the street.

Maggie woke her computer and clicked through numerous
anonymous files and bland icons to reach the camera feeds.
Camera Four was in the birdhouse with a wide-angle view from
the three-way street corner to the left, across the front and three
houses to the right. She selected infrared mode, tapped the
screen and hit play.

It took a few minutes but then she saw a Jeep Cherokee—
Cam and Grace—turn left at the corner and then into the
Randall driveway. In the distance on the far left of the screen
there was another vehicle parked at the corner. It started
turning and flicked off its headlights.

"Here it comes," she murmured quietly.

The second vehicle, a lighter-colored SUV pulled quickly
in front of the Randalls' house. The muzzle flashes were rapid
fire. The SUV pulled away, sped past the front of the house and
then out of view to the right.

Maggie ran the footage back again and as the SUV
approached the front of her house, she froze the video and took
a screenshot. She enlarged the screen and zeroed in on the
license plate. Even with her infrared camera, she couldn't make
out the entire sequence of letters and numbers, but was able to
make out two letters on the left side, she could see the right side
of the D followed by an R, and two numbers to the right, 9, and
what she was certain was an 8, and maybe, just maybe a 7 for
the third number, as she could just make out the very bottom of
it. As for the state, she squinted. "Illinois. Huh."

Maggie closed her eyes and sat still, breathing slowly, thinking, contemplating what happened if she took this step.

You're safe. Nobody knows who or where you are.

If she handled this right, that would still be the case. And that assumed the plate turned anything up to begin with.

After a moment she sighed and opened her eyes and powered up the smartphone she'd retrieved and went into the contacts, of which there was but one. She tapped on it and started tapping out a text: *I know it's been a long time. I hope all is well. I need a favor...*

The text complete, she hit send.

Creak... creak... creak...

She stuffed the iPhone in her desk drawer, exited out of the security camera program on her computer and flipped to an online article about spring fashion.

"Couldn't sleep?" Rob asked when he came into the salon, leaning down and kissing the top of her head.

"No. Thought I'd read about something... light, you know. Dresses... not..."

"It was a day," he said as he tenderly massaged her shoulders. "You should come back to bed."

"Will you still rub my shoulders?"

"Always."

SIX

"MY HEARING IS FINELY TUNED."

Braddock lay on his back, the light slowly brightening as it seeped in around the curtains covering the bedroom windows. The ceiling fan whirred. Tori lay to his right. He smiled at the vision of her, curled up in a little ball like a kitty under the comforter, breathing lightly, as if she were purring. He gazed about their bedroom, the boxes and tubs stacked along the far wall, pre-packing for the pending remodeling project that would start in a little over a month. The house would be a disaster for the better part of three months. However, when the project was completed, they would have an expanded master bedroom, closet, and bath, a fully remodeled second floor along with an extension of the house out and over the detached garage. With a prime lot on the lake, he couldn't imagine them ever leaving.

His alarm buzzed on his nightstand. Tori popped right up. "Hey."

"Good morning."

She tossed off the comforter and stretched her arms. "I suppose we need to get going."

"Yeah, I guess so."

Tori jumped out of bed, whipped off her nightshirt and threw it into the closet, skipping naked as a jailbird into the bathroom, giving her butt a little shake for his benefit as she did. He laughed at her little exhibitionist display. He heard the shower door close and swung his legs out of bed. A minute later he joined her. She looked back at him, her eyes raised.

"Don't get all excited," he said. "I'm just saving time."

"Don't flatter yourself," she replied, slapping him playfully on the ass as he closed the shower door. "Besides, it would appear you are at least mildly excited or is your thermometer just testing the water temperature?"

Braddock laughed, kissed her, and then reached for the soap, letting the warm water wash over him and her. "Did you sleep much?" he asked.

"Much? No. Hard? Yes. I crashed," Tori said, turning him around and quickly soaping his back. "You?"

"A bit. Although I woke an hour ago and all I could think about was whether this was all about what Jensen and Horn saw at Gresh's apartment building. If he was innocent. If he had nothing to do with it. He'd have appeared. He hasn't."

"He's on the run. It's been eleven, twelve hours now. He could be a long way from here."

After a stop for coffees and bagels, the whole team met in the conference room. Steak and Eggs were present, and Reese and Nolan were brought in. Sheriff Boe joined them.

"Thoughts?"

"Gresh," Braddock said. "If, and I emphasize if, he did this, then he's hiding or on the run, or getting ready to run. There are alerts out for him, but we can't wait for him to pop his head out like a prairie dog. We need to hunt him down. Reese and Nolan, that's you. If he's running, he's going to need help. Who does he get it from?"

"On it," Reese said.

"You said *if?*" Nolan said.

"Right," Braddock started. "If he was the shooter, there was a driver and a spotter. Who are they? If there was a body rolled up in that rug, who was it? If that was a murder, did someone make the call for the kill?" He looked to Boe. "Gresh was in the drug world. Did it, as you posited, have something to do with the other missing drug dealers? We're all going to take some pieces of that. Steak and Eggs, you two work your sources, see what they're hearing. Steak when you reach out to your little bartender buddy, I want to go on that one."

"Copy that."

"Who are you talking about?" Boe asked.

"A source who is particular about who he talks to. He won't go on the record, but he can point us in the right direction sometimes."

"Is he your Deep Throat or something?"

Steak shrugged. "He'd be amused by that particular reference, but, yeah, he's something like that."

"In the meantime, Tori and I will go over the scene in Holmstrand in the daylight," Braddock said. "And we need to talk to the families some more."

The first meeting was with Grace Horn's parents who had driven overnight from Milwaukee. They had first stopped to see their daughter's body and now were in Braddock's office, completely broken and angry. Tori attempted to lay out where the investigation stood but Mr. Horn went right to it.

"This old boyfriend, the one that was stalking her, is he the one responsible? Did he do it?"

"We're trying to find him," Braddock said.

"You got a manhunt on?"

"He's a person of interest that we want to talk to."

"But he hasn't come forward, has he?"

"No, sir."

"Sounds to me like he killed my daughter."

"I thought that had died down," Horn's mother said, dabbing at her eye. "I thought when she started dating Cameron all that was over."

"How often did you talk to your daughter?" Tori asked.

"Oh, we texted every day. I bet we talked two, three days a week," the mother replied. "She seemed very happy the last couple of months."

"Were you aware that on Monday night, she and Cam went to Ron's apartment? She wanted to retrieve some things that were still at his place. Did she tell you about that?"

"No," Mrs. Horn said and looked to her husband. "Did she say anything to you?"

"No. Did that trigger all this?"

"That's what we're trying to find out," Tori said.

The Horns left, intending to drive to Cameron Jensen's house. "That will be hard," Tori said as she watched the parents walk to their car. "They feel responsible because of Grace's relationship with Gresh."

"Not Grace's fault."

"They shouldn't feel any guilt, but that doesn't mean they won't."

"I'm going to need to catch-up with you," Braddock said, looking at his phone. "I need to meet with Steak and his guy."

"The source? What do you call him?" Tori asked, whispering, "Eff'n something?"

Braddock smiled. "Eff'n Jones."

* * *

Tori drove to Holmstrand and the Randall house.

In the daylight, Nokomis Lane, the Randalls' street, was a mixture of older but well cared for one and two-story homes, the yards filled with a thick mature mixture of oaks, elms,

aspens, maples, spruces and firs. In a month the plentiful decid-
uous trees would start budding. She imagined the summer, the
houses all hiding behind and under the dense tree canopies that
would provide cool shade and then in the fall, there would be a
picture postcard explosion of bright oranges, browns, yellows,
and reds as the leaves turned and fell.

That was not the scene today as she slipped under the
yellow tape and walked the driveway. Last night, the mass of
tree trunks, central stems and expanding crowns would have
served to prevent anyone watching from seeing the shooting
clearly, even if they'd have wanted to. She made a point of
slowly walking along the front sidewalk, peering to her right at
the street and the corner, gauging the SUV's approach.

She envisioned the SUV coming around the corner, slowing
in front of the house and firing—eleven shots based on what was
found in the victims, siding, and interior of the entryway. Last
night she'd looked at it as something of a kill box, but as she
looked at the blood spots on the sidewalk and steps, she was
seeing something a little different. She took out a tape measure.
There was just over nine feet between the two spots. There was
some separation between Cameron Jensen on the sidewalk and
Grace on the steps. She took her pen and pushed it into one of
the bullet holes for the siding. Her pen was angled slightly to
the right. The shots came in at a slight angle. She left the pen in
the hole and then went back to her Audi and drove the
approach, making the turn and first passing in a slow roll. She
turned around and made the pass again, this time coming to a
stop. Parked, she walked around, then got into the backseat and
took out her gun and pantomimed the sequence.

Eleven shots, huh?

Last night she thought all three of them were lined up in a
row but as she looked at it now, Grace and Leo Randall were
close but there was some separation for Cameron. Grace had
been hit twice, as had Leo, and then Cameron three times with

four misses. Given the approach and angle the first seven shots were at Grace. Leo was hit twice, and two bullets went into the entryway. She moved her hands left, two misses into the siding and then Cameron, three hits in his upper torso.

That's good shooting. Very good shooting.

Tori got out and walked back up the driveway. To her left, watching out the picture window was the neighbor they'd spoken with last night, the stylist with the shoulder-length blonde bob. What was her name again? Maggie something. Tori turned and walked over and the woman opened the front door.

"Hello. Maggie, right?"

"Yes. Maggie Duncan. I was watching you work out there. I hope that's okay."

"It's fine."

"Figuring anything out?"

"Just working through a few things. A question. If I remember correctly, you said you heard the shots, right?"

"Yes."

"Were they in rapid succession? Quick?"

Maggie took a moment. "Yes. I mean it seemed like it. You know, rat a tat, tat, tat, tat. In the midst of it all I was pushing Jenny to the floor, to get down just in case, but yeah, no hesitation that I remember."

"And then you heard the vehicle drive away?"

"Yes."

Tori looked out the front picture window. "The vehicle, when it raced out of here, your video camera caught it driving by."

"Yes. Gosh, I wish that footage was better. That camera is so old. I'm surprised it still works."

"It's better than nothing, Maggie," Tori said. "If they drive by the front of your house, then the only way out of the neighborhood is the left up another half block, right?"

"Yes. Cherry Street. Although once you're going north on

Cherry, there are a few other side streets before you get to Main Street."

"All residential though, right?"

"Yes."

Tori looked back to Maggie. "And the gunshots again. There were as many as eleven. You heard them all in succession?"

"Yes."

Tori took a few notes.

"I can't imagine what Cathy is going through," Maggie said. "She's had such a rough go."

"How so?"

"Her husband left her for another woman, the *bastard*," she said bitterly, her arms folded. "And then he made the divorce a living hell for her. Nate, her ex, had wanted her to be a stay-at-home mom for years to raise Leo, which she did. But then he up and leaves her for a younger woman and then fights her on support, the house, and all that."

"That sounds brutal," Tori replied. "And unfair."

"Infuriating is what it is. In any event, she was just starting to move on from all that. She met a nice man recently and was excited about that. I styled her hair yesterday. She was going to... have a date tonight." Maggie wiped her eyes. "Leo was a great kid and he looked after his mom. Now..."

"Are you two good friends?"

Maggie nodded. "Rob and I got married nine years ago. He was a widower and had Ellen and Brian. I'm just their stepmom."

"Hey, stepmoms matter big time."

"I like to think so. I think of them as my kids. Anyway, we lived in Minneapolis, and Rob taught at a city high school, but after we married, he wanted a change, to live a quieter life and raise the kids in a more peaceful place so we moved up here. And until last night, it had been that. Anyway, Cathy was the first person we met here. The day we moved into the house she was over with a pan dessert. She introduced us around and was the epitome of Minnesota Nice. I mean I used to laugh about that phrase, you know, 'Minnesota Nice,' but Cath made it real. Real to us anyway."

"I grew up here but lived in the concrete jungles of Boston and New York City for nearly twenty years," Tori said. "Minnesota Nice is a very real thing."

"Sure is. Cathy and I have become close over the years. She was home all day, and I work out of the house. We'd talk every day. I might be fixing a neighbor's hair and Cathy would be there, the three of us just chit-chatting, gossiping, having a bunch of laughs. Just the girls hanging out."

"She's going to need people to lean on," Tori said knowingly. "And you and others need to make sure she does."

* * *

Braddock picked up Steak at the government center and the two of them made their way west of town on Highway 210 five miles before turning right onto a gravel road that took them into the woods.

"Turn left," Steak directed.

A minute later they came to a small, open beach by a lake. A Chevy SUV was parked, waiting for them. Braddock and Steak got out and into the Chevy.

"It's about fucking time," Ryan Eff'n Jones greeted. "I've got a fuckin' bar to run you know."

"Yeah, yeah," Steak said from the front passenger seat.

Braddock knew the two had met long ago because Jones's older brother was a good friend of Steak's older brother. A stubby little man, Jones compensated for his lack of height with an exceedingly foul mouth. He was also fearless in running his business, never afraid to get in the face of someone misbehaving in his establishment. His bar, The Outskirts, was on the far western edge of town and was a place generally ignored by the vacationers. Instead, Jones's place catered to an eclectic mix of locals, from the bikers, blue-collar mill workers to the white-collar types who filled the offices and cubicles at Mannion Companies. As a result, Jones had his finger on the pulse of the town and from time to time came across information of value. He was willing to share that information on occasion in return for some leeway as his bar at times attracted patrons who might fracture an occasional law.

"What's up?" Jones asked.

"Holmstrand last night," Braddock said.

"What is wrong with people?" Jones moaned. "A fucking drive-by shooting? Seriously?"

"Do you know a guy named Ron Gresh?" Braddock asked.

Jones shook his head. "No, I don't think so. Is he your shooter?"

"Maybe."

"Do you have a photo?"

Steak pulled a photo up on his phone and handed it to Jones.

"The guy doesn't look familiar, but I'll definitely keep my eyes and ears open for him."

"If you would," Braddock said.

"Why did he do it?"

"If he did it," Steak said. "We don't know if he did but he's in the wind right now and had a thing for the woman who was killed, ex-girlfriend."

"So, he fucking smokes her," Jones said, shaking his head. "Fucking misfit."

"It could be more complicated than that," Steak said. "Word is this Gresh was in the drug scene. And on Monday night two of the victims..." He gave Jones the rundown on what Jensen and Horn saw outside Gresh's apartment building. "So, it has us thinking about—"

"The other thing we've been talking about," Jones finished, nodding. "I follow."

"Anything on that?" Steak asked.

"Any word on who is making this move on these guys?" Braddock added.

Jones shook his head. "Not that I've heard. As you know, I listen for information. I don't go digging it up. That's what gets you in trouble."

"But you'll keep listening?" Braddock asked.

"My hearing is finely tuned."

"Be discreet," Braddock cautioned. He liked the little foul-mouthed dude, and his bar.

"I'm touched. Truly."

"I'm serious, Jones. Be careful."

"I hear ya, chief."

* * *

Tori entered the coffee shop on campus and found Gresh's roommate Brandon waiting. "Can I buy you a coffee?"

"I'd take a sweet tea."

"You know, that doesn't sound too bad. I'll make it two."

They grabbed a table in the back of the seating area.

"I haven't heard from him," Brandon said.

"Tell me this," Tori asked. "You saw him with a gun that one time. Was that the only time you recall seeing it?"

Brandon nodded. "Although I wouldn't be surprised if he had one there at other times."

"Think about this. When you saw him with it, did he look like he knew what he was doing?"

"In what way?"

"Was he just playing, or did he have experience? Was he a

good shot?"

"I don't know," Brandon said after a moment. "A year ago, I don't think he'd have been doing this."

"Any history with him of hunting or using a shotgun?"

"No, I don't think so," Brandon said. "At least I never heard him ever talk about it. And hunters? They talk. You teach here. There are lots of guys at school who hunt, who talk about it all the time, especially in the fall. They pick this school because they can be in a deer stand in a half-hour after class."

"They wear the orange and camo to class."

"Right," Brandon said. "I never saw any of that with him. Why?"

"Just curious," Tori said as her phone buzzed. Braddock was looking for her.

Tori met Braddock back at his office. "I don't question that Gresh is involved here, but I wonder if he really is our shooter."

"Why?"

"Whoever it is who pulled that trigger last night was a shooter. A killer. I asked Brandon if Gresh was a hunter or something like that and he said he didn't think so."

"It was a drive-by shooting. He sprayed the house."

"Did he though?" she said. "The shots covered twenty to twenty-five yards. He took eleven shots and had—"

"Seven hits," Braddock said, nodding. He thought for a moment. "Where does that get us? Gresh was still very likely involved. Otherwise—"

"He would be reachable," Tori replied. "He was likely there and was there the night before. But he may not have fired the gun. This rug that Kristy said that Grace and Cam saw get taken away, if it had a body in it, who was it?"

Braddock sighed. "It would seem there's another homicide out there we don't know about."

SEVEN

"I FEEL NOTHING GOOD CAN COME OF THIS."

Rob, Ellen and Brian all awoke early on Thursday morning. School had been cancelled on Wednesday but was back on for Thursday. As Rob understood it, the administrators thought the kids might grieve better together than apart. Maggie sat with them all at the breakfast table as Rob gave the kids the option to stay or go. A bit to her surprise, they both wanted to go to school.

"I texted with the guys, they're all going," Brian said.

"My friends too," Ellen agreed. "I don't want to sit at home. Especially when it happened... next door. The police were around all day yesterday. They'll probably be back again today."

"I'll be there," Rob said, seeing the concern on Maggie's face. "If either of you feel like you need to leave, or even just talk, come find me."

"I'll come and get you if you need me to," Maggie assured them. "Just call."

"I will, I promise," Ellen assured her.

"Me too," Brian said.

The kids left the kitchen to grab their things for school.

"I don't know," Maggie started. They were her stepchildren.

She was not their mom, and she never once questioned a decision their father made in front of them.

"I don't either," he said, wrapping his wife in a hug. "But I'll be checking on them both through the day. I promise you that."

"Okay then," she said, looking up and pecking her husband on the lips. "I'll have a nice dinner ready for us tonight."

Rob left for school with the kids. Maggie cleaned up and then went to the salon. She'd cancelled all her appointments for the rest of the week. She thought it unseemly to continue to operate her business right next door while Cathy was grieving. Thankfully, her customers, most of whom lived either in Holmstrand or Manchester Bay, understood. Being closed, she went into the salon and took care of some recordkeeping. That work complete, she opened a drawer and retrieved the smartphone she'd sent the text with. There was a response: *I haven't heard from you in so long. Hope all is well with you up in Minny. Call me. We need to talk.*

She tapped the number.

"Hey, how are you?" her old friend greeted.

"I'm well..." They caught up for a few minutes. "Now tell me. What did you find?"

"You're not... you know... back doing—"

"I'm just trying to help a friend with something. Some damage that was caused."

"Are you sure about that?"

"Yeah, why?"

The voice sighed. "The name I ran across on this."

"Who?"

"Rudick."

Maggie froze for a moment. "Seriously?"

"Don't act surprised."

"I am though. I'm... shocked. How is that even possible?"

"What are you into?" her friend pressed. "Tell me before I give you any of this. This could be dangerous for you, and me."

"Okay, okay," Maggie relented. "On Tuesday night..." Maggie explained what had happened and how she had the license plate number. "Go online and you'll see reporting on it, I'm sure. I won't tell you how, but I have this license plate. It's for a gray or light-colored SUV that the shooter was in. I had no idea, *no idea*, this would be the outcome."

"What did you intend to do in sending this to me?"

"See if I could help find the shooter. My friend lost her only son. That's all I'm looking to do here. I'm not looking... to go back. I want to get this to the police without them knowing who I am or how I got it."

"I feel nothing good can come of this. Why not just give them the footage you have and let them deal with it?"

"I don't want them to know I have it. I'm just trying to help my friend. What do you have? Come on."

"It's circuitous. The license plate was for a car that was compacted two years ago. According to the last registered owner down here in Barrington, he was in an accident and the car was totaled. It went to Petrovic Salvage. As you may recall, Petrovic was the brother-in-law of—"

"Rudick."

"That's right."

"Okay. Is Rudick here, in Minnesota?"

"I don't know. I just don't know."

"Tell me."

He gave her the address.

"Holy smokes," she said when she mapped it. "That's only five miles from where I live. I can't believe this."

"That's close. And you're telling me you've never seen him?"

"No," Maggie said. "Never."

"You need to be careful."

"What more can you tell me?"

. . .

It had been a minute, she thought when she parked at the storage facility. She opened the padlock, pushed up the door and then immediately closed it. With her cell phone flashlight, she found the lamp on the rudimentary workbench and switched it on. She opened the safe and took out a Beretta and quick cleaned it before sliding in a magazine, stuffing it in her backpack. The gun clean, she took out two old disposable flip phones, still in their boxes. She extracted one and plugged it in to charge it. Next, she retrieved a small black plastic case. Inside, the round disc and small monitor were packed tightly in their foam compartments. Like the flip phones, it was an older model that had been sitting in the safe for a good decade plus, though never used so the set looked practically brand new. Would it work?

The unit powered right up. She packed it into her backpack.

A half-hour later, she took a sip of her mocha as she drove south on the H-4, keeping a side eye on the cell phone in the holder mounted on the dashboard. The right turn was just ahead, a turn for which there wasn't even a designated turn lane. The street sign itself was barely visible. She eased to the shoulder and turned right onto the gravel road.

She drove cautiously along the road rutted from winter damage as it wound its way through the woods, the bright blue line on the map on her phone getting ever shorter. There were a series of modest homes on both sides of the road, all set back on heavily treed lots with long driveways.

Her destination came into view on the left through the trees. It was a larger and newer two-story cedar log home. Behind the home she knew was a lake.

She slowed. While the house was set back a good hundred feet from the road, the detached two-car garage sat closer. In the paved driveway were three vehicles, a black Dodge Ram pickup truck, a rusted white Chevy Trailblazer, and a champagne-colored Ford Escape. None of them were the SUV from the video, not that she really expected to find it. That SUV had been chopped up and crushed by now.

But Ernie Rudick, a name too familiar to her for all the wrong reasons, was involved somehow. How? With who? And why would he be involved with a drive-by shooting of a couple of college kids? Rudick's address was the house she was now viewing in her rearview mirror, and she'd learned that his truck was the Dodge Ram.

She drove ahead a half-mile, turned around and then pulled to the side of the road and parked. From her backpack, she pulled the small tracker and activated it, checking it on the small handheld monitor. She stuffed the tracker in the pouch of her thick black hoodie. She pulled on a black stocking cap and her black gloves and then wraparound tinted sunglasses and slipped out of the car, locking it. Her workouts were not as frequent as they once were. These days she preferred yoga and exercise involving movements with light weights, but on occasion, especially in the summer, she would go for a run.

She started jogging along the gravel road, hewing tight to the right side. It took three minutes for her to reach the gentle bend to the left and the two-story house came into view ahead on her right. As she approached the detached garage and parked vehicles, she discreetly glanced around but neither saw nor sensed anyone else about. When she was completely behind the structure of the garage, she quick scooted to the back of the Dodge Ram, reached under the rear bumper and placed the tracker, feeling the magnetic back grab hold.

She kept jogging to the east for another half-mile before she crossed the road and turned around and jogged back. As she approached the house again, a shortish stocky man with brown hair and a mustache she hadn't seen in years approached the Dodge Ram.

Rudick.

He glanced in her direction.

"Hi," she greeted with a friendly wave, one that he perfunctorily returned before getting into the truck.

Five minutes later she reached her car. Once inside, she checked the tracking monitor. The Dodge Ram was driving north on the H-4. "And there you are."

EIGHT

"HE THINKS HE PLAYED IT SMART."

Maggie spread out the ingredients on the counter.

"I like the look of this," Rob said as he entered the kitchen and from behind leaned down to kiss his wife on the neck. "This for you and Ellen?"

"No. Cathy returned this morning. She's having family over this afternoon. I'm making something for her to serve. Lasagna is quick and easy."

"You're a good egg, Maggie Duncan."

The kids both came into the kitchen and the four of them conversed while Rob drank coffee and the kids made quick bowls of cereal and some toast. Twenty minutes later, they were all packing up to leave.

"Brian and I'll see you tomorrow night," Rob said as he leaned down and kissed her, before wrapping his wife in a warm hug. He was taking Brian down to Minneapolis to watch the semi-final and final games for the state basketball tournament, a chance to get away from the shooting. "You sure you don't want to come?"

"I'll stick around in case Ellen needs anything, and Cathy too." That might have been more a warning to Ellen to not engage in anything too crazy. She was a high school senior. Rob and she weren't so naïve as to think partying and drinking wasn't going on. It was the reason Rob would be going on spring break with Ellen and her friends at the end of next week, serving as one of the adult chaperones to keep the kids, not so much in check, but safe and looked after. Brian had a trip of his own planned with a good friend, going skiing in Colorado with his family. Maggie would be home alone, not that she minded.

Rob kissed her again. Brian followed, swinging his backpack and duffel bag over his shoulder.

"What, no hug for me, B?" Maggie asked.

Brian smiled, came back, and gave her a good one before he left with his father.

Maggie made herself a cup of tea before she started browning some ground beef in a frying pan. While the meat cooked, she slipped into the salon, opened the cabinet, and took out the tracking monitor.

At present the pickup truck was at the house. The tracking history showed that so far there were two specific locations at which the truck had stopped multiple times. One was the town of Cullen Crossing. Another one was for a location that looked to be out well northwest of Manchester Bay.

"What is even out there?" she murmured under her breath, switching to her iPad to look at the satellite map of the location. The answer was nothing. It was forested and not developed. There was a dirt road that threaded its way through some woods, but she couldn't find any structure or house where the truck had stopped. "Hmpf."

She heard the ground beef sizzling and went back into the kitchen. "Oops." It wasn't burned but was getting close as she stirred it and then turned the burner down and let it simmer. For the next hour she puttered around the kitchen, making up the trays of lasagna. Both trays ready, she put them in the oven to cook and poured herself another cup of tea.

Gazing out the living room picture window, she took light sips of the hot tea, between slow reflexive dunks of the tea bag into her oversized cup. Numerous vehicles were parked along the street outside of the Randall house. Cathy came from a large family, and they had arrived en masse in support. The wake for Cameron and Leo would be next Tuesday and the funeral on Wednesday.

Just beyond she saw a black Tahoe pull up. Will Braddock and Tori Hunter. The two detectives solemnly approached the front of Cathy's house. It would be of little comfort to Cathy, but at least the best investigators in the area were working the shooting of her son.

Letting the lasagna cook, she showered, dressed, made herself up and came back down as the timer went off. She put the sleeves of French bread in and let that bake until the timer went off again ten minutes later. The pan cooling on the stove, she peered outside and saw that the black Tahoe had left. She packed up the two trays, the bread and made her way over to Cathy's house. Jenny let her inside and led her back to the kitchen.

"My gosh, Mags," Cathy greeted. "You've brought enough food to feed an army."

"Hey," Maggie greeted, wrapping Cathy in a warm hug, holding her tight, whispering gently. "Whatever you need, whatever it is, you just call me."

Cathy stepped back. "Thank you."

Maggie nodded and they hugged again for a minute before Cathy slowly pulled away and walked out of the kitchen and back to the living room and her family.

"I don't know how she's holding it all together," Jenny murmured as she mixed up the salad. "The police just stopped by an hour ago."

"And?"

Jenny glanced toward the living room then whispered,

"They do have a person of interest."

"Who?"

"They didn't say, specifically. All they said is they are searching for him."

"For three days?" Maggie said quietly.

"I guess. The police said he didn't own a gray SUV, which is what Cathy saw after the shooting."

"But they didn't say who it was?"

Jenny shook her head, then leaned in and whispered in Maggie's ear, "After the detectives left, Cameron's mom said it was Grace's old boyfriend. She told the detectives about him the night of the shooting."

"Old boyfriend?"

"Yes. His name is Ron Gresh," Jenny whispered, stepping back and taking another look into the living room. "Apparently," she continued, mixing the salad again, "he didn't take the breakup well and he didn't like that Grace was with Cam. I guess he got into drugs and some other things."

"That sounds... promising," Maggie whispered back. "In the sense that... they might know who did it."

"Yeah, but the detectives said that as of right now, they don't have any witnesses besides Cathy, and she can't identify the SUV or shooter. Nobody else saw anything. They're like you and I." Jenny shook her head dejectedly. "They heard it but didn't see it."

"I see," Maggie answered.

"After the police left, Cathy said that even if this Ron Gresh guy did it, if nobody saw him do it, unless he admitted it, he might not—"

"Get prosecuted," Maggie said. "You said his name is Ron—"

"Gresh. This is him," Jenny said, handing Maggie her phone. "I got this from her sister, who got it from Grace's parents, in case you see him anywhere."

"But the police said he didn't own a gray SUV?"

"No," Jenny replied. "What do you make of that, Maggie?"

"I don't know. I don't know much about police and detectives, but it doesn't sound good."

* * *

After visiting the Randalls' with Tori, Braddock called a meeting with his investigative team.

"We're three days post shooting and I'm getting tired of telling Cathy Randall, the Jensens and Horns we're still looking for the shooter," Braddock said. "Heck, I can't tell them who we're after, although they know it's Gresh. Cameron Jensen's parents are throwing the name around. Do any of you have anything new?"

"No," Steak said plainly. "We've been through the neighborhood repeatedly. You know what we got out of that. We've been talking to people around the university, but nobody has seen Gresh in about a week. Gresh's roommate has not heard from him, despite trying to call him for us a few times. We've tried tracking his phone, but it's shut off so we're getting nothing there. We have eyes on the apartment, but Gresh has not returned. Eggs and I have talked to everyone we know around town, nothing. If you ask me, I'd say he's flown the coop and is far away at this point, or—"

"He's already dead," Tori said looking to Braddock.

Braddock nodded. "One of those two results are getting more likely by the day."

There was a knock on the conference room door. Braddock's assistant stuck her head inside. "There's someone here to see you and Tori. He says his name is Brandon."

. . .

Braddock led a nervous Brandon back to his office and a guest chair. He got him a soda and then sat down behind his desk. Tori took the other guest chair, curled up.

Brandon took a long sip from his soda, his hands tremoring.

"What's on your mind?" Braddock asked casually.

"Have you found Ron yet?"

"No."

"Do you have an idea of where he might be?"

"We're still looking. Why? Are you afraid of him?"

"Well... yeah. If he shot Grace and Cam and the other guy, shouldn't I be. I'm his roommate. He'll know you came talking to me. Why wouldn't I be afraid?"

"Because we have a cop watching your place at all times," Tori said good-naturedly. "You didn't come here for an update. What do you have?"

Brandon nodded and took out his cell phone. "I was going through some old texts, back when Ron and I were more on speaking terms and ran in the same social circle."

"And you found what?"

"Late one night last fall I was up studying for an exam when I got a text from him. The text said, 'Have you seen Tripp?'"

"So?"

"Like I said, we ran in the same social circle. I didn't know anyone with a first or last name of Tripp. I texted him back with a question mark. And he said, sorry, wrong Brandon. It happened again about six weeks later," Brandon said, holding up his phone for them to see. It was a text that said: *I need to get with Tripp. Do you know where he is?*

"Ron stopped at the apartment the next day and I just kind of asked him who this Brandon guy was that he was confusing me with. And he said, oh sorry, I meant to text Mitch. I just hit the wrong name."

"Mitch?" Tori's eyes shot up. "You said you didn't know any of the drug crowd he was running with. Let me see both texts."

Brandon handed her the phone.

"Brandon, you think these guys Ron was trying to text, the other Brandon, maybe named Mitch Brandon, or Tripp could be part of that?" Braddock asked.

"I don't know. I asked a bunch of the guys I and Ron both know and asked if they knew of anyone with these names and they said no. Nobody knew a Mitch Brandon, that's for sure. Tripp didn't ring a bell either."

"Brandon, I'm going to have you wait out in the hall for a minute," Braddock said. "Leave us your phone."

"Yes, sir."

Tori read the two texts over a few times. "They read like Gresh needed to connect with these guys." She looked to Braddock. "There's no overt drug talk but worth a look, don't you think?"

Braddock searched for Mitch Brandon. "I have one here in Manchester Bay. Aged twenty-four. Has an address here in town. And... what do you know, he has a record." Three years back, Mitch Brandon was arrested with marijuana, enough for distribution. It was a first offense and he got probation. Braddock printed off Mitch's DMV photo. Tori fetched the photo and went out to their Brandon. Mitch Brandon had styled brown hair, brown eyes and a small dimple in his chin. "Have you ever seen this guy before?"

Brandon looked at the photo. "Yeah. Yeah, I recognize the dimple in the chin."

"Was this at your apartment?"

"No. I think it was at the Monarch." The Monarch was one of the popular bars with the college kids near campus.

"And he was with Ron Gresh?"

"They were talking. I remember that. I remember him because of that chin."

Braddock thanked Brandon for coming in. "Mitch Brandon has a record and knew Gresh. I think we should pay him a visit."

* * *

Mitchell Brandon lived in an expansive apartment complex situated just east of the H-4. He wasn't home when Reese and Nolan knocked on his door. They waited in the parking for three hours, but he didn't return. However, the apartment complex had two security officers who constantly patrolled the premises. Reese left them his business card, a picture of Brandon, pointed out the specific apartment and handed over twenty dollars, enough for a case of beer. "Call me when this guy posts."

The call came just past 7:00 p.m. Reese called Braddock. He and Tori had been waiting to be seated at a restaurant. "Do you want us to bring him in?"

"Nah, let's do it at the apartment. Tori and I are five minutes away. We'll meet you there."

Ten minutes later, with Reese in tow, Braddock was knocking on Mitch Brandon's door. When the door opened, Mitch Brandon greeted them. "Yeah?"

They all held up their IDs.

"All of you for me?" Mitch said with raised eyebrows. "Even her?" he said, letting his eyes linger over Tori. She'd primped up a bit for a night out with Braddock, her shoulder-length hair with a little extra bounce in it, skinny black jeans, a tighter white sweater, and black leather jacket to match her knee-high boots.

"You can never be too careful," Reese said, backing Mitch Brandon into the apartment. "People out shooting other people and all," he asserted, spinning Mitch around, pushing him up against the wall and frisking him. "Is it Mitch or Mitchell?"

"Mitch."

"Do you have a weapon on you... Mitch?"

"No."

Reese finished and turned him around. "At least not on you. What happens if we take a look around here?"

"You got a warrant for that?"

"You think we won't get one?"

"Not a crime to have some self-protection in your own home, is it?"

"Depends. Where is it?"

"My nightstand drawer."

Reese took out a rubber glove and walked down the hall. He was back a minute later, holding a sub-compact 9mm semiautomatic with a full magazine. The ballistics report said they were looking for a .45. "Is this it?"

"That's it."

"And if we have this checked?"

"I've never fired it," Mitch asserted.

"Never?"

"Well, other than practice. At a range but it's been months."

"You'll let us take it then?" Reese asked.

"Again, if you have a warrant," Mitch said unworriedly and walked to the kitchen counter and took a seat on a stool.

"Again, think we won't get one?"

"Then get one," Mitch scoffed and turned to Braddock and then let his eyes drift to Tori again and asked her, "So, honey, what is this all about?"

Braddock had sized Mitch up. He wasn't a slug. In good shape wearing slim jeans and a pressed shirt, he looked like a guy who could carry himself some and probably do okay with the ladies. He also was on the cocky arrogant side. He glanced left and saw Tori was quietly evaluating as well.

"Tell me, Mitch," Braddock started. "Where were you on Tuesday night between five and eight p.m.?"

"Last Tuesday?"

"Yes."

"Ha ha," Mitch replied, wagging his finger. "Uh-huh. That was the night of the shooting up in Holmstrand. I was at Sam's Bar down in Fort Ripley drinking beers with a couple of friends. We sat right at the bar."

"You know about the drive-by shooting then?" Tori asked, nodding with her big eyes, taking the stool next to him. Sitting close.

Mitch turned to her. "Hard not to."

"Do you have any idea who did it?"

"Now why would I know that... it's detective, right? You're a detective. Detective Hunter?"

"She's a special agent," Braddock said. "FBI. Retired. Working with us."

"Special Agent Hunter. I see. I don't know who did it."

"Because if you did, you'd of course tell us, being a smart guy and all."

"Yeah. I mean who wouldn't. That's valuable information. But like I said. When it happened, I was otherwise occupied."

"Someone was pulling the trigger," Braddock asserted. "And your name came up as part of our investigation."

"From whom?"

"Do you know Ron Gresh?"

"Doesn't ring a bell," Mitch replied immediately, letting his look drift back to Tori.

"You're sure about that?" Braddock asked.

"Uh yeah. Never heard of the guy," Mitch replied, not looking in his direction. Tori's eyes shifted to Braddock. They both read people for a living. They were thinking the same thing.

"So, you don't know Ron Gresh?" Braddock pressed.

"No. Never met him."

"How about someone named Tripp?"

"Nope," he answered quickly. "Can't say that I have."

They pressed Mitch for another five minutes before Braddock said, "Thanks for your time. As I'm sure you can understand, we need to track down every lead possible."

"Wish I could have helped."

"If you think of anything, don't hesitate to call us," Tori said, handing Mitch her business card.

"Sure thing," he replied with a smile, taking the card.

The three of them reconvened in the parking lot.

"He knows Gresh," Braddock asserted. "For sure."

"You think so?" Reese asked. "I don't know about that."

"He knew exactly why we were here."

"For starters, the answers were way too quick," Tori asserted. "If he didn't know Ron Gresh, he would have at least paused, or thought for a moment, or asked who he was before he just flat out said no. He was practically answering the questions before we asked. Mitch never asked for a photo of Gresh. He never asked how it was we came to come and question him. Plus, he had an alibi at the ready," she said, snapping her fingers.

"Innocent people don't have their alibis ready so fast," Braddock said.

"He thinks he played it smart," Tori said. "Instead—"

"He confirmed he knows him, or knows it was really important to say he didn't," Braddock finished.

"So now what?"

Braddock turned. "See that black pickup truck with the trailer hitch?"

"Yeah?" Reese replied.

"That's Mitch's truck. Get Nolan back here in her car," Braddock ordered. "You two are going to sit on this guy and see what, if anything, he does tonight. If he moves, follow him. If he goes somewhere interesting, call me."

"Where are you going to be?"

"Close by at the University Diner."

* * *

Mitch locked his apartment door and scooted over to the picture window and peeked around the edge of the curtains, watching as the detectives left, taking a moment to admire the woman one more time. She was in her late thirties but did have a look to her.

He thought he'd handled their arrival well. Seeing the detectives depart, he went to the coat closet by the front door, unzipped the interior pocket of his winter coat and found his backup cell phone, then went back to the window and took one last look outside, seeing the detectives pull away.

Tripp answered on the third ring. "What's up?"

"Police detectives just stopped by. They were asking about you know who. They dropped your name. I told them I didn't recognize either of your names. I think they bought it, but you never know."

NINE

"ROAD TRIP."

Maggie noticed the glare of the headlights through the den's curtains and then heard the clatter of Ellen's footsteps as she came down the stairs and stepped into the den, giving Maggie a perfunctory hug goodbye. "See you in the morning."

"Be good," Maggie said with a hint of warning to it. Ellen was a great kid, but she wouldn't be doing her job, even as a younger stepmom, if she didn't at least say it.

"I will," Ellen answered. "I'm staying at Haley's. We're not going anywhere. Are you watching basketball? Dad and B are at the games tonight."

"I'm flipping around. I love your father and brother, but I can only watch so much basketball."

"No kidding," Ellen replied and opened the front door. "Well... be good."

"Ha!"

Maggie locked the door behind Ellen and then watched her get into her friend's car for the trip across town. Once the car pulled away, Maggie went back to the salon and checked the tracker. The pickup truck was at the two-story house. Earlier in the afternoon she had taken a quick drive up to

Cullen Crossing and it appeared the truck stopped at a strip mall that basically housed all the businesses in that little town. There was a restaurant so perhaps Rudick had gone there. The only other place he'd gone repeatedly was the place out in the woods and she was curious as to what was out there that would draw him there four times in the last day plus.

Maggie pulled on jeans, a warm coat and grabbed one of Rob's black stocking caps and black gloves. She stuffed the tracker into her small backpack, along with the iPad, a disposable phone and a Beretta. There wasn't an address for this location that she could get from the tracker. Perhaps if she'd had a newer model. That was the problem using twelve-year-old equipment. There was only one thing to do.

"Road trip," she said, a tingle of excitement pulsing through her as she tied her hiking boots.

Forty-five minutes later, having gotten turned around a few times, she thought she'd found a gravel road that Rudick's truck had taken. She drove along slowly, scanning each side, looking for any sort of a structure. *Perhaps he was just meeting someone out here on the side of the road,* she thought to herself as she motored along. She pulled to the right and stopped. She looked at the line on the tracker and compared it to the position of her car on her own phone map app. "It's still ahead," she murmured to herself. "Maybe another half-mile."

She pulled forward, creeping slowly along the road when she caught a glimpse of light through the dense trees. Stopping, she powered down her window and killed her headlights. The glow she saw was a light from a camping trailer.

Huh.

Maggie pulled forward and on the left crept by an opening in the woods for a rough driveway that led back to what looked to be an old Airstream. She drove ahead and around a bend in the road to the left and saw a small turn off to the right. Taking the turn, it was just a small jut that dead-ended fifty feet in, but it was an out of sight place to park.

She turned around and looked back.

What in the world are you doing out here?

It had been years, but she was getting the feels the way she once did when she was scouting. The oddity of driving out here multiple times each day, in the middle of nowhere, to an Airstream trailer. There was something to that.

First grabbing her backpack, she got out of the car, quickly crossed the road and then crept along the right side, maybe a couple hundred yards, to the entry to the small driveway. There were fresh tire tracks along the muddy and snowy path leading to the trailer.

She kept to the tree line and halted halfway to the trailer. A body walked past the window. She slipped into the trees, knelt and slipped off her backpack and took out a pair of small binoculars. She focused on the windows of the trailer.

There he was again, but it was just in a flash, not stopping long enough to get a solid look. *Patience.* A minute later the man stopped and looked out the window to the right of the door, holding still. He was on a cell phone.

She'd seen the face, on Jenny's phone. It was Ron Gresh. *This is where you're hiding.* Reaching back to put the binoculars in the backpack she looked to the south and saw headlights.

"Oh, oh."

She took out the small tracking monitor. It was Rudick. She worked her way deeper into the woods. Ducking down, she hid behind a downed tree as the truck made the left turn. Rudick was coming out to visit Gresh multiple times a day and now again tonight.

Why?

From her crouched position, she saw the truck as it pulled by. And then another truck. Rudick was not alone. He had others with him.

She reached into her backpack and took out the flip phone.

* * *

"Anything from Reese or Nolan?" Tori asked as she dipped her last tater tot into the little mound of ketchup left on her plate, her Cajun chicken sandwich long since finished. Braddock had done the same, polishing off his double cheeseburger. They were both drinking sodas.

"No," Braddock said as he looked to a waitress walking by, salivating at the full tray of beers she was carrying to a nearby table. "I could go for one of those but—"

"You're on duty."

"Technically *we're* on duty," he corrected.

"Eh," Tori said. "You're not paying me enough. It's why I need a second job teaching classes."

"Oh yeah, you're living in poverty."

Tori laughed. She was living quite well thank you very much. Her phone rang.

"Who's that?" Braddock asked.

"Not sure. Could be spam," she said, letting it run. She set her phone down and reached for a tater tot. The phone rang again. "Same number," Tori muttered and picked up her phone. "They're persistent."

"You've handed out your card a lot as of late."

"Good point." She hit the green button. "Hello."

"Is this Tori Hunter?" a whispered voice asked. It was a woman.

Tori looked up to Braddock. "This is she."

"Are you still looking for Ron Gresh?"

"Yes."

"I know where he is right now. I'm looking at him."

* * *

Ron rubbed his hands together as he paced back and forth. *I need to get out of here*, he thought. *I'm a sitting duck.*

He needed to get out of the trailer, away from Manchester Bay, out of the state, he needed to be gone. He was demanding it from Rudick this time when he arrived. Yeah, he'd screwed up in a way, Grace and Cameron outside the apartment that night. It wasn't his fault that bitch and her boy toy were out there. And that they would come back a second time?

He never imagined all this would come from it.

I need to take the edge off. He took what was left of the bag and spread it out on the small tray. This was the last of it. He put the small pile of coke on the table and then with the razor blade sliced and cut it into four thin lines. With the rolled-up dollar bill he snorted the first line in, feeling it burn the inside of his left nostril, then the rush and energy as it surged through him. "Oh... yeah." After a moment, he leaned down to take in the second line.

The last line complete, he went to the refrigerator and took out another bottle of beer, twisted off the cap and swigged it down, feeling drips leak out and trickle down his chin. "Ahh."

Light came in the door window, and he looked out to see the truck approaching.

Finally.

* * *

"What's out there?" Braddock asked Steak.

"Woods, ponds, wildlife, but not... people. You think this is legit?"

"It sure sounded legit," Tori replied. "The caller was... descriptive. Gravel road, Airstream, four men plus Gresh inside the trailer."

"Get on your horse," Braddock ordered.

"Hauling ass."

"I get Steak's question," Tori said as Braddock roared north on the H-4, flashing lights and siren. Another set of flashing lights came into view behind them, which she assumed was Reese and Nolan. "Dirt road barely on the map, Airstream trailer, other men there. It's awfully out of the blue."

"Sometimes tips are," Braddock said.

* * *

"Hey, Ronnie," Tripp greeted with a wave and a smile as he and Rudick, along with Nico and Gill came inside.

"Damn it, Ernie. I have to get out of here," Ron exclaimed, pacing again. "The police are looking for me. They're thinking I was the shooter. I wasn't even there but you guys have a target painted all over me."

"I know, Ronnie, I know," Rudick said easily.

"This wasn't my fault!"

Rudick nodded, holding up his hands. "I hear you, kid. We're putting you on the road."

"Where? Where am I going?"

"We're going to take you back to the house and you and Gill are driving to San Diego. From there we have someone who will get you into Mexico and onto a boat. You're going to need to go away for a long time. Pack your stuff."

"It's about time." Gresh sighed in relief as he went to the back bedroom.

* * *

Maggie reached inside the backpack and took out her Beretta and quickly chambered a round, just in case.

The men all went inside the trailer, and even through the small windows and open door, she was able to observe. From the way the men took position, she knew.

Here it comes.

* * *

"I'm ready!" Ron said as he threw the duffel over his left shoulder and stepped out of the back bedroom. "What the—"

Bap!

Tripp's first shot hit Ron dead center in the chest. "Whaaa... I did what you..."

Bap! Bap!

The second two hit him in the upper left chest. Ron fell back against the doorjamb and then onto his back and into the bedroom.

"Whoa!" Gill said, taking a step back.

"Don't worry," Rudick said, turning to Gill. "We'll get this cleaned up."

Pop! Pop! Pop! Pop!

Gill's eyes bulged. He looked to Nico, who'd shot him. He clutched at his chest. "But... Nico."

Rudick looked Gill in the eye. "Had to be done."

Nico stepped over to Gresh's body, quickly wiped the .45 and then placed it in Gresh's hand, lifted his hand, steadied it, and fired off two more rounds into the wall near where Gill's body lay. Tripp did the same with his weapon, placing it in Gill's right hand, firing two shots hitting the wall to the left of the bedroom door.

"Okay, let's get the hell out of here," Rudick said. "It'll be days, if not weeks, before this is all found out here."

Rudick, Tripp and Nico descended the steps. Tripp pulled the door closed.

* * *

Four men went in. Three came out.

So that's what they were doing.

She ducked low behind the downed tree trunk, her stocking cap pulled low, gun in her right hand as the two trucks quickly turned around and zoomed down the driveway and roared down the road.

She crawled over the log and stepped back onto the driveway.

Get out of here.

That's what she should do. Instead, she jogged to the trailer and quickly slipped inside. One man was lying to her immediate right, crumpled under the small table. He'd been shot three times in the chest. She checked for a pulse, but he was long gone. He had a S&W .40 in his right hand.

Ron Gresh was to her left, lying flat on his back, his right leg crumpled underneath him as he laid half in the bedroom. He too was dead. A .45 rested in his right hand. She had a guess about that gun's prior usage.

That's how they're going to sell it.

Thirty seconds later, she stepped out of the camper and jogged up the driveway and turned left, sticking close to the left side of the road, checking behind her. In the distance she thought she saw headlights. She squinted. No, there were multiple sets of headlights and flashing lights.

Hustle.

Her jog was now a full out sprint as the road veered to the left. A hundred yards ahead was the little notch in the woods she had parked in. She ran at a full sprint, turned to the right but hit an ice patch, slipped and crashed hard on her right side, banging the right side of her face on the ground.

"Ow! Ow! Ow! Dammit!"

Pain seared through her right shoulder. An SUV, police light flashing, came flying around the corner. *Move.*

She pushed herself up, stumbling to her car, falling against it. She turned back to see a Sheriff's Department Explorer fly by.

* * *

"There it is," Tori said, gesturing to the Airstream trailer visible through the woods. "Just like the woman said."

Braddock slowed and turned left into the narrow driveway, Reese, Nolan, Steak, and another deputy behind him. A second deputy approached from the north. Parking up, Braddock called to the Airstream. "Ron Gresh! Come out!"

Tori scanned the Airstream, the lights on inside. The exterior door opened outward. "The door is half open," she said. Braddock realized he and Tori were not vested up. Reese, Nolan, Steak, and the deputies were. He looked over to Steak and nodded toward the trailer.

Steak looked back and waved the deputies forward. He caught Reese's eyes and pointed with his two fingers toward the trailer door. With the others covering his approach, Reese scooted quickly forward to the left of the door, reached for the handle, and pulled it all the way open, ducking down behind it. Everyone held their position for a moment. There was no movement. Steak hustled forward, a deputy right behind him coming in from the right. Steak glimpsed the legs lying on the floor. "I have a man down."

"Make that two," Reese said, gesturing inside to the right of the trailer. He covered Steak as he took the step up into the trailer. Reese followed.

A second later, Steak appeared in the open door. "We're clear."

Braddock and Tori stepped up inside and took in the scene.

"Huh," Tori muttered. "Would you look at that."

TEN

"THEY DON'T KNOW ANYTHING BUT WHAT THEY'VE ALWAYS BEEN."

Sunday morning.

Boe invited Tori and Braddock to her home for breakfast.

"What do you make of meeting at the boss's house?" Braddock asked with a wry smile after they accepted the invite.

Tori shook her head and replied, "She's a politician. Is it just possible this will be a conversation she doesn't want anyone to hear?"

"It could be that she just wants to have breakfast."

"Uh-huh."

"You're such a cynic."

"Occupational prerequisite."

When Boe let them inside, the kitchen smelled richly of breakfast: eggs, sausage, and potatoes. "I've got the egg bake ready. Grab a plate."

"This is delicious," Tori complimented as they ate, knowing that buttering up Boe was no bad thing. "My dad used to make this when we were kids."

"Big Jim had a recipe?"

"He did. He'd mix in different kinds of sausages, red and green peppers, onions, everything. It was tasty," Tori said with a smile. "And then Jessie and I would burp and fart all day. Those peppers just did us in."

Boe cackled.

"Where is Craig?" Braddock asked. Craig was Boe's husband.

"I'm a hunting, snowmobiling and fishing widow," she said, smiling, explaining he was up on Lake of the Woods ice fishing. "Are you two packed for your pending vacation?"

Spring break from school started at the end of next week. Tori and Braddock were planning some downtime, taking Quinn, Braddock's twelve-year-old son, to Costa Rica for six days, along with his brother-in-law Drew, Drew's wife Andrea and their kids. "We will be," Braddock said. "Getting to some warm weather will be good."

"I agree," Tori replied. "I haven't been to Costa Rica so I'm looking forward to that."

Once they'd finished breakfast and another cup of coffee was poured, they talked shop.

The BCA had processed the scene at the trailer, fast-tracking the ballistics analysis. "Time of death was within an hour or so of our arrival," Braddock said, flipping through his case file. "The gun in Gresh's hand was the same .45 used to shoot Leo Randall, Cameron Jensen and Grace Horn. The gun had Gresh's prints on it." The other dead man was confirmed as Tony Gill. He too had been shot with the same .45. Gresh was shot with the gun in Gill's hand. "The BCA says that they lasered the shooting angles and it sure looks like those two shot each other."

"Looks like?"

"They're skepticism isn't as informed as ours, but they have it too."

"What do we know about Gill?" Boe asked.

"Aged twenty-five. He had an arrest for minor possession down in St. Cloud that he plead out. That was three years ago.

Nothing since," Braddock reported. "Friday night, we searched his apartment here in town but didn't find anything of use beyond some marijuana, an amount typical for personal use, not sale. Interestingly we didn't find a cell phone on him or at the apartment."

"It wasn't in his car either," Tori noted. "Someone took it. One of the others our tipster told us about."

"What do you two make of that?" Boe asked. "The tip?"

Braddock sat back. "One part of me thinks it was someone at the trailer who called it in after it all went down. Someone who wanted us to find that scene and Gresh and the gun."

Tori crinkled her nose at that, which Braddock expected.

"And your theory?" Boe asked her.

"I don't think the tipster was out there to mislead us. I think she was there to help us."

"Who do we think she is?"

"No idea yet. I've listened and re-listened to that call. She was whispering. The urgency of it is authentic. To me it sounded like she was there, seeing it and reporting it as it was happening. Now the part that lends credence to Braddock's theory is how in the world does she end up out there. You don't just wander by that place, see Ron Gresh, and call it in late on a dark Friday night. It's way too off the beaten path. You can't see anything from the road. To know Gresh was in there, you either had to just know it, or get up real close and see it."

"The phone used for the tip was a burner phone, a really old one sold thirteen years ago," Braddock said.

"Thirteen years?"

"Yeah. We have no way of tracing who the phone was sold too or who our informer was. For now, that's a dead end. As for Gill, we're subpoenaing his phone records, financials, anything else, see what we get come Monday," Braddock reported.

"Did he have a roommate?"

"No. He lived alone. One bedroom apartment. He was originally from Milwaukee. Came to Minnesota to go to college in St. Cloud. Dropped out and went to work and ended up here a few years ago. I talked to his parents yesterday, but they hadn't talked to him in months. They weren't close. That's what we have on Gill. And we know the story on Gresh's background."

"I can't believe he held on to the gun," Boe said, shaking her head. "What a dumbass."

"I'm not convinced he did," Braddock suggested.

"This whole thing just reeks of a setup," Tori said skeptically. "Our tipster said there were four men plus Gresh. Where did the other three go? They set those two up to take the fall."

Braddock nodded in agreement. "First thing that should have happened after the shooting is Gresh dumps the gun."

"Oh, I agree," Boe said. "However, I saw the pictures of the table, the drugs found on it. Most criminals aren't that smart. Especially ones that are all doped up on coke," Boe said, falling back on her experience in the Marshal's Service. "It's often why we caught them. They go back to their old girlfriends, their family, restaurants, bars, habits, vices. They don't know anything but what they've always been. It's a .45, a big gun. A wannabe thug who thinks he gets away clean might not be so quick to give that up, even if that's what he should have done."

"Is your theory this was all about Gresh lashing out at Horn for dumping him and taking out her and the guy who replaced her?"

Boe grimaced and shook her head. "I wish that theory truly held water."

"It would be easy and clean," Tori said. "But—"

"We can't unknow what Grace and Jensen told Grace's roommate Kristy. What they saw the night before," Braddock replied.

"And Gresh now being dead is all too convenient," Tori continued. "It is too beneficial to someone or more than one someone. We were supposed to find Gresh and Gill like that, just not thirty minutes after they were shot. Heck, we don't even truly know if he was the shooter. He was found with the gun, had motive, was hiding, on drugs. He looks guilty. And that's all someone would have to argue. Even if we suspected someone else, the evidence on Gresh alone creates more than ample reasonable doubt for anyone else."

"Which is why, for now, what we tell the family is that Gresh is dead. He was found with the gun that killed those kids. Whether he pulled the trigger or not, he *was* involved. The families think Gresh did it and they think they know why. In the meantime, we also have an open investigation of missing drug dealers and perhaps that includes whoever was wrapped in that rug coming out of Gresh's building. You keep working that and if more develops on the Holmstrand front in investigating, all the better."

"That's not telling the family the whole truth," Tori contended.

"No, but it does tell them what we do know for certain. They think they know who is responsible and now he's dead. This gives them some closure."

"And if we can give them more later, we will," Braddock said.

"I don't know—" Tori started.

"Let me talk to the families about it," Boe said. "I'm the boss. If we're not telling them everything, that decision falls on me, not on you two. That way, if you have to go back to them later, you weren't the ones who didn't tell them everything."

* * *

Maggie bundled up and made her way over to the Randalls' house, carrying the roaster full of chili next door. She rang the doorbell with her elbow. Cathy opened the door.

"Hey, Maggie. Geez, let me help you with that," she said,

stepping out onto the front stoop and taking the roaster. "You've done so much."

"It's nothing, Cath. I just whipped it up quick this morning. Thought you and all your family could use an easy lunch is all."

"Thank you. The Jensen's are coming down. The police are stopping by. They have news for us."

"In that case," Maggie whispered in her ear, "I should go."

"No, no, no. Stay," Cathy said, slipping her arm through hers. "You're like family to me too."

She'd expected it would be Will Braddock and Tori Hunter, but it was Sheriff Boe instead. Everyone gathered in the family room, encircling the sheriff, who sat in a high-backed soft chair.

Boe explained that they found the man they strongly suspected of killing Leo, Cameron and Grace late Friday night. He was found dead in a trailer out in the woods, along with another man. "It appears they shot one another. One of the guns we found in the trailer was the one used here."

"Why? Why did he do it?" Cathy asked.

"Was it that Grace used to be this man's girlfriend?" Karin Jensen said.

"We can't know motive for sure. He did not take the breakup well. He had continued to pursue Grace." Boe mentioned a picture display of Grace that Gresh had in his apartment. "He doesn't appear to have moved on. He also was mixed up in drugs. In the trailer where he was found, we also found cocaine. We'll know more when we get the toxicology report on the two men."

"Is the investigation over?" Cathy asked. "Is it solved?"

"For now, yes. He had motive and the gun."

"Well... at least we know," Karin Jensen said, holding Cathy's hand. "At least we have some answers now."

Maggie remained stoic, but she knew.

The sheriff wasn't telling them everything.

ELEVEN

"IT WAS PART OF HIS DETAILED NATURE."

Maggie let her eyes close behind her sunglasses, attempting to stem the tears she felt forming yet again. Rob stood to her left, his arm gently around her shoulders. Brian and Ellen stood to her right, their heads bowed, the tears slowly streaming down their cheeks. They were on the left edge of a massive grouping of Holmstrand High School families. The support from the community in the week since the shooting had amazed her. There had been many hundreds between the wake last evening and the church service this morning. And if the miles long procession of cars and trucks had been any indication, it seemed as if the entirety of the towns of Holmstrand and Pequot Lakes had come to the cemetery to pay their respects.

Just in front of them, Cathy stood arm-in-arm with her sister Karin, the caskets of Leo and Cameron resting in front of them as a light misty fog enveloped the area, adding an extra layer of dreariness to the burying of two good young men who had so much life yet to live.

The words of the priest, while earnest and heartfelt, didn't reach her like they may have some of the others standing about. She'd had a tenuous relationship with her faith given her own past. What she focused on was her friend, the alternating period of heavy sighs followed by the flow of tears. Her sister Karin had her husband, her other children to lean on but Cathy was alone. Her ex-husband Nate stood on the opposite side of the casket, his new fiancée standing to his left. Rob, a man not prone to violence of any kind, had muttered of his desire to go and, "rip that assholes head off." It only made her love him that much more.

Letting her eyes drift about the mass of humanity, she gazed to the left, up the rise to two lone people dressed in black, standing back from the crowd, present to pay their respects. Will Braddock and Tori Hunter.

She had wondered why, following what happened at the trailer in the woods, they were not the ones to come and see Cathy. She had read up on Tori Hunter and her own history of loss as well as of her career in the FBI. Her own interpretation was that if the sheriff were unwilling to let the whole story be told, Hunter wasn't going to be part of telling the families less than the whole truth. She suspected the same of Braddock.

As she looked further about, out beyond the fence surrounding the cemetery, she caught a glimpse of another familiar face.

Rudick.

Standing with him were the other two men from the trailer.

They were not present to mourn.

* * *

It struck her as an odd juxtaposition, hiding behind sunglasses on such a dreary day. The cold, damp weather conditions were much like those on that late March Thursday twenty-one years ago when she buried her father. Two days later she left Manchester Bay and didn't return for nearly twenty years.

After the funeral service concluded and the crowd began to

slowly disperse, leaving the immediate family to gather round the caskets one last time. Braddock held Tori's hand as they strolled across the cemetery to visit the graves of her parents and Jessie. She knelt to Jessie's grave plate, placing her right hand on it.

"Hey, sis. Miss you. Every day," she said softly as she cleared away some loose leaves and twigs.

"We should have brought some flowers," Braddock murmured.

Tori nodded as she stood up. "That's okay. It gives us a reason to come back after our vacation and spring clean. The grass is encroaching on the grave markers."

They slowly walked back across the cemetery and found Cameron Jensen's father waiting for them at Braddock's pickup truck.

"Detective Braddock, Agent Hunter, thank you for coming today. It was very kind of you."

"Of course," Tori said, stepping in to give Mr. Jensen a quick hug. "Your eulogy of your son was truly moving."

"Thank you," Mr. Jensen replied, but then lingered.

"Mr. Jensen, is there something, anything, we can do for you?" Braddock asked.

He nodded. "Um... on Monday, I was able to go and collect Cam's personal items, his wallet, watch, keys and phone." He held up the phone and then handed it to Braddock. "We spent the last couple of nights going through all the photos on it. We used some for the video that played at the funeral home yesterday. It was a true joy to see all the fun he'd had at the university and, of course, his photos with Grace. He was..." Mr. Jensen caught himself. "He was so happy."

"I understand, sir," Braddock said softly.

"There was, however, something on his phone that I thought was... odd. It was in the Notes app. He used that quite a bit. He used to say that if you don't write it down it—"

"Never happened," Tori said, completing the aphorism.

"It was part of his detailed nature," Mr. Jensen said of his son who had been studying to be an engineer. "If he thought of something that he wanted to remember, that was important, he would write it down. He'd tap it or speak it into the phone."

Braddock looked to Tori. He was leading to something.

"In any event, after we looked through all the photos, we thought we might get a chuckle out of some his notes and there were a couple of funny ones. Quippy things or sayings his friends might offer. We found a date checklist in there from a few months ago. I think for his first date with Grace."

"A date checklist?" Tori asked.

"That was Cam. But what else caught my eye was this note." He showed the phone to them. The note read: 786-AWF. "He put that in his phone the night before..." He choked up for a moment. "They were shot. I know the night before the shooting he and Grace went to this Ron Gresh's apartment. Grace's roommate told her mom that and she told us."

"That's right," Tori said.

"I know Ron Gresh is dead, and I'm not sorry to say I'm glad of that, but still, I thought this might mean something given all that's happened. I just thought you should know about it."

"I'll check it out, Mr. Jensen," Braddock said.

"Thank you and thank you again for being here today."

"That was a license plate, don't you think?" Tori said when they got into the truck.

"Let's go see."

A half-hour later Tori was looking over his shoulder as Braddock sat at his desk and typed 786AWF. It was a Minnesota license plate.

"Paul Marrone," Braddock muttered. "Cadillac Escalade. Address that is Crosslake although I think... yeah, his address

puts him on Bertha Lake." He was fifty-four years old. 5'10"
two hundred twenty pounds, graying hair, per his DMV
photo.

There was a knock on the door. They looked up to see
Steak, Eggleston, and Nolan in the doorway.

"What's up?" Braddock asked.

"Something on our missing drug dealer investigation."

"Yeah?"

"We have another one missing. Reardon Banz." Steak
handed over a photo. "Here's the kicker. He's been missing
since the night before Holmstrand and lived a block away
from—"

"Ron Gresh," Braddock finished.

"Yeah," Steak replied, his eyes wide. "How did you connect
that?"

Braddock held up a yellow sticky note. "Cameron Jensen
put this license plate number into the Notes app on his phone
the night before Holmstrand. That plate is for a man named
Paul Marrone."

"Who is he?" Steak asked.

"We don't know much yet but if Jensen took down the plate
number, it must mean something."

"Let's say it's Reardon Banz's body that was wrapped in
that rug and put into the back of that van outside Gresh's apartment. Cam and Grace see it," Tori posited. "They were noticed,
maybe by Gresh, maybe by this Marrone fellow, or somebody
else, but they were seen, and they saw something, or these guys
think they saw something they shouldn't have. Before they
could tell the police—Boom!" She let out an annoyed laugh.
"And Gresh never got over his old girlfriend angle gives it all
cover."

"And they saw the display of Grace in Gresh's apartment,"
Braddock said. "Because Banz was killed inside it."

"One part doesn't fit in all that," Tori interjected. "The

woman caller. What was her role in all of this?" She sighed in exasperation, looking to Braddock. "Great timing, huh?"

"Don't even think it," Braddock said, hearing the tone. "Not for a minute. It isn't happening."

"But—"

"We're on that plane tomorrow. I'm not doing that to Quinn, to Drew, to Andrea. We're back in six days."

"This doesn't feel right," Tori insisted. "How can we sit on the beach in Costa Rica with this..."

"Because it's covered," Braddock replied. He turned to Nolan. "Start digging on Marrone, where he's from, what he's done, jobs, home, family, pets, unusual proclivities. Who is this guy? Who does he run with?"

"Done."

To Steak, he said, "Assume Banz is connected to Holmstrand and the other missing dealers, so what turns up? Keep on that, add this Marrone name to the mix. If you find something that you have to act on, call. We're reachable."

"Do we clue in Boe?"

"Let's see what we find first."

Tori examined the stacks of clothes laid out on the small couch and coffee table in her office. Braddock stuck his head inside. "You do know we're only going for six days, right?"

"Yeah, yeah," she replied dismissively, evaluating what she wanted for their trip.

"I packed for this thing in about ten minutes," he snickered.

"Reason number eight-hundred-twenty-four why the world is easier for men than women."

"Jeez, look at all that stuff," Quinn said, chomping on a square piece of pizza. "If you take all that the plane won't get off the ground."

"Listen, you," Tori said, turning around and then noticing

Quinn dressed in a sweater and pressed pants, his hair combed. "Are you going somewhere?"

"I'm going to a movie with some of the guys," Quinn answered.

"And some of the girls from school too," Braddock mentioned and then with a wry grin, added, "One of whom I assume is his girlfriend."

"Izzy is going?" Tori said.

"She's not my girlfriend," Quinn replied with a headshake. Except she really kind of was. He and Izzy Farner "liked" each other, which as best Tori could tell, was the middle school equivalent of "dating." At this point, from what Tori had surmised, it amounted to a lot of texting and not much else.

A horn honked. "That's Andrea," Quinn said. "See if you can do something about these piles before I get back, Tori."

Tori laughed inwardly at the snark, the maturity of it. "Are you packed?"

"All ready," he said and then grinned. "Just waiting on you. Like always."

"Get out of here," she replied, taking a quick step at him.

Quinn fled, laughing. "Don't make us late for the plane."

After the back door slammed, Tori smiled. "His wiseass game is developing."

"A little too well I think," Braddock replied. "I blame you."

"What?"

"You're the queen bee of snarky repartee. He picks up on it."

"Yeah, yeah."

Braddock examined the clothes piles. "Seriously, do you need help with this?"

"No!" Tori replied. "I know what I want. I've just been... slow. You know, thinking before I act. You should try it."

He knew the tone. "What's on your mind?" He already knew the answer.

"The funeral, the plate number, and just going on vacation while all this is still... unresolved. I just don't feel right leaving."

"And I can't think of a better reason to get away," Braddock said, leaning casually against the door frame. Tori was not one who could easily just shut things down and compartmentalize. "Days, weeks like this are exactly why we have to get away for our mental health. And I have good people on it. If something truly vital breaks, they'll call. If something truly vital breaks, they can handle it."

"I know, I know," Tori said, folding a small top and placing it in her suitcase. "It's not stopping me from going on vacation. I just want to be on the record that I don't feel... completely right about it."

"Duly noted."

"Don't mock me."

"I'm not. But everyone's tragedies are not our burden to bear," he said.

"But—"

"They're not. This job is hard enough without adding that to it. I, for one, plan on forgetting all about it when I feel the first bit of Costa Rican sand in my toes."

"It doesn't bother you in the least that we're leaving this behind?"

"If we weren't going on vacation, I'd still be at the office. Problem is," he said, a smile forming, "I'm worried you'll need help packing. You're very indecisive."

"Whatever," Tori replied.

"Hey, Tor, it eats at me a bit too."

Tori looked back. "You're good at hiding it."

"I try to be like a doctor, you know, clinical. It'll be here when we get back. I'll deal with it then."

Tori nodded as she folded a small tank top.

"There is one thing I've been ruminating on."

"What?"

"Our informant."

"Ah, the *mysterious* woman X. I'm intrigued by her as well. She used a burner phone, was whispering, wasn't there when we got there."

"And in my experience, innocent people don't use burner phones or leave the scene when they could be a valuable witness. That Airstream is out in the middle of nowhere. You don't just stumble upon it. So either she knew it was out there or to find it required tailing, which wouldn't have been easy," he said, pursing his lips.

"For an amateur," Tori said as she picked up a pair of cut-off white shorts and folded them. "Banz, what those kids saw, there is a lot more going on here than we know. But."

"But?"

"You're right. It'll be here for us when we return," she said walking to him, letting him wrap his long arms around her. She tipped her chin up so that he could lean down and kiss her.

TWELVE

"WE DIDN'T GO INTO WITNESS PROTECTION."

Friday morning. One week later.

The famous adage of Chaucer percolated in her mind: *All good things must come to an end.*

It was apt given what she was putting at risk.

The sun was at her back, rising. Shortly, it would be blinding were anyone looking out the east side windows of the house. With her gloved right hand, she raised the miniature binoculars to her eyes one last time. The two-story house was quiet.

Maggie, why are you here?

She didn't have to be. She shouldn't be. This was a choice.

Was it the right one?

There had to be a hundred times over the last week where she said to herself, just let it go and move on. You have a good life. A husband who adores you. Two great stepchildren. A business to call your own. As one of the coffee cups in her kitchen said: *Life was good.*

But then she would see how it wasn't for Cathy. She was with her daily and saw a little bit of life drain from her each time. The loss of her only child caused by a brutal and senseless act. Maggie told herself that whatever it was she did could not bring Leo back for Cathy.

The logical side of her said tragedy strikes good people all the time. It's random, like a car accident or a tornado. Nothing you could do other than give your condolences, support and be there for them and, in the end, be thankful it wasn't you and those that you love.

Except she could do something. She possessed... certain abilities. And she couldn't get past the thought that there ought to be a cost for killing innocent people.

After driving out to the trailer and witnessing Gresh's murder, she'd linked the tracking monitor to her iPad. Now the iPad, stored in her salon desk drawer, was like gravity, its polarity pulling her in. It contained actionable intelligence if one were inclined to act on it.

The police had not caught the people truly responsible for Leo, Cameron, and Grace's deaths. They might have identified the shooter, if Ron Gresh was the one who actually took the shots. But Gresh wasn't the one who made that call. Rudick's presence at that trailer confirmed that. The others at the trailer were involved as well. And as best she could tell, they were facing no consequence for it. And then, after all that had happened, to see Rudick and those men in the distance at the funeral. That was rubbing salt in the wound and while Cathy didn't know who they were, Maggie did.

From the monitor she could see that each day, Rudick drove long loops through Shepard and the surrounding counties. Every day there was also a trip to Cullen Crossing around noon. Four days ago, Monday, her calendar open save for a late afternoon appointment, she drove to Cullen Crossing and watched as Rudick arrived at the strip mall and went into the restaurant. He was inside a good hour before re-emerging. On Tuesday, the middle of her day was open. She drove back up to Cullen Crossing. This time she was sitting inside the restaurant and at the bar when Rudick entered. She monitored him in the reflection of the stenciled mirror behind the bar as he sat down alone in a booth in the corner that allowed for some privacy.

She had ordered a bowl of soup and half-sandwich, and took her time dining, waiting, reading her phone while occasionally glancing up to the mirror for the next forty-five minutes. The soup and sandwich nearly finished she was starting to think perhaps Rudick simply liked the restaurant and that was why he went there. Just as she was reaching into her shoulder bag for her wallet, she glanced up to the mirror and saw two men walk out of a door from the staff section of the restaurant and join Rudick in the booth.

This can't be happening.

It had been twelve years.

Jimmy Mileski. Paul Marrone.

How? How is it that those two were here? In of all places a little strip mall in Cullen Crossing, population less than one hundred. Six hundred miles from Chicago. Twenty miles from her home.

She had little worry they would recognize her, not with her significantly altered nose, sharper jawline and blonde bob, her eyes hidden behind stylish dark-rimmed glasses, wearing a white stocking cap, loose black sweatpants, white turtleneck and silver puffer vest, looking for all intents and purposes like the soccer mom that she had been for the last decade.

However, seeing those two with Rudick put the shooting in a whole new light.

Were the police investigating them?

Not that she perceived. She saw Cathy daily and the police had not provided any updates.

Mileski and Marrone were the sharp ones back in the day. They weren't the leadership, that was their older brothers, but they were around, involved, making moves and were no friends of the people she'd once cared about: and undoubtedly played some role in their demises. Despite the seemingly legitimate restaurant she was sitting in, there was no way Mileski and Marrone were here operating it strictly legitimately. It wasn't in their DNA. If they were up here, they were up here for a reason and Rudick, an old hand from Chicago, was here with them too.

What was it they were into? Why would they need to kill Cameron, Grace and Leo?

There were drugs at the trailer. Cathy and Karin Jensen said that Ron Gresh got into drugs and drug dealing. She'd heard something about Cameron and his girlfriend going to Gresh's apartment the night before the shooting. Was that it?

Looking in the mirror she knew that if Mileski or Marrone had given such an order, Cameron and Grace must have seen something significant. If Ron Gresh was involved in drugs, the mere presence of these men told her he was involved with Mileski's operation. And if Gresh was the shooter at the Randall house, he was acting on orders. That kind of an order, regardless of who communicated it, always came from the top.

This confirmed that what she saw at the trailer that night was a clean-up operation. Eliminate Gresh and the other man and cut off all possible lines back to Mileski and Marrone. They keep their heads down for a few months, ride out the storm and things return to normal.

Same as it ever was.

Not wanting to leave a credit card record, she left a twenty on the counter and walked out.

What to do?

She wondered that as she drove home that afternoon. Nothing was the logical answer and by the time she'd reached Holmstrand she'd had herself believing that. That night, Cathy knocked on the door, desperate for someone to talk to. It all came pouring out of her.

"Maggie, I hear those shots every day, every night, I see

them, I feel them. They wake me up at night," Cathy said over tea in Maggie's kitchen. "I see... Leo every day. I can't..."

There was a time in her life when she would have been numb to what Cathy was going through. But now, ten years married with stepchildren she loved as her very own, she was no longer so anesthetized.

She wondered if she'd been able to talk about what *she* was feeling maybe she wouldn't be here. Of course, nobody in her life would understand it if she did so confide. There had only been one person she could talk, really talk, about these things with years ago and even Angie wasn't the most sympathetic of shoulders to lean on. He was more of a gruff reality check than anything else. He had warned her of the path she was going down. When he couldn't prevent her from following it, he helped her instead, working with her and in ways protecting her, but when she would lament what it was she had to do, he would often say: *I warned you.* She wished Angie was here now.

Should she do this? If she did, how should she do it? Should she walk away?

Of course, with Rob and Ellen away on spring break and Brian skiing in Colorado with a friend's family, she'd been at home by herself for the past week, alone in her thoughts. Had they been home, would she be here? Probably not. They would all be home by tomorrow so if she was going to do this, it had to be now.

Maggie refocused on the two-story house with her binoculars. There were three men inside, all with a bedroom upstairs. Rudick had the master on the far side of the house. The other two had the smaller bedrooms along the front. She also had seen that they were night owls, sleeping until nine or ten a.m. daily. She was counting on that now. The house was asleep. No interior lights on.

To her right on the opposite side of the property was the

detached garage. There were three vehicles parked in front of it, including Rudick's black Dodge Ram.

After one last quick scan of the house, she put the small binoculars into a side pocket of her tight black-leather jacket. She pulled her black leather gloves tight to her fingers, before reaching down to the black holster strapped to her left leg and pulled out the gun. Ejecting the magazine, she checked it one more time before sliding it back in and chambering a round. She quick screwed a suppressor to the end of the Beretta before sliding the gun back into the leg holster. She repeated the same ritual with the gun in the holster strapped to her right leg.

Her combat boots were tied and secure. Her hair pinned tight to her head, she pulled the ski mask down over her face, securing the bottom around her neck and then zipping her leather jacket tight, making herself as sleek as possible.

She closed her eyes and took in a long breath.

Go.

Light on her feet, she moved to the edge of the wood line, and then sprinted fifteen yards across the narrowest part of the yard to the house's backside and down a slight incline to the back door for the basement. She pulled out her lock pick.

* * *

Alisha's eyes fluttered open. She looked across the room and saw that Nico was sleeping on the air mattress on the floor, his back to her. She'd been scared in the middle of the night and he came down to keep her company.

She threw off her blankets and went to the bedroom window and peered under the bottom of the window shade and out the window. It was blustery, the branches whipping in the wind. However, in the bright early morning light, she could see down to the lake. There were white caps in the roiling waters.

She watched intently through the small crack between the shade and bottom of the window.

There was a flash of movement to the left. A woman was coming quickly down the hill. She was dressed all in black, including the face mask. She went to the door and started doing something to the lock. A few seconds later, she opened the door and stepped inside.

Alisha rushed over to Nico and shook his shoulder.

Nico sleepily rolled over to see his sister and the look on her face. He signed: *"What's wrong?"*

* * *

Holding the Beretta high in her gloved hands as she crept up the stairs she stopped three steps short of the first floor and listened. The house was still. The only sound was the blustering of the wind clattering against the house and the light hum of the furnace. She took the last three steps and turned the corner and started slowly up the steps to the second floor.

The second-floor landing overlooked the open family room. At the top of the steps a bathroom was to the immediate right, the door open. There was a bedroom door straight ahead, the door closed, though not fully she could tell. It would push open with a nudge. To the left, another bedroom was halfway down the landing, the door fully closed, and then the master bedroom at the end.

Light on her feet, gun up, Maggie stepped quietly down the hallway to the door to the master bedroom. The door was open a crack. She peeked inside. Rudick was lying on his back, his mouth open, snoring.

With the toe of her right boot, she gently nudged the door open. It creaked just enough. Rudick's eyes fluttered open. He never made it out of the bed. "What the—"

Bap! Bap! Bap!

She spun right and took three rapid steps to the second door and with her left hand opened the second bedroom door, throwing it open and stepping inside.

The man was throwing off his blankets. "No! *No!*"

Bap! Bap! Bap!

She pivoted to her right, rushed down the hall and kicked the last door fully open. The bed was on the far wall, a perfect angle to fire.

The bed was empty, as was the room. She immediately spun to the stairway and looked down into the family room, expecting an attack from below.

Ca Chunk!

That was a car door slam, outside. She dashed to the bedroom window. The third man was getting into the Dodge Ram pickup. She turned the window lock open.

The engine started.

She shoved the window up as the truck backed out of the driveway. Dropping to her right knee, she tracked the pickup truck as it pulled away, crossing in front of her field of fire.

Bap! Bap! Bap! Bap! Bap! Bap!

The pickup sped away.

He saw her come in the house. He saw her.

Maggie sprinted down the steps, turned left through the kitchen and then out the house's side door, and sprinted through the yard and into the woods, scooping up the backpack and picking her way as planned through the woods to her black Acadia parked in the driveway for a cabin not yet open for the year. She got inside and reached into the backpack and took out the tracking monitor and set it in the center console.

Got him.

She slipped her mask up above her eyes and pulled away and zoomed east on the twisting gravel road. She glanced at the monitor to see that the Dodge Ram had turned right and was going south on the H-4. The end of the road was ahead. She reached the edge of the forest and the turn, and it was as if she'd emerged into the light and charged ahead. Coming around a right bend in the highway as it approached the Manchester Bay exits, she caught a glimpse of the pickup truck ahead as it got caught up in thickening traffic. She pulled up right behind the dual cab pickup, her left hand on the wheel, reaching for her Beretta with her right.

The driver of the pickup truck pulled onto the left shoulder and charged ahead. She did the same. The truck zoomed ahead but only into another cluster of vehicles, which allowed her to close on him again.

He abruptly veered right, cutting across the traffic and then down an embankment to an exit ramp.

She checked her rearview mirror. It was clear and she slammed on the brakes, almost coming to a stop, letting the traffic of the right lane fly. She turned hard right and cut across the right lane, veering back against the grain and then yanked the wheel left, her backend fishtailing and then zoomed down the exit ramp. The pickup truck was at the bottom, charging through a red light, making a left turn.

You're out of control. Far too many eyes. You know where he is. Calm down. Track him.

Stopped at the red light, she calmed her breathing. She straightened out the face mask on her head, so it looked more like a stocking cap and slipped on a pair of sunglasses. Checking the monitor, she saw that he was approaching the university campus.

Eyeing the monitor she kept following him around the campus. As she approached the corner there was a parking lot. She looked through it to see the pickup truck pulled to the side of the road. The man was taking a little girl out from the backseat.

She was in the truck?

Maggie observed as he dropped the girl off at a park bench.

She couldn't be but eight or nine years old. The man gestured to her, and she did the same back. Sign language. He leaned forward and hugged her and then ran around the front of the truck and got back inside, leaving her behind.

The Dodge out of view, she turned right and drove slowly along, eyeing the little girl. She was sitting on the park bench in a pink coat, her hood pulled up, her hands in her coat pockets. She was frightened.

* * *

Nico looked back at Alisha one more time before focusing on the road ahead. He weaved his way south of campus to a county road and turned left and raced east into the countryside, his hands tight on the wheel.

What to do?

He'd never spoken directly with Marrone or the boss man before, but he knew where to find them and knew Marrone's phone number. Rudick and Tripp were killed. They needed to know. There was a left turn ahead and he knew that could get him to Cullen Crossing.

* * *

Maggie was two miles behind him, observing the tracking monitor. Then the man turned left. She ran her finger on the road, tracking it north.

I know where you're going.

She made a snap decision, taking a left turn of her own, cutting northeast along a narrow road that wound its way through low lying wetlands and dense woods. She was driving at a forty-five-degree angle to the truck, observing the blue dot go north while she was driving east, northeast. They would meet a mile ahead.

* * *

Nico reached for his phone. He called Marrone, violating protocol. He didn't answer. He tried immediately again as he rushed north.

"Yeah?"

"Mr. Marrone, this is Nico. I know we're not—"

"Sorry, wrong numb—"

"No! It's not. Rudick is dead! Tripp is dead! Some masked woman dressed in black leather and combat boots broke into the house and killed them."

He caught a glimpse of a black flash in his rearview mirror. "And she's still after me. Right on my ass."

"Did you say a woman?"

"Yes! And now she's on me," Nico exclaimed, accelerating. She was coming up behind him. "I'm north on County 63."

He looked up in the mirror and she pulled into the oncoming lane.

"Shit!"

* * *

The road ahead was straight and the oncoming lane was clear. She powered down the passenger window, veered left and accelerated. She lifted the Beretta in her right hand.

The pickup truck accelerated, but she matched him. She could see the back of his head. He saw her coming and it looked like... he was on the phone.

Bap! Bap! Bap!

* * *

Nico ducked as the window glass shattered.

"Ahrg!"

A shot had nicked his upper left shoulder.

"Nico! Nico!"

* * *

The magazine was spent.

The truck angled into her, and she eased back to avoid colliding as the truck pushed her across the road onto the far shoulder. She braked and let the truck get ahead of her again.

With her left hand, she grabbed the Beretta from the left leg holster and quick passed it to her right hand and pushed the gas again, closing in the oncoming lane.

Oh, oh.

A car was coming right at them. She braked and veered right in behind the pickup truck again.

The car ripped past, and she veered out left again. Another car was coming. She pulled back behind the pickup truck. Letting the car pass, she knew the road was straight for another good two miles before they reached Cullen Crossing.

* * *

"Nico! *Nico!*" Marrone called.

"Here she comes again!"

* * *

Maggie veered left and accelerated alongside the truck. She could see him. *Time to hit him with all of it.*

Bap! Bap! Bap! Bap! Bap! Bap!

* * *

"Nico!" Marrone exclaimed.

"Ah... ah... I can't... I can't."

* * *

She eased back on the gas as the pickup truck started weaving and then headed across the far lane, tipped to the right and flipped over twice before crashing into a massive tree trunk.

Maggie zoomed by and looked to her rearview mirror to see the truck upside down and there was a truck, perhaps a half-mile back of her that was slowing and pulling to the shoulder. She drove ahead, glanced at the map on the small monitor and took a quick right, getting out of sight.

* * *

Twenty minutes later, Maggie pulled the Acadia into the garage-sized storage unit located around the backside of the storage facility in Deerwood. After she pulled the door down, she quickly took stock of the situation.

She got out of her black leather jacket, pants and combat boots and stored them back in the large trunk that contained other like clothes. One mildly odd yet satisfying feeling she'd had in putting it all back on for the first time in so long was that it all still fit, albeit a hair snugger. At the workbench she removed the two suppressors and then quickly disassembled the two guns that she used and stuffed their parts into two separate weighted duffel bags.

Quickly, she slipped into her workout clothes, black yoga pants, sports bra, sleeveless gray shirt, and long-sleeve yellow-quarter zip top. In a small round mirror, she checked her appearance, allowing her hair to remain disheveled if not sweaty, her cheeks flushed, the looks of someone who had just worked out.

She checked to make sure the area was clear before slipping

out of the garage and walking quickly around the corner to her dark blue RAV4. She pulled away and a couple of miles west of the storage facility, on a back gravel road, stopped and threw the duffel bags out into a pond, watching them sink below the surface. She drove back to Holmstrand, stopping along Main Street to buy her favorite specialty drink at the local coffee shop, chit-chatting with a few neighbors inside. When she slipped in the back door of the house, it was not yet 9:00 a.m. She had a couple of hours until her first appointment.

* * *

"Okay. Get out of there... Yeah, stay out of sight but keep an eye on it." Marrone hung up the phone. The two of them were hunkered down in the office.

"What did Stevie find?" Mileski asked.

"Rudick is dead. Tripp is too. I can only assume Nico is as well."

"Dead how?"

"At Rudick's house, three shots to each, tight, center mass. Professional."

"And this Nico. He said it was a woman?" Mileski asked Marrone. "He was sure of that? A woman."

"He said in all black leather, wearing a mask and combat boots."

"Have the police arrived yet?"

"No. Stevie is staying on watch. If the cops show, he'll know."

"Rudick didn't have anything there that—"

"No. He knew better than that. Even at his office there should be little tying back to us. My more immediate worry, Jimmy, is we're vulnerable." The two of them had already pulled guns out of the safe and had them tucked under their sweaters. "After Gresh and Gill, we were down guys. With

Rudick, Tripp and Nico now gone, we're down to Stevie and his brother Joe, but we both know Joe's not up for anything heavy. We might have to back off."

"No. I'm not doing that," Jimmy replied. "Bobby won't go for that either."

"But—"

"I don't know what this is yet, but I ain't closing up shop," Mileski said bitterly. He took a drink of his coffee. "You don't suppose? After all these years?"

"I'm really skeptical," Marrone replied. "It's not like we were unfindable. We didn't go into witness protection. We've been here in the open all this time. If she wanted to come for us, she could've done it any time. It's been what? Twelve years?"

"Still?"

"If it's her, why now, Jimmy?"

"I don't know, but we can't take any chances."

"You going to make the call?"

Mileski checked his watch. "I already have. He's on his way and bringing help with him."

THIRTEEN

"YOU NEED TO GET TO ME."

Her eyes drifted open, the light creeping into the room through a crack in the curtains. Tori glanced to the nightstand to her right. 5:50 a.m. Her alarm would go off in ten minutes. Why not get an earlier start, she thought and flipped off the blankets, and started to swing her legs when a long arm wrapped around her. In one motion, Braddock pulled her back and turned her so that she was straddling him.

They had gotten home last night from their spring break vacation from Costa Rica. It had been a relaxing six days in the house they rented with Drew and Andrea that had its own private swimming pool and was situated on a bluff overlooking the Pacific Ocean. The best news was the kids all had their own space in a lofted area that they retreated to at night, while the adults cocktailed and played card games. She and Braddock had their own secluded bedroom that had a double door to a patio that overlooked the pool and further out, the Pacific. With the light ocean breezes billowing the curtains each night, they made good use of it.

"Look at you with those bedroom eyes," she said, peering down at him. "You didn't get enough of me in Costa Rica?"

He smiled as his hands started slowly wandering about, starting low on her thighs, just above her knees, slowly, tantalizingly working their way up.

Stirring to the feel of his touch, Tori slowly pulled her hands back and with her eyes locked on his, deliberately slipped her long nightshirt off over her head, seductively twirling it twice before tossing it away leaving her fully naked.

"Watching you do that puts impure thoughts in my mind."

"How impure."

"Very."

She leaned down. "That's the idea, Braddock," she said before kissing him, one he eagerly returned.

He'd indeed had impure thoughts, ones that left her feeling light, as if her feet didn't hit the steps as she made her way down to the kitchen dressed in black jeans, a white blouse and light-blue casual blazer. Chic comfortable clothes for going over to campus to check in on things.

Braddock turned around and smiled. "Good morning."

"Right back at you," she said in a low murmur, leaning up, kissing him again, letting him wrap her in a hug, taking in the fresh scent from his shower and shave. And she liked the black-and-gray patterned sport coat and black slacks combo with light-blue dress shirt ensemble he was wearing. He looked and smelled good.

Quinn came into the kitchen. "Jeez, you guys. Didn't you get enough of each other on vacation?"

Tori looked up to Braddock who simply laughed as if to say, *what are you gonna do?* Quinn was the perceptive son of a detective. He wasn't missing much of anything these days.

Pushing away from Braddock, Tori turned to the little smart aleck. "That's enough out of you, wise guy. Cereal or some quick eggs?"

Quinn was already digging out a large bowl. "Cereal."

"On it," Tori replied, retrieving the cereal options and the milk from the refrigerator. Braddock's phone rang. "It's Steak," he said. "What's up, buddy? Whoa, slow down. Say again... Uh-huh... Really? Hot? Several times? No, that's an odd one for sure. Man, you think I could have a day to get back into the swing of things, wouldn't you? No. I'm on my way."

"What is it?"

"Homicide from the sounds of it," Braddock said, stuffing his phone in his pocket. "Road rage incident of some kind out on County 63."

"Road rage? Out there?" Tori asked skeptically. "Seriously?"

"I hear ya. There isn't much out that way but woods and deer," Braddock replied, collecting his Tahoe keys and various other items, stuffing them in his pockets. "A deputy is out there. A driver of a black pickup truck was shot five times. Truck is crashed upside down against a tree. He's reporting it looks like a road rage deal. I gotta hustle out and meet Steak and Eggleston."

"How do they know that?"

"There's a witness," he said. "Vacation is over," he said, giving her a quick kiss. "See ya later. And can you drop wise guy here off at Rog and Mary's?"

"Of course. We'll talk about toning down the wise guy."

"Why would I want to do that?"

"My point exactly."

* * *

Braddock made his way quickly through Manchester Bay and rushed east on Highway 210, following Steak and Eggleston, while his mind drifted back to the morning, and he scoffed a

laugh. It had been a very good morning. It had been a phenom-
enal vacation.

When he'd met his late wife Meghan, it was like a lightning
bolt. It happened at a party in a Manhattan apartment while
they were in college in New York. He was working the tap on
the keg when he'd spotted this pretty brunette with beautiful
brown eyes walking toward him. She smiled brightly and asked
for a refill and never left. For him it was love at first sight. It took
Meghan a little longer, but not much. They married three years
later. Meghan had this effervescent personality that made every
day an adventure. There was never a cross word between them,
just laughter. They had Quinn and things were even better. He
was a detective first grade with the NYPD, on a fast career
track, and her clothing design business was flourishing. There
was some money in the bank, mostly Meghan's but a little of his.
Life was going so well, the future exceedingly bright. They
were talking about another child. Then the headaches started
for Meghan and not long after the diagnosis. Two years later she
was gone, glioblastoma.

He'd been a widower five years when Tori came along.

At first, she hardly seemed like the antidote to the loss of
Meghan. Tori was alluring like Meghan, with her petite athletic
figure, auburn hair, deep green eyes, pretty smile and love of
clothes and fashion.

That's where the comparison stopped.

Unlike Meghan, the first time he met Tori they argued,
loudly, about how to pursue the killer Tori was certain had
murdered her sister twenty years before. For the first few weeks
they worked together, they fought and bickered and almost
seemed to revel in getting under each other's skin. He thought
Tori abrasive, combative and opinionated. She didn't seem too
impressed with him either. They were two alphas fighting for
control.

Now and then, when he and Tori looked back on it, they

euphemistically called those first few weeks the long foreplay. It took him that long to figure her out.

Like him, she was wounded. He had lost the love of his life. She had lost her twin sister and father within eighteen months of each other when she was a teenager. Tori had experienced all that loss at such a difficult age and felt, unreasonably in his view, responsibility for both losses. She ran away from Manchester Bay and tried burying the pain with distance and her work with the FBI. When he started to understand that, and when she realized he understood it and, more importantly, was and wanted to be there for her, was when her walls started to come down. He knew that he was the catalyst for her to make peace with her past so she could start living life and live it with him. She told him as much. She put in a lot of work to get herself there, along with a well-timed push or two from him along the way.

Tori was all in now. He could tell that was true with him and most importantly, with Quinn. His son, wary at first, had come to adore Tori and the feeling was quite mutual. She was not his mom, nor did she try to be. Nevertheless, the way she interacted with, influenced, and cared for him, gave Quinn something he'd been missing and needed, another person to lean on. Plus, the two of them liked just giving each other the verbal business.

While nobody had said out loud that they were all a family now, that's what they were.

He never thought he'd have that contentment that he'd had with Meghan ever again but the last few months with Tori and especially after the vacation, he was starting to feel like maybe he would.

Flashing police lights appeared ahead on the left and Braddock shook himself back to the present. Deputy Frewer was along the left side of the road. Braddock parked behind Steak and took in the scene. A Dodge Ram was lying upside down against the tree. Lying outside the opened driver's side door was a body under a white sheet. Standing with Frewer was a man looking nervous, smoking a cigarette.

"What do we have?" he asked Frewer, checking his watch. It was just short of 9:00 a.m.

"Driver's name was Nicholas Sweeney," Frewer answered, handing the driver's wallet over to Braddock for a quick look.

"His pickup truck sure took a beating. And some bullet holes," Steak observed.

"The interesting thing," Frewer said, "is it's not his truck. While I was waiting for you guys, I ran the plate. The truck is registered to a company, EBR Enterprises."

Braddock looked to Eggleston. "Let's dig in on that. See if we can get a name attached to the company."

"On it."

"What's this about a shooting?" Steak asked Frewer.

Frewer turned to the witness. "Mr. Stinson, tell Chief Detective Braddock and Detective Williams what you saw."

"I live a few miles south of here. I was coming out my driveway to go to work up in Jenkins."

"What time?"

"Seven-thirty a.m. give or take. I got to the end of my driveway and that pickup truck goes flying by, hauling ass north and as I looked, the other black SUV was on its left side and..."

"And what?" Braddock asked.

"It didn't look like the SUV was trying to pass, it was paralleling the pickup. I followed because I was curious to see, but I stayed back, man. The truck and SUV were weaving on the road and the SUV kept having to drop back in behind because vehicles were coming in the opposite direction. But then we hit that last two-mile straightaway to Cullen Crossing and the SUV made the move."

"How far back were you?" Steak prodded.

"A couple hundred yards. But we hit that straightaway and

the SUV swerved out to the left side and then... I saw the gunshots. The shooter must have unloaded a whole magazine. They kept firing and firing and firing. Then the pickup truck started swerving all over the road."

"What did you do?"

"I dropped back and called 911. I didn't need to get mixed up in that." Stinson exhaled a breath. "I've seen road rage before, but this was next level."

"What happened next?"

Stinson took a breath. "I was on the phone with the 911 dispatcher when the pickup truck crossed all the way over off the road, flipped over a couple of times before it stopped against that big tree."

"And the SUV?"

"It just kept on going."

"Where?"

"Other than north, I don't know," Stinson said. "I pulled over and ran to the pickup truck. I pulled him out, but he was... dead. I just waited for the police and ambulance then."

"Okay," Steak said. "Please wait here."

Braddock and Steak stepped down through the ditch to the truck. Steak lifted the white sheet and then rolled Sweeney's body onto the right side.

"Four hits," Braddock observed, gesturing with a pen. "Three in the upper back and then the one just left of the spine here that goes through the back of his neck and out the front of his throat."

"That's the fatal one most likely."

Braddock stood up and started walking around the pickup truck. "Do you buy the whole road rage thing?" he asked.

"Well..." Steak started before exhaling a breath. "I was until I heard your skeptical tone. However, from what our witness describes, it sure as heck sounds like that's what it was."

"Out here?" Braddock shook his head before crouching

down to look inside the truck cab. The interior was a mess, the glove box, and center console compartment both open with papers, coins, not to mention shattered glass strewn throughout the cab. "Looky there."

"What?"

With his gloved hand, Braddock reached inside and pulled out a cell phone.

"Burner," Steak observed.

Braddock looked at the display and the call history. "When was this happening?"

"Guy said seven-thirty a.m., give or take."

"Call history says he was on the phone at seven thirty-two a.m.," Braddock noted. "People usually use burners to call other burners, but we should check the phone number anyway. Call lasted several minutes. See who was on the other end."

"Will do."

Braddock stood up and started walking around the pickup truck, making a complete circuit around. The truck had flipped over a couple of times. There was no way of telling what damage was from that or playing Dodgem Cars on the highway. "He was on the phone and then he was shot several times," he said, looking to the rear bumper.

"Right. It puts the whole rage in road rage," Steak replied.

"Or does it?" Braddock said as he peered more closely at the rear bumper.

"What is it?" Steak asked.

Braddock gestured to a small silver metallic disc attached underneath the rear bumper. "Is the BCA coming?"

"Eventually. The call has been made."

"Take a few pictures of that with your phone."

Steak pulled out his phone and snapped several pictures from a few different angles. He quickly checked the quality of his pictures. "We're good."

Braddock reached under the bumper. The silver disc was

magnetized but he pulled it from the bumper. There was a small red light on the side, still alight. "This is a tracker. An older one but it hung on despite this thing flipping over. If our shooter was tracking this truck, this might be something other than road rage."

"Maybe. Maybe not," Eggs said, coming over to the two men with her phone in her hand. "There were calls into Manchester Bay PD this morning. A black Dodge Ram pickup truck was being chased by a black GMC Acadia on the H-4 early this morning just north of Manchester Bay, a little after seven a.m."

Braddock's phone started buzzing. It was Tori. "I got a weird one out here."

"Does it involve a black pickup truck by chance?"

"Uh... How do you know that?"

"You need to get to me."

FOURTEEN

"WHITE CAPS."

Psychology Professor Hannah Lane zipped up her jacket. It might have been early April, but the early morning temperature was not yet thirty degrees. She reached for her Starbucks tumbler and got out of the car and saw a friendly face.

"Happy Friday morning," she greeted, raising her cup as Tori Hunter slammed the door on her Audi Q7. "I thought you were on vacation."

"Just got back last night. Thought I'd come over and check in on things."

"It must have been good. You look tan."

"Costa Rica is highly recommended. If you haven't been there, go," Tori replied and then looked down the sidewalk. "Huh?"

"What?" Lane asked.

"The little girl on the bench," Tori said, gesturing to two students with backpacks, crouched in front of a little girl in a pink coat sitting on a park bench. Tori recognized the students. They were in her criminal procedure class. The little girl she did not recognize.

"What's going on, girls?" Tori asked when she and Lane approached.

"Morning, Professor Hunter," one of the students greeted. "We found her sitting on the bench. She's alone. She looks scared, and cold, her teeth are chattering. We've tried to talk to her but she just kind of looks at us shaking her head."

"Let me try." Tori had a thought and knelt in front of the girl, smiling. "Hi," she said and then with her right index finger touched her ear and mouth.

The little girl's eyes brightened, and she made a fist, moving it up and down.

"You know how to sign?" Lane asked.

"I can manage a bit," Tori replied, smiling, and lightly patting the girl on her leg. "I learned some on a lengthy investigation years ago. I'm a bit rusty though." Tori slowly gestured with her hands, saying: *I'm Tori.* Then she signed to the girl, asking: *What is your name?*

Tori watched the girl's reply. "Hi, Alisha," Tori signed and said it out loud. Lane and the two students smiled and waved to her.

Pretty name, Tori signed and then took a moment, thinking through the motions needed before asking: *Why are you here?*

The little girl made several gestures. Tori had trouble following so tapped her open palm with her other hand, asking for her to tell her again but then added the sign for her to do it more slowly.

The little girl nodded and then signed again, and Lane watched as Tori nodded along and then raised her eyes. Tori made a fist with her hand, and then stuck out three fingers, her thumb, index, and middle finger. *You're sure?*

The girl nodded, signaling yes with her fist again.

Tori made a quick, wary scan of the area before looking back to Alisha. She signed: *Will you come with me?*

The girl nodded.

"Girls, thank you for stopping and checking on her. Professor Lane and I will look after her, okay."

The two students nodded, waved to Alisha, and sauntered off none the wiser. "Hannah, take Alisha's hand."

Professor Lane watched as Tori reached inside her shoulder bag and transferred her Glock 19 into her coat pocket.

"Tori?"

"Come on," Tori said, leading them toward the Administration Building, scanning the area.

"Tori, what is going on?"

"We need to get inside, for Alisha's safety."

"For her safety? What is it?"

"She was dropped off at that bench by her brother."

"Why?"

"Because someone is trying to kill them."

"*What!*"

"Hannah, not here, move!"

Tori and Professor Lane hustled along the sidewalk with Alisha, rushing inside the double doors and finding a small conference room in the Administration Building. Campus security showed up two minutes later and Tori put her gun back into her shoulder bag. She looked to the clock on the wall. It was just after 9:00 a.m.

"Hannah, do we have a sign language interpreter we can call?"

"We have a few on staff for ADA purposes," Lane replied.

"Let's get one here," Tori said and noticed the small refrigerator in the corner stocked with beverages. She led Alisha to the refrigerator and the little girl picked out an apple juice.

Lane returned. "Trish Adams is coming."

Ten minutes later, a woman with long red hair came into the conference room and Tori recognized her as the one who did the sign language for the university president's speech to the faculty a few months back. Tori brought Trish quickly up to speed, watching her eyes get wider.

"I don't imagine this is what you expected when you came to work today."

"Ahh... no."

"I'm a marginally functional but far from fluent signer. I need someone more proficient to get me the details quickly. Alisha told me outside that she and her brother were being chased. Someone shot at them. That's why she was dropped off. She said others were shot as well and that's as far as we got before I got her in here."

"I see."

"I need to know more right now."

Tori sat down and signed that Trish would ask questions. Alisha asked: *Are you staying?*

Tori smiled and nodded.

Trish pulled a chair up to Alisha such that the three of them formed a triangle. Trish started communicating with her, smiling, and nodding as she introduced herself. The two of them had their hands moving rapidly. Tori was able to follow along with bits and pieces of the conversation.

After some back and forth, Trish started. "Alisha's mother died a few weeks ago. She was staying at a house with her brother. Before that she was staying with an aunt, but she didn't like it there. Nobody could communicate with her, and she didn't feel safe. She says she was hit."

Tori grimaced. "Oh man, poor thing."

"Alisha's last name is Sweeney. Her brother is Nico Sweeney. He visited her at their aunt's yesterday and then took her with him."

"And where was Nico living?"

"At the house they were at in the woods. It was on a lake. She'd been there before a few weeks ago and liked it. That gets us to this morning," Trish said, before smiling to Alisha. She turned to Tori. "This morning she woke up early and was looking out the window down at the lake. She liked the waves and that they changed colors."

"White caps."

"Yes. Then she saw a woman dressed in all black and wearing a black face mask come around the back of the house and do something to open the back door."

"A woman? She's sure?"

"Yes."

"And she picked the lock?"

"That's what she described to me. The woman came inside the house. That's when she went to her brother and woke him up. He snuck out of the bedroom and went up the basement stairs a bit and then all of a sudden came rushing back down. Next thing, he's putting her coat on and running her out the back door, around the house and to a black pickup truck. When they drove away, Nico was ducking, and glass was breaking all around her and she felt something hit the truck."

"Gunshots?"

"Yes, I think so. Nico drove. Alisha couldn't see much over the edge of the passenger windows or the front window. She says Nico was agitated, constantly looking behind them and then driving, and this is my word not hers, erratically."

"Ask if they were being chased."

Trish gestured quickly to Alisha. Alisha replied with a fist, rocking it up and down: *Yes.*

"And is that why he dropped her off at the university?"

Alisha made the fist sign again.

"Ask her about the others at the house?"

Trish signed the question. This time Alisha replied with a series of gestures. "There were at least two others at the house. They were sleeping upstairs. She said Nico usually slept upstairs in his room but stayed down with her last night."

"Does she know their names?"

Trish asked the question and Alisha replied with no.

"Had she seen them before?"

Trish turned and asked. "Yes, they lived at the house. She says one person who was not there this time was Tony. She remembered him. He was nice to her before."

"Does she know where this house is?" Tori asked.

"No."

"And she said they were in a black pickup truck?"

"Yes."

Tori stood up and called Braddock.

"I got a weird one out here," Braddock said when he answered without preamble.

"Does it involve a black pickup truck by chance?" Tori asked.

"Uh... How do you know that?"

"You need to get to me."

* * *

Braddock, Steak and Eggleston, all made their way back to Manchester Bay. Steak and Eggs went to the government center to follow up on the truck ownership, Nicholas Sweeney, and the phone call he made. Braddock went to the university. Tori introduced him to Alisha and Trish and then explained what they'd learned. Braddock gave them a quick rundown from what they had on County Road 63.

Braddock handed Trish a photo of a driver's license. "Can you ask Alisha if this is her brother?"

Trish showed the picture to Alisha, who replied: *yes.*

Braddock looked to Tori, whispering, "That's our driver. He's dead. Shot several times."

Alisha pulled on Tori's arm then signed and Tori understood the question: *Where is Nico?*

"She's asking about him," Tori said and then closed her eyes, sitting down. "Trish, can you help me with this."

"Yes," Trish replied. "But, Tori, I think she reads lips a bit too."

Trish nodded and the two of them re-sat down with Alisha. Tori looked Alisha in the eye and reached for her hands and spoke while Trish signed. "I'm very sorry, but we found Nico. He..." She sighed. "I'm so sorry, but he died."

Trish signed slowly and Tori watched as the tears slowly formed in the anguished little girl's eyes and she started shaking her head in disbelief. Tori reached for Alisha, pulling her to her and embracing the little girl in a hug. "Oh, I'm so sorry, sweetie. I'm so sorry."

Braddock let them have a few minutes, stepping out of the conference room to check in with Steak, updating him on what he'd learned. When he stepped back into the room, Tori was kneeling to Alisha, Trish by her side. Alisha signed a question. Tori thought she understood it but looked to Trish for confirmation.

"She asked what is going to happen to her. What should I tell her?"

Tori didn't know. "Tell her... we'll figure it out."

Trish turned and conversed with Alisha who eventually nodded. "I told her we'll make sure she's safe." Trish turned to Tori. "We will, won't we?"

"I'll do everything I can. For starters, we need to get child protective services here."

"I'll have someone make that call," Braddock said, dialing his assistant back at the government center.

"In the meantime, we'll keep her here," Tori said to the campus security guards. "You'll keep guard until we figure some things out?"

"Yes, ma'am," a guard affirmed. "Stay in here as long as you need."

"Is there a security camera covering the bench she was found on?"

"My guess is it'll show up somewhere. I'll go check," a second security guard replied, reaching for his radio.

Braddock pulled Tori to the far side of the conference room and took out his phone. "I found this on the back of the pickup truck." He showed her the picture of the tracker. "The kicker is the truck wasn't her older brother's. It was registered to an EBR Enterprises. Steak and Eggleston are digging into that. And Nico was making a phone call when all the shooting was going down. But the truck had the tracker on it. And Alisha is telling you a woman dressed in all black and a mask came to the house and then she and her brother were being chased and then her brother ends up dead, shot multiple times. What the hell is going on? I mean, a woman hitter?"

"Now wait—"

"I'm not making a sexist comment. A woman can be a killer. It is, however, unusual to hear of something Alisha has described is all. I mean, have you heard of something like this?"

"Well, back when—"

"Detective," the security guard interrupted. "We don't have a camera specifically focused on that bench or area. However, it is visible in the distance on two fixed cameras for two buildings." Tori and Braddock followed him down the hallway to a security office. Inside, another security officer was sitting at a computer.

"This is the camera over the east door for the Administration Building." The bench was to the right, in the upper right-hand corner. The officer pushed play in the time window. The pickup truck pulled over and Alisha's brother rushed around the front of the truck, carried her from the truck and sat her down on the bench and he signed quickly to her, hugged her, and then rushed back to the truck. A few vehicles pulled by before the two students finally noticed Alisha sitting alone on the bench and stopped to check on her. She sat on the bench for nearly an hour.

"We have a second camera on the exterior of Brooks Hall. It looks north and covers the bench." The bench was in the upper left-hand corner. Alisha is dropped off again and her brother rushes away. This time they see Alisha watching as her brother pulls away. The officer let the footage run out for a minute and was ready to press stop.

"Wait," Braddock said. "Let that run for a sec?"

The officer started the video again.

"Run it back about thirty seconds," Braddock ordered. The officer did as he was instructed. "There. The Acadia. Eggleston said there was a report of a black Acadia and black Dodge Ram chasing after each other just north of Manchester Bay this morning."

"Can we make out a plate?" Tori asked the officer who worked the mouse, enlarging the area of the screen. "That's as good as I can do. It's a little fuzzy but—"

"Iowa license plate," Tori said.

Braddock made a call to run the plate. "Call me back."

Tori watched the video of the Acadia again. "You can kind of see the driver's face a bit."

"White. Wearing sunglasses with a black stocking cap on her head. Black gloves on her hands. Not much to see," Braddock said.

"But we suspect that's a woman, so that's something. Every little piece counts. Maybe forensics could do something with this. Enhance it."

Braddock's phone buzzed and he answered. "Yeah... uh-huh...." He looked to Tori. "The plates are for a Subaru. They were reported stolen a couple of days ago."

"From where?"

"Pequot Lakes."

"Hmpf," Tori murmured. "What was so important about this Nico? Or anyone else at this house?"

"If we find it, maybe we'll get a better idea."

"In the meantime." She walked back down to Trish. "Does Alisha have any other family? Other than her aunt?"

Trish turned to Alisha and the two of them talked for a minute. "No other family that she knows."

"When child protective services arrive, I'm sure their first thought will be to send her back there. I'm not wild about sending her back to her aunt if there were issues there—"

"She could stay with me and my husband for a bit," Trish replied brightly. "He signs as well. One of our children was like Alisha so that's how we both learned to sign. That and we fostered children. We haven't done it in some years, but we're still certified."

"You'd be willing to do that?"

"She's a little cutie this one," Trish said. "And she's been through an awful lot. She'd be very welcome at our house while things get worked out and we see if she has some other family we can find."

Tori looked to Braddock who nodded. "Let's get the bureaucratic ball rolling then."

Braddock's phone buzzed. It was Steak. "Yeah," he answered, listening for a moment, "We'll meet you there."

"What?"

"Steak found the house Alisha told us about."

FIFTEEN

"THAT'S NOT EVEN THE BIG THING?"

"EBR Enterprises is owned by Ernest R. Rudick," Braddock explained as they drove north on the H-4, Steak and Eggleston just ahead and now a sheriff's deputy right behind them. "Rudick is the truck owner. He also owns a house on the north side of Little Rock Lake. I've got Nolan and Reese digging further on him."

The cedar sided two-story appeared through the woods to their left. Braddock pulled to a stop in front of the driveway, he and Tori were followed by Steak and Eggleston. Two deputies arrived just seconds later to provide backup. Everyone vested up and spread out to surround the house. Braddock led Tori and a deputy to the east side. A side door to the house was partially open and Braddock held his fist up.

"Will?" Steak called on the radio. "The door around back under the deck is not locked. We're going in."

"Copy. We're coming in the side door that is part open," he reported. He and Tori made their way to the steps and pushed their way inside. The other two deputies went to the front of the house to cover.

"Sheriff's Department!" Braddock called but there was no

response. "Anyone here?" The house remained quiet. He called down to the basement. "Anything?"

"Nobody down here. There is a bed and blowup mattress in a bedroom but nothing else."

Tori knelt at the first step of the stairway to the second floor and noted the dirt on the carpet treads. It was fresh. She and Braddock slipped covers on their shoes and cautiously made their way up the right side of the stairs to the second floor. The first bedroom was empty, although the window was open and there were holes in the mesh window screen. At the second bedroom, a man with gunshot wounds to the chest laid against a wall. Braddock quick checked for a pulse. "His body is cold."

"The whole house is," Tori noted. "Doors and windows open for hours."

In the last bedroom, they found Ernest Rudick, lying on his back in the bed, he too with three gunshot wounds to his upper chest.

"Tight pattern," Braddock noted. "Boom, boom, boom."

"Same thing with the other man," Tori remarked as she walked back to the second bedroom. "If I had to guess, she started with Rudick, then rushed back to here. This guy hears the shots and tries to get out of bed to the gun on the dresser, but he didn't make it."

Braddock went to the first bedroom. "She expects Alisha's brother to be in here perhaps?"

"But he's in the bedroom in the basement. Our killer doesn't see Alisha when she comes around the back to the door, but Alisha sees her, sees her come inside and tells Nico. They get out of the house to the pickup truck in the driveway. He pulls away and the shooter fires at them from here."

Braddock nodded and took out a pen and knelt and with the pen tip, picked up an ejected shell casing. "9mm." He set it back down and led Tori down the steps. "Then she rushes down the stairs, out the side door and runs for her Acadia."

"She knows exactly where Nico is going because of the tracker you found," Tori said, standing at the open side door. She turned to him, pursing her lips.

"What?"

"If she has the tracker, why play demolition derby on the H-4 with him? Or do what she did out on County 63. Just track him until you get a shot at him. Those acts are in conflict, unless..."

"Unless what?"

"She couldn't let Nico warn someone about her?"

"He recognized her?"

"Or... could describe her."

"That could have motivated our killer to chase him down like that, stop him before he could let someone know," Braddock said, scratching his head. "Who the hell are these guys? Rudick owns this place. Nico or Nicholas Sweeney is who exactly? And who is the other dead guy?"

"All good and relevant questions."

"Do you have any answers?"

"Not ye— Hang on."

Tori made her way back to the second bedroom, Braddock right behind. She found a wallet on the top of the dresser and opened it. "Kevin Waltripp. Waltripp. We've heard that name before. When we were trying to find Ron Gresh. His roommate had the texts looking for Mitch Brandon and—"

"Tripp. Kevin Waltripp?" Braddock said. He and Tori shared a long look. "Does today tie back to that?"

Tori shrugged. "I have a sneaking suspicion it does. We knew there was more to it. And this professional killer, if that's who she is, adds an interesting new twist on things."

"Professional killer?" Braddock asked, eyebrows raised. "How do you know that?"

"You saw the bodies. This is not the work of some amateur. No," Tori smirked, "she's a pro."

"A pro you've seen?"

"Come on. Let's go back and talk to Alisha again," Tori said, walking away, leaving Braddock to catch up.

"Why?" Braddock said, chasing after her. "What aren't you telling me?"

Alisha and Trish had moved to the office of one of the university's administrators. Alisha was watching cartoons with closed captioning on. Trish was sitting with her. Alisha's eyes lit up when she saw Tori coming back.

Tori sat down crossed legged on the floor with Trish in front of Alisha. To Trish she said: "I need her to describe the woman she saw again."

Trish turned and she and Alicia talked for a minute. "It was a woman, dressed in all black and with a mask."

"Like a ski mask?" Tori said.

Trish asked Alisha, who signed and nodded. "She said it had a gap in it for her eyes."

"Was the woman short or tall?"

"Tall," Trish replied after a moment. "She was thin. She had on boots that were laced up with big thick heels."

Tori pulled out her phone and tapped in a search for combat boots. She pulled up a photo for black lace-up boots that went just over the ankle. "Like these?" She showed the photo to Alisha.

Alisha shook her head and then gestured to Trish, who said, "They were longer up her leg."

Tori recalibrated her search for black lace-up combat boots with thick heels up to the knee. "How about this?" she asked, holding up her phone.

Alisha nodded.

"How about the black clothes?" Tori asked. "Jeans, yoga pants?"

Trish turned to Alisha and asked. "She says they were shiny."

Tori looked to a coat hung over the chair that was brown leather. She went to it and held it up. "Leather? Like this."

Alisha nodded and then signed to Trish, who said, "Black leather gloves too. Everything was leather except the mask."

"Tall, black leather head to toe, combat boots. Did she see hair color?"

Trish asked Alisha who quickly answered no.

"How about white, Hispanic or African American?" Trish signed to Alisha who replied by pulling her open hand from her chest into a ball.

"She was white?" Tori asked, making the same motion and Alisha nodded.

"How about guns?" Braddock asked. "Did the woman carry a gun?"

Tori knew that sign as well, which was her thumb up and two fingers pointed out.

"Two guns?" Tori asked, surprised. "She had two?"

The little girl nodded and then made some quick gestures. "She says the guns were on her... legs," Trish said, confused.

"On her legs?" Tori asked, questioningly.

"A holster maybe. On both legs," Braddock replied and then did a quick phone search of his own and pulled a picture of a tactical leg holster that strapped to a thigh. "Something like this?"

Alisha squinted at the photo. Tori gestured with her right hand, slowly rocking it back and forth.

"Sort of?" Tori said.

Alisha nodded.

"But there were two guns?" Tori asked.

Yes.

"She was tall. Wore all leather, combat boots and two guns and picked the lock to the house? You're sure of all that?"

Alisha nodded.

There was a knock on the office door from a woman from social services. As she and Trish talked about Alisha, Braddock took Tori by the arm out into the hallway. "That description is registering with you, isn't it?"

"Maybe," Tori said, and she pulled out her phone, and started scrolling her contacts and hit the number.

"Maybe my ass."

"I need to confirm with Tracy."

"Tracy? FBI Tracy? Tracy Sheets?" Braddock asked.

Tori nodded. "I'm getting her voicemail." She waited for the beep. "Tracy, it's Tori. Twelve years ago. Cleveland. What if I told you I had a case today where the shooter was a tall woman wearing all black leather, combat boots, took out three men, shots to the chest in a tight pattern. Does that ring any bells? Give me a call."

Tori and Braddock stayed at the university for a half-hour until it was determined that Alisha would spend the weekend with Trish and her husband.

Tori sat with Alisha a minute to make sure she was okay with that arrangement.

Yes, Alisha signed. *Trish is nice! Will you come see me?* she asked.

"Yes," Tori said with a smile. "I promise."

Alisha leaned in for a hug. If the case wouldn't be taking up all their time, Tori would have been willing to watch her for a few days. She felt bad. The road ahead for Alisha was likely to be tough.

A half-hour later they were back at the government center and Special Agent Tracy Sheets called back.

"Do you think I'm crazy?" Tori asked, relaxing in the chair in front of Braddock's desk, her phone on speaker.

"I haven't thought of that case for a long time," Tracy replied. "I assume you want me to see whatever came of that?"

"Yes. I mean we worked it a week then got back to our own case, but I swear it sounds just like her."

"Let me make some calls," Tracy said and rang off.

"You worked what a week?" Braddock asked.

"I worked this case once in Cleveland—"

There was a knock on the office door and Nolan burst in and handed a stack of papers to Braddock. "Rudick has a small office in Manchester Bay. Looks like some sort of real estate business. He has a real estate license and I'm seeing his name pop up as owner on other residential properties, many over by the university. I'm guessing he owns houses over there and rents them to college kids. I called the county attorney's office. We'll get into the office maybe yet tonight, for sure tomorrow. And Steak called. He's still up at Rudick's. The BCA is on site and has started processing."

"That's good news."

"That's not even the big thing."

"What's the big thing?"

"The phone number Nicholas Sweeney was dialing. It's for Paul Marrone."

Braddock's eyes shot up. "Holy shit."

SIXTEEN

"MAYBE ON HER OWN SIDE."

Braddock burst into Boe's office. "I need you to come down to my office. Right now."

She looked up at him with a frown. "As the sheriff, I usually have people come to *my* office. You know, because it's the biggest one, and I'm the boss."

"Everybody is in mine and there is something you need to hear about."

"About today?"

"Today, yesterday, the last month, maybe more."

With Boe inside, Braddock closed his office door and pointed to Nolan who started handing out binder clipped documents. "Paul Marrone. Let's hear it."

"And Paul Marrone is who?" Boe asked.

Braddock explained how he and Tori noted the license plate in the Notes app on Cameron Jensen's phone, entered the night before he and Grace were shot in Holmstrand. "That was a week ago. This license plate that Cam noted down linked to a vehicle owned by Marrone. While we were away, I told Nolan to dig into him, and Steak to go back through the investigations on Banz and the other missing dealers to see if there was a tie to Marrone. I never even got to the office before the shooting this morning. Then Marrone's phone number shows up today; Nicholas Sweeney was calling him as he was racing along County 63."

"And who is this guy."

"Paul Marrone, age fifty-four. He was born and raised in Chicago where he lived for the first forty-three years of his life, until he moved up here twelve years ago. Married to wife Connie. In addition to the black Escalade, Marrone owns a house on Bertha Lake near Cullen Crossing as well as a pontoon. If you flip over the page, you'll see the satellite and street level photos of the house."

The house was a beige one-story walkout down to Bertha Lake, which was one of the lakes on the Whitefish Chain of lakes. "Nice but fairly modest for that lake," Tori noted. "What is his employment?"

"Marrone is the store manager at CC Hardware."

"That's the hardware store in that small strip mall in Cullen Crossing, right?" Boe said.

"Yes."

"And we know Marrone is the store manager how?"

"I followed him to work on Wednesday from his house," explained Nolan. "His office is in the back of the hardware store. Nameplate on the door says store manager. I did a little more checking and found that he has been the store manager ever since the place opened."

She flipped over a sheet of paper. "I was curious about the strip mall. It's odd."

"Why?" Boe asked.

"Because Cullen Crossing isn't even a town really," Tori said.

"It's a flashing yellow light over the crossroads of two county roads," Braddock noted. "The population is maybe a hundred, if that. Yet there is this longish strip mall eating up one side of the northeast corner of the crossing."

"Six shops. A bar and restaurant, liquor store, hardware store, drycleaners, gift shop and convenience store," Nolan said. "I walked them all a few days ago. Legit businesses. I bought a nice hoodie at the gift shop. It was full of cute knick-knacks. I dug into the records and it's the same six stores from when it first opened twelve years ago. No changes."

"Who owns it?" Tori asked.

"This is where it starts getting interesting if you ask me. The owner is listed as M Enterprises."

"M Enterprises?"

"Catchy," Boe remarked.

"Opaque," Tori said.

"That's what I thought," Nolan continued. "The name behind that is James Mileski. Mileski also owns a house on Bertha Lake, three down from Marrone. He is age fifty-nine. Married to wife Lois. Mileski moved here from Chicago twelve years ago."

"Are they partners?" Tori asked as she flipped open her laptop.

"Could be," Nolan said. "I looked up if they had criminal records."

"And?"

"They do. A couple of assault and racketeering charges for Marrone. A racketeering charge for Mileski as well."

"And where were these charges made?" Tori asked.

"Funny you should ask," Nolan replied. "Illinois. Chicago to be exact. Interestingly, they both have family with more significant criminal records. James Mileski's older brother is named Robert 'Bobby' Mileski."

"And he is who?"

"The current head of organized crime in Chicago."

The room went silent for a moment.

"Seriously!" Tori finally blurted, reaching for her laptop. "He's running the Outfit? And his little brother is up here running this strip mall and his store manager was on the phone with our murder victim today?"

Boe's eyes got big and looked to Braddock, who muttered, "Hoo boy."

"Did you know this when you came down to grab me?" Boe asked.

"Uh... no," Braddock replied. "We hadn't gotten quite this far. I undersold and way over delivered here."

"Jolted me too," Nolan said. "I spoke with a friend of a friend of a friend with the Cook County Sheriff's Office. He says Bobby Mileski is running the show. He keeps his head down and is low profile but he's in charge."

"And Marrone?"

"His brother John 'Big Johnny' Marrone was a capo for what was then the west side crew. He died twelve years ago in a gangland shooting. But, before that, he did six years for racketeering. Bobby Mileski did time on the same crime. He's been clean ever since."

"Huh," Braddock sighed, sitting back. "Twelve years ago, these two made guys move to northern Minnesota and build a strip mall in the out of the way township of Cullen Crossing. Why twelve years ago I wonder."

"That gangland shooting," Tori said, peering at her laptop. She spun it around. It was a lengthy newspaper article in the *Chicago Times*.

"From what I'm reading it appears the west side and south side crews got into a war with one another about that time. Twelve years ago. The heads of both crews were murdered within weeks of one another along with other higher ups that included Marrone's brother. The FBI and CPD had a joint investigation of Chicago organized crime. There were a series of prosecutions. Twenty-three members ended up in prison for any number of transgressions, mostly racketeering and drug related. It left the Chicago Outfit, Syndicate, Mob, whatever you want to call it, in a state of total disarray. It was thought that between this last 'war' between the factions and the prosecutions out of the joint FBI and CPD investigation, that the Chicago Mob was essentially dead." Tori thought for a moment. "I remember this joint investigation. It wasn't just Chicago. The Bureau had an organized crime investigation that spanned the Rust Belt at that time. Cleveland, Detroit, Chicago, a few more places."

"All that is perhaps why Mileski and Marrone moved up here," Nolan said.

"Could be," Tori said as she ran her finger along the computer screen. "This article suggests, however, that predictions of the Mob's demise were premature. What was left of the Chicago Outfit was reorganized and the new leader is—"

"Bobby Mileski," Nolan finished.

"I didn't even really think there was a Chicago Mob anymore," Braddock said.

"It still is out there," Nolan said. "Some of the lucrative things they used to profit from are now legal, like gambling. It's been legal in Illinois for years. Marijuana is legal. There still is racketeering, union and public corruption, hijacking, distributing stolen goods, narcotics, maybe a little loan sharking although money is easy to get legitimately these days, even for people with questionable credit or backgrounds."

Tori nodded. "I heard of this in New York too. These guys went semi-legit. They bought or assumed regular businesses, restaurants, bars, convenience stores, businesses that are... more cash based, even these days when nobody really uses much cash anymore."

"I get it. If they find a good illegal enterprise or hustle, they'll run the cash from it into the legit business and it gets laundered." Braddock shook his head. "For twelve years Mileski and Marrone have been up here, and nobody even really knew it, at least until now."

"Cullen Crossing is not a crime bastion, that's for sure," Nolan said.

"Let me summarize then," Braddock started. "The night before they were murdered, Cameron Jensen and Grace Horn were parked outside of Gresh's apartment when they saw a rug dumped into the back of a van and driven away. There was probably a body in that rug, and we now suspect that is Reardon Banz. In Jensen's phone we find the license plate note for an Escalade owned by Paul Marrone. Paul Marrone and Jimmy Mileski are two guys with ties to Chicago organized crime who are quietly operating a strip mall in Cullen Crossing."

"We know this about Banz being the body how?" Boe asked.

"Banz was last seen earlier on the night before Holmstrand. He lived a block away from Gresh's place and was a drug dealer. Gresh was into drugs. We found drugs at that trailer out in the woods."

"Now we have Banz missing. We have a few other drug dealers nobody has seen in months," Tori said. "And then we have what happened out at that trailer with Gresh and Tony Gill three nights after Holmstrand. Our tipster tells us of five people out there, yet we only found two dead."

"You think it's odd we haven't heard further from her?" Boe said.

"We did," Tori said. "Today. She's the shooter. She's the pro."

Braddock raised his eyebrows.

"How can you possibly know that?" Boe said.

"Think about it. How in the world do you find that trailer out in the woods to begin with?"

Braddock smiled and nodded. "You'd have had to have been following. But that would be tough out there with minimal traffic and you'd probably have to stay somewhat close, which might be dangerous."

"Or—" Tori led. "If you had a tracker on Rudick's truck. You could follow at a safe distance. It's what probably happened today. Why not out to that trailer?"

"Huh," Braddock snorted. Everyone else was quiet, taking in what Tori was arguing.

"It's all connected," Tori continued. "All of it. I'll bet you Rudick was out at that trailer that night with Nicholas Sweeney and Kevin Waltripp, and they staged that shootout between Gresh and Gill. They leave the gun out there for us to find so that we would conclude that Gresh killed those three kids. Ties it up all nice and neat. But it wasn't the truth. Our killer today, she knew the truth."

"Okay, say I buy all that," Boe asserted. "Why set Gresh up like that?"

"So that you would go tell the families that we caught the killer. That the investigation was over. And you know what? It probably works but for Cameron Jensen's father going through his son's phone. Gresh may or may not have been in Holm-strand for the shooting, but it had nothing to do with his obses-sion for Grace. It was because of what she and Cameron Jensen saw the night before outside of Gresh's apartment."

"Who is our killer today then?" Boe asked. "Who is she? And if she's a pro, is she still even here?"

"You know, I think she is," Tori said after a minute. "What I don't get is calling us about the trailer but then today, killing these men. That's an escalation. Informant to assassin. Why?"

"Maybe she killed Gresh and Gill, and just told us a story," Nolan suggested. "She called to make sure Gresh was found."

"I get that logic, but not the same way," Tori said. "I do

think she wanted us to find Gresh, so we could get answers, but I don't buy that she was the killer out there."

"Is that based on gut or something that is, you know, tangible?" Boe asked.

"Both. Look, nothing about what she said that night fits with setting us up or that she killed them. She was out there. She called me to bring us in. We were there twenty minutes later, if that. The bodies were still warm. And when we found that scene, we publicly concluded what? Gresh was dead and he had the gun for Holmstrand, so he was guilty, case closed."

"It wasn't case closed, though," Boe said.

"That's not what we told the families," Tori said. "And I understood why you did what you did. And we were still working it, albeit quietly."

"But if you're right," Boe said. "She, this woman, didn't know that."

"And she acted. Because she was at that trailer and saw what they did. Saw it was a set-up. And who knows, maybe she knows more than that. But she's here and she's a player in all this."

"On what side?" Boe asked.

"Maybe on her own side."

"What's the play here?"

Braddock looked to Boe. "Your call. I know you kind of suggested to the Jensens, Horns and Randalls that the case was solved."

"I left myself some wiggle room because we had suspicions then because of the call from this woman," Boe said, nonplussed. "You've now developed new evidence that confirms those suspicions and that there is more to all of this. If you're right, if Tori is right, then a great deal more. I think you all best start working on figuring that all out. I'd prefer we handle this instead of her."

* * *

Tori took the reheated pieces of chicken out of the microwave, cut them up and spread them atop the chef's salad she had quickly concocted for the two of them. Braddock handed her a beer.

"Kind of defeats the purpose of the salad," she noted, before taking a long pull of the Northern Pine Lumberjack, a local brew.

"A beer is a reward for eating a salad. It creates balance and harmony."

"Okay there, Obi-Wan."

They both took care of themselves, working out frequently and staying fit, but Tori often lamented that whenever they got into a case their diet instantly suffered and it took weeks to undo the damage. So instead of stopping and getting a quick pizza, as Braddock had suggested, she instead whipped up two large chef's salads. They ate in relative quiet, the two of them deep in thought before eventually turning to their cell phones, reading. It was as if they were avoiding talking about the case.

Braddock finally broke the ice. "When we were talking to Boe, you left out what you know about this woman."

"Because I'm not sure I know anything."

"Tell me what you suspect then. You can hold back from everyone else but not—"

"From you." She sighed and took a drink of her beer. "A black *leather-clad* woman pro in combat boots. Not a lot of those out there."

Braddock knew the tone. "What about her? Or maybe the better question is, what do you know about her?"

Tori savored another drink of her beer, thinking an extra second before speaking. "I've heard of someone like this before."

"Heard?"

"Yeah," she replied and pushed herself up from the table,

picked up his bowl with hers and dropped them in the sink, before grabbing another beer for each of them and going to the living room, and curling up in the soft sitting chair.

"The woman?" Braddock prodded.

"Twelve years ago, I was in Cleveland on a missing child case, or series of them. It morphed into this human trafficking investigation. I'd only been with the Bureau a few years, was still stationed down at Quantico when the case came along. It was a case with some profile, and I jumped at the chance to work it. It was the case where I ended up making an early name for myself."

"You got one of your meritorious service awards for that case, didn't you?"

"Yeah. That case." She shook her head, a wry smile. "I lived in a hotel in Cleveland for nine months. Nine months in a hotel is... a long time, in any city. God I was so tired of that place."

"Yet, you smile."

"It's where I met Special Agents Geno Harlow and Tracy Sheets."

"Your buddies."

She nodded. "After that, we all ended up in New York City. But in Cleveland we lived in the hotel and worked out of the Bureau's field office. It was during that time that I later learned that the Bureau had ongoing coordinated organized crime investigations in Cleveland, Chicago, Kansas City and St. Louis."

"The ones you mentioned today."

"Going after organized crime in the Midwest and Rust Belt. The Cleveland one was operating just down the hall from where I was. When I was there though, an undercover special agent named Como was murdered along with two men high up with the Cleveland Mob. The special agent had been under for a couple of years and, as I learned later, was getting ready to make the move on them."

"Flip them?"

"Right. You know, the old 'You two can go to jail for twenty-five years or you can tell us everything we want to know'. But one night the three of them, while walking to a car in an alley, were shot and killed at close range. They were executed, by a professional, a woman. An employee for the bar was dumping garbage out back when he saw the men all leave. As they walked down the alley, they were following a woman. She was dressed in black leather pants and jacket and high heels. They all went around a corner and then *bing, bing, bing, bing, bing, bing*. It was done in a flash. The dishwasher and another man waited a minute and then ran down the alley and around the corner and all they saw were the three men sprawled out, lying by a car, dead. The woman was gone."

"A professional hit."

"Yes."

Braddock nodded. "The Mob find out about Como being a Fed?"

"Must have."

"Was it from the inside?"

"I never knew. Maybe the special agent got made or there was a leak. I don't know. I never learned anything about that part of it. I do know that Tracy, Geno, and I were temporarily assigned to the investigation of his death, canvassing the area around the bar. I remember seeing Como's wife at the Cleveland field office. I couldn't believe he was undercover for two years, being married and all."

"Did Como's murder end the case?"

"No," Tori replied. "I recall hearing sometime later that the Bureau and U.S. Attorney's Office eventually got the higher-ups in the Cleveland family, despite the setback. It just took longer. I was in New York by the time that all happened."

"I take it this assassin was never found."

"Not that I'm aware of. That's why I called Tracy."

"The Bureau hunted for her?"

"If you kill a special agent, the Bureau will never stop looking for you," Tori replied, taking a drink of beer, reaching for a blanket, and draping it over her legs. "And if it is her, and she is here, then neither will I."

SEVENTEEN

"I NEED TO FIND HER BEFORE SHE FINDS ME."

Max pulled into the parking lot and into a slot in the second row for the bar.

"Bar CC. Cullen Crossing. Clever," Carlo observed lightly as he unhooked his seatbelt. "What do you think, boss?" he asked looking to Vince in the backseat.

"I think it took us a long ass time to get all the way up here," Vince Smith replied as he yawned, ran his hand over his short blond hair and then stretched his arms wide before he unfurled his long legs out the back of the Lincoln Navigator, the nine-hour drive from Chicago complete.

Vince led his men inside the dimly lit bar. The three of them took seats at the corner of the bar, a perch that allowed them to observe the interior of the bar on a quiet Friday night, a basketball game playing on the big screens mounted in the corners. The bartender waddled over.

"Three whiskeys," Carlo requested.

"Is the kitchen still open?" Max asked.

"Yeah. Some stuff," the bartender replied, sliding over a small menu. He looked to Vince. "Down the back hallway and through the door."

Vince let his eyes sweep the bar while he downed his whiskey. He slipped off his barstool and headed down the back hallway, past the bathrooms and through the door where he found a hallway for the whole strip mall and then a stairwell. He took the steps down to the basement. At the bottom was a small hallway leading to a private room.

Marrone and Mileski were sitting at the poker table, a small ice bucket and a bottle of whiskey in front of them.

All three of them shook hands. "It's been a while, gentlemen," Vince said.

"We're glad you're here," Mileski said, pouring a drink for him. He got right to it. "Do you think we're dealing with Marta?"

"One thing at a time. Give me the details that led up to today."

Marrone and Mileski ran through what they knew about the day and the past three weeks.

"If I'm hearing you right, all the trouble started when your boys disposed of this Banz guy. You think that these two kids you're telling me about, Horn and Jensen, saw your boys remove the rug from the apartment building, then saw you two and you were worried they would go to the police."

Marrone and Mileski both nodded.

"It was Gresh's old girlfriend who saw us," Marrone explained. "She had been to the building earlier in the night, ringing for him with her new boyfriend. I guess he had some of her stuff. They ignored the buzzer and the two of them left. However, after we pulled away and Gresh went back inside the apartment building, he took one last look out and that's when he saw them parked out there, and then pulling away."

"Do you know if they actually saw anything?"

"No," Mileski replied with a headshake. "But we don't need people poking around, asking questions."

Vince didn't necessarily disagree with that. "Fine. But a

drive-by shooting was hardly the most subtle way of fixing the problem there, Pauly."

Marrone nodded in frustration. "Our guys followed Horn and Jensen around all day. In Holmstrand it was night. The street was tree-lined and dark. Not ideal but it was urgent before they went to the police."

"And you're certain they didn't?"

Mileski nodded. "If they had, they'd have likely gone to the sheriff's office in Manchester Bay. And if they did, that would be a problem."

"How so?"

Mileski looked to Marrone, who said, "Will Braddock is the chief detective for the county. He's a former NYPD detective. He worked homicide and later terrorism back there. He came here some years ago. A serious guy. Word on the street is he lives now with a woman named Tori Hunter. She's former FBI, moved back here a couple of years ago. She was a special agent based out of New York City for years. Her specialty is missing children, but she works for the sheriff's department now in an investigative capacity. They've had a couple of big cases the last few years."

"And?"

"They may not have a lot of resources, but they're very formidable. They investigated the shooting in Holmstrand. They'll be the ones investigating what happened today."

"They're no joke, those two," Mileski said.

"And the man who did the shooting?"

"He was killed today. Plus, the one the police thought did it is no longer an issue," Marrone replied. "We had him hideout for a few days after to see what the fallout was going to be, but the police were immediately on him, even quicker than we thought they'd be."

"This Braddock and Hunter?"

"Yes," Mileski said. "If the police got him, well..."

"He was a liability that we took care of out at this trailer out in the woods. Left him with the gun that was used at the drive-by shooting. Staged it to look like he had a beef with one of the others with him the night of the shooting. Plus, he still had the hots for the girl, so we figure..."

"He's jealous. Kills the girl and the new boyfriend. Simple story."

"It should have held," Mileski moaned.

"Why didn't it?"

"The police found our two dead guys in that trailer within a half-hour of the shooting. How, we don't know. Maybe someone heard the shooting, or, maybe someone was out there watching. We just don't know."

"And you think that all led to this morning?"

"Our three guys killed today were the three who staged that shooting out at the trailer. One of those guys, Nico, called me as he was being chased. A masked woman dressed in black leather and combat boots was after him."

"What else?"

"Nico was driving Rudick's truck and ended up upside down against a tree. She got him a few miles south of town. Shot him several times. I sent Stevie Bianchi to Rudick's house for a quick looksie. He said Rudick and Waltripp were executed, three shots each to the chest. Rudick was shot in his bed. Waltripp barely made it out of his."

"How'd this Nico get away?"

"He had a room upstairs at the house as well, but he may have been sleeping in the basement," Marrone stated. "Stevie found a small suitcase in a spare room in the basement that had child's clothes. I think he had his little sister staying out there again. It's all I can think."

"Dammit, Pauly—" Mileski protested.

"I know, I know, Jimmy. I told Rudick that shit couldn't go on, but after losing Gresh and Gill, we needed Nico. His mom died. His sister is nine and deaf. She needs to be with someone who can communicate with her. Nico knew she couldn't stay out there. He was trying to figure out what to do."

"And did this nine-year-old girl see any of you?"

"Me," Marrone replied, shaking his head. "A few weeks ago. The night of the drive-by shooting. I stopped at Rudick's several hours after, and she was there, snuck up from the basement late that night."

"Dammit," Mileski moaned.

Vince took a drink of his whiskey, taking a moment to think. "Other than this girl. Who can hurt you right now? Is there anyone else who's a liability?"

Mileski and Marrone shared a look before both shaking their heads. "After today we're wiped out," Marrone said. "We have the Bianchi brothers. Stevie drives us around and Joe is running the warehouse."

"Any chance Stevie was seen?"

"I don't think so," Marrone said. "Most of the houses near Rudick's are summer cabins. He parked at one and worked his way through the woods to the side of the house. He was in and out in five minutes."

"Was Stevie driving the night you were at that apartment?"

Marrone nodded. "But it was my SUV. Jimmy was there too."

Mileski understood Vince's question. "You want to do Stevie, you'll need permission from Bobby. We keep sacrificing our own people, we won't have anybody left to work for us."

"We'll cross that bridge if we ever get to it," Vince said.

"In the meantime, our operation is suffering," Marrone said. "Heck, I have Stevie making the runs for us now. That's what we're down to. I'm leery of going home tonight. We put our wives on the road to Chicago this afternoon."

"Tonight, you stay here," Vince stated. "Let Max and Carlo

get the lay of the land. We're staying at condos in Crosslake. We'll be five miles away and always have two men here."

They all paused for a moment, sipping their whiskey and all thinking the same thing. "Vincent, is it Marta?" Mileski eventually asked.

Vince took another sip of his whiskey, savoring the taste before letting it slowly flow down. He shook his head. "Makes no sense that it is."

"Why?" Mileski said.

"For one, you guys have been up here for what? Twelve years?"

Marrone nodded. "Yeah, after the shit hit the fan back home."

"Point is, you're not hiding up here. You're in the phone book, for Christ's sake."

"We had the same thought earlier," Mileski said.

"If she wanted to kill you two, she could have done it easily at any time over the last twelve years and you'd have had no idea she was coming. And besides, where has she been? Not a peep for twelve years and now she comes out of hiding up here? For this? I don't get it."

Marrone exhaled a breath. "I have to tell ya, when I heard that description this morning. It sent a shiver down my spine, to think she's still out there lurking around."

"We hunted for her for a long time," Vince said. "She disappeared after Philly. We never found a trace of where she went or who she became."

"Who else would it be? Who else meets that description?" Mileski asked. "And would come after *us*?"

Vince took another long drink of whiskey. He slowly rotated the heavy glass in his hand, considering if it was Marta they were facing. *If it was her, why after all this time would she emerge? Why? What has triggered that? If she's been in hiding, she'd done it awfully well. She would only risk it for something or for... someone that truly mattered to her.*

"If it is Marta, what would make her come out of hiding after twelve years and risk it all? What could reach you like that?" Vince asked.

"Family," Marrone said immediately.

"She's related to one of these people?" Mileski asked.

"Not family. I'd remember if she had family up here and she didn't. I think it's more likely one of these victims mattered to her greatly for some reason," Vince said. "That is what we need to find out."

Vince checked his gun before slipping it under the pillow on his bed and then grabbed his bottle of water and sat down in the chair and peered out the window. The back of the condo overlooked the north end of Crosslake. It was a clear night. The full moon reflected off the calm waters.

Marta.

It had been twelve years.

They figured she would come after Philly and his crew after what they'd done to Angelo, and after Cleveland. They'd had the boss under heavy guard, and the club had been like a fortress. He had eight good men inside and had for two weeks.

The redhead.

He'd seen her repeatedly in those two weeks, the smoky redhead with the long wavy hair halfway down her back who worked at the club. She'd had the stiletto heels, the long legs in her sleek black pants with the white button-down collar blouse tight to her body, her breasts firm with just a hint of bounce, one extra button left open to give you that slightest hint of what lay beneath. If he had a type back then, she was it. He'd contemplated whisking her off after the danger had passed.

He was reading the *Sun-Times* when she walked right by

him, her head down slightly, carrying a stack of towels to the steam room, two bottles of water lying on top. She'd done it several times in those two weeks. He paid her little mind. Then thirty seconds later.

Bap! Bap! Bap! Bap! Bap! Bap!

The steam room.

He spun around, pulling his gun. She came rushing around the corner, the red hair, the gun, the suppressor. Marta.

Bap! Bap! Bap!

Boom! Boom!

He took two in his chest. He'd managed to get two strays off before falling to the floor. He saw her in the hall. It was Marta. She recognized him and took two quick steps forward, her gun up, dialing in on his head, coming to finish the job. As if she knew he'd been the one to kill Angie. Her own boss. Her guy.

There were voices and footsteps behind him.

Men were coming. Working their way back.

She froze and then started backtracking when the first shots came from behind him.

Crack! Crack! Crack!

She'd returned fire.

Bap! Bap! Bap!

The rest he had only faintly heard as he bled out.

Bap! Bap! Ba...

He had awoken two days later in the hospital and learned she had killed two more men while escaping out the back of the club. Despite five more men being on the premises and giving chase, she had disappeared into the night.

The real redhead had been knocked out. She was found bound and gagged in a closet by the laundry room.

Marta?

She'd vanished and hadn't been heard from since.

Until now.

EIGHTEEN

"YOU LOOK AND SOUND TOTALLY RETIRED."

"How did you sleep?" Braddock said when he came into the kitchen. The sun was just over the eastern horizon on the far east side of the lake.

"Like you, fitfully," Tori said with a wan smile as she handed him a cup of coffee. "I got up and took out my frustration on the exercise bike."

"Did you make it your bitch?"

"When don't I?"

He laughed, kissed her on the cheek before taking his coffee cup. Tori's phone beeped. "Huh. Interesting."

"What?"

"Tracy wants to get on a call about our woman killer. She's looping in the special agent in charge from the Chicago office."

"Chicago you say?" Braddock said. "Interesting. The connections continue."

"You should call Boe."

A half-hour later, situated in Tori's home office, the video conference included Braddock, Tori, Boe, Tracy Sheets and Special Agent in Charge Joe Bahn from the Chicago FBI field office. After introductions were made, Tracy explained that Tori had called her with the description of the woman killer. "Because Tori and I worked a case twelve years ago in Cleveland that involved a killer matching that description. What I didn't know when I talked with Tori is the history of this woman killer. I made a few calls that led me to Special Agent Bahn in Chicago."

"That got me curious," Bahn said. "Very curious, actually."

"Does this have anything to do with Special Agent Como being killed in Cleveland twelve years ago?" Tori said.

"It may," Tracy replied. "Tori, if, and I emphasize if, this is the woman you and I are thinking of, what Special Agent Bahn is going to tell you is that she has nineteen kills to her record."

"*Nineteen!*" Tori blurted.

"Yeah, this goes way beyond what happened that night in Cleveland."

"Who is she?"

"That's the thing," Bahn said with a shake of the head. "We don't know her identity. I have my doubts it's her, but if it was, yesterday was the first time we've heard of her operating in at least twelve years."

Twelve years? Tori looked to Braddock questioningly. "Trace, what *do* we know about her?"

"The thought is that she was a contract killer with the Chicago Outfit although there is no confirmation of that. Just rumors and supposition."

"Did we know any of this twelve years ago?"

"No, I don't think we did."

"So what is it about yesterday that harkens back to these nineteen murders?"

"Description," Bahn said. "Tall, wearing black leather, combat boots, three tight shots to the chest. It's not the most detailed I know, but enough to give my memory a jolt."

"Agent Bahn, does the name Paul Marrone mean anything to you?" Braddock asked.

A wry grin creased the special agent's face. "I remember his brother John Marrone vividly. He was a Mob guy out on the west side, a capo. Paul was his younger brother, although I haven't heard of him in years. Why?"

"He's up here, running a hardware store," Braddock replied. "And, at least on paper, the hardware store is owned by a man named James Mileski."

"Jimmy Mileski?" Bahn said, surprised. "I'll be."

"Who is that?" Tracy asked.

"Jimmy Mileski's brother Bobby is the boss for the outfit in Chicago these days. Johnny Marrone and Bobby ran side-by-side back in the day for a boss named Philly Lamberto."

"I didn't think there was much left of organized crime these days in Chicago," Tracy said.

"They're still around," Bahn said. "They don't have the overall numbers or power they once did but they're still a menacing presence. And these days, Bobby Mileski is the boss. He keeps quiet and operates out of an upscale neighborhood restaurant. It's a legit place, well thought of, won a food award or two, but he's running his crews out of there as well. With Paul Marrone and Jimmy Mileski up in your neck of the woods you've doubled my interest, to say the least."

"You think they're operating up there?" Tracy asked Bahn.

Bahn snorted a laugh. "Leopards don't change their spots."

"True that," Tori echoed.

"Marrone was but a blip on my radar until the last week or so and I'd never heard of Mileski until last night," Braddock said. "The strip mall he owns is in a place called Cullen Crossing. It's just a speck of a town, your basic intersection with a flashing yellow light."

"What businesses are in the strip mall?" Bahn inquired.

"A hardware store, gas station, bar and restaurant, tobacco shop, liquor store, and a gift shop, I think."

Bahn nodded. "Sounds about right. This is what Mileski's

crew has done down here. They've bought up or assumed distressed cash type businesses like restaurants, diners, convenience stores, liquor stores, coffee shops and run them legitimately, but then run other money through them. You deposit that money in the bank and into the system and it gets laundered. If this strip mall is out of the way and they've kept their heads down since they've been up there, you wouldn't have given them a second thought."

"At least until we ended up with as many as ten dead bodies over the last several months," Braddock replied disgustedly. "Agent Bahn, is narcotics part of what these guys are still in?"

"Oh yes," Bahn said, "and prostitution, counterfeiting, robbery, weapons dealing, racketeering, all the usual stuff."

"I want to get back to our killer," Tori said. "You said she worked for the Chicago Mob? We know that how?"

"That was the supposition, Special Agent Hunter," Bahn replied.

"Special Agent Bahn, you can call me Tori. I'm no longer a special agent. I'm retired," Tori said with a smile.

"Yeah, you look and sound *totally* retired," Bahn replied sarcastically. "As to this woman, I was working out of this office when she was active. The nineteen killings were not limited to Chicago. There were killings tied to her in St. Louis, Kansas City, Milwaukee, Wichita, Philadelphia and as you and Special Agent Sheets noted, Tori, Cleveland."

"Ever in Minnesota?" Boe asked.

"Not that we know of. There were few visual sightings of her. She was described as tall, long thin legs, wearing all black leather and high heels or stiletto boots. One time she was thought to have long dark hair.

"Nobody ever saw her face or at least nobody ever lived to describe it. Beyond the physical description, there is also some commonality to the kills. She gets in close. Often, a tight pattern of shots to the chest. On occasion, if she had the time, she would finish people off with a headshot, execution style. A few times there were multiples, but often just singles in her victims. She would use different guns each time but favored Berettas and used small caliber ammunition such as 9mm parabellums. So between physical description and method, we've zeroed in on her and the nineteen kills I noted. Do you have ballistics yet?"

"Not a report, although there were 9mm casings at the house scene yesterday," Braddock answered looking over to Tori. "A Beretta certainly would fire that kind of ammunition."

"How long was she active?" Tori asked.

"About six years," Tracy noted.

"Why do you think she was a killer for the Chicago Outfit and not just an independent?"

"Agent Bahn and I talked about that earlier," Tracy started. "The Bureau backed into that view, but only after she seemingly disappeared."

Bahn jumped in. "It's a long story and we can send you our file on her, but yes, we think, and I emphasize think, she worked in Chicago and her shot caller might have been Angelo DeEsposito."

"What ties her to him?"

"Twelve years ago, the night she's doing the job on our guy Como in Cleveland, DeEsposito and two of his men were murdered getting into their car behind Dudek's, a southside bar that DeEsposito owned and operated out of," Bahn said. "Angelo and his men were taken out by a rival crew that was run by Paul Lamberto who went by Philly. Lamberto was born in Philadelphia and moved to Chicago as a kid, hence Philly. Where this gets interesting for you is Lamberto's top two lieutenants were Bobby Mileski and Johnny Marrone. Back then, times were challenging for the Outfit. There was shrinking territory for their usual business avenues, law enforcement was paying them a lot of attention and there was a leadership vacuum at the top. It was anarchy. Lamberto and DeEsposito were not friends and Lamberto's crew felt like Angelo's boys were encroaching on their turf. Something had to give and Philly made his move.

"When DeEsposito was killed, things got ugly and that's where the woman comes back into play. Two weeks after DeEsposito and his men were killed, Lamberto was under heavy protection as he expected what was left of Angelo's guys were going to come after him. Lamberto was hunkered down at his private club. One night he's sitting in the steam room with Johnny Marrone, his guys on guard watching all the hallways, when a red-headed woman looking like an employee of the club familiar to everyone, carried a stack of white towels right through all Lamberto's guards to the steam room. In the stack of towels was a gun. She put three each into Philly's and Johnny's chests, killing them, severely wounded another of his men outside the steam room and killed two more of them as she escaped out the back."

"And you're certain it was her?" Tori said.

"We think so. And after that night, she completely disappeared."

Tori understood the Mob tie. "You think she worked for Angelo DeEsposito? And killing Lamberto, Marrone and the others was revenge?"

"Yes. Angelo was sixty-one when he was gunned down. He was old school, a canny operator who had connections well beyond Chicago. If someone in the Outfit needed help in another city, they went to see Angelo and he could facilitate things."

"Like taking out a rival," Braddock suggested. "Or someone who was getting in the way."

"Correct," Bahn affirmed. "All nineteen of her confirmed kills were related to organized crime. She might have had others we don't know about, but we have nineteen we think for sure are hers."

"Seems like she limited her killing to people who were criminals or had Mob ties," Tori observed. "She never killed your run of the mill citizen, other than Special Agent Como. Do you think she knew he was with the Bureau?"

"I think someone did," Bahn said. "Whether they clued her in to that or not, I do not know. She took the contract and pulled the trigger. Doesn't matter if she knew or not."

"If I'm hearing you," Braddock started, "the connection of the woman to DeEsposito is based strictly on rumor and then the timing of the hit on DeEsposito, followed by the retaliatory hits on Lamberto and Marrone."

"She was tied to DeEsposito. You think Lamberto had DeEsposito killed? Who killed DeEsposito?" Tori asked.

Bahn shrugged. "We never knew the specifics. Nobody saw it all go down. It was a bloody scene in the alley behind Dudek's, which was the bar Angelo operated out of. They hit Angelo in his car, getting the driver and his other man. It was assumed Lamberto called the shot and the fact that he was gunned down two weeks later by the woman rumored to be Angelo's mysterious killer confirms it. That's how the Bureau and CPD backed into it. But again, until yesterday, nobody has heard from her in twelve years. So the names Mileski and Marrone have me curious. What have they been up to up there?"

"My people are about to start finding out," Boe said.

"Well, if you have a Mileski and Marrone operating in your neck of the woods, I'd like to know what else you find."

"Given what they've told you, Joe," Tracy said. "Do you think they're dealing with... her?"

"The first question I'd ask is why come out of hiding after twelve years? We thought she might have been—"

"Killed."

"Yes. We were hunting for her because of Cleveland and the Chicago boys were hunting for her over killing Lamberto,

Marrone and the others. After a few years, and no sign of her, we figured the Mob hunted her down and killed her. It was that or she successfully disappeared and started life anew. Not many people escape that profession. If she accomplished that, why come out of hiding now?"

Braddock glanced to his right. Tori was sitting back in her chair, staring off. She was thinking something.

"That's all I know. I'll be curious to learn what you find," Bahn said. "Maybe we can help each other."

They talked for another five minutes before Bahn dropped off. Tracy hung for a minute to chit-chat with Tori. "Keep in touch. My curiosity is piqued, Tor."

"You know I will," Tori replied. "Talk soon."

Boe hung on the video conference. Braddock looked to Tori. "What do you think?"

"It's her. Has to be."

"Convince me," Boe said.

Tori sighed. "I get Bahn's logic. She escapes the life and goes into hiding. I think that's what she did, and what better place to hide than northern Minnesota."

"Hypothetically, say she is here, and she did escape the life and establish a new identity and life," Boe said. "Answer Bahn's other question. Why get involved now? Did she unretire? Or did she never quit. She only changed her look and methods."

"But then goes back to her old style for this one?" Tori replied, not buying the idea. "She called to direct us to Gresh," Tori said. "She wanted us to find him. Gresh either killed those kids in Holmstrand or knew who did. If we'd have gotten to him, we'd have gotten some answers."

"Or she killed him, and the call was just intended to get us to find his body."

"Nah," Tori scoffed. "If she killed him, she doesn't call us at all."

"Why not. We find him. We tell the families..."

Braddock snorted a laugh, shaking his head.

"Is something I said funny?" Boe asked angrily.

"No, Janette," Braddock said, sitting back himself. "It's just that knowing what we know now, what Bahn just told us about this killer, what happened at that trailer plays way differently to me."

"How so?" Boe asked.

"She was tracking Rudick's car. Our woman sees it all go down at the trailer. Rudick, Waltripp and Sweeney set up Gresh and Gill, leave the murder weapon, and at least publicly, based on what the Jensens, Horns and Randalls have been told, we found the man most responsible killed. Publicly at least, our case is closed."

"She knows otherwise," Tori said as she stood up and started pacing, going in and out of view of the camera. "Huh. That's how it happens."

"What happens?" Boe asked.

"She's out there and sees these guys set up Gresh," Tori replied, leaning back into the camera. "At that point, she's not committed to anything other than tracking Rudick. She's done nothing more than dip her toe in the water. She's being careful, using a burner phone and a tracker. She doesn't want to reveal herself. She wants *us* to get the man responsible. She calls me, figuring we get to Gresh, we either get the guy or find who ordered the killings up in Holmstrand. But then... those other three—"

"Set Gresh up."

"And she witnesses it. And what's the public story?"

"Gresh was the killer," Boe said, grimacing.

"She knows there's more to the story. And she figures we're not going to pursue it any further," Braddock said. "Even though we quietly were."

"Still," Boe argued. "Why get involved? Why emerge and

bring on all the attention this is now going to get? I don't get why she's risking it."

"It's personal," Tori said. "That's the only way it makes sense."

"Mileski and Marrone?" Boe asked skeptically.

"That isn't the only way it gets personal," Tori said. "There are three victims in Holmstrand—"

"Someone she cared about. Family maybe," Boe said, seeing it now. "What do we know about the Horns, Jensens and Randalls?"

"Might be time we find out," Braddock said.

"But still, what about Mileski and Marrone? Why not just kill them?" Boe posited. "Under your theory, they may have been the ones to order the drive-by."

"Who says she's not going to," Tori replied.

"I was afraid you were going to say that," Braddock muttered. "Now that she's started—"

"Why stop. Plus, if she killed Lamberto and Marrone's older brother twelve years ago for killing DeEsposito, what's to say she won't want to finish off that old business now that's she's started up again."

"Do we warn them?" Boe asked.

"No," Tori said with an evil grin. "Make them squirm."

"But—"

"We don't have to, Sheriff," Braddock replied. "Mileski and Marrone are operating up here and I'm betting with Mileski's brother's approval if not his orders. If we assume guys like Waltripp and Sweeney were muscle for these guys, now that they're gone, they're exposed. You can bet that if Mileski and Marrone are still hooked into Chicago, that they may have paid a call to Chicago for reinforcements."

"And they're going to want to find her."

"Oh yeah. They won't let this go."

"And they'll rip the area up to do it," Boe said. "We can't have that. We have to go after Mileski and Marrone and now."

"With what, Janette?" Braddock said. "We don't have anything concrete on them, just a lot of suspicion."

"They're dirty."

"You know what the problem is? You're a marshal."

"What does that mean?" Boe said defensively.

"Marshals see the target and go get them. They don't need proof because the targets have already been proven guilty. I don't have proof on these two. All we do by going at them right now is alert them. I want to catch them at whatever it is they're doing and who they're doing it with. I want them looking for her, not us."

"The long game," Tori said. "Build the case."

"Not too long but I want to throw everything we have at it. I want a tight team of Tori, Reese, Eggs, Nolan, myself, and a few others to watch these guys every move. Steak keeps working the investigation on Banz and the others to see if we can tie them back to Mileski and Marrone now that we have someone to look at."

"And our woman killer?" Boe asked.

"If we're watching Mileski and Marrone—"

"She'll show up," Tori finished. "It's a two-fer. She has them in her sights too."

Braddock looked to Boe. "That's my plan."

"Go do it."

NINETEEN

"YOU'RE STILL NOT ONE OF US."

Braddock made a quick phone call after they finished with Boe and then he and Tori drove northeast toward Cullen Crossing to get their own look at matters, passing the city limits sign on the right. Cullen Crossing, Population 94.

"I'd like to check on Alisha at some point today," Tori said.

"Good idea," Braddock replied, his arm draped casually over the steering wheel.

They came around a sharp ninety-degree bend to the left and the strip mall was on the right, just before the flashing yellow light, a carved wood sign encased in massive boulders with medium-sized spruce trees framing it all: Cullen Crossing Plaza.

At first blush, the front of the mall looked like a classic piece of northern Minnesota with the dark pine log exterior, deep forest-green awnings and classic cedar shakes on the multiple peaked roofs nicely dressing up an otherwise long rectangular building. The centerpiece of the mall was CC Hardware, occupying the wide middle of the building, the entry under a log archway. The expansive front sidewalk was filled with mowers, tillers, edgers and wheelbarrows, along with two stacks of green plastic Adirondack chairs. A large Spring Sale sign was strung tightly high over the entrance. A We're Open sign alighted in the front windows.

To the right of the hardware store was the tobacco shop, followed by the kitschy Lakes Gift Shop, and then the CC Deli, which served as the grocery store and gas station on the end. To the left was the liquor store that then led into the CC Bar and Grill. It was late on what should have been a busy early spring Saturday morning, yet there were only a few vehicles in the open parking lot. Across the street from the mall was a small post office, city hall and the volunteer fire station. Further down the road was a boat repair and rental shop and then a small church and finally a self-storage facility.

"Not much to the town," Tori said. "Just a few houses, hardly even a street grid."

"It's an unincorporated township, not a city, so there isn't much to it. However, Jenkins is back five miles west and Crosslake five miles east. Nothing but lakes in between so I'm sure that's what drives business."

"The houses are all old, but they look mostly well-tended to. It's quainter and cuter than I remember."

"You remember this place?"

"I rode the county with my dad all the time when I was growing up. You see everyplace when you're pounding in lawn signs. *Big Jim for Sheriff. You know him, you trust him.*"

"No last name required."

"Nope. Everyone knew him."

"Oh, I hear that," Braddock said. "People still talk about him, ask about him, ask me if I'm shacking up with his daughter."

"Shacking up?" Tori said, smiling.

"Yeah. I actually had someone say that to me not long ago. 'I hear you're shacking up with Tori.'"

Tori laughed. "Our living arrangements are public knowledge I guess."

Braddock drove through the town and then did a U-turn and made another pass through. "I want to hunker down and observe these guys. The problem is how?"

"And from where," Tori added as she scanned the area. "Even though we haven't given them cause to think we're watching, they'll be conscious of any attention from us. If Reese and others are sitting up here in Tahoes and Explorers or even a surveillance van, they'll be spotted in about five minutes."

"What would you do?"

"We need to get into a couple of these houses to get front and back views. Then maybe station an unmarked mobile unit somewhere just out of town in case you want to give someone a follow."

"Capital idea," Braddock said. "Let's go to lunch and hash it out."

They made another pass by the strip mall before they continued east another five miles and into Crosslake and to the Manhattan Beach Diner, a small café overlooking the water. Inside, they found their old boss Cal Lund sitting in a secluded booth, reading a newspaper, drinking an iced tea.

"Hi, kids," he greeted cheerily, folding his paper. He stood up and shook Braddock's hand warmly. "Victoria," he greeted, wrapping her in a big bear hug. Cal had been her father's best friend. In a way, a hug from Cal was like getting one from her dad and she always held on to them for an extra second.

The waitress quickly came by and took their lunch orders. The three of them caught up for a bit. Cal and Lucy had just returned from their first full winter of retirement in Tucson. He'd survived being shot in the chest last summer. Nine months later he still had a bit of gauntness to him, but it wasn't the lifeless gray kind and to Tori's delight, he looked tanned, healthy, refreshed, and happy as he regaled them with stories of his first winter south. "Lots of nice folks in our complex. I even played two rounds of golf a week and didn't hate it."

"You, golf?" Braddock asked. He'd taken the game up himself in recent years at his brother-in-law's urging. Athletic to begin with, he enjoyed playing in a men's league a few days a week. He'd asked Cal to play often, but he'd refused. It was Minnesota. He lived on a lake. There were fish to be caught. But now, he golfed. "Two days a week, huh? Next thing I know, you're going to be in the Wednesday men's league at The Pines with all of us."

"Signed up just the other day," replied Cal, smiling.

"Yeah?"

"I'm retired. I have time to fill. Now," he said, dropping his voice. "I'm in Arizona, and I'm reading about drive-by shootings? And I get back a few days ago and we have this crazy stuff yesterday? What's going on around here?"

"A lot," Braddock replied. "And it's all connected."

"Do tell," Cal asked, his curiosity piqued.

They spent fifteen minutes bringing Cal up to speed. "And Janette, she's giving you free rein?"

"Yes." Braddock had worried about a new boss. He'd grown accustomed to Cal letting him run investigations as he saw fit. He hadn't been sure Boe would be so accommodating. "Of course, I haven't completely screwed the pooch yet, so she's letting me do my thing for now."

"What do you think of her, Victoria?" Cal always called her by her full-given name.

Tori took a moment. "She's a smart, savvy... *politician*."

"It's a component of the job, Victoria."

"Yes, but you were a sheriff first, a politician second. With Boe, it seems like it's the other way around."

Cal nodded at that and then looked to Braddock. "So, what's your plan to go after these two fellas over in Cullen Crossing?"

Braddock and Tori laid out their thoughts for a multi-pronged investigation of Mileski and Marrone.

"I've always wondered how that place stayed in business," Cal remarked. "You know, you drive by and look at it and think how odd it is something as large as that is in Cullen Crossing and making it."

"You ever talk to Marrone or Mileski?"

Cal nodded. "A few times, just to stop in and say hello. They would be out front talking, the one always smoking a cigar. They said all the right things, but you could tell they weren't natives. They had that big city attitudinal edge to them. Kind of like you had when you got here," he said to Braddock. "It's dissipated in you over time."

"But the New York, it's still there," Tori said, smiling. "The attitude."

"Really?" Braddock said dismissively.

"You're still not one of us," Cal said, echoing a common Minnesota euphemism for non-native Minnesotans. "But you're more like us. Now, what about this killer from yesterday?"

"I'm on that," Tori said.

"Doing what?"

"Figuring out who she was to determine who she now is."

"The Bureau has a dossier on her, if it's her," Braddock said. "And given Tori's Bureau ties."

"And the admiration they oddly retain for her for some reason," Cal quipped.

"Hey, hey, hey."

"Oh, it's well earned, Victoria, of that I have no doubt. But if she were a pro, isn't she gone by now?"

"We're not so sure about that. Tori has a theory that I'm starting to buy." Braddock explained their hypothesis that she was in the area, perhaps living, certainly hanging around. "I figure if she killed these guys, she might go after Mileski and

Marrone. If we keep a close eye on them, she might turn up too."

Cal nodded. "So how you going to keep that close eye on them?"

"It's a little vexing," Braddock said. "We need a place or places where we can set up shop and watch the strip mall. I don't suppose you know an old constituent or two who might be willing to lend a helping hand."

"You know I just might."

* * *

"Maggie, I love it! Love it!" Emily exclaimed, looking in the mirror at her long wavy black hair, but now with stylish bangs in the front.

"I really like the look too," Maggie said with a big smile, standing behind her, fluffing strands of Emily's hair. "It kind of reminds me of Anne Hathaway in *The Devil Wears Prada*. You know, when Andy was waiting outside the restaurant after her fashion makeover by Nigel."

"Yes. *Yes!*" Emily replied, her eyes lighting up. "It so does. It's exactly what I was looking for."

"I have a feeling Glen is going to like it as well," Maggie said as she swept the smock off Emily and then blow dried some last clumps of hair away. "All done."

The two of them chit-chatted over a cup of tea for a few minutes while Maggie ran Emily's credit card through and then showed her out the door, just as Rob and Ellen came inside with their suitcases.

"You're home!" Maggie greeted them, hugging Ellen and then quick kissing Rob. Brian had returned earlier in the day and was upstairs napping from the overnight drive from Colorado and his ski trip. "And you both look very tan."

"I got burned yesterday," Ellen said. "My shoulders, trying to get a little extra so I'd look tan for prom in a few weeks."

"I think you'll be fine," Maggie said. "Hungry?"

"Yes," Rob replied quickly.

"Good. I'm going to make spaghetti. Give me an hour."

Ellen headed upstairs. When she left the kitchen, Maggie pulled Rob down for a kiss, this one a lingering one.

"Hi there," he said, smiling. "What was *that* for?"

"I'm just glad you're home," she said, before leaning in for another kiss that he eagerly returned, wrapping his arms around her, lifting her up for a two count. "Plus, you look all tan and sexy."

"And I've missed you all week."

She smiled and nuzzled his nose. "We'll have to do something about that. For now, how about you open a bottle of wine while I cook."

"Done."

The two of them spent the next hour talking about the spring break trip while sipping wine and Maggie cooked. "She was actually very responsible and well behaved for the week," Rob noted. "Of course, they couldn't leave the resort. She was home by her curfew every night so we were good. How was your week?"

"Nothing too exciting." Maggie was steady as she casually talked about Cathy and her customers.

Rob helped her with the French bread and salad and in the hour-long cooking process, they polished off the bottle.

"I'm going to open another," he said, flicking his eyes.

"Splendid idea."

The kids came down when called and the four of them sat around the kitchen table for a good hour, long after dinner was finished, talking about their trips, current events in the kids' social media feeds and the upcoming prom. Ellen had a date. Brian said there were a couple of girls he was thinking of asking and got his older sister's input. It was nice for the family to be back to talking about normal things, though the shooting next door was never far from anyone's thoughts.

After clearing the dishes from the table, Brian and Ellen each left for the night, having plans with friends. She and Rob moved to the family room and perused the streaming services before Maggie admitted to Rob that she'd never seen *You've Got Mail.*

"How is it possible you haven't seen that?" Rob asked. "You're the romantic comedy movie chick extraordinaire. I thought you'd seen them all."

"Not that one. Remember, buddy, you're older than me." Rob was forty-five and he believed Maggie to be thirty-five. Her true age was thirty-seven but that was just one other thing he didn't need to know. "That movie came out when I was like ten."

"Ouch," he replied with a laugh. "Well, I'm pretty sure you'll like it," he added, before finishing off his wine glass. "Before I start it do you want a refill?"

"Of course. Let's downshift to some white though."

"Okay."

Their wine glasses refilled, Maggie curled up on the couch, leaning into her husband while they watched the movie.

"The AOL sound for dial up Internet!" Maggie cackled.

"Those were the days."

She liked the movie. Tom Hanks and Meg Ryan were always good, and she had a certain appreciation for the duplicity of the Joe Fox character in wooing Kathleen. As the credits rolled, Rob moved to lean forward for the remote when Maggie stopped him, turned into him and kissed him, this time deeply. "I'm glad you're back."

"I can tell."

She stood up and reached for his hand and then led him up to their bedroom. She closed the door, turned around and began to undress him, lifting his long-sleeved shirt up over his head and then pushing him backward onto their bed, landing on top of him, kissing him on the neck.

"I take it you're in the mood," he said as he fumbled with her jeans, shoving them down her thighs, using his right foot to push them the rest of the way off.

"Oh yeah," she said, looking him intensely in the eye, cupping his face with her right hand. "Way in the mood. Let's go!"

A half-hour later, they lay on their bed, naked, the sweat cooling on their bodies, both still breathing heavily. "That was... intense," Rob said with a light laugh. "You were on fire."

"I think passionate is the word you're looking for," Maggie said with a giggle, lying on her back.

"Well, it was, but you were... very ardent," he said, smiling.

"Ardent? I was ardent?" Maggie teased, rolling onto her side, eyeing up her husband.

"You were like possessed. When you looked me in the eye and said: let's go! That was new."

"You didn't like it?" Maggie asked playfully, leaning in, pecking him on the lips. "I kind of think you liked it."

"No, I loved it. It's just that it wasn't the... usual sex, you know."

"Wait, wait," Maggie said, smiling, all naked, relaxed, and loose, sitting up and rolling to straddle him. "What's usual sex?"

"Well, you know."

"It's checklist sex, right? Ten minutes of foreplay, missionary for five minutes, ten-fifteen pumps, you cum, I *maybe* orgasm, and we roll over and go to sleep five minutes later. Like we're getting the weekly sex out of the way."

Rob cackled. "Well, I like to think I've got a little more game than that."

"You still do. You put in the effort tonight. Once I got you going."

"That you did. Tonight, you were like that one night when we were on vacation down to the Bahamas. That was the night you had me on the table in the room and—"

"Oh, I remember." Maggie smiled, leaning down to kiss him. "That was our five-year anniversary trip."

"So why tonight? I mean what happened today that had you so revved up?"

"Nothing really," Maggie replied, lying. "Maybe I just felt the need for you. I missed you all week. Isn't that enough?" she asked, rolling off him and lying her head back down on his chest. "It's been a long few weeks."

"Yeah, it has."

"I saw you come in the door tonight and I just... I needed you is all. There's nothing more to it than that."

"Being needed is good," he said, looping his left arm around her, lightly scratching the soft skin of her back. "Everything is alright though?"

"Yeah," she replied. She reached down to the end of the bed and pulled up the comforter and then rolled on top of him, letting her long body intertwine with his. Leaning in, she nuzzled his nose and then kissed him. "I love you."

"I love you too."

An hour later she lay awake on her side, Rob, his back to her, contentedly asleep. She replayed their last conversation, her husband asking if everything was alright.

Was it?

TWENTY

"SOUNDS INTERESTING."

Vince and his men spent the morning evaluating Marrone and Mileski's homes as well as the routes and alternate routes from Bertha Lake to Cullen Crossing. On the most direct route, it took five minutes door to door. For the time being, they would spend the night at Mileski's house.

"That lets me put two men for sure with you at all times," Vince said over a late breakfast. "Plus, Jimmy's house is on a more open piece of land so we can see someone coming and he has a security system."

Vince and Max left Carlo to coordinate security for the day at the strip mall, though he expected few problems there in the daylight. It was the nighttime he was leery of, particularly in such a lightly populated area.

"While we're here, what are you doing?" Mileski asked.

"Max and I are going to take in some sights."

An hour later, Max drove through downtown Manchester Bay, making his way around the southside of the lake. "Small town America, man. We stick out like sore thumbs around here."

"Nah," Vince replied. "Just say 'ya' and 'ya know' and 'jeez' and you'll blend right in with local yokels."

"Oh yeah," Max replied, jet-black hair, square head, unibrow, bulky shoulders, gold chain to go with his black T-shirt and leather jacket. "I blend right in with all these Finns, Swedes, and Norwegians. I've never seen so much blond in my life."

Max wasn't wrong, he thought, evaluating his own leather jacket and dress pant look. They probably needed to work on their wardrobe. Jeans, fleece quarter zips or flannel and hiking boots might allow them to better meld with the locals.

Through the town and to the west they followed the GPS until they turned off County Road 44 to the east and found the house along the paved road, a wavy Northern Pine Lake visible between the houses and through the leafless trees.

Max did a slow drive-by of the house to their right, the back door opening as they did. He saw a red-headed woman inside.

"Ease up," Vince ordered as he adjusted the passenger side mirror to look back. "And there they are."

A woman and a young girl were walking out the back of the house. As they got to the car, the woman signed with the younger girl, who quickly signed back. "That's them."

Max drove around a bend and out of sight before completing a quick U-turn. "Should I follow?"

"Not right now," Vince replied. "Just drive by the house again."

Max did another slow drive-by of the one-story white clapboard house with a detached garage. The house itself was set well back from the lake, providing for an expansive yard down to the shore. "Thoughts?"

"Is it me, or are most of the houses and cabins around here unoccupied?"

"I think you're right. We're a long way from summer yet."

Vince nodded. "We should come back and check it out in the dark tonight."

Their next stop was Rudick's house. The crime scene tape was still fluttering in the wind as Max pulled by but there was no police presence guarding the property. He drove another hundred yards down the road and pulled into a driveway for an unoccupied cabin. The two of them walked down the road a bit and then slipped into the woods and picked the rest of the way through to the house. Based on what Marrone told him, he could envision how Nico and the girl slipped out of the house and ran around the west side to Rudick's truck parked in the driveway.

Vince looked over to Max. "If Marta approached this house early in the morning, how would she have done it?"

Max took in the property and got his directional bearings. "She'd come from the east I'd think. The glare of the rising sun would cover her approach."

"Nico gets away in Rudick's truck. If you're right, Marta is parked somewhere to the east. She runs on foot to her vehicle while our guy is hauling ass out of here," Vince observed, looking to the east through the trees. "Next house is what? Fifty yards away? Next one another fifty?"

"She had to get out of the house, through those trees and to her vehicle. He has a thirty second head start at least," Max said.

The two of them made their way back to the Navigator and drove to Rudick's house. Max hit the gas and accelerated down the winding road, driving at a high rate of speed to the highway.

"Thirty-six seconds," Vince remarked. "And I bet our guy was driving faster."

"Which way did he turn?"

"Right. He drove south into Manchester Bay. According to Mileski, he dropped his little sister off at a sidewalk bench at the university. Our killer caught up to him on County 63 twenty miles to the east, driving north up to Cullen Crossing."

Max shook his head. "She was thirty to forty seconds behind him. How would she know which way he turned? How would she know where to go?"

"She had a fifty-fifty shot and guessed right," Vince answered.

"Where to next?"

"Holmstrand," Vince said.

* * *

"What is it exactly you're looking to do?" Eunice Michaels asked Braddock. Eunice was in her seventies, a widow, with a small two-story house, out the back of which they could watch the front of the strip mall.

"Eunice, I'm going to have Detective Reese, and some others, engaging in some surveillance," he replied as he peered out the upstairs spare bedroom window. It provided a perfect view across County Road 16 to the strip mall. "They won't bother you at all."

"For how long?"

"At least a week or two," Braddock said as he pulled back a curtain before looking back to Eunice.

"Sounds interesting. Does this have anything to do with the shooting on Friday? Everyone is talking about that."

Braddock looked back at Eunice and smiled. "Now what would you give you that idea?"

"Well, okay then," Eunice said, now curious. "Do I get paid anything for this... accommodation?"

Braddock laughed. Cal said she was a little brassy. "Yes, there is a stipend for your trouble. Now, I'll leave so you and Detective Reese can get acquainted."

* * *

"Ol' Cal said a lady detective would be along," Harold Keen said as he let Tori inside. "He didn't say she would be so dang pretty." Cal warned that Harold could be a charmer. Now well into his eighties, he'd been married three times, though sadly, his three wives had all predeceased him.

"You said your name is Tori?"

"Yes," Tori said, shaking his hand. "Victoria Hunter is my real name but everyone, except Cal, calls me Tori."

"I like Victoria."

"Then, Harold, I'll permit you to use it."

"That puts me in good company then," Harold said as he ambled along the narrow hallway with his cane, leading Tori into the back of his boxy one-story house.

"The room hasn't been used in years," Harold said as he opened the door to a spare bedroom. "I'll probably need to vacuum it for you all."

"We'll take care of that," Tori said as she gazed out the window. "How long have you known Cal?"

"Thirty years at least, maybe more. He and I took more than one fish out of Clamshell Lake, let me tell you. That and he came up to my deer hunting land a few times over the years. He was a good sheriff. Knew everyone. Now you said your last name was Hunter. You any relation to Big Jim?"

Tori smiled broadly. "He was my father."

"Oh my," Harold said with a grin. "Now your pops, what a guy. And he could catch a fish too."

"That he could," Tori replied. "How'd you know Big Jim?"

"Same way I know Cal. I owned a small resort with my first wife, Edith. Your father would stop by every so often just to check in and see how things were going, have a cup a joe and investigate how and where the fish were biting."

"That sounds like him," Tori said as she peered out the

window. The house sat southeast across a gravel road from the strip mall. The window provided an unobstructed view of the gas station and back of the strip mall. "This will be perfect."

"Will *you* be here watching?" Harold asked hopefully.

"Now, I could be convinced to take a shift or two if you're here," Tori replied with a big smile. "And I have a few women detective friends that I'm sure will be by as well. You'll really like them, Detectives Eggleston, and maybe Nolan."

"Well," Harold replied with a big smile, "if you promise that, the room is yours. Whatever you need, Victoria."

"We appreciate it. Now, Deputy Frewer will be along shortly."

"Frewer!" Harold replied. "Oh, he's a beauty too."

Harold would work out just fine.

* * *

It was later in the afternoon, the sun now down behind the trees to the west, darkening the neighborhood. The Randall house sat a quarter block ahead to the southeast, a *Coming Soon - For Sale* sign in the front yard.

Vince envisioned Mileski's boys following Jensen and Horn to the corner ahead, making the left turn and then opening fire as they slowly drove by. There was a streetlight on the corner, but he didn't notice any others nearby. Other than the exterior garage or front door lights, he imagined the tree-lined street provided for a thick darkness when it all went down.

"The house might be a tough sell," Max remarked, leaning against his door, his right arm casually draped over the steering wheel.

"Are you a real estate agent now?"

"No, but it does beg the question, what do you hope to glean from sitting here?"

"Not sure," Vince answered as he took a sip of his gas

station coffee. "Except that what happened here really seemed to set all of Jimmy and Pauly's problems into motion. I wanted to see where it all began." He bit the end of his cigar and spit out the window. "That tobacco shop at the mall is convenient."

"Are you going to light up in here? Really?" Max questioned as a dark blue Toyota RAV4 pulled by and then turned left at the corner ahead.

"Lighten up," Vince replied as he took out his lighter and lit up. "I've got the window cracked."

"Oh yeah, like that makes all the difference."

* * *

Still sweating and parched from her workout, Maggie took a long drink of water as she turned right, eagerly anticipating the shower she would take, the glass of wine she would later drink and then the stir-fry dinner she planned to make. As she approached the left turn for her street, she noticed the Lincoln Navigator parked along the street to the right, the light cloud drifting up from the exhaust pipe. As she drove by, she noted it wasn't parked near a driveway or sidewalk to a house.

She passed the Navigator, turned left, drove past Cathy's and then pulled into the garage. From inside, she hit the button to open the rear lift gate for the RAV4. She walked to the back, peering northwest across Cathy's yard to the Navigator. She leaned in, grabbed two bags of groceries, and took them inside, dropping them off on the center island. Taking a new bottle of water out of the refrigerator, she walked into the living room and peeked between the gap in the curtains out the front picture window. There were two men sitting in the front. The exhaust continued to float up from the rear but then she noticed smoke wafting from the passenger side, as if it was coming up out of the window. It wasn't cigarette smoke. This was thicker and hung in the air. A cigar.

From the front hall closet she extracted a pair of binoculars and rushed upstairs to Ellen's bedroom. She raised the horizontal blinds a couple of inches and then sat cross legged on the floor and focused the binoculars first on the driver and then to the passenger, the cigar in the fingers of his right hand perched to let the smoke billow out.

The man she was looking at had killed Angie twelve years ago, of that she had no doubt. He didn't call the shot but he'd executed it as Lamberto's hired gun. The last time she'd seen Vince Smith was two weeks later, in the hallway just outside that steam room where she'd found them all. He was just a hair slow that day and she put two in him while he fired wildly. If only she'd finished him then, but she hadn't had that extra second of time.

He'd taken on some years and the slicked-back blond hair looked to have lightened to more of a gray, but it was him and he could only be here for one reason.

To find her.

TWENTY-ONE

"YOU CAN EITHER TAKE ON RISK OR ELIMINATE IT."

With Frewer and Reese set up on surveillance at Cullen Crossing, Braddock and Tori went to check in on Alisha.

"What's social services doing?" Braddock asked as they made the short drive north on County 44.

"Conveniently dragging their feet," Tori answered. "Plus, it's the weekend. Who knows what happens come Monday."

Braddock turned right off the county road and weaved his way toward the lake and to the home of Trish and Paul Adams. Alisha was fostering with the Adams until a more suitable long-term solution could be found.

Trish let them inside.

"How is she doing?" Tori asked.

"Okay, all things considered. I took her out shopping and we got a few things for her today, some new clothes which she seemed to like."

Tori nodded. "Missing her brother?"

"Yes. There have been some tears, for her brother and her mother," Trish said. "It's so much for a nine-year-old. She's old enough to wonder what comes next."

"Any word from her family down in St. Cloud?" Braddock asked.

"Not a one. It appears they have as much interest in her coming back as she does in going back," Trish replied as she led them to the family room. Paul was sitting with Alisha, the two of them playing a game of Connect 4 on the coffee table. Alisha smiled when Tori said hello and then went to sit down with her. Braddock chuckled inwardly as Alisha signed to Tori and Tori then slowly went through the thought process of how to reply.

"It's cute to see her just dive in and talk to her."

"Tori told me that she learned to sign on a case years ago," Braddock said. "She said by the end of it she was developing some fluency, but she'd hardly used it since."

"It looks to be coming back," Trish said of Tori's efforts. "You can see the motions getting quicker, more natural, and automatic. That, and she just has a way with her. You can see the smile Alisha has when she's here."

Braddock nodded. "She's particularly good with kids."

"Do you two have children?" Trish asked.

"I have a son, Quinn. He's twelve. And she's great with him."

"You two aren't married?"

Braddock smiled. "We live together, but, no, we're not married."

"Well," Trish said, patting him on the arm, "not yet anyway. Dinner is ready."

The five of them enjoyed a chicken dinner in the dining room. Paul and Trish each had a glass of wine. Since Braddock and Tori had more work ahead, they stuck to water, although Tori stole a sip of white wine from Trish. "Oh, I like that." The two of them started discussing their love of wines and Tori showed Trish information about the wine club she was in.

"My friend, you're about to spend more money on wine," Braddock warned Paul.

Paul smiled. "That's okay. I like drinking it as much as Trish."

After dessert was cleared from the table, Tori took out a folder. She and Alisha sat at the corner of the table. For this Trish signed for Tori while Braddock observed.

"Trish, my first question is how many times or how long was she out at that house?"

Trish asked the question and she and Alisha signed back and forth. "She stayed out there three times. The first time was when her mom was sick. She was there for about a week or so. The second time was just after her mom died and then the third was a few days ago." Trish paused and then looked to Tori and Braddock. "You know, I hear all that and I start getting worried about her schooling."

"Me too," Tori said.

"By the way, Tori," Trish said. "Remember, she reads lips pretty well too."

Tori immediately turned to Alisha and held up a photo of Rudick. "Do you recognize him?"

It was his house.

Next, was a photo of Kevin Waltripp. "Him?"

He was Nico's friend. They talked a lot.

Tori nodded and then took out a picture of Ron Gresh. "How about him?"

Alisha took a moment to review the photo and then nodded. *Just a couple times.*

The next was for Tony Gill.

Alisha nodded, adding: *He was there a lot. He was really nice to me.*

She took out a picture of Reardon Banz. "How about him?"
No.

Tori set a photo of Jimmy Mileski on the table. "How about this man?"

No.

Tori felt herself sag just a bit. The last photo was Paul Marrone. "How about him?"

Alisha immediately nodded and looked to Trish. Tori couldn't keep up with the conversation, their hands were moving rapidly.

"What is it?" Tori asked.

"He was the man who said Alisha had to leave the house. That Nico needed to find a place for her, which is why she ended up at her aunt's house in St. Cloud."

"Did he say why?"

"The house was no place for a child. It was a place of business, or something to that effect. He came with another man."

"Another man? I need a description."

Trish engaged Alisha, signing with her back and forth for a moment.

"The other man had black hair, some gray at the temples. His head was like a square she said, and he had no neck. And he was... I'm interpreting here, but she said a little chunky."

Alisha motioned like she had a big belly.

Tori smiled. "*Big* guy."

Yes.

"A place of business?" Braddock asked. "What did she mean by that?"

"I bet I know," Tori said, thought for a moment before signing Alisha a question: *Did Nico have a gun?*

Alisha slowly looked down and away, which was an answer in and of itself.

Tori reached for her hand. "Hey, it's okay. I just need to know. Did he?"

She nodded and signed: *It scared me.*

"Trish," Braddock said. "Can you ask her if she knows how to read a calendar?"

Alisha nodded before Trish even asked.

"You really can read lips," Tori said with a smile.

"I saw a calendar hanging on the fridge," Braddock said to Paul. "Can you get it?"

Alisha asked Tori a question: *Was Nico a bad guy?*

Tori thought for a moment before replying. "He had bad friends. But he loved you and saved you."

Paul returned with the calendar. Braddock sat down next to Tori. He looked Alisha right in the eye. "Can you tell us *when* you were at that house?"

Alisha pointed to April 7th and 8th, which was last Thursday and then Friday, the day Nico was shot. She flipped the calendar back and pointed March 15th through the 23rd.

Braddock and Tori shared a quick look.

Alisha then pointed to the last week of February for the first time she was there.

"Alisha," he asked and then held up the picture of Marrone. "Do you know when you saw this man at the house?"

She looked to the calendar and pointed to the 22nd of March, a Tuesday.

"You're sure?" Braddock asked. "You're absolutely sure?"

Alisha signed back and forth with Trish.

"What is she saying?"

"The twenty-second was the night... she was told by Nico later that she had to... leave," Tori said. "And that... everyone was shouting and yelling that night."

"Shouting and yelling?" Braddock asked. "Really. What did they say?"

Alisha shook her head and signed and pointed at Marrone's picture.

"What?" Braddock said.

"She said she saw the shouting and pointing but then Marrone turned around and saw her," Tori said while Trish nodded. "When Marrone saw her, Nico put her into the bedroom down in the basement and told her to stay put." Tori spread out the pictures on the table. "Who else was there *that* night?"

Alisha pointed to Gill, Waltripp and Marrone.

"How about him?" Tori asked, pointing to Gresh's picture.

No.

"But there was the other man you described, right?" Tori asked. "The block head with the big belly?"

Yes.

"Anyone else?"

No.

Tori smiled and signed: *Good job!*

Alisha smiled and then took Tori by the hand back to the family room and sat down at the coffee table and pointed to Connect 4. She wanted to play a game.

"You're on."

* * *

"Where are you going?" Rob asked. She was dressed in black skinny jeans, turtleneck, and zip-up top. It was a stealthy look.

"I just realized I need a couple of things for this week," she said with self-annoyance. "Some supplies for the salon."

"How long will you be?"

"You know me, I get shopping and—"

"You lose track of time," he said, a basketball game playing on the big screen. "Do be careful. I mean, you're in all black, somebody might not see you."

"Good point. I'll grab my white ballcap by the back door. I don't expect to be super long," she said as she leaned down to the recliner and kissed him. "Is there anything you need, or I can get you while I'm out?"

"Coffee creamer. We're out."

"I'll see what I can do."

Her first stop was the storage unit.

The Acadia was still parked inside. For tonight she didn't think she needed it.

From the gun safe she retrieved two more Berettas, and extra magazines and stuffed them in her large black backpack. She had one more tracker that she quickly tested. It still worked. She grabbed the small single eye range scope and a set of miniature binoculars.

* * *

After two Connect 4 games and several hugs, Tori and Braddock took their leave and made their way up to Cullen Crossing.

"She's a little cutie that one," Tori said.

"Careful. You're getting attached."

She smiled. "A little but not like you think. Now Paul and Trish. They might be getting... attached." Changing subjects, she noted, "Alisha says there was shouting and anger the night of the twenty-second at the house."

"That suggests to me that those were the people involved in the shooting. I doubt Rudick was in Holmstrand for it, but the others at his house probably were. I could see Marrone being very angry about what they did or more likely—"

"How they did it," Tori finished. "For two men who have operated quietly for twelve years that was too much exposure."

"Is Marrone there?" Braddock asked, holding the walkie-talkie, two miles out of Cullen Crossing.

"Yes," Reese answered. "Or at least I think so. Eggs, you haven't seen him leave, have you?"

"No. Nobody has come out the back."

"Who would have the best chance of seeing him? You or Eggleston?"

"Probably me," Reese replied. "Marrone's Escalade is parked in front."

"We'll be behind Eunice's place here shortly."

* * *

Her hat pulled down low and dark-rimmed glasses on, she drove by the front of the mall, peering to her right at the vehicles parked in front of the mall and she spotted a black Lincoln Navigator. At the far north end of the mall, she turned into the parking lot and made a loop along the front, slowing slightly as she approached the Navigator and checked the license plate. Illinois.

Kind of sloppy.

In all there were perhaps twenty to twenty-five vehicles in the parking lot, congregated on the end where the bar and liquor store were located.

To park or not to park?

If Mileski and Marrone were the least bit careful, and with Smith and Company in town, they were being extra careful, they likely had some sort of surveillance system in place. She kept going.

Exiting the parking lot, she pulled across the county road into the small residential neighborhood. It was a short one block square loop with maybe twenty modest one and two-story houses on the inside and outside of the loop. She pulled to the curb in front of a darkened house and killed the engine. It was 8:40 p.m. Sitting low in her seat she peered to her right between two houses and across the county road to the mall and its front parking lot.

Bright light flashed in her rearview mirror, and she slid lower in her seat. An SUV pulled by on her left and then turned right into the driveway three houses ahead. A man and a woman got out.

"I'll be damned," Maggie muttered at the sight of Braddock and Hunter going in the front door of the house.

They were on this.

But what were they on? Mileski and Marrone? And for how long? And what exactly was it they were they looking for?

She looked up at the house they'd gone into, but it was mostly dark, just a light or two on for the first floor. The upstairs was dark. If they were watching, that would be the perch from which to do it.

Maggie, do you withdraw?

She debated whether to move.

Who knows how fast Hunter and Braddock would move or how far they were into their investigation? Vince was parked outside Cathy's house, which meant they were parked outside her own house.

No choice.

She reached behind her seat for her backpack and took out the small silver tracker disk and shoved it into the side pocket of her top and then grabbed her shoulder bag from the passenger seat. Taking one last look around for prying eyes, she slipped out and walked south to the outlet to the county road. As she edged past the last house, she stopped and looked to the house that Braddock and Hunter entered. The second story was all dark but there were two windows along the back with the curtains just slightly open.

With her right hand on her purse strap, she jog-walked across the road and into the parking lot and then walked down the row behind all the vehicles parked against the curb and the front walkway for the mall. The Navigator was fifty feet ahead on her right. She stopped and leaned down to re-tie her shoe. Shifting her gaze left, she scanned the windows of the house but couldn't see anyone. If they were watching, they were being careful.

Not sloppy.

She stood up and walked slowly and then stepped to her right between two parked vehicles and to the walkway and reached inside the side pocket for the tracker when the front door of the bar opened. Marrone and another man stepped outside, each holding cigars.

Not good. She didn't want to walk past them. The liquor store. She quickly stepped inside.

"Hiya, hun," the cashier, a blue-haired lady, greeted. A man was in the back of the store stocking the shelves. "Everything okay?"

"Uh, yeah, fine, just fine, just glad you're still open."

"Anything in particular you're looking for?"

Maggie smiled. "I'm going to peruse the wine aisle. I was driving by and suddenly had the thirst for something."

"Sure thing. Just so you know, we close it up at nine."

* * *

"That's Marrone," Reese said, peering through his camera resting on a tripod. A video camera sat underneath it, also on a tripod, recording. "The guy with no neck, he's been around much of the day. The other guy I've seen a couple of times as well. Interestingly, he arrived in a Lincoln Navigator, Illinois plates last night."

"Hmm," Tori murmured. "He's a big guy, shaved head. In the context of Marrone and the driver, the third guy screams muscle."

Braddock had binoculars on the men. "The guy with no neck matches Alisha's description, don't you think?"

"Yes," Tori replied. "We need a few pictures of him, but I don't think we'll get them tonight. Too dark and they're all standing under the canopy smoking cigars."

"What have you seen these guys do?" Braddock asked.

"The shaved head guy arrived a few hours ago in the Navigator. He's been inside. As for the guy with no neck, like I said, he's been around, in and out."

Eggleston piped in. "The first time I saw no neck today, he arrived in a black panel van and parked behind the mall at the liquor store back door. He delivered some boxes inside and then he left. He came back a few hours later in an Escalade, so there was that."

"Anything else?" Braddock said.

"Other than their sojourn to Crosslake for lunch," Reese said, "the two of them haven't left. Is that normal? Don't know. It's our first day. We'll need a few to get the rhythm of things."

* * *

The CC Liquors wine selection was far from robust, but she made a point of taking bottles off the shelf, reading the labels while at the same time glancing left to see the two men standing on the sidewalk, smoking their cigars.

"We're closing in five minutes, hun."

"Okay."

Marrone and the other man were still out front. She could hear them talking and laughing, the cigar smoke billowing. They weren't standing directly in front of the Navigator but to the driver's side. She looked down to the wine bottle in her hand and then to the gap between the Navigator and pickup truck parked next to it on the passenger side.

That could work.

She set the bottle on the shelf and leaned to grab two cheaper ones off the bottom before heading to the counter.

The cashier rang it up. "Thirty-two dollars and sixty-four cents."

Payment? Don't use a credit card and leave a record, dummy.

She quick checked her cash pouch and pulled out her small wad and was relieved to see she had three twenties. These days she used cash so little she didn't always know what she had.

"You want a bag?"

"No, that's okay. I have my shoulder bag." She stuffed the wine bottles inside along with the receipt. After she put the bottles inside the bag, she quickly checked her pocket for the tracker.

"Good night now."

"Night," Maggie said as she stepped out the door and then quickly between the Navigator and pickup truck, took two quick steps and then pulled the tracker out of her right pocket.

She intentionally stubbed her toe. "Oh!" She fell face first to the ground, the wine bottles and other items from her shoulder bag spilling out onto the pavement. "Ow!" she exclaimed in real pain as she quickly stuck the tracker under the back bumper. She pushed herself up to limp after a wine bottle. "What a klutz!"

"I'll get it, I'll get it," the man with no neck said as he scampered after one of the bottles as it rolled across the pavement. She picked up the other and while down on one knee made a show of checking for a crack, her hat pulled low.

"Are you okay, ma'am?" the man asked pleasantly. "That was quite a spill."

"Yeah," Maggie replied sheepishly. "I'm so embarrassed," she added as she scooped up the contents of her shoulder bag quick and stuffed one wine bottle in her bag.

"No need to be," the man said as he handed her the wine bottle.

"Thanks so much."

"You be careful now, ma'am."

"I'll try," she replied and walked across the parking lot and county road into the neighborhood. In her RAV4 she quickly reached into the backpack and checked the iPad. The tracker was working.

* * *

"That's a good photo of him," Reese said as he showed Tori and Braddock the photo. "Right when he was under the light. Full face and everything."

Tori gave the photo a look. "We could show it to Alisha."

"Yes, but tomorrow," Braddock said.

* * *

"You had the day," Mileski said. "What do you think?"

"You took out these two kids because they could hurt you," Vince answered. "I question the how, but not the why."

"Is there anyone else out there that can hurt us?"

"First, if it is Marta out there stirring up this trouble, she can hurt us."

"On that," Mileski replied and gestured to a stack of documents, "our friends in Chicago sent along all this on the families of Horn, Jensen and Randall."

"And?"

"The three families don't have any ties to Chicago or our girl."

"At least familial," Vince replied, taking a drink of his whiskey. "But that isn't the only problem. We have another perhaps more immediate one. Carlo has been observing it tonight."

"And what do you propose to do?"

"What do you think?"

Mileski grimaced, knowing what that meant. "Do you really think it's necessary? That could bring a lot more heat."

"It's what Bobby ordered me up here to do."

"This isn't Chicago."

"It doesn't matter. Look, Jimmy. You can either take on risk or eliminate it. You want to play insurance company on this?"

Jimmy sighed and shook his head. "When?"

"Tomorrow night."

TWENTY-TWO

"WHAT'S WITH ALL THE CLOAK-AND-DAGGER?"

"As we thought, 9mm parabellums," Boe said, handing over the ballistics report from the shooting at Rudick's house.

"That fits our killer," Tori said, gazing over Braddock's shoulder. "And likely from a Beretta. That matches up too."

"It's her," Braddock said. "Too many things matching up."

"How are you going to find her?"

"We start by digging through all this," Tori said, holding up a brown expandable file.

"Which is what?"

"The Bureau's file on her. Plus, we have another photo or two to show Alisha. She's already tied Rudick, Gill, Gresh and Waltripp to Marrone and on the night of the shooting in Holmstrand. Tying them to Marrone, ties them to Mileski. And she saw our woman killer."

"That's good, I guess."

"Now, why is this killer doing what she's doing? All we know is she started getting involved after Holmstrand. Perhaps digging through the FBI file will shed some light on that."

"That's our plan, unless you have a better one. I'm all ears," Braddock said.

Boe sighed and shook her head. "No, I don't. I do wonder about you two sitting in a house watching a strip mall and whether that's the best use of your time. Can't Nolan do that?"

"She'll take her turn. For now, she's working the paper trail on Mileski and Marrone and digging on the Jensens, Randalls and Horns to see if there are any Chicago connections. She's my best on that so we let her work it for a few days and see what comes. And besides, Sheriff, that's not all that's going on."

"Anything you care to share?"

"Not yet. Just know that I've got more than one iron in the fire. I'm throwing everything we have at it."

They made a quick stop at Paul and Trish's house to show Alisha photos of the man with the squared head they saw last night.

Is it him? Tori asked.

Yes.

"Now we need a name."

"We'll get it," Braddock said. He and Tori made their way twenty-minutes north to Cullen Crossing, relieving Eggleston at Harold's house. Braddock set up a chair, adjusted the video camera for the back window and made himself comfortable. Tori dug the brown expandable file out of her backpack. She laid the binder clipped stacks of documents on the bed, organizing them and then opened her laptop.

She spent the better part of the next four hours reading through the paper files as well as reviewing the photos on her computer. Braddock kept an eye on the mall although to keep from getting bored, he found himself scanning some of the file as well.

At 12:30 while he was eating a sandwich, he murmured, "There's our guy." He picked up the camera, focused and snapped photos of him. He checked the small display screen on the back of the camera. "Eh." He maneuvered his chair and waited for a few minutes. "There he is again."

Click, click, click, click, click.

Tori dropped her file to move to look over Braddock's shoulder at the man Alisha identified. "He's a thick dude."

"He arrived in the black van. He's running stuff inside the hardware store."

"Huh," Tori said. "Didn't Eggleston say yesterday that he delivered to the liquor store?"

Braddock nodded. "I guess if you're working for Mileski, you have all kinds of tasks. That or because of recent events, they're down people."

"And only using people they really trust."

"Closing ranks."

"Exactly. Have you seen either Mileski or Marrone?"

"Once. The two of them came out the back of the hardware store to stand outside and drink a cup of coffee. Marrone smoked a cigar. It seems like it's routine."

"These guys just basically hang around here all day?" Tori said. "Morning, noon, and night?"

"Appears so," Braddock answered. "Although interestingly, they did leave to go home last night but Frewer, who was at Eunice's in the morning, nor Steak, who was at Harold's, saw either of them arrive yesterday."

"Do they sleep here?"

"Or it's a fortress. They're not leaving themselves exposed."

She went back to the binder clipped documents. "She's like a ghost."

"That's the idea, isn't it," Braddock said. "Although if she was a hitter for the Chicago Outfit, *someone* knew her."

"As Bahn said, that someone was probably Angelo DeEsposito," Tori said, holding up a picture of an older DeEsposito with thick gray hair, bushy eyebrows, a wide nose and a jowled appearance. "It's interesting," Tori observed, having now consumed the files. "The time window on her being active is only six years although she was quite prolific in that short period of time. It ended with her killing Lamberto and Johnny Marrone in the steam room at his club, along with two of his bodyguards."

"When did she start?"

"She first appeared when two Chicago Mob guys are murdered late at night in an alley behind a bar. One of the guys is Ed Kranz. He was Lamberto's predecessor apparently. In any event, she got them near their car, each of them three times in the chest and then finished both off with one to the head from close range execution style."

"How do they know it's her, though?"

"It's late and a worker at the bar is dumping garbage out back and he notices these two guys exit the bar and walk down the alley. He doesn't pay much attention to them. They left out the back all the time. He pulls down the dumpster lid and sees the two of them reach their car at the other end of the alley. But now he sees what looks to be a tall woman, long coat, legs, and hair, very sleek looking, approaching them. Both men stop and then just like that, quick as can be, she pulled a gun and shot both men multiple times and then stood over each of them and finished each of them with a headshot. The witness claimed the gun looked long, and the shots were somewhat muffled."

"Suppressor."

"Right. The witness said she turned around and walked briskly away and was around the corner seconds later."

"The witness didn't see her face?"

"No. It was dark. She had long hair. He was too far away. He saw the outline or silhouette of her, backlit by a streetlight. Then, six months later it's late at night and two guys with KC Mob are meeting in the back of a barbeque restaurant south of downtown Kansas City. She gets the bodyguard in the hallway and the two guys never even get out of their chairs. All are shot three times in the chest, boom, boom, boom. Two other body-guards were in the front of the restaurant, they come running in the back and think they see a woman dressed in all black, this time with a mask on, flee out the back door. They chase after her but all they hear is a vehicle driving away around a corner and by the time they get around that corner, the car is two blocks away. All they see are tail lights."

"So, they saw a woman in black and that ties it all together?"

"That plus a similar shot pattern to the two guys in Chicago. Similar ammunition, 9mm parabellums, as we've found here. Beretta, Beretta, Beretta, etc. Method is alike as well, late night attack at a common hangout. These guys are always there so she could scout for some time and then hit them when most vulnerable. In fact, you look at a lot of her kills, she kills where these guys are most comfortable, where their guard is down and they feel safe. Plus, she's a woman and I'd guess an attractive enough one. Men let her get close, they want a look-sie. They don't sense the danger until it's too late. She got nineteen of them over six years."

"Her victims?"

"All organized crime or men affiliated with organized crime. The only exception was Special Agent Como in Cleveland." She flipped a page. "Huh."

"Huh what?"

"The thing about the Cleveland hit is it was literally at the same time that Angelo DeEsposito was killed."

"When you say same time, was it the same night, same time at night or—"

"Same night and nearly time," Tori murmured and flipped between binder clipped stacks. "Angelo was killed just after midnight central time. The hit in Cleveland was around one a.m. eastern time so literally at the same time."

"She took out the guys in Cleveland and someone got DeEsposito. What does the file say about the DeEsposito murder?"

"Classic Mob hit. Got Angelo and his men coming out the back of a place called Dudek's."

"Lamberto's guys?"

"It's apparent she thought so, although DeEsposito's shooters were never identified by CPD. It's two weeks later when she does her revenge killings: Lamberto, Johnny Marrone, two of his men and severely wounding another, some guy named Vince Smith."

"And then she disappeared," Braddock said. "Or so it seems." He reached inside the cooler they brought and took out a bottle of water and took a long drink. "The timing is interesting of Cleveland and the DeEsposito hit. Whoever took out Angelo, they knew who she was."

Tori saw where he was going. "She does Cleveland, because they want her to, but then they lie in wait for her in ambush somewhere, maybe in Cleveland or Chicago, but she sees it coming. Maybe she got warned or in learning that DeEsposito was killed, figures her cover is blown." Tori smiled. "I have to respect her."

"How so?"

"I think your insight is right, they knew who she was. Or maybe they identified her at the Cleveland hit. They were watching. Whatever it was, she knew her cover was blown. But they missed her. And because they missed, Lamberto, Marrone's brother, all these guys are holed up in this club in Chicago because they know she's coming."

"That's what I'm thinking."

"Yet despite the fact they know she's coming for them, she still slips into that club, gets Lamberto and Marrone and a couple of others and gets out unscathed. That's about more than luck. But after that, she's done. She walks away from the contract killer gig, disappears, establishes a new identity, and moves up here and lives quietly as your average citizen."

"Until now." Braddock's phone beeped, a text, from Steak which read: *Eff'n Jones. One hour. Pick me up.*

He showed Tori the text. "You have the con, Number One."

* * *

"What's your approach?" Vince asked, eyeing the house through binoculars, a quarter mile to the south.

"From here or along the shoreline," Carlo said. "Max and I were here last night and again today. Most of these places between here and there aren't occupied right now. Past the house, several others are not opened either. It's still early April and it's a Monday. It'll be quiet."

"And darkness hits when?"

"It'll be fully dark by seven fifteen, seven thirty at the absolute latest."

"You go tonight?"

"I think we have to."

* * *

"This is out of the way," Braddock observed as they approached Harding from the west.

"Jones's call. He's a careful little shit," Steak replied.

The miniscule town of Harding, population 156, sat at a crossroads in the vast desolate farmlands of northeastern Morrison County well to the southeast of Manchester Bay. The town, such as it was, consisted of thirteen houses, a Catholic church, ten large trees, yet two bars, one of which was the Harding Saloon. There were three vehicles parked in the rough gravel parking lot when Braddock pulled in with Steak.

Inside Steak made eye contact with the bartender who nodded for them to meet him at the far end of the bar. "He's in the basement. Go through the swinging door and turn right. Can I get you guys anything before you go?"

"Captain Morgan Diets in a tall glass," Braddock said as he set a twenty down, and then murmured, "But hold the spiced rum."

The bartender offered a toothless grin, kept the drink glasses down below the level of the bar top but made a show of looking to pour the spiced rum into the Diet Coke, his thumb expertly placed over the nozzle. Drinks in hand, the two of them made their way to the basement and found Jones sitting at a small table, talking on the phone, jotting notes into his little black book. He hung up and laughed. "NBA playoffs are starting soon, lots of action today. You were a hoops player, Braddock, you want in?"

"I'll pass."

"Just thought I'd be polite and offer," Jones said as he stood up and walked over to close the door. "Thanks for meeting down here."

"I've never been to Harding," Braddock quipped lightly. "I didn't even know it existed."

"Nobody fucking does, which is why we're here," Jones said, before taking a drink of his coffee. Steak and Braddock shared a quick look. Jones, for all his normal bravado, was nervous.

"What's with all the cloak-and-dagger?" Steak asked.

"You guys are asking about fucking Mileski and Marrone."

"And that means you have to be *this* careful?"

"There are a few people who know I'm friendly with you guys," Jones said to Steak. "And they assume I might provide a little info about things I hear from time to time."

"Sure."

"And they're fucking cool with it because they know it's never about them and that you guys look the other way when I take the occasional wager," Jones said as he tapped his black book.

"I got bigger fish to fry," Braddock said. "As long as nobody is getting hurt. But right now, people *are* getting hurt."

"That's fucking right," Jones said pointedly. "And Steak here is asking me about Mileski and Marrone. Talking about them could get a fucking guy hurt."

"Why is it that we've never heard of these guys before?" Braddock asked. "Why is it you haven't told us about them?"

"Because until recently, they've been very careful and never gave me a reason to share anything with you. It seems now, they might have fucked up."

"You know them?"

"Know? No."

"But you've dealt with them?" Steak asked.

"A few times, yeah. Wasn't a real pleasant experience."

"Enlighten us."

"The first time was a little over four years ago, during football season." Jones tapped his black book. "I only deal with people on referral."

"Someone has to vouch," Braddock said, nodding.

"Right. A guy named Gary was referred to me and I took a few decently sized bets from him, a little larger than normal shall we say. He gave off the vibe that he had some money to play with. His bets were odd, though. So odd that I wondered if he had some sort of inside information. I questioned whether to take the wagers, although I ultimately did. I liked my odds. I was right."

"Good for you then."

"It was, until Marrone and a big guy show up at my joint late one night a week later and stay past closing to have a chat."

"About Gary."

"And apparently a few others I'd taken bets from."

"You were competition?"

"Yeah," Jones said. "Look, I'm just this little five-foot-four motormouth, and the goon was six feet tall, built like a brick shithouse with no neck and the bulge inside his coat said he was carrying. I wasn't afraid per se, but I sure took notice of the nature of the guy."

Braddock pulled out a photo. "This guy?"

Jones slipped his reading glasses on. "Yeah, that guy. Stevie Bianchi. When these two showed up, it was, at a minimum, to send a message."

"Which was?"

"That I should just get out of the wagering business altogether," Jones said.

"To which you said what?" Steak replied, anticipating the answer.

"Fuck off," Jones replied with a wry smile. "And then my bartender set his old 44 Magnum on the bar top."

Braddock smiled at Steak. Jones had balls. "You had a standoff."

"I'd heard through a few of my regulars that there were these guys up in Cullen Crossing at the strip mall taking bets like me. And I'd heard there was some muscle behind it. Another guy got a whiff of Mob off them and maybe that's true. They're from Chicago, I think, so I wouldn't be surprised. However, until Marrone showed that night, I didn't know who they were. Clearly, they didn't like me moving in on their competition."

"But I know you're still doing it, so?" Steak said.

"I told them I didn't know they even existed, which was a bit of a fib, but I didn't know *them*. It's a free country, but I wasn't looking to move in on their business. I preferred to keep my clientele small. It's nothing more than a side hustle. My financial future was the bar."

"Side hustle. Good one," Steak muttered.

"You don't have to con us. Remember, I don't care," Braddock said. "Okay, so what was the outcome of this standoff?"

"I think they came down to take the measure of me and what I was about."

"Have they been back?"

"Bianchi a few times to suggest I should steer clear of certain people. That, quote 'he belonged to the guys up north,' and if I didn't want issues..."

"Don't take bets from them."

"Yeah. I learned later that the reason some of their guys found their way to me is the interest, the vig, these guys were charging, but whatever. I liked the money, but it wasn't worth the risk, you know. There's enough risk in taking bets to begin with. Why compound it."

"And Bianchi was the one that would come down and deliver the message?"

"Yeah," Jones said. "But get this, he places bets with me."

"After all that—"

"Yeah, I know," Jones replied, shaking his head. "Maybe not my brightest move but the guy wanted the action and he's not laying wagers with his boss. I see him every so often. He and his brother."

"Brother?"

"Joe Bianchi. He runs a warehouse out east of town here."

"And what happens at the warehouse?"

"No idea, but look, there's something else. The real reason I asked to meet down here is last time you guys asked me about drugs."

Braddock had been letting Steak take the lead and mostly observing. With Jones you usually had to really pull things out of him but today, he was just going, talking, stream of consciousness like. Braddock was seeing two things as a result. Jones was defiant, fronting fearlessness. Yet he was also a bit uncertain, as if he knew he was wading into more dangerous territory if he kept talking, especially about drugs. Steak had shifted his eyes over to Braddock a couple of times. He was seeing it too. In a case like this, let him keep talking.

"Jonesy, you said you didn't know much about that," Steak said.

"Yeah, *well*," Jones shrugged. "I know a guy who knows a guy. Last time we talked, you both mentioned missing drug dealers."

"That's right," Braddock said.

"We think there's another one now," Steak said. "Guy named Reardon Banz."

"Ahh fuck, I knew Banz," Jones said, shaking his head, angry. "You know, he was an okay guy."

"For a drug dealer?"

"Shocking, someone comes into my bar and they aren't the world's most upstanding citizen. The reprobates have to go somewhere."

"When I called you the other day, I asked what you knew about the drug trade around here. You said not much."

"Maybe I'm getting informed. I asked a couple of guys in that world about what they're hearing."

"And?"

"They say my guy Stevie is working for some guys moving in on the drug trade in these parts. They're offering a deal you literally can't refuse."

Steak nodded. "You either sign on with them or—"

"You end up dead?" Braddock said.

"That's the inference. And like how they make book, the cut they take is *substantial*," Jones said. "All these guys are skittish. They have no protection. I mean it's not like they can come to you with their problems."

"I see the point," Steak replied and then looked to Braddock. "You know, boss, it all fits."

"Yeah, it might," Braddock agreed.

"We have to deal."

"Jonesy, do you know anyone who has dealt with Mileski and Marrone who will talk with us, without us... having to force them to?" Braddock said.

Jones shook his head. "Boy, I don't know."

"I have a sweetener."

"A get out of jail free card if you will," Steak added.

"Immunity or some shit like that?"

"Yes."

"You got that kind of juice, Steak?"

"Braddock does."

"I can hook it up with the county attorney if the information pans out. If you had someone like that we could talk to, off the record, no strings attached, and test the information."

"You have to be discreet, Jonesy," Steak cautioned.

"No shit, Sherlock."

"Jonesy. This is serious shit, man. For us, and you, too."

"Yeah, I feed you info, you don't want to lose your source."

"Come on, pal, it ain't just that," Steak said seriously. "We both kind of like you."

Jones nodded. "I hear you, man."

"Be careful with this," Braddock counseled. "We have enough dead bodies around here. Don't add yourself to the count."

"And you stay in touch with me, daily," Steak ordered, looking Jones right in the eye. "I mean it. Every damn day. Just check in with me whether you know anything new or not. Call it proof of life."

"Will do."

Braddock and Steak left the bar and began driving back to Manchester Bay.

"Inch High Private Eye in there is ballsy," Steak said. "I'll give him that."

* * *

Maggie took a drink of her tea while she checked the iPad and the location of the tracker. *You're back there again? Why?*

Knock! Knock!

She looked up and her 1 o'clock was a few minutes early. She placed the iPad into her desk drawer and went to the salon door. "Hi. You must be Colleen."

"And you must be Maggie."

"The one and only."

After Colleen got a cut and color, along came her friend Lisa with her boys Jared and Jacob, hockey players, who needed quick trims of their lengthy hair. "It's all about the flow you know," Maggie said to Jared as she trimmed his hair, his brother watching intently.

"I'm pretty much done with the flow," Lisa said, rolling her eyes. "They both look so mangy but it's one on three in our house."

"One on three?" Maggie said.

"Their dad thinks it's cool. I'm out voted."

"Ah," Maggie replied as she kept trimming around the hair at Jared's shoulder. "You just need to fight fire with fire, Lis."

"With what?"

"Food. Cooking strike unless I take the boys' hair a little shorter."

"Ah come on, Maggie," Jared complained.

"This is an idea with some merit," Lisa said with a smile.

Maggie stood in front of Jared. "Well?"

"You're killing me here."

"You heard her. She's going on strike." She held up the scissors and comb. "I can prevent that. I'm your best friend right now."

"Okay, okay, take a little more off."

She looked to Jacob. "You too when it's your turn?"

"Fine."

It was just after 5:00 p.m. when she let a happy Lisa and her slightly less happy sons out the door and she heard a ruckus in the kitchen. Brian was digging in the refrigerator, Ellen behind him and Rob standing nearby.

"Hold it! Before you take anything out, I've got extra-large take and bake pizzas in the garage refrigerator from Reynold's," she said as she set the oven temp. "It's clear you're all hungry. Half-hour on the pizzas."

Brian and Ellen evacuated the kitchen. Rob sat down at the table, and they talked for a bit until he decided to go change his clothes. With the pizza having twenty minutes left to cook, she snuck back into the salon and retrieved the iPad. The tracker was still in the same vicinity as before.

They're watching something or someone. Who?

TWENTY-THREE

"WE'RE NOT ALONE OUT HERE."

With dinner finished, Maggie bagged up the four extra pieces of deep-dish pizza for later. Rob was sitting at the kitchen checking his phone, scrolling through texts, antsy.

"Are the Timberwolves on again tonight?" They were having a great season and were a must watch for an NBA junkie like Rob.

"Yes. It's a late game, nine o'clock against the Lakers out in LA. A couple of the coaches and other teachers are going to the sports bar to watch. Would you mind if I joined?"

"Of course not. Besides, I need to run a couple of errands myself."

"Well, I'll get going then."

"Already?"

"It's almost seven. There are other games on tonight and the boys are already heading up there, so..."

"Go." Maggie waved playfully. "Go."

He kissed her on the cheek and rushed out of the kitchen. A minute later he was out the door.

She ran upstairs, quickly changed into dark clothes and told Ellen she was going out to run a few errands. From her hidden cabinet in the salon, she pulled out the backpack she retrieved last night. Taking one last look at the iPad and the location of the tracker she drove south out of Holmstrand and then around the north end of Northern Pine Lake over to the west side.

Glancing right at the monitor, she saw the tracker location still stationary halfway down the west side of the lake, just south of a point angling out into the water. She turned left and weaved her way south southeast out to the end of the point where the road then swung back southwest. Driving slowly, she was nearly on top of the tracker when she caught a glimpse of the Lincoln Navigator to her left, parked by a garage on a cement slab. It was running. She pulled by and drove a quarter mile down the road and then made a wide loop back around to the north side of the point. She pulled on her black mask, but left it on top of her head, and tight black leather gloves, checked her gun and slipped out of her SUV.

She made her way to the large house set out on the point. The house was dark with no signs of life, and she suspected that despite its massive size, it was a summer place only.

Crossing across the front yard of the house she made her way to the back of the next house, which was also dark. In fact, most of the houses and cabins along this stretch were dark, except for two. She made her way to the first one that was alight and from the cover of the garage, saw in a side window through the kitchen into the family room. It was a couple that looked to be in their seventies sitting in a recliner and on the couch, watching television. Two houses down the lights were on. She crept along the side of the house again and managed to peer into the bottom of a window to see a woman sitting on a couch wrapped in a blanket, the television on, the gas fireplace aflame, and she was reading a book. Close to the front of the house, she made her way to the corner and peered around the edge.

The one question foremost in her mind was: *What were these guys after?*

* * *

"They're on their way back," Vince reported. "I'd say ten minutes to your position."

Max turned to Carlo. "You better go."

Carlo nodded, pulled his gun, chambered a round and slipped out of the Navigator. He slithered north, hewing close to next three houses. Past the third house he turned to his left and ran to the side of the next house and then inched his way to the back of the house and then across a small gap in the yard to the side of the detached garage.

He stood with his back against the side of the garage and pulled down his mask. A minute later, to his right and behind him he saw the glow of headlights approaching.

"Carlo is in position," Max reported to Vince.

"I'm a half-mile south of you on forty-four. I have a view in either direction for a good mile."

* * *

Her eyes had adjusted to the light now, the half-moon providing illumination, a thin white stripe of reflection rippling in the wavy water. She gazed ahead, her northeast approach along the shoreline allowed her a good angle to see the remaining seven houses between her and the Navigator.

There.

A flash of movement. If you were looking for it, you could see it. A man walking tight to the houses.

She held her position, observing him come along the lake-side of the houses until he darted and disappeared to the right. She scurried to the back of the house she was at. She saw his silhouette in the backyard of the house two doors down.

What was so important about that location?

* * *

"Hi, Mary," Tori greeted as she and Braddock stepped into Roger and Mary Hayes's house. Quinn was sitting at the dining room table at his laptop computer and a textbook open.

"What's he working on?" Braddock asked.

"Math," Mary said.

"Come on in, you two," Roger greeted. "You look hungry. We have chicken left over from dinner."

"Perfect," Braddock said. "We're starving."

"Tori?" Mary asked, holding up a wine glass.

"Please," she replied and reached in her back pocket for her buzzing phone. It was a number she didn't recognize. However, it was a 312-area code. Chicago. "Hello?"

"Is this Tori Hunter?"

It was her.

"This is she," Tori replied and snapped her fingers, drawing Braddock's attention, waving him over. "Who is this?"

"I'm the one who called you about Ron Gresh out at that trailer. Tell me, do you know someone on the northwest side of Northern Pine Lake at 61533 Baycliffe Pass?"

* * *

Paul opened the back door to let Alisha down from his dual cab Chevy truck. Trish walked around the back and the three of them walked toward the house. At the door, Trish slid her key into the deadbolt.

Cliiiick

Paul and Trish spun around.

* * *

"We're coming! We're coming fast," Tori exclaimed.

"How far away?"

Braddock raced north on County 44, police lights flashing. "We're less than three miles."

"He has them at gunpoint. If he gets them inside the house, they're done," the woman said in a hoarse whisper. "I gotta go."

"Wait! Wait! Dammit!"

"Shit!" Braddock buried the accelerator and reached for his radio mic. "What's the call?"

"Homicide," Tori replied, pulling her gun, chambering a round.

"Dispatch. This is Braddock, send all units in the area to 61553 Baycliffe Pass. Possible 10-89 in progress."

* * *

Maggie pulled her gun and screwed on the suppressor. She pulled the mask down over her face and edged around the corner of the house. The terrain was relatively flat. There were two large trees between her and the next house. Keeping the first large tree in the line of sight between her and the man, she crept ahead.

* * *

"Not a word," a man in a black mask said, his finger to his mouth.

Alisha grabbed Paul's arm in fear, and he stepped in front of her and Trish. "We don't want any trouble," Paul said hoarsely. "Y-y-you can have my wallet. M-m-my keys. Take the truck. It's yours," Paul said, holding up his keys. "Just take it. Go."

* * *

"That's not why he's here!" Maggie called.

The man pivoted to her.

Bap! Bap! Bap!

Boom! Boom! Boom!

She ducked back behind the massive tree, shards of bark plinking. She'd clipped him.

* * *

Vince peered right and then left, County Road 44 was quiet. "Are they there?"

"Just pulled in," Max reported.

He peered to the north and then back to the south again. He saw flashing lights in the distance. He reached for his binoculars. The mix of red and blue flashing lights were from the... grill of a truck.

"I see them... Wait a... We're not alone out here," Max exclaimed. "We're not alone!"

"What?"

"Carlo is under fire. Shit!"

Vince looked to his right. The flashing lights were for a Tahoe that blew right by him.

"We're blown. Get out of there, Max! Get out of there! Police are coming!"

* * *

Peeking quick around the tree, she charged ahead to the next thick tree.

Boom! Boom!

She reached the tree. Sirens were faintly audible in the distance, but she knew coming fast. She switched the gun to her left hand and swung her arm around.

Bap! Bap!

"Get in the house!" She pulled back and switched hands

again. Looking around the right side, she rushed forward to the corner of the detached garage. The sound of sirens was getting closer. Stepping out she walked speedily, gun up, hunting, her view obscured by several thick trees. Shuffling right, she saw him running, angling to the right and the road.

Bap! Bap! Bap! Bap! Bap!

* * *

"Carlo, I'm coming to you," Max's voice exclaimed in his earbud.

Tree bark shards hit him in the face as he stumbled over a small hedge and then kept running. To the right, he saw the Navigator approaching. He veered to his right. The passenger door flew open as the SUV skidded to a stop.

"Come on! Come on!" Max yelled.

* * *

She moved ahead, veered right toward the road and saw the passenger door open for the Navigator closing in the distance.

He was at the truck reaching for the door.

She set her feet.

Bap! Bap!

He turned. *Boom! Boom!*

Bap! Bap! Bap!

She hit him again, this time in the chest, twice. He collapsed, his right arm sliding down the truck.

Crack!

She felt it slice the skin on her upper left shoulder as she slid left behind another tree.

Crack! Crack! Crack!

"Get in! Get in!" she heard the driver call.

She peeked around the right side of the tree. The runner

was down, not moving. She spun back left. She had three shots left. Sirens were closing. She quick peeked to her right. The driver ducked back into the cab.

Go! She bolted from the tree. Firing as the truck pulled away.

Bap! Bap! Bap!

The truck veered left, off the road and into the trees.

The sirens were close, really close now. The night sky filled with flashing red and blue police lights. She pivoted to the left and ran down between the houses and toward the lake.

I need to get out of sight. I need to get out of here.

* * *

"Come on! Come on!" he heard Max yell and then fire.

Crack! Crack! Crack!

"Get in! Get in!"

"Max! Max!" Vince called out.

Bap! Bap! Bap!

"Oof. Ahrg. Vin..."

He heard a crash and then the engine.

"Max!... Max!"

There was no response. He glanced to his right. More flashing lights were coming from the south.

"Max!"

* * *

"Hustle!"

"Almost there," Braddock said.

The police radio burped. "Be advised. Report of shots fired, Baycliffe Road."

"Careful," he warned. "We're not geared up."

Braddock braked hard and turned right and roared ahead,

took a quick right, re-accelerated down the road and then skidded to a stop at a forty-five-degree angle, blocking the driveway. Ahead at another house was a pickup truck, crashed into a tree, a body slumped over the steering wheel. Tori was out of the truck in a flash.

"The back door is open," Tori whispered and then called: "Trish! Paul!"

"In here!" Trish replied.

Tori and Braddock rushed into the house and found the three of them huddled in the living room that looked out to the lake.

"What happened?" Braddock asked. "We heard a report of shots fired."

"We got home from dinner," Paul said, breathing hard and holding Alisha. "We were walking to the house. A man stepped out from behind the garage. He had a gun and ordered us inside."

"And then there was this woman," Trish said. "She defended us."

"Where did she come from?" Tori asked.

"The north side," Paul said. "She called out from the Nielsen place next door. And then all heck broke loose, gunfire, it was nuts."

"She yelled for us to get inside," Trish noted.

"It all didn't end but a second or two ago. Did you see her?"

"No," Tori replied as she rushed to the front window. "Trish, you said she came from the north, right?"

"Yes." Tori looked out the front windows for the house, looking north. "There's someone out there still, I see them," she exclaimed, stepping to her left and opening the sliding glass door.

"Tori, no," Braddock warned.

"Come on."

More police were coming. Sirens approaching.

"Dammit, let's go!" Tori said. "It's her."

* * *

Maggie jogged ahead, feeling the sting in the skin and the wetness of blood in her left shoulder as she picked her way with some care, her head on a swivel, checking behind her, the sirens approaching. As she looked back, she saw the sliding glass door open to the deck and two people come rushing out. A tall man. A smaller woman. *I knew I was cutting it too close.*

Her jog turned into a sprint.

* * *

"There!" Tori gestured. "There, there, you see her."

"Yes," Braddock said. "She's no friend. She doesn't want to be caught."

* * *

Maggie sprinted ahead and needed to get out of sight. A cluster of bushes was coming up on the left. She reached in her back pocket and pulled out a new magazine and jammed it into the gun.

She glanced back and the two of them were coming. More would come soon. She spun around.

* * *

They saw her two houses ahead. The woman went up an incline. Then spun around.

"Get down!" Braddock exclaimed, shoving Tori to the right and then diving left behind a tree.

Bap! Bap! Bap! Bap!

He looked right to see Tori behind a small, landscaped rock wall. The shots sailed high over them. He looked over to her. "You hit?"

"No, You?"

"No."

Tori peered up over the rock wall. "Where now?"

"Not sure."

They moved forward cautiously, maintaining cover. She could be laying an ambush. They approached a cluster of bushes up on the left. Tori pulled up behind a tree and peered around the right side. Braddock skip-walked to his right to another tree to create an angle on the bushes.

He carefully inched out from the cover of the tree, his gun up to the area behind the bush cluster. But there was nobody. They were nearly all the way out to the point, several houses north of the Adams' house now.

"Go left," Braddock whispered. "Cut across the point but keep cover."

Tori took off, running from tree to tree along with Braddock, the two of them covering for one another.

* * *

The big house on the point was next and she ran through the front yard the same way she'd come. Her SUV was right ahead in the driveway for the next house, lights off but still running. More police and sheriff's units were flooding the area, lights beaming through the trees.

Maggie reached her RAV4 and quietly opened the door, quickly slid down inside, put it into gear and slowly rolled forward. Keeping her headlights off, she checked her rearview mirror.

* * *

Braddock crossed in front of the massive house out on the point, hurdling through the landscaping areas near the house, while Tori veered more left toward the street. What was that? She held up her hand and looked back to Braddock who had stopped.

What was that sound? She ran to the road and looked first to the north, but it was dark, then back toward the Adams' house and all the police lights and then again to the north and squinted.

"What do you see?" Braddock said.

"I don't see anything."

"She's gone."

TWENTY-FOUR

"I'M RELIEVED SHE'S GOING TO SEE TEN."

When they got back to Paul and Trish's house, Boe had arrived, as had Steak and Eggleston, along with a slew of deputies and two patrol units from Manchester Bay.

"Whoever she was," Steak said. "She got two hostiles."

"She's a hostile herself too," Braddock said. "She popped four off at us."

"And missed," Tori said and then added, "Wildly."

"You think she tried to miss us?"

Tori shrugged. "I think if she was truly trying to kill us, the misses would have been a helluva lot closer. She slowed us down, made us cautious. It gave her the room to slip away."

"Well, my friend," Steak mused. "She may have missed you two, but not these guys. She mowed them down."

One man lay face down in a yard near the road. He was hit twice in the chest as well as the upper left shoulder. The other was the driver of the pickup truck that had veered off the road and into a tree.

"I'd say our girl likes to shoot drivers and run them into trees," Steak said wryly. "The driver is Max Gryzlik. Chicago, Illinois. It's his Navigator. He has a Glock 19, fired it six times.

The corpse in the backyard over there is Carlo Gianni, Barrington, Illinois based on the license in his wallet. He had himself a Springfield XD, a common handgun. He fired it six times. It was a shooting gallery around here. Ejected shells everywhere."

Tori walked over to the Navigator. *How did these two end up here?* she wondered as she evaluated Gryzlik, the driver. He was hit in the upper right shoulder and then the fatal one was through the right side of his face, coming right through the windshield.

Looking back to the Adams' house, she could envision how it all played out. Gryzlik was waiting to the south and Gianni approached from there. The woman approached from the north and attacked when Gianni made his move. He retreated and she gave chase, gunning him down and then Gryzlik when he arrived in support.

How does she know they're here?

Tori walked around the truck and then looked underneath the rear bumper of the truck. "She's consistent and they don't learn."

Steak and Braddock came to the back. With her gloved hand, Tori reached underneath and pulled the silver disk from underneath the bumper. "She must have a lifetime supply. Same as the other tracker. This is five guys now. She's just mowing them down."

"Illinois plates, Illinois IDs. Addresses in Chicago and Barrington, which is a Chicago suburb," Steak noted.

"And they came after Alicia," Tori said through gritted teeth. "They were sent by Mileski and Marrone. She's a witness and a threat to them."

"We don't know that for sure," Steak cautioned.

"The fuck we don't!" Tori growled. "Those two are the only ones who would have a motive to do so."

"Comes down to what we can prove," Braddock murmured, angry.

"Then we better get some goddamned proof. A nine year old? I'm inclined to help our mystery girl just wipe them out."

Braddock nodded. "We're going to get them. If it's the last fucking thing I do, we're getting them. I don't care how long it takes." His phone buzzed. He looked at the display and showed it to Steak and Tori. It was Jones. Braddock answered. "We're kind of in the middle of a homicide here."

"Does it relate to what you've been talking to me about?"

Braddock sighed. "Yeah, I think it does."

"Then all the more reason for you to meet me right now."

"Give us a half-hour."

Tori's phone started buzzing. She looked at the display. "I think it's her."

* * *

Maggie checked the dashboard clock. It was 8:45 p.m. She pulled off the county road along a gravel one, parked up and reached for her left shoulder. The wound was superficial but still bled. From the backpack, she took out a T-shirt and ripped off a long strip of fabric and wrapped it tightly around the wound. Ideally, she'd be able to give it a stitch or two. Her face stung. She pulled down the shade and looked in the mirror. She had a laceration on her face, on her upper left cheek. Not deep but a definitely visible scratch, from a tree branch no doubt.

How will I explain it?

It was worth it. She saved the little girl. Or at least she hoped so. *But for how long?* She took the burner flip phone out of her pocket. From the backpack, she took out an old-school voice modulator and plugged it into the phone and recalled the last number.

"This is the third time you've called me? Don't you think we ought to know each other's names?"

"You know I'm not going to do that."

"Your voice is different. A little deeper."

"Just being careful. I'm sure you understand."

"No name. Okay, I'll just call you Angie. Or would prefer DeEsposito? You know what, we'll go with Angie. It's easier. Rolls off the tongue a little better."

"Doing your homework, I see. Then you'll know I wasn't trying to hit you out there."

"Could have fooled me."

"Come on, Tori. If I wanted to hit you, I would have. Not ten feet above your head."

"Thanks," Tori Hunter replied. "I guess."

"Are they all alright?" Maggie asked as she drove north on the H-4, keeping a keen eye on her rearview mirror and the tracker. "Is the little girl safe?"

"Uh... yeah, she is. They are," Hunter replied. "What are you, a guardian angel now?"

"They're after the girl."

"*They're* after? Who is this 'they're' you're talking about?"

Maggie smiled. "You know who."

"We do?"

"Don't play stupid, Tori. It doesn't suit you."

"Enlighten me."

"Cullen Crossing. The oddly located strip mall you're watching from the second floor of a house across the county road," Maggie said. "Stay on it. Your investigation, your instincts tell you it's dirty. Trust them. Mileski and Marrone are thugs. Nothing is out of bounds, including children now, which is a line even I didn't think they'd cross."

"With them, there is no line," Hunter said sharply.

"Then my work here is done. Good—"

"The girl's name is Alisha by the way," Hunter continued. "She's nine."

"I'm relieved she's going to see ten. That's all I have to—"

"Here's what I don't get. You killed her brother, but you let her live. You drove right by her that morning. She was sitting alone on that bench. She saw you."

"I have a line."

"I'm sensing that. Tell me, what were those kids in Holmstrand to you?"

"They were—" She caught herself. Careful. She's a cop, a good one. She should just hang up but couldn't, not like that. Some things needed to be said. "Those kids were murdered senselessly by men who think they can just kill people who get in the way. Something needed to be done."

"And you're going to kill them and keep killing them?"

"I'll do what I have to."

"Why escalate from just calling us about that trailer to all this?"

"You knew that was me?"

"I assumed it was. Why escalate?"

"I... don't work me, Tori."

"Why?"

"I'd much prefer you and Braddock catch them, and for them to go to prison, but you have evidence to collect, cases to build and rules to follow. That takes time I don't have."

"Meaning."

"You better hurry."

"Who are you protecting?"

"Just know I won't hesitate, Tori. I'll do what I have to do."

"You don't want to do that. It's not—"

"Focus, Tori. *Focus!* They're distracted, looking over their shoulder for me now. You and Braddock are on the right track but I'm telling you, make haste. These guys are dirty, and you know it. Prove it, but don't take two months to build the case. Move fast because they know only one way and that's to kill their threats. Alisha was a threat to them. Get her out of here."

"It's not just Mileski and Marrone though, is it?"

"No, Tori, it's not. You worry about them."

"And the others?"

"What did I say, Tori? Focus. Mileski and Marrone are the ones who give the orders. Them and people down in Chicago. Focus on them. Hunt them. Rapidly."

"You know, you talked about lines earlier. You said you have a line. What about Cleveland?" Hunter said. "You killed someone like me. Was that not crossing the line?"

She grimaced as she crooked her neck and squeezed the steering wheel, her muscles tightening. "That... was a mistake. A very, very, bad mistake."

She hung up, powered down her window and threw the phone out.

* * *

"If we'd have been setup on your phone, we could have traced her," Boe said. Braddock returned and re-listened to the call with Steak. After it finished, she looked to Braddock. "Do you buy what she said about us being on it?"

"Hell, yes. And she's telling us to get our asses in gear. To that, I may have another lead."

"What?"

"Steak and I need to go meet with someone. Now."

"Who?" Boe asked.

"A source. We have to go."

"Go," Boe said, and Braddock and Steak ran off, taking Steak's Tahoe.

"Thoughts?" Boe asked Tori.

"You listened to the call, how she talked, it makes me wonder if tonight isn't over just yet. Who is up in Cullen Crossing?"

"Reese and Frewer. They better be on alert."

"I'm going up there to have a look. She's right. These guys might be a bit anxious."

"Go," Boe said. "I got this."

* * *

Some mistakes you never stop paying for. There was a line she never intended to cross. Yet she did, once.

Cleveland.

She never would have taken the contract, nor would Angie, had they known of the FBI agent. There was a rule that was never to be violated, by either of them. She would never kill a citizen or law enforcement. If they were in the game, really in the game, then they were fair game. If the job was to take out some market owner because he wouldn't play ball, they could find someone else. In her mind, to do that would have made her one of them. To some that might have been a distinction without a difference, but to her, it was real, it mattered. The people she killed had accepted all the rewards, and all the risks of being in the trade, all of them, except one.

Even now, all these years later, with complete clarity, she could replay that night in her head. To her, Special Agent Como was John Sylvester, a Mob guy, just one of a group of three that the powers that be in the Cleveland family had determined had to go and they reached out to Angie to have it done. The money was wired. The job would be done.

She'd watched the three men for several days, as she always did when she hunted and never got a whiff, a sense, that Sylvester was anything other than another wise guy.

Her plan came together as envisioned. The three of them exited the rear of the bar, maybe not drunk, but certainly feeling no pain. She pushed out of the doorway and walked ahead of them in the alley, hearing the catcalls, her skintight leather having its usual desired effect, drawing their attention, lowering their defenses.

When she turned left around the corner, she turned her

head just slightly to get a last view of the three of them, walking close together, laughing, one man had his arm around the other's shoulder. After the turn, she pulled her gun from inside her thick leather jacket and stuffed it in the waistband of her pants, the small suppressor already attached and slowed the cadence of her walk, allowing them to slowly, almost imperceptibly, close on her as she approached their parked car on the right. When she was even with their car, one of them called out to her, "Hey, honey, that's my car. Want a ride?"

They were twenty feet behind her and based on the laughter, they were close together. "I'll take you anywhere you want to go."

She pulled the gun and spun around. "I don't think so."

The three of them were one huddled mass. She fired right to left, the three of them collapsing in rapid succession. Moving in, she finished the three of them off, with Sylvester being the last. Gasping, he pleaded with her, "Please, no. I—"

He never finished. She whipped around and ran out of the alley, around the corner to the right and to the small stolen car she had waiting and sped away, driving ten minutes to her hotel. While on the way, she called Angie as was their standard practice to let him know it was done. He didn't pick up. That was odd.

At the hotel, she went up to her room, quickly changed her clothes, put her hair into a ponytail and put on a White Sox ballcap. Normally, she would have already ditched her gun, but there wasn't a good place to do so on the way to the hotel. She decided she would do so once she was clear of the city. She stuffed the gun and a spare magazine into her small black shoulder duffel bag and hustled her way out of the hotel. As she walked to the front door, the man at the check-in desk called to her. "Do you need a cab, ma'am?"

She halted. "I do in fact."

"One just pulled up and is waiting."

When she stepped outside, she looked to her left and the cab, parked out along the street, saw her and quickly pulled up. "Where to?"

"Cuyahoga Tap. You know where it is?"

"Uh... yeah. I do."

The drive would take ten minutes from her hotel to her Jeep Cherokee she had parked a block from the bar.

As she rode in the backseat, she noticed how the cab driver kept checking her in the rearview mirror. That in and of itself wasn't that unusual. A leering look from a man wasn't all that uncommon. However, in this case, the man was... nervy. The first time she noticed it she thought it was late at night and a cab driver always had to be on watch, but his nervousness did not abate, which was odd. She was a woman. In her experience, cab drivers relaxed when she got into the car. She wasn't perceived as any sort of a threat. Instead, she often found the cabbies would make light conversation, if not talk her ear off, even if she wasn't in a bantering mood. Not this guy. Not even a warning about being a woman going out to a bar on her own so late at night, a warning she had received many times over the year. Rather, he asked her twice, "The Cuyahoga Tap. I just want to be sure."

He was twitchy, nervous and kept checking her in the rearview mirror. Careful in her own right, she peered back to see if they were being followed, but there was no vehicle behind them within following distance.

They were a few minutes away from the bar. She thought back to the hotel. The check-in desk man, from his perch he wouldn't have been able to see that a cab had just pulled up. He had no window, no angle to see. Was it that he knew it was there because it was *supposed* to be there?

"How much?"

"How much what?" the cab driver asked. "The fare?"

"How much were you paid to be at the hotel to pick me up?"

"Uh... excuse me. What are you talking about?"

"You expected me to give you a different destination, didn't you?" Maggie said, holding her gun up enough for him to see in the rearview mirror. "You were expecting me to say the South Garage for the Wolstein Center."

"I... I..."

"I won't kill you. They might, but I won't." She checked behind them again. "Pull over."

The driver did as she ordered, trembling as he parked along the curb.

"What's your name?"

"Uh... Ben."

"I'm going to give you some advice, Ben. Whoever paid you? If they don't get what they want, they will come back for you and it won't be to just get the money back."

"What do I do?"

"Take whatever money they paid you and get as far away from here as you can."

Out of the car, she called Angie again. They had a code to speak of matters. Again, he didn't answer.

Had he set her up?

She found that hard to believe. He wasn't her father, but he looked after her, had taken her under his wing after her own father's passing.

Two cab changes later she arrived at an all-night restaurant where she sat in a booth allowing her to see anyone who entered. She tried Angie again, but there was no answer.

First thing in the morning, she took another cab to a car rental place. As Cleveland disappeared behind her, she tried Angie again, but there was no answer. She tried another number.

"I was wondering when you were going to call."

"Why?" Maggie answered warily.

"You haven't heard?"

"Heard what?"

"Angie was gunned down last night, right around midnight. He and two of his guys were ambushed in the alley behind the bar."

Cleveland had been a setup. Four days later, she learned why. John Sylvester was FBI Special Agent Como.

She had crossed the line. It was a sin she would never stop paying for.

TWENTY-FIVE

"I WITHHELD INFORMATION UNTIL IT WAS NO LONGER NECESSARY TO WITHHOLD IT."

Vince held his position as four more police vehicles zoomed by from the south, making the turn on the road leading to the lake.

Max's earbud was still operating. He heard the creaking of a truck door opening.

"He's dead," a male voice he didn't recognize called out. "How about the other guy? The one lying in the yard? Him too? Who the hell are these guys?"

Vince tossed out the earbud and drove north on the county road and was able to see the flashing of the multi-colored police lights through the woods. The scene was now swarmed with police.

As he drove away, he patted his own coat pocket to check for his gun.

We're not alone.

Marta was out here.

How? Was she following them?

Or... tracking them.

He checked his rearview mirror to make sure it was clear before he made a left turn and drove down a dirt road for a quarter mile before pulling over. Her turned on his cell phone flashlight and walked around the Escalade, searching underneath the vehicle. He didn't find anything. That didn't mean she wasn't tracking Max's Navigator.

Where was she off to now?

Back inside the truck he made a U-turn and accelerated back to County Road 44 and made for Cullen Crossing. Twenty minutes later, when he reached the strip mall, he made a careful circuit of the parking lot, his gun in his right hand, inspecting every vehicle in both the front and the back before he parked behind the building. He found Mileski, Marrone and Stevie out front smoking cigars.

"Is it done?" Marrone asked softly.

"No," Vince said and pulled everyone close. "Max and Carlo are dead."

"What?" Mileski blurted loudly.

Vince put his finger to his lips and then looked around. "Marta was out there. I don't know how, yet, but she was there, and she got the drop on them before they could take care of the problem. She had to have followed them or had a tracker of some kind on Max's Navigator."

He nodded for them to follow him inside. The four of them walked to the back hallway.

"We're under attack," Mileski growled in anger. "You need to find Marta. This little girl, whatever her name is, can wait. Hell, I didn't think we needed to take her out. Now, the police are going to be all over this."

"And yet they haven't been here, have they?" Vince said. "That tells me they haven't tied anything back to you guys. And Jimmy, you may be right, maybe we didn't need to take the step tonight, but it would have eliminated all risk."

"If it worked. It didn't. Now we have more."

"We have to deal with this problem," Marrone said. "You have to find Marta and now you're down two more men."

"That is a problem which is why we're changing some

things up," Vince replied. "We're hunkering down right here. We'll go to your houses tomorrow in the daylight to get clothes and supplies. But for the time being, this is where we're going to be. With what I have, I can protect you here. We can see anyone coming. Limit yourselves from the hardware store to the bar and then basement. We can cover that."

"And business?"

"Close the bar for tonight," Vince said.

"And the rest?"

"Keeps going. The rest of the mall and everything else. No interruption. One person, one woman, is not going to shut the operation down. Things need to look normal. We avoid suspicion if we act normally."

"You don't think she can get us here?"

"I think she can get us anywhere because we don't know who she is right now. However, this makes it as hard as possible," Vince said. "She gets you when you're isolated. Here neither of you are. I can keep a tight grip on things, especially when it's dark, which is when she usually hits. At night we're in this bar or the basement, that's it."

"But we just can't sit in here forever. How are you going to find her?"

"I'm working on it."

* * *

Jones was waiting for them underneath the grandstand at the county fairgrounds.

"This is a hell of a place to meet," Braddock said.

"Yeah, nobody will see us. Is that offer you talked about the other day still good?"

"Yes."

Jones nodded. "T, come on out."

They glanced left to see a slight man with a hoodie pulled

over his head, wearing a baseball hat, come out of a grandstand stairway tunnel and approach them.

"And this is?"

"Tristan Wilcox. I told you I knew Banz. T worked for him."

"I hear you're offering immunity," Wilcox said.

"Is there something you need immunity from?" Braddock said.

Wilcox turned to Jones. "Can I trust these guys?"

"I fuckin' do. They've never done me dirty. They're straight shooters."

"Even if he's not," Steak said snarkily, gesturing to Jones.

Jones shrugged. "Touché."

"Did you kill anybody?" Braddock asked Wilcox.

"No!"

"Did you see anybody kill anybody?"

"No. No, no, no."

"I'm assuming you know about *somebody* getting killed?"

"I think that's what happened to Reardon."

"Tell them what you know," Jones urged.

"I'm not sure, Jonesy. My best play is to walk."

"Yet you're here," Braddock said calmly. "Clearly you have something you want to talk about. Let's talk. That's all we're doing here. I have a lot of dead bodies. Can you help me with that?"

"Talk about what you told me. About business," Jones suggested.

"Let's hear it," Steak said. "No judgments."

"Well, we had a nice thing going. A steady supply from a contact down in the Twin Cities. We had a small tight group of four, including Banz. We were careful about what and where we sold and were doing alright, more than alright actually."

"Where were you dealing?"

"Here in Shepard County, a few of the others around here.

The market is fertile enough. Kids on campus mostly like weed, some shrooms, nothing too crazy. Outside of Manchester Bay it's the harder stuff. We could get what people wanted. Then a few months ago, Banz is leaving a bar up in Pequot Lakes. Four guys put a gun on him and took him for a ride out into the countryside."

"To where?" Steak asked.

"This trailer. He said it was one of those silver ones. What do you call them?"

"An Airstream?" Braddock asked, glancing to Steak.

"That's it. He said there was this big dude, square head, broad shoulders inside and they had him at gunpoint."

"Who was the guy?"

"I learned it was Steve, Stevie, something like that."

"And what did he want from Banz?"

"To tell us that they were going to replace our supplier."

"And if Banz didn't agree?"

"He didn't think he was leaving the trailer alive. But it was a bad deal."

"Most deals at gunpoint are," Steak retorted. "Let me guess, their cut was significant."

"Huge. Before that we were doing well. But having to pay them, we were making a lot less. We had to work twice as much just to get back to level. Our other two guys were going to bail on us. Banz went to the guy, this Stevie and tried to renegotiate the deal, get us closer to what we had."

"Where? Where did he go do this?"

"Met him at a bar in Pequot Lakes. Banz tried changing the deal, but it was a no-go. This guy tried buying him off with five thousand dollars. He had it in an envelope in his coat. Called it a bonus for doing a good job. It didn't get us anywhere near where we were."

"So, what happened next?"

"Reardon said fuck it. He took the five grand, called his old contact in the cities and we rolled for a few weeks that way, back the way we were. Then I dropped Banz off at his townhouse on the Monday after we got back from the Twin Cities, re-upping with our guy. I was going to pick him up the next day. But I went and he wasn't there. He didn't answer his phone. I've seen no sign of him. He's vanished."

"You think it was these guys coming back on him? He didn't just leave town?" Steak said.

"Banz had a serious girl, a pretty little thing. They'd been together a couple of years. No way he skips town without her, no way. She told me she hadn't heard a peep from him and none of his stuff was missing from his townhouse."

"In other words, no sign he'd packed quick and ran."

"Right. He's just gone."

"What did you do?"

"I drove him to that meeting at the bar. The guy saw me. I figured I was next. I bailed," Wilcox replied. "I'm from Fargo. I didn't go back there in case they knew who I was."

"Where are you now?"

"I'm not saying. At least for now but it's a long way from here and I just took a landscaping job. It's hard work, the pay is for shit, but nobody is trying to kill me at least."

"Why are you back here then?"

"Through a mutual friend, Jonesy reached out to me, told me you were investigating Banz missing and what you were offering. Look, Reardon was no saint, but he never harmed anyone. But killing him? And he's not the only guy who has gone missing. There were some others. Jones says you're looking into that too. I think those guys took a pass on this deal with these guys. My guess, Reardon ended up just like them. These guys are no joke. They have some heavy dudes. Shit, Reardon and I never used a gun. We just bought for a dollar and—"

"Sold for two," Braddock finished.

Steak took out his phone and swiped through some photos. "Is this the guy? Stevie?"

Wilcox examined the phone screen. "Yeah, that's him alright."

"And he was what? The supplier?"

"Reardon told me he was the guy who gave him the ultimatum. I never saw him supply anything."

"How did they supply you?"

Wilcox took a moment. "At Reardon's house. If he needed supply, he put this locked bin on his front stoop with payment inside. He had a key; they had a key. The payment would be picked up and then a new delivery would come the next day or two. After the deliveries, he'd put the bin inside until he needed another delivery."

"And who made the deliveries?"

"I don't know who it was."

"You ever see it?"

"Just once. A black van pulled up. Guy was wearing a plain black full body zip-up uniform, ballcap, looking like a delivery guy. He unlocked the box, picked up the payment and away he went. Delivery came the next day."

"Hang on a second," Braddock said as he hustled out to his Tahoe and rushed back. He opened his file folder that had photos. "Any of these guys look like the delivery guy?"

Wilcox sifted through the photos and stopped on one. "Any more for this guy?"

Braddock pulled out a couple of additional photos and handed them over.

"This guy I think made the delivery. It was October or November I want to say. Fall for sure."

Braddock held up the photo to Steak.

"Gresh."

"He was a minion for these guys," Braddock muttered. "Is anyone from your crew still operating?"

Wilcox shook his head. "No. We disbanded. After Reardon it wasn't worth it, you know."

"I hear that," Steak agreed.

"This helps us, Tristan," Braddock said.

"Is it worth the free pass?"

"Jones as my witness, I really don't give a rip about what you've done, especially if you've left the area. I'd suggest you stay away until we finish this all up."

"So, I can leave?"

Braddock nodded. "Stay reachable, through Jones. This free pass may require your further assistance. If we call, you answer. Understood?"

* * *

Tori got to Eunice's house and rushed upstairs to the second floor. Reese was on the edge of his chair when she got up there. "Glad to see you in one piece. The radio was going nuts."

"The night has been nuts. What's going on here?" she asked, reaching for a pair of binoculars.

"Something is definitely stirring," Reese replied, looking back with raised eyebrows. "Marrone, Mileski and a couple of their goons were out front, smoking cigars, just like the other night. Twenty—" he checked his notes "—three minutes ago, another guy comes outside, a tall blond I hadn't really seen before. He talks to them for a minute. I see a bunch of gesticulating and then they went back inside the bar. Then, ten minutes ago, things got kind of weird."

"How?"

"Closing time is one a.m. and they are usually open that late. There is a group of regulars who usually close it down. But all the sudden, everyone files out of the CC Bar & Grill and the lights turn off inside. They shut it down."

"By everyone, how many?"

"Twenty, maybe twenty-five people," Reese said. "I could play back the tape. Not a huge crowd but not nothing either. What do you make of that?"

"It's confirmation they're spooked. Marrone and Mileski sent those men to the house Alisha was at tonight and it didn't go according to plan," Tori said as she peered out the window at the darkened bar. All the businesses were closed. "Now they're wondering what comes next."

"Who is this woman?" Reese said.

"I don't know," Tori replied. "Whoever she is, she's got these guys on edge."

"That ain't all bad."

"Ain't all good either."

* * *

Maggie grimaced nervously, gripping the steering wheel tightly, as the door for their double garage slowly raised.

Phew.

Rob wasn't home yet. She snuck inside the house and immediately into the salon, stuffing her backpack into her hidden cabinet. She left her muddy tennis shoes outside the salon door. Walking lightly, she made her way upstairs.

She tiptoed by the kids' rooms and into the master bedroom. She stripped out of her filthy clothes and stuffed them to the bottom of her dirty-clothes basket. That's when she got the first real look at the long scrape on her upper left arm. That was a bullet coming a little too close for comfort. The cut wouldn't require stitches, but she was feeling the sting of it. Then there was her face. There was a deep two-inch scratch on her upper left cheek, just under her eye. From a tree branch no doubt as she was fleeing. And she smelled of musty outdoors. It was in her hair and on her hands.

She showered quick to ditch the smell. In the mirror, she

examined her wounds. She applied ointment to the bullet gash on her left arm and then placed two large Band-Aids over it. On her cheek, she cleaned the scrape and then applied some light makeup. It wouldn't completely hide it but it was good enough for now.

Thump!

Rob. She swiped her makeup into her vanity drawer. Turned off the bathroom light and rushed to the bed and jumped in, turning off the lights. She had her back to him when he came into the room.

To her relief, he came into the bedroom and tiptoed to the closet himself and was as quiet as could be, slipping gently into bed five minutes later, not saying a word.

* * *

"I've got dead bodies coming out the wazoo here," Boe said, agitated. "And we don't have any damn answers."

Braddock shook his head. "Actually, I think we have the answer to the biggest question we have. We know who we're looking at now. And not just the shootings. Drug distribution too, which may explain what happened to Banz and others." He explained what he and Steak had learned.

"Drugs? Where are you getting that?"

"Steak and I have a source feeding us some intel. Banz was in the drug world. Our source is putting a Mileski and Marrone meathead in the middle of the muscle side of it and identifies Gresh as one of their delivery boys."

"And the source is?"

"Confidential. Two confidential informants, in fact."

"Names?" Boe asked.

"We're keeping those to ourselves for now."

"I'm not sure I like being left in the dark."

"I don't imagine you do," Braddock replied. "You need to trust us on this."

"Who is us?"

"The three people in the room with you."

"I need to trust you, but you three don't seem to trust me," Boe asserted. "And I am the boss."

Braddock snorted and shook his head. "That's fair, Janette. If our sources names get out, these guys will do to them what they did to Banz, what they tried to do tonight. What they did to those kids in Holmstrand. To Gresh and Gill at that trailer. Our one source is very reliable. The other one is to be determined in the next few days. We get something, then maybe we can say who he is."

"And I'm guessing you're offering immunity of some kind?"

"Yeah."

"And you think this will work?"

"We don't know," Steak replied. "But our reliable guy... he knows people who know people we don't know. He brought us someone we wouldn't otherwise have found."

"And you trust him?"

"For someone who operates in the gray, yeah."

"Good. Keep at it then," Boe said. "But in the meantime, this woman is running around up here killing people."

"At least she's killing the right people," Steak blurted with a chuckle.

"You think this is funny, Detective?"

"No, Sheriff, I don't," Steak grimaced while scratching his head. "But I saw two dead guys tonight who tried to kill a nine-year-old deaf girl and the two kind souls who've taken her in. A bad joke is how I cope with shit like that."

"Yeah," Boe nodded. She opened her desk drawer. "I know my predecessor liked bourbon. I prefer Scotch." She poured everyone a small drink and passed them out. "What is our plan now?"

"Twofold because we have two problems," Braddock replied. "The first is Mileski and Marrone. You've heard part of that strategy already. They caused all this shit. That's my focus."

"When are you going to go at them?" Boe demanded.

Braddock sighed. "When we have something to go at them with."

"But—"

"They're looking over their shoulder right now."

"Or so our killer says," Boe needled.

"I think she's right," Tori replied. "They shut down their bar tonight after this all went down. Cleared everyone out. They're nervous."

"Then if they're nervous and you go at them—"

"With what?" Tori replied. "It's one thing to know it, and another to—"

"Janette, we don't have anything concrete," Braddock said. "We go at them right now, we're giving them a lifeline. We're telling them we know about them and what they've been up to. They've already shutdown their bar tonight. They did that why?"

"To hunker down," Tori said. "To protect themselves. She has them spooked."

"If I go at them right now, they might shut *everything* down. The mall, their operation, the whole kit and kaboodle. If they do that, we won't ever catch them. I need them to keep operating. I want them to keep being dirty while Steak and I—"

"Do whatever it is your doing."

"Right. Janette, it's taking every fiber of my being to not go into the strip mall, grab those two and beat them to death with my bare hands after tonight. But if we're going to get them, we have to be a little patient."

"I wanted to go from Eunice's and walk in the front door and shoot those bastards," Tori said, before she took a long drink. "The damage they've done to Alisha. She lost her mom, her brother in the last month and now they tried to kill her. She's nine. *Nine!*" Tori gripped her glass as if she were going to throw it.

"Easy," Braddock said quietly, tenderly patting her on the shoulder.

Boe came around her desk with the Scotch. "I'm right there with you," she said as she held Tori's hand and refilled her drink glass.

"Tori's comments notwithstanding, I agree, going right at them now, is not how we get them," Boe said and took a sip of her drink. "You were right before. My marshal instincts get in the way. I'm a hammer and the whole world is a nail. I didn't have to worry about proof. You do," she said and took another drink. "But you said twofold earlier."

"The second problem is our woman killer. You're right. We have to find her. And to your marshal point, we don't have to prove she's guilty. We already know she is. We just have to identify her."

"How exactly?" Tori asked.

"You hunt her down," Boe said with a wry smile, and she knew what Braddock was thinking. She turned her gaze to Tori. "I do believe you're going to Chicago."

"I am," Tori said, eyes raised.

"She is?" Steak said.

"Yep," Braddock said.

"I think you're right, Tori. She's been living here, new identity, new life," Boe said. "But she's smart. She knows her old life could still be looking for her. Especially now. I'm betting she's always had someone down in Chicago she could call and check-in with. Someone who is keeping an eye on things. Someone with an ear to the ground to warn her if need be. And given all that is going on, I'm betting she's talking to them now. That's what I'd be doing if I was her.

That's what the people I used to chase for a living would be doing."

"And Tori's job is to find out who that is?" Steak asked warily.

"Before I can do that, I have to figure out who she is, or was," Tori said.

"That's right," Boe agreed. "Whatever bad blood she had with Mileski and Marrone down there, it's now being spilled up here. We have to stop it."

"Look, that's not something that happens overnight, if at all," Tori said. "It's not like I can jump on a plane in the morning and do it. It's going to take some planning and resources. I'm going to need some real time down there."

"Whatever it takes," Braddock said.

"I don't know about this," Steak protested. "You're sending her down there alone? To Chicago, with no backup? And Tori isn't with the Bureau. A Shepard County badge isn't going to mean shit down there." He looked to Tori. "And then, there's the fact that you're you and all that comes with that."

"What's that supposed to mean?"

Steak smiled. "You have an innate ability to piss people off."

"That's coming off the top rope," Braddock warned.

"Really? Need I remind you of the first time you met her?"

"You think I'll need protection?" Tori said.

"I know you can handle yourself, but... yeah," Steak replied worriedly. "You're going down to Chicago to look for a killer who worked for the Chicago Mob. Some people might not be too hospitable to your inquiries. Particularly if you're alone."

"I'm touched by your concern," Tori said half-heartedly.

"Don't mock me on this, Tori. Don't you dare do that."

Tori took the measure of Steak's concern, surprised by the intensity of it. "Then I'm going to need some friends with me, aren't I?"

"Who do you have in mind?" Boe asked.

"Special Agent Bahn was a fountain of information. I can reach out to him. I think this case intrigues him. And—" her eyes lit up quick at the thought "—if I'm taking some time down there, and with a few days lead time, I might have another friend who could help me. And she too has some investment in this case."

"You're going to make a call to New York City," Braddock said.

"In fact, I think I might."

TWENTY-SIX

"LIVE FOR TODAY FOR TOMORROW IS NOT PROMISED."

Vince sipped coffee out on the deck.

The morning was clear, the sun bright, the waters of Bertha Lake a brilliant reflection of the clear blue sky. The air crisp, the distant calls of birds and gentle brisk breeze soothing to the skin.

The tranquility of it all was the antithesis of his daily life.

For twenty-five years he'd been doing this. Cleaning up messes, whether it was Chicago or Kansas City or St. Louis or Omaha or Cleveland or even an occasional assignment further east. He'd never shown an aptitude for much of anything else, certainly not for something as lucrative as what he did.

When he started, he didn't figure to see old age. Not many in this line of work ever did. In doing what he did not only did you have to hit the target you were hired to take out, but after you did, you always had to be mindful of the people who hired you lest they now viewed you as a liability. He'd often been hired to eliminate human links in evidentiary chains. However, in doing so, that too in a way made him such a link, particularly were he to be caught. There was one time when someone viewed him as such a liability and acted upon that concern after he'd finished a job.

At the last moment he saw them coming.

They missed. He didn't when he came back on them.

That sent a message to those who hired him in the future. Nevertheless, someone could try again and while he was still very good, he was feeling the creep of age. Fifty was six months ahead. The blond hair was turning to gray and much to his dismay, it was thinning. There were scars, and the aches and pains lingered a little longer each morning. There was money put away and it was plenty to live comfortably.

The problem was that in this line of work, the moment you said you were done, you became a liability. The hunter became the hunted.

He exhaled a long breath.

There was irony in this assignment. He was now hunting someone who had done what he now often thought of doing. Disappearing. And at least on this morning, as he gazed out to the blue waters of Bertha Lake, he understood why she may have chosen here.

The door slid open behind him. Mileski joined him.

"I get why you like it up here."

Mileski nodded, leaning on the deck railing. "I was angry when Bobby sent us all up here. All I knew was Chicago. What the hell am I going to do up here? I was certain I was going to be bored out of my mind. It took me about two months to realize I was wrong. You should see it in the summer when the trees are all green. Or even better, in the fall in late September and early October when the colors are changing. It rivals anything you've seen on the shoreline on Lake Michigan or Grant Park."

"I notice you didn't mention the winter."

Mileski shrugged. "It isn't much different than Chicago. It's a bit colder and longer, but I didn't have a problem adjusting to that. I love it up here. I'd never go back. My question to you, Vince, is am I going to keep it? Marta's picking us apart."

"Which is why we're being careful. We stay at the mall for now."

"You know, this feels a lot like what Philly was doing twelve years ago. Hunkering down. And she ended up getting him."

"I told Philly we should be moving around, especially in the city. A new place every night but you know he loved that club. He felt safe and thought it was a fortress. But here, Jimmy, where is there to go other than here or the business?"

"I don't know," Mileski said. "I never thought it would be a problem."

"It's never a problem until it is."

"Bobby," Mileski lamented. "My brother is the boss. What he says goes. Move up here and run this, I did it. Pauly and I were up here eleven, twelve years, operating quietly, setting him, us, and everyone else up, the money clean as a whistle. Nobody paying us any attention. It was a brilliant move. But now, the last couple of years, he's gotten less smart and greedier."

"He says branch out," Vince replied. If there was one thing he'd learned over the years, guys like Bobby Mileski never had enough money. They always wanted more. They never, ever, left money on the table. "But that raises your profile."

"Yeah. He comes up here and sees the area in the summer and says we could kill it. He has a good drug connection and boom, there we go. I argued why rock the boat, but—"

"He's the boss."

"That's right. And he was right, the money? Big. More than I thought it would ever be."

"It came with risk."

"The greed wasn't just the business opportunity; it was the terms. He had us putting guns to heads up here. It was bound to cause problems, but he wasn't hearing it. What we do in Chicago we do here."

The door opened behind them. "I'm set," Pauly said, and they caravanned it back to the mall.

At the mall, Vince retreated to a private room in the basement and placed a call.

"Vincent," Bobby Mileski greeted gregariously. "How are Jimmy and Pauly?"

"Alive. We're hunkered down for now."

"You're certain it's Marta? You're absolutely certain?"

"After last night, I have no doubt."

"What is her tie up there?"

"No familial tie to the families that were victimized by that shooting. It could be a friend but right now I don't have the manpower to hunt her and protect these two at the same time."

"I'm working on that. Any problems with the police up there yet?"

"No, but it has to be coming. Law enforcement up here is of an unexpected caliber." He explained Braddock and Hunter, not to mention the sheriff's background. "They have ability if not the resources. I think you can assume they would have reached out to the FBI by now. You may want to make some discreet inquiries of your own."

"I will. Have the police been sniffing around our operation up there?"

"Not that we have detected thus far."

"That's good."

"Still, they're out there," Vince said. "Jimmy and Pauly have done enough up here with the drug operation that there are people out there who know of them now. That's going to be an issue sooner or later."

"What else? I can hear it in your voice. There's more."

"Pauly says one of their guy's named Nico, last Friday, before Marta got him, used a burner phone to call Pauly on his personal phone. Pauly was on while Nico was being chased. If the police recovered that phone, they could trace it back to him.

And as you know, what precipitated all this was the fact that Pauly and Jimmy were seen outside that apartment."

"Those two kids didn't go to the police. Why? They didn't know what it was they saw if they saw anything. Jimmy and Pauly had to eliminate the problem. How they did it wasn't ideal, but it was taken care of. And the police, good as they may be, don't have any tie back to Jimmy and Pauly."

"What about Rudick?"

"Rudick just ran the money through his rental properties for us and got a nice spiff for it. That and he oversaw the drug operation, but his name isn't tied to the mall, or the warehouse. He was compartmentalized, intentionally so. They can dig on Rudick, and they might find dirt, but on him, it won't go back to Jimmy and Pauly. It won't go back to the mall."

"There is still the problem of my two men she killed last night. They're Chicago boys. They'll raise suspicion."

"You couldn't have cleaned that up?"

"Bobby, there was no time. She killed Max and Carlo. The police were there moments later. I had to get my ass out of there myself."

"And where did Marta go?"

"I can only assume she had to do what I was doing."

"How did they get there so fast?"

"It's curious that is. Maybe it was chance. It could be the police were on their way for another visit as they had the prior night. Perhaps a neighbor called 911. The timing of it is concerning. As I said earlier, they have some capabilities up here that you've been fortunate to avoid thus far. But here's the thing, this little girl saw Pauly at Rudick's the night of the shooting. Stevie Bianchi too."

"Yet the cops haven't showed?"

"No. Jimmy and Pauly keep expecting it but nothing so far."

"This girl. She's nine. She probably doesn't know their

names. If the police don't have a name or anyway to identify them, then they've got nothing."

"As of now. Things can change."

"If she's told them anything, anything of value, wouldn't she have done so by now?"

Vince sighed. "You would think so."

"And that would trigger at least a visit, wouldn't it?"

"Again, I'd think so."

"Yet it hasn't," Bobby said. "Look, keep a low profile today, and if nobody shows, then tomorrow we get back to business. Not operating draws attention too. If we're not open, people will wonder why, even up in that backwater town."

* * *

Maggie yawned and stretched her neck as she opened the bathroom door.

Rob was right there.

"Oh, jeez, you startled me," Maggie blurted, jumping back. She thought he'd already left for school with the kids.

"How did you scratch your cheek like that?" Rob said, reaching for her cheek, turning her head. "Gosh, looks like it hurts."

"Oh," she replied, ducking away, and walking into the closet. "I went out to check on a noise in the backyard last night and a tree branch jumped out and got me."

"It got you good."

"I know. I put some first-aid cream on it right away last night," she said and coughed.

He stepped into the closet, and she knew it was to get close and check on her. It's what he did. She coughed again, and then harder as she leaned down and pulled out a pair of fresh jeans.

"Are you feeling alright?"

She stood up and smiled wanly. "I think I might be getting a cold, probably from being stupid and stepping out into the cold last night without a coat while scraping my face." She coughed again. "You might want to keep your distance."

"I probably should. Do you have a busy day?"

"I'll be fine. I'll throw down some cough suppressant and fight through."

She did have two appointments on the day. Her second was Sally Ullman from four doors down. And Cathy came over, just to hang out, in need of company, the three of them doing their best to chit-chat in the salon. To Maggie's amazement, Cathy carried the conversation.

"I've got a building contractor coming tomorrow. He's going take out the front steps and sidewalk."

"With the Coming Soon sign up?" Sally asked.

"Yeah. If I'm going to sell it, I can't have those blood spots there."

"I'm so, sorry," Sally said, mortified, her right hand to her mouth. "Cath—"

"It's okay, Sal. I have to talk about these things. It does me no good to just keep them bottled up. Just bear with me because sometimes..." She wiped a tear away. "You know... it catches me."

"Of course. Of course. Anything you need," Sally urged, leaning forward. "You can call at any time. Stop over at any time. Ask me for anything."

"I know, and I appreciate it. Both of you," she said, looking from Sally to Maggie, "have been so great. Maggie, I've been living in this salon, and your refrigerator the last month it seems."

"And you just keep on coming over," Maggie said.

"Thanks. I can't tell you what that means, but you know, I was thinking that Leo would be mad if I just sulked around. I must mourn him, but I have to... move on too. I'm forty-four. I have a lot of life left to live."

"Darn right you do," Sally affirmed.

"So, I just have to... press on, keep going and hope it'll get better with time."

"One day at a time, sweetie."

"How about the man you went on those dates with?" Maggie asked. "Has he... called?"

"Yes, and well, I reached out to him too."

"You did?"

"Well, he's the contractor removing my steps," Cathy said with a sly smile. She exhaled a big breath and offered a wane yet hopeful smile. "Live for today for tomorrow is not promised. I have to move on, you know, and live. I need to live for me and for the memory of Leo. We all do."

* * *

After dinner, Maggie took her leave, telling Rob she wanted to go shopping for a few things. "I'll be an hour."

She went into the salon, opened the hidden cabinet and took out a new previously unused disposable phone. Then she headed down to the shopping area of Manchester Bay.

* * *

You win again! Tori signed to Alisha, who won their third game of Chutes and Ladders. Tori kind of let her win the first game, competed a bit harder in the second and played it straight in the third, losing all three.

Alisha clapped and smiled, happy to win, signing: *I'm unbeatable.*

"Ha!" Tori smiled. *I'm going to go talk to Trish, okay?*
Okay.

"Kids amaze me," Tori remarked to Trish as they shared a cup of tea in the kitchen, Alisha sitting on the floor, cross legged, watching television with closed captioning. "How quickly they get past traumatic events."

"I know," Trish replied. "Paul and I are still rattled from last night."

"Me too."

"You don't seem like it."

"I've been through things like that... more often than I care to admit. That doesn't mean it doesn't stick with me."

"Will they try again?"

"I don't think so, but we're not taking any chances. There will be an officer on guard and another patrolling the area for the time being."

"And these men who came after her? What of them? Do you know who sent them?"

Tori took a sip of her tea and thought for a moment before nodding slightly. "We do. And trust me when I say, they are getting our undivided attention twenty-four hours a day."

Trish nodded, dunking her tea bag into the water before looking to the living room. "Paul and I were talking about what a tough road Alisha has ahead of her."

"Her road was already tough and then all this added on," Tori said. "A lot for a little girl to take in."

"Yeah," Trish said with a nod. "No family, or at least no family interested in taking her in. It has Paul and I thinking and talking."

"Really?"

"Neither of us is retiring any time soon and we don't have grandkids yet..."

An hour later, Tori pushed through the back door for the house. Braddock was off running an errand. Quinn was upstairs in his bedroom, completing his homework. She took out the half-finished bottle of white wine and poured herself a glass and wandered back into her home office and her suitcase. If she was going to Chicago, she needed to pack.

Her phone buzzed in her back pocket. She examined the screen. It was a number she didn't recognize, other than it was another Area Code 312 number. She hit the record feature she'd installed on her phone and then answered. "People are going to start wondering about us," Tori greeted.

The modulated voice laughed. "I'm like an old friend calling." Her voice was lighter, more playful.

"We're not friends."

"I kind of think we could have been though, were circumstances different. What are you up to?"

"You just call to chat?"

"I have a point. I'll get to it. But seriously, what are you up to right now?"

"I'm having a glass of wine," Tori replied, taking a drink. She wasn't going to tell her she was packing for a trip to Chicago. The call was being traced, though with a new number from what was undoubtedly another burner phone it would be nearly impossible. "A lovely, sweet California Chardonnay."

"Ah, a good choice. I like a chilled sweet white."

"You like wine?"

"Started drinking it when I was twelve."

"That's an early start."

"My dad, he didn't shelter me from much."

"Would that be Angie DeEsposito?"

The voice laughed. "Tori, Tori, Tori. Been reading the FBI file, have we?"

"It makes for an interesting read. Leaves one with a lot of questions."

"That I'm not going to answer. Are you still hunting me?"

"What do you think?"

"I think you are what you are, Tori. You're a hunter," the voice chuckled. "Sorry, no pun intended."

"I'm a hunter, eh?"

"You left the FBI, yet you continue to chase. New venue, same pursuits. You might be happier doing it here, but you're still the same. No change."

"Oh, is that what you did? Changed?"

The voice laughed. "Yeah. I think I've changed quite a bit. And, while I reverted, it's been momentary. I think I've done enough."

"You're stopping?"

"Yes, though I will be keeping a wary eye out."

"For me?"

"Or anyone else who wishes me harm."

"I don't wish you harm."

"Ah, but you do want to catch me because that's who *you* are."

"You have something to answer for. I don't give two shits about Philly Lamberto or Johnny Marrone, or anyone else you killed, but Special Agent Como? His family? His wife? Did you know he had a wife?"

A pause.

"I didn't."

"They need justice. Even if you didn't know he was an agent, it really doesn't matter. You murdered an agent. We're not going to forget that. Ever."

The woman's voice went quiet for a moment. "Tell me, Tori, do you have a motto you live by?"

"A motto?"

"Yeah. Words to live by."

Tori snorted a laugh. "You know, I've never really thought of it. I just try to be true to myself, to who I am I guess."

"Do you succeed at that?"

"Better now than I used to."

"You know, I didn't really have one until today."

"What happened today?"

"Call it a moment of clarity."

"Hmpf." Tori shook her head. "Moments of clarity. Those I understand. And what did this moment of clarity tell you?"

"Live for today for tomorrow is not promised."

"Sounds like you have a lot to live for?"

"I've done enough, Tori. I have faith that you and Braddock will finish it."

Click.

Tori made another instant call. Braddock answered right away.

"Any luck?"

"No. If she'd used the disposable number we had, we might have had a chance, but it was a new phone. You glean anything from the call?"

"I got the coffee cup motto that told me one thing."

"Which is?"

"She has someone to live for."

TWENTY-SEVEN

"JUST DO IT OUT IN FRONT OF GOD AND EVERYONE."

Friday morning.

The coffee maker clock reported it was 4:02 a.m. as it burbled to its brewing finish, a little steam filtering out the top, the warm smell of fresh coffee enveloping the kitchen like a warm blanket. Tori came rushing down, dressed casually in skinny jeans and a hoodie, her hair in a wet ponytail, wheeling her suitcase and carrying her backpack and shoulder bag.

"I so have to boogie. My flight is at eight thirty." She was driving down to the Minneapolis/St. Paul International Airport, just under three hours to the south.

Braddock poured her a large tumbler of coffee and then followed her out the back door, wheeling her suitcase to the Audi and stuffing it in the rear compartment. "A long weekend in Chicago. It should be fun."

"Ha ha," Tori replied before leaning up to kiss him. "Wish you were coming."

"Me too. Just be careful and watch your back."

"Will do," she said as she jumped into the Audi.

"And call me with any updates."

"I'll do that too."

And just like that she was gone. There was no sense going back to bed. And with Quinn staying at his grandparents' house last night, he didn't need to get him to school. He quick showered, dressed and went into work. In the early morning quiet of the investigation offices, he started the coffee maker and went to the conference room.

On the whiteboard the whole case was laid out. The problem was they were stymied on much of it. They had worked through every shred of paper and every computer file from Rudick's office. If he were alive, they could have prosecuted him for tax evasion and money laundering. The problem was there was hardly a shred of documentation tying him to Mileski and Marrone. They knew he was part of their operation, but they couldn't prove it.

The murders were all detailed. Holmstrand, at the Airstream trailer, Banz, the other drug dealers, even what happened at the Adamses. The frustration was that in the case of Banz and the others they didn't have a body or a live witness to testify as to their disappearances and suspected murders. They knew it. They couldn't prove it.

Same for Holmstrand. That was all tied up neat with a bow when the gun was found with Gresh. He had motive. Even if they developed evidence that Mileski and Marrone did order that murder, unless it was someone in the room with them at the time, it would be hard to obtain a conviction given Gresh's existence and the evidence pointing to him. And the others who were in Holmstrand for the shooting? Some combination of Gresh, Gill, Waltripp and Sweeney? They were all dead.

Then there were the reasons for all the murders. Given what Wilcox had told them and what they'd learned of Gresh, it appeared every action taken was to prevent the uncovering of the murders that were meant to clear away anyone who didn't play ball on the drug operation. However, now, with all the murders, including the attempt the other night on Alisha, could they even afford to keep the drug operation going? If so, how were they doing it? The woman killer had taken out much of Mileski and Marrone's team, or so it appeared. Who did they have left?

That was the thought that percolated in his mind when he checked his watch just before 7:00 a.m.

He decided to get some fresh air and went down the street to the coffee shop. He bought a large double shot espresso and a bagel and slowly walked back, breathing in the refreshing early April morning air. The temp was going to get into the low fifties today and he could sense a hint of spring warmth in the air. It made him think of the summer months ahead and the lake.

He returned to the conference room and the laptop computer and began to click his way through all the photos that everyone had taken over the past several days while stationed in Cullen Crossing. Hundreds of pictures in, he stopped on photos of a black panel van that kept popping up. There were several recent days of photos of it stopping at the strip mall, the driver, Stevie Bianchi, making the deliveries. What he noticed was the plain black zip-up coverall.

He thought back to the meeting under the fairgrounds grandstand. Wilcox talked of a black panel van making deliveries, the deliveryman wearing a delivery uniform. He identified Gresh, but he was dead. If Mileski and Marrone were still operating their drug network, someone had to be making the deliveries. In the photos, the man driving the black van the last several days when it arrived at the strip mall was Stevie Bianchi.

What was it that Wilcox had said about the delivery process?

An hour later, after placing a call to Steak, Braddock stopped at home, changed into jeans and a gray hoodie and navy-blue Twins baseball cap. He left his department SUV at home, grabbed his portable police radio, and drove his pickup truck to

Harold's. Inside, he found Eggleston in the back bedroom chomping on an egg salad sandwich.

"What are you doing here?" she asked, surprised to see him.

"Have you seen this van arrive today as of yet?" He handed her a series of photos from Monday through Thursday.

"Not yet. That looks like Stevie Bianchi though. Is he the driver?"

"It looks like he has been the last few days this week."

She checked her watch and then notepad. "It's just after eleven a.m. The van usually arrives midday. Why the sudden interest?"

"Something we got from a source."

"Jones."

Braddock snapped a sideways glance at her.

"What? Steak and I have been partners a long time," she replied, binoculars to her eyes. "And what do you know. Here it comes."

"Will!" Steak called over the radio. "Where do you want me?"

"Pick me up at Harold's," he replied. To Eggs: "Stay on the radio." Then he called for Nolan, who was back in Manchester Bay. "Get Reese and get up this way."

"To do what?"

"Help me with a hunch."

Two minutes later, Steak, in his black Ford F-150 dual cab pickup, swung by Harold's and Braddock quick jumped inside.

"What's the plan?"

"Follow and observe," Braddock said as he took out a camera and attached a zoom lens. "Nolan and Reese will be making their way up here as well."

Steak drove them to the fire station and pulled around the north side, a position that allowed them a look at the back of the black van parked behind the strip mall at a door for the liquor store. "And our interest in this black van?"

"Something Wilcox said the other night."

* * *

"Tori!" Special Agent in Charge Joe Bahn greeted cheerily from his car as she walked out the front doors of her hotel. "Welcome to Chicago." They shook hands. "I know your time is tight this afternoon. Where to first?"

"I want to look at where Lamberto was killed and then maybe DeEsposito."

* * *

"I was reading through the notes and reports this morning since we've been watching that strip mall," Braddock said as they followed the black panel van north on the H-4, approaching the town of Pine River. "Every day this week this black van shows up with Bianchi driving it and he's carrying boxes inside. One day it's the bar. The next it's the liquor store. Yesterday the hardware store. Today he was taking boxes inside the gift shop. Same driver, same van, same uniform but different store every day."

"It is a little odd when you think about it," Steak said mildly, his wrist draped casually over the steering wheel.

"Maybe it is, maybe it isn't. Only one way to find out."

The black van was a quarter mile ahead of them as it entered the town and signaled a right turn. Steak accelerated closing the gap, making the right turn onto the main drag just seconds after the van. Steak maintained a one-block gap, now sitting up, two hands on the wheel.

Through town, the van took the bridge over the Pine River dam and Steak followed, no longer having other traffic with which to blend. Braddock ordered Nolan and Reese to hang back in the town.

"Here's where it gets a little tricky," Steak murmured as the van made a right turn. Steak reached the same right turn and held his stop for a moment.

"Left turn, second block," Braddock said, looking south.

Steak turned right and then took the first left.

"Wrong t—"

"Trust me."

Through the gaps between the houses scattered along the right side of the street they were able to see the black van as it slowly motored along and then pulled to a stop. Steak pulled to the side and parked. They could see the black van through a wide gap between houses. He used binoculars while Braddock snapped photos.

Bianchi went to the back of the van and stepped inside. A minute later he stepped back out, closed the doors and walked to the house with a package slung under his right arm. He walked up to a one-story rambler with a shaggy yard and uneven roof.

"What's that on the front stoop?"

"Lockbox," Steak blurted as Braddock snapped photos. "You don't suppose?"

"What Wilcox told us? Yeah, that's exactly what I think it is," Braddock said as the man unlocked the lockbox and set the package inside. "And there's your delivery."

"Just do it out in front of God and everyone."

"Sometimes that's the best way," Braddock replied, continuing to take photos. "These days nobody looks twice at a delivery to a doorstep. I swear, Tori has something delivered every day." He snapped two photos of the driver getting back into the van. "Okay, he's going to come around the block, right at us."

Steak made a quick left and pulled into a driveway and killed the engine. The two of them slumped down in their seats. Braddock looked back between the seats while Steak tracked the van in the rearview mirror. They both turned to the left after the van passed behind them and watched as it took a right turn.

"He's going back the same way."

They followed, catching a view of the van going over the dam bridge.

"Reese, he's coming back your way. Stay on him. We're hanging back here in Pine River."

"We are?" Steak asked.

"I want to know who Lockbox guy is and what he does next."

* * *

"This is it?"

"This is it," Bahn said, having driven them ten blocks northwest of the Chicago field office.

"The building looks ancient, at least by Midwestern standards," Tori remarked of the two-story red and brown brick building with a restaurant fronting the structure.

"There's a date block on it, 1887. When she killed Lamberto and Marrone it was a private club attached to the back of the bar. Basically, Philly Lamberto ran his crew out of here. He had an office and bedroom upstairs. The bar for the public was at the front of the building. The club was in the back."

"And the club had what?"

"A separate small private bar for the members and their guests, along with a steam room, a masseuse, a card room, and then a few other 'private' rooms upstairs."

"For the girls."

"These guys always have something on the side," Bahn said. "It's been twelve years. What do you think you'll learn here?"

"I'm not sure I'll learn anything," Tori said. "However, this was the last place she was ever seen. I wanted to get a look and feel for it."

Bahn parked and they went inside. What was once a bar was now a trendy restaurant. The owner had been briefed by Bahn and was ready for them. Bahn introduced himself and Tori. The owner led them back.

"Structurally, the building is largely the same as it was back then," the owner said. "We haven't moved many walls and the ones we did are upstairs to open that area up for private dining events. I have a book of photos of what it looked like when we bought it. Kind of a before and after."

"And you bought it when?"

"Two years after the shooting. It was shuttered by then."

"Between their own internal war after DeEsposito and Lamberto, and then the Bureau moving in on them, the Outfit had to consolidate their interests," Bahn said. "The crews all basically merged. This place was left behind."

Tori took the photo book and flipped through the pages. "The interior was dark back then. Not white and bright like now."

"Those guys didn't like bright," Bahn said. "They liked dim and shadows for quiet conversations."

"So how did the hit on Lamberto and Marrone go down?" Tori asked.

"We *think* she got into the building via the restaurant."

"*Think?* Let me guess," Tori said. "We don't know how because there was no surveillance system. These guys don't want surveillance evidence of... anything."

"Correct."

"And who was here at the time?"

"In addition to Lamberto, there was Johnny Marrone, a few of their regular men, and this guy, Vince Smith." He handed her a photo. "Tall blond guy. He was the one shot twice but who survived."

Tori lingered over the photo. "I should send this to Braddock. I think this guy might be up our way right now." She stuffed the photo in her folder. "The day of the shooting here. Johnny Marrone was here. How about Marrone's brother or Mileski's?"

"Yes, they were all Lamberto guys. According to the bar staff, the two Mileski's and Paul Marrone left with a group twenty to twenty-five minutes before the shooting."

Tori nodded. "Alright, they leave, it's a little less populated and she makes her move. She comes into the restaurant. Then what?"

"She gets into the back. There was a woman who worked the private area, a redhead, long wavy hair, skinny, long legs. She'd been here for a few years and was liked and trusted."

Tori looked at a photo of the woman.

"Our girl got back here, knocked the redhead out, tied her up, taped her mouth, blindfolded her, and stuffed her in a small closet. She didn't kill her though she certainly could have."

"That would have crossed the line for her," Tori said, remembering her phone call. "So, our killer dressed like this woman. White long-sleeved blouse, black pants and shoes, long red hair, almost certainly a wig. Interesting."

"That's right," Bahn said. "She carried a stack of towels to the steam area. The thought was she had a gun hidden in the towels. She opened the steam room door. Lamberto and Mileski were both sitting on the far bench in nothing but towels. She lit them both up, six shots, not a miss. Lamberto in the head, Marrone in the upper chest. Turned into the hallway here, hit Smith twice, putting him out of action. He survived, but two other men gave chase and were killed by her as she made her way out a back door. She got out, down the alley and away before anyone else got back here. A witness thought they heard a motorcycle roaring away in the distance through the neighborhood to the north, but nobody ever confirmed that."

Tori nodded. "The stack of towels, where did she get them?"

Bahn flipped through his notes. "I'm not sure."

"There was a laundry room just behind the kitchen for the restaurant," the owner noted. "It was the next room from the closet she'd stuffed the other woman in."

Tori found the laundry room and the closet. She mimicked picking up the towels and then walking the hallways with the stack in her hands, weaving her way to the steam room, getting lost twice and having to backtrack along the way. "If I remember right, you said he had men on guard throughout the place, right?"

"That was the word," Bahn said. "Mob guys don't exactly talk much and didn't after the shooting. But restaurant employees said there were. The two dead guys and the third one severely wounded certainly show that was the case."

"And this was two weeks after DeEsposito was killed. Thus, one could assume Lamberto had his guys securing him for those two weeks."

"Yeah, I suppose."

"And here?"

"That was the word. What are you thinking?"

"That it was highly unlikely that in that two weeks' time she was able to get back in here and scout."

"I agree. But you've read the file. She was very good at this."

"I've seen firsthand. But I don't care how good you are, you don't come in here and do this cold. It's a labyrinth back here. I got lost twice making my way to here from that towel closet. She had one chance at this. She couldn't be lost back here, not with all these men on alert for her. And how does she know about this woman and what she wore? She had to look and act like this woman employee people knew and trusted and wouldn't look twice at."

"What are you saying?"

"She'd been back here before. She knew who worked here, what they looked like and how to get to the steam room and then how to get the heck out. She wasn't on a suicide mission, just her last one," Tori said.

"Huh," Bahn said after a moment, nodding in agreement. "I'll buy that. She was prepared. Not sure, after all these years where that gets us."

"We can at least conclude she had some tie to someone who came here, perhaps often."

"DeEsposito?"

"Maybe. You would know better than me if he frequented the place and brought a woman along. Show me where he was killed."

"That would be Dudek's," Bahn said as he checked his watch. "I think we have time, at least for a quick look."

"Dudek's Polish Palace?" Tori said as Bahn pulled to a stop.

Bahn smiled. "It has a certain local neighborhood fame down here in south Chicago. It's been around forever. It was just plain Dudek's back in the days of Angelo DeEsposito. Back then it was mostly a bar that served a basic menu of burgers and pizza. It was a neighborhood hangout joint."

"DeEsposito was Italian."

"It was an Italian and Polish neighborhood. The owner before DeEsposito was Stan Dudek, as Polish as they come."

"Hence now Dudek's Polish Palace. It still has a kind of neighborhood look and feel to it," Tori said as she took in the refurbished exterior and peeked inside to see the open kitchen concept. "Albeit a little upscale."

"New owner. He's turned it into a bit of a foodie place with traditional polish dishes and whatnot."

"Have you eaten here?"

Bahn nodded. "Yeah. It's not bad. Now, I imagine what you

want to get a look at is where DeEsposito was killed," he said, waving Tori around to the back of the building, which sat on a corner. He handed her a photo. "This place is all windows and open concept now but back in the day it was your typical neighborhood joint, all brown brick and small glass block windows. You couldn't see out, nobody could see in." He turned a corner into the alley. "See this row of parking spaces? Angelo DeEsposito's Cadillac El Dorado was parked nose in. It was in his reserved spot."

Tori nodded. "No secret he was there then."

"Nope. Anyway, as was customary, he and his two men came out the back door around midnight. The bar was still open but there were just a few people inside. Angie gets into the car, as do his men and just as they're about to back out another car blocks them in, and another pulls up on the street. Two men get out and you can see the rest."

Tori held the picture of DeEsposito and his two guards, riddled with gunshot wounds.

"Two weeks later, you've seen what happened to Lamberto and Johnny Marrone."

"And this hit on DeEsposito took place at the same time as she made her hit in Cleveland."

"Yes."

Tori pondered the photos she was holding for a moment, thinking through the timeline. "Lamberto's guys knew who she was."

"You think so?"

"If they fear her as much as it sounds like, then they moved on DeEsposito and her all at once. I'll bet there were men waiting for her in Cleveland after she killed those three men. There is no way you'd want her to get back here and find out about this. That's what I'm thinking and seeing here. They retreated to that club because they knew she would come for them. They knew that because she was... close to DeEsposito.

They knew he meant enough to her that she would come back on them."

"You're assuming they tried to get her in Cleveland."

"That would have been a good place to do so. She kills those three men. They kill her. DeEsposito is killed here. The competition and his hired gun are wiped out in a single night. You never identified the men who shot DeEsposito, right?"

"No. For the most part, people heard this all go down. We only had one distant eyewitness from down the street who was out walking his dog. He couldn't see a license plate. He just saw the car, dark colored, pull up, two men jump out and fire at will. There was another car that pulled up behind DeEsposito and someone fired from there as well. It was all over in ten, fifteen seconds. Very quick and very bloody, Chicago style."

She held up another file. "Is this everything you have on DeEsposito? Full history. Family, financial, the works?"

"Yes."

Tori checked her watch. "Is there anyone who works here now, that was around back then?"

"Not sure," Bahn said. "I think the current owner has some history with the place. You want to talk to him?"

"I don't know that we have the time right now," Tori said, checking her watch. "Is there a history of this place in the file?"

"No. But I can have one done."

"If you would."

Bahn drove them back to the field office and Tori made a beeline for the airport, calling Braddock. "Hey, I might have figured a thing or two out today," she said excitedly, recapping what she'd deduced at Lamberto's old club.

"We had an interesting day too," Braddock explained what he and Steak had discovered about the vans. "Stevie Bianchi is driving the van right now. And he has a criminal record. Two prison stretches."

Tori saw where this was going. "You need someone on the other side of his deliveries."

"We're hashing that out. You on your way to pick Tracy up?"

"Yeah. It'll be a night on the town."

"Might be for Steak and I too. The only difference being we won't be drinking."

"Pity."

They talked for another five minutes before she hung up and pulled up into the arrival lane at O'Hare, looking to her right, searching for where to pull in when she saw the arm waving. She pulled to a stop and popped the rear tailgate.

"Hey, you!" Tracy Sheets called, rushing between cars, her roller suitcase behind her. She reached the Jeep Cherokee, shoved down the handle on her roller bag and tossed it in back. "It's so good to see you," she said, embracing Tori, squeezing her tight. "I've missed you."

"Thanks for coming."

"A weekend in Chicago. A little shopping, a little drinking and dining, and some investigating on a case I have absolutely zero responsibility for but sounds interesting as hell. I am so in."

"Then let's go."

* * *

"There he is," Steak said as Braddock snapped photos of a front door opening. A skinny man in a white T-shirt, blue jeans and sandals stepped onto the porch, picked up the whole lockbox and took it inside.

Steak's phone beeped. He looked at the message. "The homeowner is Justin Devers. Age twenty-six. Here's a photo."

"That's him."

"What do you want to do about him?"

"I think we see where he goes and what he does."

The radio burped with Nolan's voice reporting that Bianchi had driven to a warehouse east of Manchester Bay. "It's small. A black Escalade and a pickup truck are parked in front." She sent a cell phone photo. The warehouse was basically a pole barn with a panel roll-up door and then a cinderblock office space built to the right side.

"Nothing fancy," Braddock remarked.

"Who owns it?"

"Don't know. We'll have to find out but I'm betting it's Mileski or Marrone or one of their opaquely named companies."

Steak looked at its location on the map. "Hmpf."

"What?"

"It backs up to the Quarry."

"The Quarry?"

"It's right behind the warehouse."

"What's this Quarry? I can hear it in your voice."

"Ask Tori about it," Steak said with a big smile as he raised his own pair of binoculars to his eyes to scan the house. "Are you thinking about making a buy from this guy?"

"Maybe. I was thinking of making a call into the narcotics unit. See if this guy registers." He used his own binoculars to eye up the house. "What is it you and Tori would know about this quarry place?"

"The Quarry is what we called it. It's an old mine that's been inactive for, gosh, forty years, maybe more. It sits on the far western edge of the Cuyuna Iron Range. Back in the day it was where many of the youth of Manchester Bay drank their first cheap beer, had their first kiss, perhaps saw the opposite sex naked for the first time."

"Ahh," Braddock said, eyebrows raised. "And I should ask Tori why?"

"We partied out there as high school kids is all."

"What you're telling me is you saw Tori naked out there?"

Steak laughed. "What? You never went skinny-dipping in your youth?"

"I grew up on Long Island. Nothing but concrete, roads, and people."

"And an ocean."

"And public beaches. So how was it you went swimming out there?"

"There was a small mine lake out there we'd swim in. It was the summer spot," Steak explained. "For years we went out there. It was anything goes."

"And Big Jim and Cal Lund were okay with that?"

"I don't know that they were okay with it, but as long as things didn't get too out of hand, they both looked the other way. Kids needed to have their fun that they weren't yet legally entitled to have," Steak said. "But as luck would have it, someone did get hurt out there maybe eleven, twelve years ago and then the fun police stepped in. The county fully fenced it up. I'd heard someone looked at the land for a golf course, but nothing ever came of it."

"Who owns the land now?"

"Not sure. It's abandoned. Could be the mine company, the county, not sure."

"I see," Braddock said as he examined photos on the display screen and then looked back to the house. "You never answered my question."

"I didn't see Tori naked," Steak answered. "But I did see Jessie in the light of a full moon."

Braddock glanced over. "They were identical twin sisters."

"Then you're a very, very, *very*, lucky man," Steak replied playfully.

"In other words, she was there too."

"I can't recall."

"Right. As I understand it, those two never went anywhere without the other."

"We were sixteen-year-old kids figuring things out," Steak said. "Just having some fun. I can remember the night like it was yesterday. Jessie was the ringleader."

"Tori says she always was."

"And because of that I had a lot of fun as a kid, until that... one night," he said, letting out a long sigh. "I would never speak of this in front of Tori but from time to time I still wonder about what might have been had Jessie not been taken. How life would have been different."

"For you? For her?"

"For all of us. All of us here lost two of our best friends. Jessie was dead and Tori left and didn't come back. That had a profound impact on all of us. I mean, it's one of the reasons I became a cop."

"Yeah?" Braddock said. Steak had never told him this.

"I was kind of aimlessly going through college, trying to figure out what to do with my life. What happened to Jessie, to Tori, to their father, just always... stuck with me, but I didn't know what to do with all that. One night, I ran into Cal and he asked me what I was doing after college and I told him I didn't have a plan then. But we got to talking about all that happened with Jessie and Tori and their father. I told him how I felt about it all and he said we couldn't do anything about what happened to them, but that I could come to work for him, and we could stop it from happening to someone else. So, I graduated from college and came to work for Cal. What happened that night impacted Tori the most, of course, but the loss of Jessie hit all of us."

"She was your friend."

"She was more than that even," Steak said. "It's hard to explain, but Jessie had this gravitational pull that drew everyone to her, like she was the sun. And it wasn't that she was just the hottest girl in school either. Jessie was the singular leader of our class, of our friend group. She was the straw that stirred the drink. When she disappeared, when we all came to the realization that she was dead and gone, it was devastating. Cal gave me a chance to feel like I was doing something to make it right."

"You should tell Tori that."

"If she wanted to go down that road, I'd talk about it, but she's doing so good now the last thing I want to do is dredge all that up."

"She's doing pretty good with her history these days," Braddock said. "She's made her peace with what happened to Jessie, and her father. Wait... there's Devers. It looks like he's leaving." A red Jeep Wrangler Sahara backed out of the garage.

Steak started the engine and slowly pulled forward as the Jeep crossed in front of them a half-block ahead.

"Let's give him a follow."

"Will," Nolan called.

"Yeah."

"Reese and I are following Bianchi. He's in the Escalade now, driving back up to Cullen Crossing. Do we stay on him?"

"Follow him to the mall. Then join us."

"Where?"

"I'll tell you when we get there."

TWENTY-EIGHT

"VERY ON BRAND FOR CHICAGO."

They got Tracy checked into their downtown hotel, had two drinks in the bar, dressed, called for a car, and went to dinner at a small neighborhood restaurant just south of downtown that Bahn recommended.

"So how much work are we really doing?" Tracy finally asked after they were served their first dirty martini and ordered their dinner.

"Give me half the day tomorrow. I want to go look at a place where there was a Mob hit and talk to some people who work there. I'll go through it all tomorrow morning over breakfast. Bahn is supposed to get me a file of the history of the place, so we'll swing by, pick him and the file up and go to this place. After that, we go shopping, dinner, girl time."

"And after I leave?"

"I see where I'm at. My return ticket and hotel reservation are open ended. Could be a day, a week, we'll see."

"Ahh, you just wanted to see me," Tracy said, raising her glass.

"God, I needed to," Tori said. "We need to work on seeing each other more often. Zoom calls just aren't enough."

"Agreed. I want to hear all about Braddock, Quinn, life in the Yukon Territory."

"Ha. Ha. Very funny."

"But first, about this case."

"You want to do this now?"

"I don't get out in the field much these days. I'm a desk jockey. I'm geeked up for this. Tell me where things are at."

As they finished their first and then second drink, Tori walked Tracy through the last month, from three kids being killed in Holmstrand, to the call to the Airstream where they found Gresh, to the shootings a week ago and then the attempt on Alisha.

"And your job is to find this woman killer then?" Tracy said.

"Basically, yeah. We think she's living up somewhere near Manchester Bay."

"And while I've read the file a bit on her, you're going to tell me who she is, right?"

"I don't know."

"B.S. This is me you're talking to," Tracy said, before she gulped the last of her martini, seeing their waitress approaching. "You've got *some* inkling."

"I have what I would call a concept," Tori said as her sea bass arrived. Tracy ordered halibut and they both had shifted from martinis to white wine.

"And this concept?"

"Tomorrow."

"You're leaving me hanging here."

"You'll see. How is Sam?"

Tracy smiled. "Sam is good. He became a full equity partner in his firm."

"More money?"

"Yes. Before he was salary and bonus. Now, his book of business is such that they made him an equity partner so now he's on a draw and he gets a piece of the profit pie at the end of the year."

"He's making more then."

"Yes. It has us thinking."

"About?"

"A child. I'm nearly thirty-seven. My biological clock is ticking—loudly. When you called for this trip, this was my last little drink fest before..."

"You two get busy."

"If we can remember how. Speaking of getting busy. Braddock."

Tori laughed. "We just went on vacation. He and I and Quinn, and his brother-in-law's family. Six days in Costa Rica."

"And you had a good time, did you?"

Tori nodded, smiling. "We did."

"You went on a sexcation, didn't you!" Tracy said loudly, grinning ear to ear.

"Tracy!"

"Come on, you can tell me. I won't tell anyone."

"You just told the whole restaurant."

"Hey, throw me a bone here. Sam and I were laughing because we'll need to greatly increase our activity level if we're going to get me preggers," Tracy said, taking a long drink of wine. "Sounds like you two—"

"We definitely got our time together in," Tori said, shifting gears to safer terrain. "You're going to be a mother."

"I hope. What am I in for?"

"How would I know?"

Tracy looked at her. "Because you're one now."

"I am not a mom."

"Seriously? The way you talk about Quinn. His hockey games, how worried you were when he got hurt last fall, the funny stories about him and his little girlfriend. Maybe you don't carry the title of mom, but you're now clearly a big part of his life. You're helping Braddock raise him."

Tori sighed. "I suppose I am."

"And I see what it's done for you."

"Which is?"

"Relaxed you, big time," Tracy said. "Oh, I know the tiger lady is still there, I saw some of it on the video call the other day. That'll never change. But you're settled and happy. That's Braddock and Quinn. You have family now. It changes things. And this home expansion?"

"What about it?"

"Braddock is building you two a forever home."

"Trace, just stop."

"Come on, you've texted me about it repeatedly," Tracy said boisterously, going into HGTV mode. "A spacious master bedroom, cavernous walk-in closet, spa-like master bath, fireplace, new bedroom furniture. An additional fifteen hundred square feet of house out over the garage. On a gorgeous lake with a big boat!" She took a gulp of her wine, just getting warmed up. "And the person who never had a photo on her cell phone is on Insta now. You don't have a lot out there, but I've seen the photos that are, you and that hot little rock-hard body of yours in the skimpy two-piece swimsuits, the water skiing, tubing, floating, cocktailing. And the pictures of your mountain of a man all tall, dark and handsome."

"He is tall."

"I bet you climb him like a tree."

"Tracy! Shhh."

"I bet he picks you up and carries you all over that house!"

"Oh my God," Tori said, looking around, smiling but beet red. Tracy was a loud and happy drinker. She was on a roll.

"Pfft. Like you'll ever see any of these people again. My point is, you're happy and I couldn't be happier for you."

Tori nodded and took a long drink of wine and then exhaling, everyone around them having returned to their meals. "Sometimes I look back on the last two years and I can't believe what has happened. And how fast."

Tracy laughed. "I didn't see it coming either. I miss you, sister, you know I do. But it was worth seeing you go to see where you're at." A sly smile emerged. "The way I see it, the only thing you're missing is a big old diamond on that ring finger."

"Now, stop."

"Tell me you haven't thought about it."

"I haven't."

"You lie. To use one of your favorite phrases, you are a lying liar who lies, Tori Hunter."

Tori paused for a moment before shaking her head. "Honestly, I haven't... much. It's been a less than two-year whirlwind. My sister's case, Braddock, going to therapy, moving back, moving in, Quinn, now expanding the house. It's been a blur."

"I bet."

"It's like I've been on this wave carrying me and I'd just like some time to just sit back and enjoy it all." Tori sat back and exhaled a breath, taking a drink of her wine. "You're right. I'm happy, Trace. I have a life now, a good one. I'm content. I want nothing more right now other than a couple of days with my bestie."

"Cheers to that."

The two of them clinked their wine glasses. Tori decided to change the topic. "Now, since you're so interested in the case, I have an idea for where we could go for a couple of post-dinner cocktails."

* * *

Braddock and Steak teamed with Nolan and Reese for the next several hours as Devers made stops around the county, eventually making his way to Manchester Bay and working his way around the college campus, making stops and what they thought were sales.

Devers was no amateur. In many cases, he went inside apartments or houses to make what they suspected were in-person sales. They had also observed and photographed what looked to be several sales inside his Jeep. Braddock snapped plenty of photos of Devers and the buyer inside the Jeep. The problem was they didn't have a photo of drugs and cash being exchanged. It was all done out of view.

"Do we have enough to work him?" Steak asked, knowing the answer.

"Only if he's really dumb," Braddock replied as Devers turned left down his street and a moment later, pulled his Jeep Wrangler into his garage. "While being a drug dealer is dumb, how he operates his business is not. He's careful. I'd bet his customers are regular and my guess is they only come on some sort of referral. That way he's selling to people he trusts."

"He's made a lot of sales tonight it seems."

Braddock nodded. "It has me thinking."

"About?"

"What Wilcox said about the cut of the sales Mileski and Marrone take. It's a big chunk meaning if he wants to make money, he has to hustle. He has to build his clientele and make the sales."

"What do you want to do?"

"Sleep on it. Then go see Boe in the morning."

* * *

It was after 11:00 p.m. when Tori and Tracy got out of their Uber and arrived at Dudek's Polish Palace.

"Welcome," a man greeted as Tori and Tracy stepped

inside. "Are you dining? Our kitchen is still open though not for long."

"I think just drinks," Tori said, gazing around the open concept interior.

"There is room at the end of the bar. Cordelia will take care of you," the man said as he walked them in that direction and gestured to the bartender, who was finishing mixing a drink. He headed through the double door into the kitchen.

"This is the place, huh?" Tracy asked as she slid onto the stool.

"This is it."

The evening dinner rush had long since passed. Of the twenty or so tables and booths, but a handful still had diners. There were a few groups of two and four at the bar, but they largely had the far end of the bar to themselves.

"It didn't look like this twelve years ago. It was very much a dive. Now it's more a foodie place specializing in Polish dishes, or so Bahn says."

There was a menu on the bar and Tracy perused it when Cordelia strolled over. "Evening, ladies. Can I get you two a drink?"

"Grey Goose Martini, extremely dirty," Tracy said, still examining the menu.

"Now we're talking," Cordelia said with a raised eyebrow. "And you?"

"Better make it two," Tori replied and then glanced to Tracy who she could tell was very happily buzzed. "You're really going out with a bang, aren't you?"

"I'm just checking to see if you can still hold your liquor."

"That part of my game remains in mid-season form. Winters are long in the Yukon Territory."

"You ever going to invite me out there?"

"Come out this summer," Tori replied instantly. "Pick a week in July or August and come out. No better time to be away from New York City than then. Spend a week with us on the lake."

"Yeah?"

"Heck, yeah. The contractor says the remodel will be done by the Fourth of July. Come out sometime after."

Cordelia was back with their drinks. "Here you go, ladies."

"Cordelia," Tracy started. "Are you from around here?"

"Chicago? Yeah."

"This neighborhood?"

The bartender smiled. "How would you know that?"

"How you say 'that.' It sounds like 'dat'," Tracy replied, before taking a drink of her martini.

"I guess I'm from around here like you're from... I'm guessing New York, maybe Boston, but I think New York, the way you're dropping your 'r's."

"It really comes out when she drinks," Tori said.

"And you're not Chicago, but Midwest for sure," Cordelia observed of Tori. "Iowa, Wisconsin maybe."

"Minnesota."

"See I didn't hear the *ya* out of you."

"*Fargo*," Tori said smiling. "That damn movie labeled us all forever."

"So, what is this? Minnesota and New York. A girls' weekend?"

"Something like that," Tracy replied, taking a quick sip of her martini. "The reason I ask is that you wouldn't know it to look at me, but I'm a history buff. I love learning the history of places I travel to, and I understand this place has some interesting history."

The bartender smiled. "It does, back in a different era."

"Tell me about it."

Cordelia leaned in. "This was a Mob place back in the day."

"How so?"

"A Mob guy named DeEsposito operated out of here for years."

Tori smiled. Cordelia was happy to tell stories. That was good.

"Now, I heard he was gunned down out back, is that right? At least that's what a bartender down at Krazicky's told us an hour ago." Tracy was pulling out all the stops. They drove by Krazicky's on the way down. They didn't stop there.

"Yeah, I wasn't working here then. I was downtown but Angie, that was what everyone called him, was gunned down out back. St. Valentine's Day Al Capone-type stuff. Very on brand for Chicago."

"Any photos of that around here," Tracy asked, noting the numerous black-and-white pictures mounted on the walls.

"No," Cordelia replied. Instead, she pointed to a black-and-white photo on the wall to their left. "That's DeEsposito right there, sitting at the table. Cigar in the finger."

"Who are the others in the photo?"

"Is this a test?"

"I'm grading," Tracy said, reaching for a pen on the bar and flipping over a napkin. "I'll note in my Yelp review how knowledgeable the bartender is."

"You're a hoot. It's not too hard actually," Cordelia said, moving to the photo. "Standing on the left is Jeff Tomassoni. He owns the place now but worked here back when he was in high school and college, bartending, fry cooking in the back. He got his start in the industry that way. I'm not sure of the other woman standing next to him. The man sitting next to DeEsposito is Stan Dudek. He owned the place until he was killed in a shooting in the alley out back."

"Two shootings?" Tori asked.

"That's right," Cordelia said. "The old story is Stan was mistaken for Angie. They looked a lot alike. It was a Mob hit, and the shooters mistook Dudek for DeEsposito, or so the story goes."

"Rough neighborhood," Tracy noted. "Kinda like the stories my pops used to tell me about New York back in the day."

"It was seedy back then, for sure. Much better now," Cordelia said. "Anyway, behind Stan, the one on the left was his daughter, she hung around here when her dad was alive, and then the other, the blonde, is Anna Symanski. She works here now again too."

"Is Anna here tonight?"

"She was."

"I see. What's this place like on weekends?" Tracy asked. "I kind of like it. Tori, maybe we should come back tomorrow."

"I was thinking the same thing."

"We're open for breakfast," Cordelia responded. "The way you two are going tonight, you might need Hair of the Dog. Great Bloody Mary's for brunch. Heck of a way to start your day."

"I like it, you know the history of the place and you're selling. Now, to seal the five-star rating on Yelp, how about an order of perogies?"

Tori snapped Tracy a look.

"What? I'm hungry."

"Coming right up."

Cordelia went off to place the order.

"Well done, Special Agent Sheets."

"I still got game," Tracy replied. "And now, you know even more about this place."

TWENTY-NINE

"THERE IS A REASON PLASTIC SURGEONS NOW HAVE REALITY TELEVISION SHOWS."

Bahn and another special agent picked them up at 9:00 a.m. and they drove back to Dudek's Polish Palace. Tori brought him up to speed along the way of what they found out last night.

"A bit surreptitious of you two."

"I don't know that we intended it but it turned out that way."

"And hey, the perogies were outstanding," Tracy said.

"The owner will be waiting for us," Bahn said. "He has another employee who has been there for years who will join. In the meantime—" he handed back a folder "—here is the history of the place you asked for."

Tori opened the folder while Tracy leaned in for a peek as well.

The owner Jeff Tommasoni greeted them at the door and immediately recognized Tori and Tracy. "Last night, right?"

Tori smiled. "We just thought we'd come down and check it out. Special Agent Bahn and I walked the exterior yesterday as well."

"Cordelia was terrific by the way," Tracy noted, waving to her as she walked over.

"She should be good, being my girlfriend and all," Tomma-soni quipped, throwing his arm around her. Another woman strolled into the room. "This is Anna Symanski. Anna worked here for years when Stan and then Angie DeEsposito owned the place. She's back with us now after a long stint downtown."

Breakfast ordered, they let Tommasoni talk about the history of the bar.

"Twenty years ago, Stan Dudek owned this place, but it was always touch and go if he could keep it open. I worked here for peanuts while I was in culinary school. So did Anna."

Anna laughed. "Stan paid us cash half the time. Pulled it out of his pocket."

"The area was rough and tough. Angie DeEsposito was the king of the neighborhood. He and Stan were good friends, grew up together, they looked a bit like brothers."

"To help Stan, Angie started operating out of here. That brought paying customers in here. Were they reputable? Eh. But it kept the place open, and Stan looked after us. Then one night eighteen years ago after bar close, Stan walks out the back door with two of Angie's guys and boom."

"There were no witnesses but word on the street is the hit came from Ed Kranz. He ran the west side crew at the time. He was trying to take out DeEsposito but mistook him for Stan," Bahn explained, his file open in front of him.

"And then did DeEsposito buy the bar?" Tracy asked.

"Yes," Tommasoni said.

"From whom, if Stan was dead?"

"Stan had a daughter," Symanski explained. "She was a friend, behind me by a year in high school. She inherited the place after Stan's death. Angie bought the bar, and it left her with some money. Angie kept us all on the payroll."

"And he ran it pretty legit and took care of us," Tommasoni said.

"And lulled everyone to sleep," Bahn said. "He didn't immediately retaliate on Kranz. But it's about six months later that our woman killer makes her first appearance."

"Jeff or Anna, you know anything about any woman who might have hung around Angie?" Tori asked.

"Woman?"

"There is a woman killer that the Bureau thinks worked for or was contracted out by DeEsposito," Tracy said. "She retaliated on the men who tried to kill DeEsposito, when they killed Dudek by mistake. And she retaliated for DeEsposito. So we can assume they were close."

"What did she look like?" Symanski asked.

"Reports are sketchy, but she was described as tall, thin, wearing all black, usually leather, and high heels or boots. One report referenced long dark hair, but that could have been a wig, nobody really knows for sure. She killed this Kranz fellow and two of his men, took them in an alley six months after Dudek's murder out back. In total, she killed nineteen people between Kranz and then Philly Lamberto and Johnny Marrone six years later. Then she disappeared."

"We think she worked for DeEsposito," Tori interjected. "She went quiet for a long time but now it looks like she's active where I live up in northern Minnesota. There was a witness who saw a tall woman wearing a mask with long legs, a black leather outfit, combat boots, enter a house where two other men were killed. In all, she's killed five people in the last few weeks."

"Why?" Symanski asked.

"There was recently a drive-by shooting in the small town of Holmstrand and after that she emerged. We think it's possible she lives up there now and something about the shooting triggered her to act," Tori said, not giving all the information on Mileski and Marrone. "We need to find her. DeEsposito ran this place. She first surfaced six months after the murder of Stan Dudek. We wondered if maybe she hung around here, maybe even worked here."

"I can't think of anyone Angie hired who fits that description," Tommasoni said and then looked to Symanski. "You?"

"No. Not that worked here that I remember. I mean, what Angie did away from here, we wouldn't know anything about that."

"Take work out of it. How about someone who came to see DeEsposito? A frequent visitor. A girlfriend maybe?"

Tommasoni smiled. "Ms. Hunter, this place is in an ethnic Italian and Polish neighborhood. There were women with black hair in here all the time seeing Angie or the guys who worked for him. I knew who Angie was and what he did and what the people hanging around the bar back then did. We all did. It wasn't a secret by any means, but I wasn't about to start poking around his business, you know. Ask the wrong question or see or hear the wrong thing and you could get into trouble."

"How about Stan Dudek? Anyone visit him that looked like that?"

"That's like eighteen, twenty years ago. That's ancient history," Tommasoni replied. "I can barely remember last week sometimes."

"It was definitely a long time ago," Tori replied. "Still, you didn't answer my question, Mr. Tommasoni."

"The same people were in here operating when Stan owned the place as when Angie did. Same crowd of people."

"You said DeEsposito bought this place from Dudek's daughter. What was her name?"

"Marta, I think," Tommasoni replied.

"Marta," Tori said, taking a note. "Did she know DeEsposito well?"

"I'd assume so," Tommasoni replied.

"You assume?"

"Well, yeah. I didn't know her really, but her dad Stan and Angie were very close friends. Then Angie bought the bar off her when her dad died. So, I just figure she knew him well. What about you, Anna?"

"I knew Marta from school mostly," Symanski replied. "I wouldn't say we were close friends, but we were certainly friendly with each other, but I don't know how close she was to Angie. After her father was murdered, she didn't come back around here very often."

"That's understandable," Tori said. "Do we have a photo of Marta Dudek?"

"Umm, I don't right now," Bahn said, flipping through the file.

"There's the one on the wall I showed you last night," Cordelia said. She retrieved the photo. Marta was standing behind her father and DeEsposito, as were Anna and Tommasoni. "That was taken maybe a year before Stan was killed."

Tori took a longer look at the photo. Marta had a pronounced nose but otherwise thin features and a longish neck. "Was Marta tall?"

"Pretty tall," Symanski said. "I'm five-six and she was two, maybe three inches taller than me and rail thin."

Tori looked over to Bahn. "Let's track her down. Maybe she knows a thing or two."

"I'll look her up."

* * *

Braddock was up early. He threw Quinn's hockey gear into his pickup truck, picked him up at his grandparents' and took him to breakfast at the Wavy Café in town, the two of them enjoying a leisurely breakfast, father and son catching up on the week that was. There was still a full day of work ahead, but he needed some face time with his boy.

"When do you think your case will be over?" Quinn asked as he devoured his loaded omelet.

Braddock took a moment. Sensitive to how much time he'd been away, he didn't want to overpromise and under deliver. At the same time, he felt there was some momentum. "I think I'll know more on that in a couple of days," he said. "I think we're getting somewhere."

Quinn's eyes raised. The son of a detective, he knew the tone. "You catch a break?"

"Maybe," Braddock hedged. "Like I said, we'll see if it pans out."

"Is Tori having fun in Chicago?"

Braddock smiled. "Based on the text I got earlier this morning, I'd say she did have some fun. She has a friend from New York there with her."

"Ah, Tracy."

"You know about Tracy Sheets?"

Quinn looked up with raised eyebrows. "Dad, Tori tells me about her friends. She said to me that if she had to name a best friend, it was Special Agent Sheets."

"That she is."

"I'd like to meet her in person. She sounds cool."

"You just might. Tori extended the invite for her and her husband to visit this summer."

"Sweet! I'd like to hear some old Tori stories from when they worked together. You know there has to be a doozy or two."

Braddock chuckled at his son's humorous insight. Quinn was twelve, but wise and mature beyond his years. His wisdom came in part from being the son of a detective. He was far more observant than most kids his age. The maturity came from some accelerated growing up with a single dad with a demanding job. It led to stretches of living with his grandparents and aunt and uncle. That Tori was living with them now had allowed for a little more stability and provided another adult in the house to lean on and confide in. That he and Tori had bonded the way they had was a comfort to him.

. . .

After Quinn's cousin and uncle swung by to pick him up, Braddock drove over to the government center and met with Boe, Steak joining them. They brought her up to speed on their investigation from Justin Wilcox's tip, to Bianchi, the lockbox and then following Devers last night.

"You don't have it yet, do you?" Boe said. "At least to move on Devers or Bianchi but damn if you're not on it."

"And we're staying on it. I have eyes on Devers and Bianchi as we speak."

"Tell me how you got on it."

Braddock and Steak shared a quick look.

Boe saw the look. She stood up and walked around to the front of her desk and leaned against it in front of Braddock. "I've given you free rein to run this thing but it's costing a shit ton in overtime. I'm going to get questions about that. If I'm going to defend it, I need to have confidence it's defendable. Where are you getting this information on Mileski and Marrone? The gambling, the drugs, this Wilcox as a source. Who's funneling this to you?"

Braddock turned to Steak. "I think she's earned it."

Steak nodded. "Agreed."

"Earned what?" Boe demanded.

"Our trust. The source is Ryan Jones. He owns The Outskirts."

"That bar just outside of town?"

"He's also a bookie and whatever else he might be into."

"The Outskirts is a tough place," Boe noted.

"It is," Steak said. "It draws a rougher crowd that he and his crew keep under control, but his clientele might fracture the occasional law in or out of the bar."

"Or *he* does. Bookmaker?"

"We look the other way on that, and he tells us things from

time to time that he hears that he figures we might want to know about."

"I assume not on the record, though."

"Nope," Braddock said. "He points in a direction. It's not like we talk all the time but when we do, his tips are generally legit. That break-in crew late last fall we caught, you remember? It was just before you started?"

"Three-man crew, going into the lake houses of the wealthy out of staters? That was him?"

"He heard a few things that pointed us toward the fence."

"A cop is only as good as their informants," Boe said. "After last night, what's next?"

"Devers. I have an idea. We'll need some cash."

* * *

"We can't locate Marta Dudek," Bahn said to Tori and Tracy when he came back into his office.

"What do you mean?"

"It's like she doesn't exist anymore. Marta Dudek had an address, a driver's license, and a passport until twelve years ago." He handed her a copy of Marta Dudek's full driver's license. "We find no record of her anywhere and we're pretty good at that sort of thing. Her last address was Evanston, Illinois. But she never renewed her license, passport, anything the next time they were up after the DeEsposito hit and Lamberto and Johnny Marrone were killed."

Tori looked to Tracy.

"Five foot nine," Tracy murmured. "One hundred twenty-five pounds. She was modelish thin. Put a five-foot nine woman in combat boots or stiletto heels walking down an alley and she'd look awfully tall. And while her hair looks shoulder length and straight in this photo..."

"It could have been longer."

"Or she could pin it up tight and wear a wig."

Tori looked to Bahn. "Marta Dudek is your killer. Tall, thin, dark features. She has motive after her father was murdered behind his own bar. Six years later, DeEsposito, maybe a father figure, maybe her business partner, perhaps a bit of both, gets killed outside this same bar. The Mob has now killed her father, and maybe father figure. What does she do? She takes out Lamberto and Johnny Marrone and disappears."

"To northern Minnesota?"

"With a new identity and a new look," Tori said. "There is a reason plastic surgeons now have reality television shows. Because they can transform faces. I bet she had work done on that nose. Throw in blond or red hair and that's transformative. At five-foot nine and one hundred twenty-five pounds, she was rail thin. What can you add to that body to add some weight and curve?"

"Breasts," Tracy said.

Tori looked to Bahn. "Now you know who she is."

"We think."

Tori glared at him.

"Okay it's her."

"We need to find her," Tori said. "Before they do."

"You think they know who she is?"

"It's why she disappeared," Tracy surmised.

"My educated guess here is that she pulls the job in Cleveland where she unknowingly kills an FBI agent," Tori said, now standing and pacing the room. "After, she gets word DeEsposito was murdered. She's immediately on alert. She sees the move on her coming either in Cleveland or when she returns. She gets to Lamberto disguised as the worker in the club because she might have otherwise been recognized. The redhead made sense for her to use because she was not only tall, but the red hair was big and wavy and hid her face just enough. And think about it. Marta was around her father and DeEsposito for years.

I bet she was in that club Lamberto used more than once so she had knowledge of the interior layout."

Bahn looked to Tori. "You think she's still up there?"

"Yes. She lives up there and based on what she has said to me—"

"You've talked to her?" Bahn asked, surprised.

"She's called me a couple of times with burner phones. My sense, though, is she is living up there and not alone."

"Family?"

"She definitely has someone there and I don't think she wants to give them up. She's been urging us to move on Mileski and Marrone."

"Because if you don't..."

"She will. Braddock and his team are working Mileski and Marrone, but it takes time. I'm looking for her. Now I have a better idea of what to look for. But they'll be looking for her too. It's a race."

"But if they're looking and you're looking, how can she stay?"

Tori smiled. "Well, I suppose it all depends on how different she looks and how well she's covered her tracks." She reached inside her coat pocket for her phone. It was Braddock. "I have news."

"So do I."

THIRTY

"BEHIND ENEMY LINES."

Steak peered at the dashboard. 10:52 p.m. "How much longer you want to give it?"

"Until he goes home."

They were down the street from the Monarch, a popular college bar. Their lead was in his Wrangler and had made one sale and now, there was another kid coming out who got into the passenger seat. Once again, the transaction was handled slickly.

"We could just pull him over," Steak suggested.

"For what?"

"We could make some shit up."

"Patience."

"Yeah, yeah. I just want a beer of my own is all. I've had about enough of this case."

Devers pulled forward and motored down the hill from the campus back toward town. However, he didn't take the H-4 north as they'd anticipated. Instead, he took the loop around the south of Manchester Bay on Highway 210, past the town and cruised west.

Braddock looked to Steak. "He wouldn't go there, would he?"

"Where do all the miscreants go to hang out?"

Devers turned right onto the narrow country road and a half-mile later turned right into the gravel parking lot for The Outskirts. Steak eased back, slowly passed the bar and observed as Devers got out of his Jeep. Reese reported from behind that he and Nolan were pulling into the parking lot.

"You know how Jones feels about drug dealing in his bar," Steak noted.

"I know what he said but was that just for our consumption or did he really mean it? I doubt he really thinks such transactions never take place inside his bar. Certainly, it happens outside."

Steak pulled out his phone and made the call. Jones didn't pick up the first time. Steak tried again. Jones finally answered on the fourth ring. "It's awfully late for you to be calling."

"Braddock and I are coming in."

"I'm awfully busy."

"You want to make time," Steak pressed. "Where can we talk out of sight of your patrons?"

Five minutes later they walked in the back door of the bar and Jones met them in a small side room off the kitchen.

"What the fuck?"

From the side room they were able to look through a door crack to the bar. "At the far end of the bar. The guy sitting alone, black hoodie, jean jacket, messy hair. You know him?"

"Yeah, name is Justin if I recall. Justin Devers. He's a carpenter, I think."

"Not tonight." Braddock tied him to what Wilcox told him. "We have an idea if you're willing to help us—"

"Set him up?" Jones finished. "How does this shit come back on me?"

"If things go according to plan, it doesn't."

"If?"

"Has anything you've ever done with us come back on you?" Steak asserted. "Come on. Have a little faith."

"We have a plan," Braddock said. "Will you help?"

Jones reluctantly nodded. "What do you need me to do?"

"Which bartender do you trust the most?"

* * *

Devers finished off his tap beer and then held up his mug and caught Tony's eye. The big man sauntered over, grabbed a new handled mug, spun it in his fingers and poured him a new one. As he slid it to him on the bar, Tony leaned in. "I've got a friend looking for a pick me up. Can you help her out?"

Devers took a drink of his beer and slowly nodded.

Tony turned his head and looked back across the bar to a woman in a hoodie and baseball cap, hunched over, rocking on the balls of her feet, fidgety.

"Now you know Jonesy doesn't go for anything in here."

"I'll take her out back to the Jeep. Save my seat."

"I got you."

* * *

Nolan watched as the large bartender casually made his way to the end of the bar, poured another tap beer for Devers and then leaned in. They talked for a moment then Devers nodded lightly. The bartender looked back in her direction and Devers' eyes shifted to her. He took a sip of his beer and then pushed off his stool before walking in her direction and tipping his head to the back door.

"Tony says you need something," Devers said, when they exited the bar and walked out to the parking lot.

"Yeah, I ne-ne-need to take the edge off."

* * *

Maggie sat up in bed, Rob to her right asleep, snoring lightly. He'd drifted off a couple of hours ago after *Weekend Update* on SNL. A night owl, she let him sleep while she channel surfed for a movie and stumbled across an old favorite, *Grosse Point Blank*. Perhaps because it struck a little too close to home, she always got sucked in. Martin Blank, an assassin burned out by his profession returning home to his ten-year high school reunion to reclaim his high school sweetheart. Would Rob have understood if she told him the truth? What would he think? Unlike a movie, she could never tell him. She reached for the remote on the nightstand when a text popped on her screen. It was an alert that she had a message, on her other cell phone.

She snapped her head to the right to check on Rob. Gingerly, she raised the down comforter and slipped out of bed, down the hallway past the kids' rooms and downstairs to the salon. The text message was brief: *Call me!*

She hit the preset number. There was an answer right away. "Hey."

"The FBI and a sheriff's detective from up your way have been down here poking around, asking questions about you the last couple of days."

"Was one Tori Hunter?"

"Yes. The FBI was with her. One of the last things she said today was she wanted to find Marta Dudek to talk with her. Well, they're not going to find Marta Dudek, are they?"

Her heart thudded. "And when they don't find her... they'll know it was me."

* * *

Devers hit the garage door opener and pulled inside. He reached behind his seat for his satchel and got out of his Jeep.

He hit the garage button at the side door, stepped outside and walked to the back door.

"Don't move."

He spun around.

The white light was blinding.

"Stand still," Steak called, not yelling, his gun in his hands crossed with his flashlight.

"What the—"

"Sheriff's Department," Braddock said calmly and not too loudly, his right hand on his gun handle, the flashlight blinding Devers sight.

"What's this all about?"

"It's about the twenty or so drug felonies we watched you commit the last two nights," Braddock replied and held up two small vials of cocaine in an evidence bag. He reached for the satchel Devers was carrying and looked inside. "What do you know," he said as he held up the same kind of vials.

"That's not good," Steak said as he quickly frisked Devers.

"You could have gotten those from anywhere," Devers asserted.

"I have a camera full of photos from the last two nights of you dealing from here to Manchester Bay," Braddock said flatly, fudging the truth some.

"Hmpf," Devers shook his head. "You guys with the narcotics unit?"

"No, we're investigating homicides," Braddock said. "And believe it or not, that's really good news for you."

"What do you guys want?"

"Would you believe to help you," Steak said.

* * *

"One more?"

"Yes," said a very tipsy Tracy, smiling, her eyes happy slits as the clock over the bar neared 2:00 a.m. "Let's do a lemon drop."

"You do love your martinis," Tori said, holding up her glass to get the bartender's attention.

"Martinis are our thing," Tracy replied, leaning her head on Tori's shoulder. "Always was."

"I hear that." She ordered the lemon drops and then handed her credit card to the bartender to close them out. Her phone buzzed.

"Is it Braddock?"

"Yes."

"Booty call!"

"Ha!" Tori laughed. "I'd be more than willing, but there are logistical issues."

"Phone sex then. Do you two need a minute?"

"Just stop," Tori retorted, lifting Tracy's head off her shoulder. She answered the call. "You're up late."

"As are you."

"I'm with Tracy. My girl is a big old sloppy mess again."

"I resemble that remark," Tracy muttered with a laugh. "Hi, Braddock!"

Braddock laughed. "Okay, she's a puddle."

"Yeah, I'll be tucking her into bed shortly," Tori said. "What's up?"

"It's been an interesting night. Get on the first flight you can back tomorrow."

* * *

Vince walked down the back hallway of the mall, checking the doors to make sure they were all locked until he reached the bar. It was late, just a few patrons remained in the bar as closing time approached. He'd been around enough days now to recognize them all as locals of Cullen Crossing who came to the bar nightly to catch up with their neighbors.

He stepped behind the corner of the bar. The bartender turned to see him and nodded as Vince poured himself a small whiskey. As he took a drink, his phone buzzed. It was the boss.

"You need to get down to the Twin Cities. You're booked first thing on a flight back down here," Bobby Mileski ordered.

"Why?"

"Marta."

"Is she down there?"

"No. But I've found someone who may know where she is."

THIRTY-ONE

"THAT'S A LOTTA G'S."

It had been a late fun night and now it was a very early morning and they both were feeling it. Sunglasses, large coffees, raspy voices.

"Our voices. We sound like two pack a day smokers," Tori said with her tired, gravelly voice as they walked through the airport.

"My head is so killing me," Tracy muttered, her hair in a ponytail pulled through a baseball cap, moving slowly. She took a long drink of her tall coffee, followed by a long swig of water.

"I think you tried to drink Chicago out of vodka."

"I set ambitious goals," she said, when they reached her gate. She stopped and hugged Tori, kissing her on the cheek. "I love you, girl."

"Right back at you," Tori said. "Now, you and Sam pick a week after the Fourth of July to come out and visit. We'll have a ball."

"You can count on it," Tracy replied and hugged her one last time, holding it an extra second, giving Tori an extra squeeze. She pulled back and looked Tori in the eye. "Do be careful. Marta Dudek is no joke, nor is the Chicago Mob."

"I'm always careful."

"Yeah, right. I noticed a couple of those careful scratches on your body when we went to the spa yesterday afternoon. Just—"

"I know."

Tracy turned with her roller and disappeared down the jetway. Fifteen minutes later, Tori was buckling her seatbelt and took out the bottle of water from her bag. She took four aspirins and a long swig of water, then sat back and closed her eyes.

In the midday cool overcast, Tori walked down the narrow alley, a baseball cap pulled down low and then hustled to the back door of the house where Braddock let her in.

"Hi," he said, hugging her. "Missed you," he whispered in her ear.

"You two are so cute," Steak chirped.

"Don't make me kick your ass," Tori replied, her eyes shifting menacingly to him. "What's going on here?"

"The wait."

"On Bianchi?" Tori asked as she walked into the front of the house. A man was sitting on the couch, a pensive expression on his face as his eyes shifted between the window and the people in his house. "You must be Justin Devers."

The man nodded.

Tori stepped to the window to the left side of the front door, peered around the curtain and saw the lockbox on the step.

"We anticipate he'll be by sometime this afternoon," Braddock said and nodded for her to follow him down the house's hallway. In a back bedroom, the shades pulled, the curtains drawn, basic blackout conditions, there was a folding table where Steak had a laptop and two monitors set up. There was a camera set to the left of the front door showing the stoop with the lockbox. Another camera was focused on the street and the sidewalk to the front door.

"Check this out," Steak said as he moved the mouse on the laptop and pulled up another file and opened a photo. "That right there is the cash before Justin put it in the delivery envelope."

"That's a lotta g's," Tori mused.

"Indeed."

"I assume we're tailing Bianchi?"

"Frewer and another," Steak said. "He's still at the warehouse."

They waited much of the afternoon. Justin anxiously paced nonstop around the house, fidgety, downing repeated Diet Cokes, while Steak watched over the computer monitors. Braddock watched the monitors too, making sure everything was covered. Tori retreated to a quiet corner and napped for a couple of hours; the last few days having taken their toll. After 2:00 p.m. she woke. "Anything happening at the strip mall in Cullen Crossing?" she asked through half-opened eyes, yawning and stretching.

"Quiet for now," Braddock said. "It's Sunday. One guy we've only gotten occasional glimpses of as we've been watching the strip mall was up and on the road early this morning. He was alone. We didn't follow him."

"Has he returned?"

"No, not yet."

"Hmpf. Interesting," she murmured. "What did he look like? The guy?"

"Uh, blond or blondish."

Tori snorted and pulled a file out of her backpack and took out a photo, "This guy?"

Braddock examined the photo for a moment, "Maybe. Hard to say for sure. Who is he?"

"Vince Smith. He was the survivor of the Philly Lamberto hit. We should keep an eye on him going forward."

The radio crackled just before 4:00 p.m. "Will, he's coming into Pine River now," Frewer's voice squawked.

All of them huddled around the computer and watched as the van parked on the street, just past the front sidewalk. Bianchi was out of the van, a ring of keys in his hand, wearing a black front-zip full-body uniform and baseball hat.

He got to the lockbox, used a key, and opened it and extracted the three delivery envelopes inside, stuffed them under his left arm, locked the box and walked back to the van, opening one of the rear doors and stepping inside.

"He's got a locked cabinet in the back of the van," Frewer reported over the radio. "I saw it on the last pickup."

Bianchi stepped back out of the rear, closed the doors and was on his way. Five minutes later Frewer reported that Bianchi was heading east.

"There might be one more stop over by Crosslake," Steak said. "Then we think he'll stop at the strip mall to drop off the cash before returning to the warehouse."

"And tomorrow?"

"He should deliver," Justin said.

* * *

"See ya, Jeff."

"Night, Anna. See you tomorrow," he said as he started shutting off the lights in the bar and restaurant areas of Dudek's Polish Palace, everything cleaned and ready for tomorrow. He went back to his office and took one last look at the day's final numbers and then shut down his computer and turned off his office light. At the rear door he set the alarm before stepping outside and locking the back door.

Thud!

The blow to his neck crumpled him to the ground. Then came another one.

Blackness.

* * *

Vince pulled on his leather gloves, secured his face mask, picked up the basic wood chair and set it down in front of Tommasoni and sat down.

"Jeff? Jeff?" He leaned forward and lightly patted his face. "Wake up, Jeff."

Tommasoni stirred awake. He was secured to a chair, his ankles taped to the legs, his arms secured to the chair's armrests, duct tape over his mouth. When his eyes fully opened and focused, his head snapped upright, his eyes wide in terror, his breathing through his nose no doubt matching the racing of his heart. He instinctually pulled against his restraints but there was no give. His eyes frantically searched his surroundings but all he could see was a masked man and the bright light hanging overhead.

Vince leaned forward and yanked away the tape.

"Who? Who? Who are you?"

"Wrong question, Jeff."

Jeff Tommasoni took in rapid-fire breaths. "What? What? What do you mean? What do you want with me?"

"Now, Jeff. I think we both know what I want."

"No, I don't—"

Vince burst out of his chair and slapped Jeff across the face.

"Oh..." Jeff groaned, grimacing, his eyes closed. "Somebody, help me! *Help me!*"

"Nobody can hear you down here," Vince said, standing

slowly back further and further, feeling the stretch of the tendons, them pulling away from the bone.

"Ahrg," Jeff grimaced. "No, no, no..."

"I can break it, easily," he said, the finger bent back well past ninety degrees, applying more pressure, leaning forward. "And then another one. And then another one."

"I don't know where, at least... exactly."

He brought the finger back down, although with the damage it hung up above his others.

"Ahh... jeezus... dammit..."

"What do you know?"

"She called me and asked for a license plate check," Jeff said, panting. "It was a month or so ago. It was after some shooting. I looked it up on the news. I can't remember the name of the town. Holmes or something like that."

"And who was it for?"

"I just gave her the name."

"Who was it?"

"It was for a plate that came from a car that was supposed to have been destroyed."

"Destroyed where?" He lifted the index finger and started to push it back. "Jeff," he warned.

Jeff gritted his teeth. "Fuck!"

"Where?"

"Petrovic Salvage. It was for a car sent there to be compacted, destroyed. Petrovic's brother-in-law was Ernie Rudick. He's living up in northern Minnesota. All I know is she said she lived like five miles away from where he did."

Vince did some quick math in his head. That would put her in either Manchester Bay or Holmstrand.

"Why did she want the plate?"

"She didn't say," Jeff grunted, breathing heavily.

He reached for his left index finger and started pushing it back. "I can do this all night."

with his hands on his hips, peering around. "Call for help a you want, there is no help coming. You want to help yoursel You want to walk out of here? Tell me what I want to know."

Jeff took in deep breaths, trying to regulate his breathing.

"Marta Dudek," Vince said. "Where is she?"

"I don't know."

"Wrong answer!" he yelled as he punched him in th stomach.

"Oh... hooo... eh..."

"I'm wearing a mask, Jeff, what does that tell you, huh? don't want to hurt you. I want you to walk out of here." Vin pulled his chair back and sat down.

Jeff was regulating his breathing, trying to catch his breat He was a cook, a restaurateur. He might go to the club thr days a week, maybe ride an exercise bike but he wasn't remote conditioned for this.

"You know, I can do this all night. Can you?"

Jeff closed his eyes, sucking in air.

"The mistake you made was telling the FBI, telling T Hunter, that you hardly knew Marta. We both know that's n true. You and Marta were a thing when you were both college, before her father was killed. Then she broke it with you. Why? Because she became a very dangerc person."

Jeff didn't respond, his eyes drifting down and away, whi confirmed he was hitting his mark.

Vince whispered. "Where is she?"

His prey looked away again.

Vince backhanded him across the face. Hard, but he h plenty back. "Where?"

"I don't know where she is."

"I don't believe you," Vince said, as he leaned to his ri and started evaluating Jeff's left hand. "I believe you know sh in Minnesota," he said, taking his left middle finger, bendin

"You're going to kill her."

"She's a killer, Jeff. She is killing my people up there. Five of them."

"You're a killer. You're going to kill me."

"I don't have to, Jeff. I don't have to. Marta's a big girl. She can defend herself. What do you owe her?" He pushed the index finger back.

"Ahhhh!"

"Jeff? Give it up. Save yourself."

"She said a friend of hers, her son was killed. She had the license plate and called and asked me to have it checked. I had it checked for her. That was it."

"Tell me about the friend?"

"I don't know a name."

"Jeff, don't lie."

"I don't know. I didn't ask. Marta didn't tell. She said it was a friend. She lost her only child, her son. That was all she said. She said she wanted to help her."

"I need a name."

"I don't have it."

Vince leaned in and started on the ring finger.

"I don't know the name!" Jeff screamed as his finger bent back.

* * *

Vince wiped off his hands, looking through the one-way mirror to Tommasoni slumped over in the chair, his left hand mangled, blood dripping from his face.

"And?" Bobby asked.

"She's up in either Manchester Bay or Holmstrand. Her friend was the woman who lost her only child. Marta's friend is Cathy Randall."

"Your next move?"

"Get back up there and have a chat with Cathy Randall."

"You think this Randall woman knows who Marta really is?"

Vince took a moment. "I really doubt Cathy Randall knows that her friend is Marta. No way she tells her who she was and what she did. But if you're Marta, you don't put yourself at risk like this for some casual friend either. I start asking questions, I'll eventually start getting some answers."

"What about him?" Jimmy asked, gesturing to Tommasoni.

Vince reached inside a duffel bag and pulled out his gun and silencer. "I'll take care of it. Get me a flight."

THIRTY-TWO

YOU'RE FAMILIAR WITH THE POSITION."

With his wide stubby fingers, Joe pecked computer entries into the Excel spreadsheet on the laptop.

"I still shake my head seeing you operate a computer, brother," Stevie Bianchi said with a sly grin. "Using a spreadsheet even."

"Go figure," Joe replied. "I liked it better when I could keep track of things in a spiral notebook," he said as he put in the last of the delivery entries for the day. "Okay, done. The five usual deliveries today. On the sixth, you need to have a discussion with him. He was short yesterday, four grand. He says he'll have it today. If he doesn't..."

"I'll deal with it. I sure as shit hope we get some more guys soon. I don't mind coming here everyday, brother, but I hate this drug delivery shit. Plus, after this, Pauly has me at the bar."

"You are his driver and security."

"More like bitch."

Joe chuckled. "Speaking of bitches, they anywhere on finding Marta?"

"I don't know." Stevie sighed. "Smith is gone now."

"Like as in gone, gone?"

Stevie shook his head as he pulled on his delivery jumpsuit. "Jimmy and Pauly were tight-lipped about it. That tells me Smith is into something." He looked to his brother while stuffing his Smith and Wesson Micro-Compact in his side pant pocket. He had Glock 17 under the driver's seat in the van. "She's still out there though and has no love for us old Chicago guys. Watch it."

"My gun's loaded too," Joe replied as he hit the garage door opener.

* * *

Braddock stood between Tori and Steak, looking over their shoulders as Steak checked and rechecked everything on the closed-circuit feed. Steak had come overnight and mounted another camera out in the street to be able to record the van, its license plate and Bianchi's delivery, should he come. Bianchi had been on the road for a couple of hours now but had not yet made his way in their direction.

"How many on the tail?" Tori asked.

"Reese and Nolan rotating."

"And where is he now?"

"Pequot Lakes."

* * *

Parked around a corner, the back of the van visible to the southeast of her position, Bianchi walked to the front door, packages under his arm. Nolan raised the camera to her eyes and quickly took photos of him opening the lockbox and placing the delivery packages inside.

As he walked back, she powered up her window and placed the camera on the passenger seat.

* * *

He retrieved the delivery, two packages, from the bin in the back and walked to the front of the townhouse and the gray steel lockbox. From his key ring he found the proper key for the lockbox, opened it and set the packages inside and then relocked it before hitting the doorbell. As he walked back to the van, he peered right and then left, catching a glimpse of a black SUV, the window powering up, a woman in the driver's seat, looking the other way.

* * *

Justin was in the front of the house, his television on, the sound low, watching sports replays, anxious. Tori stood in the hallway observing. She took the last sip of what remained of her iced latte and then tossed the plastic glass in the garbage. Looking to Justin, she said, "As the wise man Tom Petty once sang: The waiting is the hardest part."

Justin looked back to her. "Then why do I feel like 'I'm Free Fallin'."

"Look at the bright side, with what they have on you, you could have gone to prison for years."

Justin nodded. "True, but what do I do now?"

"What did you do before you did this?"

"I was a union carpenter, but I couldn't get regular enough work and I had to drive a lot to get to what work there was."

Tori nodded; her arms folded. "Prison isn't a risk with that work. As a union guy, you get medical and a pension. That's a far better long-term bet than doing this." She stepped down the hallway and looked in the back bedroom to see Steak and Braddock testing. "You two are going to foul it up, you keep checking and rechecking that stuff."

"We're done with all that," Steak replied. "Now we're just watching porn."

"Well, he is anyway," Braddock said. "I'm placing NBA bets."

* * *

Stevie rang the doorbell and then walked back to the van. He drove two blocks and turned right on County Road 66, the main street through the town of Crosslake. He caught a flash of movement in his rearview mirror, a black SUV. It had turned onto the road behind him.

He drove north through the town, the lake visible through the leafless trees to his left. He let his eyes drift up the rearview mirror and the black SUV was a vehicle back. As he reached the northern edge of town there was a gas station. He took a quick left into the gas station and pulled up to a pump and decided to fuel up. As he was getting out of the van, the SUV rolled by. It was driven by a woman, in a black baseball hat. He watched as the black SUV, an Acadia, continued north on County Road 66.

He paid for gas at the pump and went inside the store, grabbing a bottle of water and then a bag of chips, all the while peering out the windows of the station. The black Acadia was gone.

He went back out to the van. Before he started the engine, he reached under his seat and retrieved his Glock 17 and set it in the center console, along with his cell phone and wondered about calling Marrone.

* * *

"He made a stop in Crosslake to fuel up," Reese reported. "He turned left and is going north on 66. If he takes a left on County 1, then I think he's rolling your way."

* * *

"Copy," Braddock said. "We're all set here." He looked over to Tori, who was biting her bottom lip. "What?"

She grabbed the radio from Braddock. "Reese, didn't he fuel up in Manchester Bay earlier?"

"Yeah."

"Unless the van is a complete dog from a gas mileage standpoint, he shouldn't have needed gas."

"Agreed. I think it was more about a snack. He came out with water and a bag or two of potato chips. He didn't stop anywhere for lunch. He probably just needed a bite to eat."

* * *

Reese followed in his pickup truck, perhaps a quarter mile back, his eyes tight on the van. "Nolan, where are you at?"

"I'm anticipating as you are. I'm four miles west on County 1, looking for a spot to hide."

* * *

He turned west onto County Road 1 and relaxed some as there was only a silver pickup truck in his rearview mirror, well back. It was fifteen miles to Pine River and he leaned down and turned on the radio to the Power Loon, catching "Dust in the Wind" about halfway through.

* * *

"Nolan, where are you at now?" Reese called.

"Swanberg Road. I'm waiting behind a storage shed."

"I'm going to fall back a bit. He should be passing you in about fifteen, twenty seconds."

"Copy that."

* * *

He took a long drink of his water. A storage facility was coming up on his left. He always thought it odd it was placed so far out in the woods. A long cinder block building with roll-up garage doors surrounded by a cement apron. There wasn't even a chain-link fence around it. He gave it a look as he rolled by and then in his side mirror, gazing back.

He saw it. The black Acadia again.

It turned onto the road behind him.

Was it the same one? It sure looked like it.

Marrone had told him when Nico called that Marta was chasing him in a black SUV.

There was a good fifteen miles left to reach Pine River and there was very little in between. He slowly pressed the accelerator.

* * *

Nolan was holding within a quarter mile on the tail, but Bianchi started pulling away, the van getting smaller. He'd accelerated. Not all at once, but he was picking up the pace. She accelerated to keep the same interval. She checked the speedometer. She was approaching seventy-five-miles per hour to keep him in view.

What is he doing?

"Will?"

The black SUV was staying with him despite increasing his speed. If anything, she seemed to be matching him. *Are you seeing things or is this real?*

He knew the road ahead, there was a near ninety-degree turn left coming followed quickly by another one to the right.

* * *

"He's going faster," Nolan reported. "Not chase fast but he's accelerated. He's twenty over the posted."

"Is he onto you?" Braddock asked, walking over to Tori and Steak sitting at the monitors. Steak had a map up, pointing to where they were.

"I'm the only other vehicle on the road other than Reese another half mile back."

"Will, I'll close up," Reese said. "Nolan, I'll pass you and you can break off."

"Let's do it out of the S turn ahead," she suggested. "I'll come around the second turn, get an eye on him and then break off."

"Copy."

She eased back just a bit to take the left turning curve to the south safely, her tires squealing as she took the turn at fifty-five instead of the recommended forty. The woods tight to both sides of the road. As she came around the corner, she caught a glimpse of the van a good half-mile ahead, the brake lights flashing as it started the turn right to the west.

* * *

He caught a glimpse of the black SUV as it came around the corner behind him. The hard right was coming, and he took it hard, the wheels squealing as he leaned into the turn. After the bend, he quick turned hard left onto a narrow gravel road that tunneled into the woods and zoomed ahead.

He called Marrone.

"Yeah?"

"I have a tail."

"What?"

"I have a black SUV; I think an Acadia on me. Isn't that what Nico said was on him?"

"Yeah. On you now?"

"I think I might have lost it."

"Turn around somehow. Get back here. Now!"

* * *

Nolan checked back and Reese was right behind her now. She came around the bend to the right.

"Shit," she muttered.

The road ahead was clear. "He turned off! He turned off! He knows we're on him."

* * *

"That's why he stopped for gas in Crosslake," Tori murmured. "He sensed or caught a glimpse of the tail. He was checking."

Steak evaluated the map of the area. "He's going to pull in somewhere and hide or he's making a run to the south to flee." He gestured to the map. "You and Tori take this road just south of Pine River here. I'm going down the H-4. If he's going south, they can drive him to us."

"Nolan, Reese, he had to take the first left out of that last ninety-degree turn," Steak said. He knew the roads of the area as well as anyone. "Get on those roads. Not a lot of houses along either one until you get to the lake."

"You two do that," Braddock said. "We're on our way. Let me check up on Stevie's brother." He made a call to Frewer, who was watching the warehouse. "Is Joe Bianchi still at the warehouse?"

"Yes."

"You have the warrant?"

"Yes."

"Move in now but discreetly, lowest possible profile. No lights and sirens. Knock on the door. Take him into custody."

"Where?"

"Keep him mobile until I call."

* * *

The gravel road twisted and turned as it went deeper into the woods. He didn't know his way in this area other than he knew he was coming up to the lake, which was becoming visible ahead and to his left through the trees. Slowing he pulled up a map app on his phone. His only routes ahead would be to the west. He looked up to the rearview mirror, which was clear. He'd lost her for now. But she was still out there, and still probably hunting him. She could read a map too.

Marrone called. "Where are you?"

"On the northside of Upper Whitefish Lake."

"Have you lost her?"

"I think so. I'm trying to find a way out of these woods to get back. It's a maze in here."

* * *

"What I don't get," Braddock said, "is if he thinks we're tailing him, that we're not going to get to him."

"Unless... that's not who he's afraid of," Tori said, eyebrows raised. "What if he thinks Marta Dudek is tailing him."

"That's a stretch."

"Is it? Mileski and Marrone have been locked up in the strip mall, under guard. She's wiped out all their muscle. Bianchi has been keeping business going, making these deliveries in addition to being what? Marrone's driver. He's a target, out here alone. Against her."

"Or so he thinks," Braddock said. "Okay, that could be what's going on here."

* * *

"Reese, anything?" Nolan called.

"Negative. I'm west of you, coming south."

She knew she was approaching the lake, driving slowly enough to eye up each driveway she came upon. She came around a bend into a slightly more open area, the trees less dense when she saw brake lights flash a quarter mile ahead, turning a corner into another dense area of woods.

Was that him?

She didn't get a good look at the vehicle, having just seen the flicker of red light.

Accelerating, she powered ahead, reaching the corner and turning right and could see ahead for a long stretch of road, still under a canopy of tree limbs. Then the vehicle turned left. Black panel van.

"I got him!"

* * *

"He just turned south on County 15," Nolan reported excitedly. "That takes him to Jenkins."

"No lights or sirens," Tori suggested. "Not yet."

"Nolan, no lights and sirens," Braddock ordered. "Just tighten up on him. We're two minutes away. We'll hit County

15 from the west. Steak?"

"I'm almost to Jenkins. I'll crossover and come up 15 from the south. We'll have him boxed in."

* * *

Stevie turned left and cruised south, checking his rearview mirror and then side mirror. It was clear. He relaxed.

For a half-second.

There was a flash of movement in the rearview mirror. The black SUV. And this time it was accelerating after him.

* * *

"I've got sight of him," Nolan reported, accelerating to match the van. "He's pulling away again."

"Keep on him," Braddock called as he quickly approached the junction with County 15.

"There he went," Tori exclaimed. "And there's Nolan."

Braddock made the right turn on 15, right behind Nolan. Tori looked back to see Reese coming up as well.

"Steak, we just turned onto 15. What's your twenty?"

"Two miles south of your position."

Tori and Braddock evaluated the map. "Ryan Road," Tori gestured.

"Steak, block at Ryan Road."

* * *

Stevie looked back. The black SUV wasn't far behind, closing on him. He looked ahead. A pickup truck turned in the middle of the road, blocking him.

"What the fuck!"

He hit the brakes. His only option was right.

* * *

"Nolan, follow him in," Braddock ordered. "We're right behind you. There is no way out. It dead ends."

Nolan turned hard right. Braddock was right behind her.

* * *

The gravel road was tight, weaving its way through the woods. He turned hard left.

"Dammit!"

The road dead ended. He turned the wheel hard to the left, his back end skidding around. He wasn't going down without a fight and reached for his Glock and took out his small Smith.

The Acadia skidded to a stop.

Who was that behind it?

* * *

The van spun around. Nolan skidded to a stop and saw Bianchi with a gun. "Oh shit!" and reached for her own.

* * *

"Now!" Braddock exclaimed.

Tori turned on the flashing police lights. Steak and Reese came in behind, now with flashing light. Braddock and Tori were out, guns up.

"Hands up, Bianchi! Get them up now!" Braddock called. He heard Steak and Reese both getting out of their vehicles behind him. There was a cocking of a shotgun, Steak.

Bianchi was stunned, the gun still in his hand, but he wasn't pointing it at them.

"Not what he was expecting," Tori said self-satisfied, her gun up, aimed at Bianchi.

"I think you're right," Braddock said. To Bianchi he called, "I'm not going to tell you again, Bianchi. Drop the gun. Now!"

Bianchi nodded and let the gun hang on his index finger and he set it on the dashboard and then put both hands in the air. Steak moved forward, shotgun up, as did Reese and Nolan, carefully approaching the van. Standing guard in front, Steak trained the shotgun on Bianchi while Nolan opened the driver's side door and Bianchi slowly climbed out, his hands in the air. Reese grabbed him, spun him around, pushing him up against the side of the van.

"You're familiar with the position," Reese needled, while kicking Bianchi's legs apart. Reese patted him down, pulling his key ring out of one of Bianchi's pockets and tossed them to Tori.

She and Braddock went to the back of the van and opened the double doors. Inside there was a locked cabinet. Tori tried the small keys on the ring and the third one opened the cabinet. Inside were three delivery envelopes. Braddock tugged on rubber gloves and then opened the packages while Tori took photos with her phone. He looked to Tori and smiled. "I do believe that is illegal contraband."

"Lots of it."

Braddock took out his phone, calling Frewer. "Do you have him?" He offered a small grin to Tori.

Tori exited the back of the van and came around to find Bianchi handcuffed. She stood in front of him, his body wide, his head seemingly sitting on his shoulders like a boulder on top of a wall. She looked back to the Acadia and then to Bianchi. "And here you thought that was Marta Dudek tracking you."

Bianchi's eyes nearly bulged out of his sockets.

"Well now, you're going to wish it had been her."

She stuck her head back inside the van to have a look.

Bianchi's cell phone was sitting on the driver's seat, along with his wallet. The phone was ringing. She looked at the display.

"Will!"

"Yeah?"

She gestured to the phone. "Does that phone number look familiar?"

"Sure does now that you mention it."

It was Marrone's cell phone number. Braddock let the ringing run out and then examined the phone and the prior outgoing calls. Bianchi had made two calls to Marrone in the last half-hour.

He laughed to himself. Tori was inside these guys heads. He led her away from Bianchi. "Let's say Bianchi did think it was Marta tracking him. He calls Marrone twice in the last half-hour. Maybe he told Marrone that too."

Tori nodded, seeing where Braddock was going. "We don't know what Bianchi said to them, but if he did say that, and now he's not answering, and his brother isn't answering."

"Keep these guys off the radar for a bit. See what shakes loose," Braddock said. "Reese!"

He came walking over. "Yeah?"

"Are your parents still down south for the winter?"

THIRTY-THREE

"THAT TELLS ME THAT WHATEVER HAPPENED ISN'T GOOD."

Vince walked up the jetway and through the concourse. In baggage claim he met up with his two men that had arrived from Cleveland fifteen minutes before he had. They were waiting for their bags when he walked up.

"I'm going to go get my SUV. I'll pick you up outside those doors."

Both men nodded.

As he walked through the parking ramp, his phone rang. It was Jimmy.

"Where are you?" Jimmy said in a worried tone.

"We just landed in Minneapolis."

"We?"

"I'm bringing a couple of reinforcements. Friends from Cleveland. We'll be on our way up shortly," he replied. "What's wrong?"

"We got another Marta problem."

"What happened?"

"Three hours ago, Stevie called and said someone was tailing him on his route. You know what route I'm talking about right?"

"Yes."

"He said it was a woman in a black SUV. She was on him at least two different times he said. He'd pulled into a gas station and saw her as she drove by. He saw her again northwest of town as he was out on a county road. He said she came out of nowhere and was on him."

"You're certain? He said it was her?"

"No, I'm not certain, Vincent," Jimmy growled. "He was being followed, aggressively. He called Pauly twice. He was out on the route, in an isolated area. You're gone. We're hunkered down in here. Stevie was out there alone. If she knows all that, she could pick him off."

"It sounded exactly like what Nico Sweeney reported to me when he called just before she got him," Marrone added on speakerphone. "I told Stevie to beeline it back here but like Jimmy said, that was three hours ago. There has been no sign of him. He's not answering his phone, responding to texts, anything. Radio silence."

"Does anyone have access to his phone to geo locate it?"

"No. Not that I know of. He's been divorced for years. His ex-wife lives back in Chicago. He lives up here with his brother Joe."

"Call Joe?"

"We have," Marrone said. "No answer to either voicemail or texts. Nada."

"What in the hell is going on around here?" Mileski shouted.

"Let's keep our heads and work the problem. We're on our way up. Shut it all down tonight."

"Already done," Jimmy said. "You want me to call Bobby?"

"No, not yet," Vince replied. "Let's see what we're dealing with first."

"You think Stevie was right. Was it her?"

Vince sighed. "It's possible. Marta's up there. I know for a fact she had a friend she was keeping tabs with down in Chicago. He didn't know her new identity. He just knows she was up there and that one of her friend's only child, her son, was killed in the drive-by shooting in Holmstrand."

"That's the Randall woman's son, right?"

"Yes."

"Knowing that, where do you think she is?"

"I'm guessing either Manchester Bay or Holmstrand, and I'm leaning Holmstrand," Vince said. "Marta had this guy run a license plate for her. It was the plate for that gray SUV your boys used for the drive-by. Those plates were from a car compacted out at Petrovic's place. It's how she found Rudick and got onto you guys. I don't think she knew you guys were even up there until the drive-by shooting. So she's close. I just need a day."

"In the meantime?" Jimmy said.

"Sit tight. Don't move. Call me every half-hour or if you hear from either of them. Do you have any friends in law enforcement up there?"

"Not many," Jimmy said. "We've gone out of our way to avoid any interaction with them."

"I know a guy or two," Marrone said.

"Reach out to them."

"In the meantime, do we keep trying Stevie and Joe?" Jimmy asked.

Vince thought for a moment. "Do these guys usually call you back right away when you call and leave a message or text them?"

"Yes."

"And now they haven't. That tells me that whatever happened isn't good."

THIRTY-FOUR

"THE MORE YOU GOT, THE MORE I GOT."

Braddock and Tori wanted privacy. Reese's parents had a summer home on Bay Lake on the far eastern end of the county and were still in Florida. Given it was Monday night in mid-April, few of the cabins and homes nearby were occupied. Consequently, when they arrived at the house with Stevie Bianchi, there were no prying eyes.

Reese rearranged some of the basement furniture to set up an interrogation table and a camera to videotape it.

Stevie Bianchi waited, cuffed at a table in the basement, under the guard of Steak and Eggleston. Unbeknownst to him, his brother Joe was under guard with Nolan in a spare bedroom upstairs.

Trish and Paul drove Alisha over. The little girl smiled and waved eagerly to Tori, running up for a hug.

"Hey there," Tori greeted, reaching for her hand, leading her toward the house. She high-fived Braddock and Steak along the way.

Inside the house, there were other police officers. Rather than being scared, she seemed curious about what was going on. Tori led her into the den where the recording equipment was arranged. Braddock hoisted Alisha up onto his lap and let Alisha look at all of it with a childlike wonder. Tori sat down next to them and described all the equipment. Paul and Trish hovered nearby. After a few minutes, Tori looked to Alisha, signing, and speaking, "Honey, I need to know if you recognize someone, okay?"

Alisha nodded, but now with some apprehension.

Tori smiled and patted her gently on the leg. "You can see him, but he can't see you, okay?"

Okay.

Braddock pulled up the camera focused on Stevie Bianchi.

"Is he the man you saw at that house?" Tori asked. "The night Nico was told you had to leave?"

Alisha peered at the screen for a moment. Steak moved the camera in for more of a close-up and then panned back, so she could see Bianchi from a distance.

"What do you think?" Tori asked.

Yes. He was with the man who said I had to go. That I couldn't stay.

"You're sure," Tori asked, Trish signing the question as well.

Alisha nodded vigorously and signed: *That's him.*

"Good job. You're all done," Tori said with a smile, high-fiving Alisha. Braddock offered her knuckles, which she returned with a big smile. Tori held Alisha's hand as she walked Paul and Trish out of the house, their police escort waiting.

"How much longer will we have to have the security all around us?" Paul asked.

"I hope not much longer. Things are moving tonight."

Tori knelt and gave Alisha another quick hug. "I'll come see you soon, okay?"

Alisha smiled and then got into Paul's pickup truck and they all departed.

"Where is social services at?" Braddock asked after they left.

"They're dragging their feet," Tori replied.

"Why?"

"Because Paul and Trish are trying to determine how deep they want to get here. I think Alisha has gotten to them. They're trying to decide if they go all in on this."

"I see," Braddock said. "It's a big decision."

"Sure is," Tori said. "What's next?"

"Giving Steve Bianchi his options."

Tori and Braddock went to the basement and sat down at the table, Bianchi waiting.

"I want—"

"Don't say it!" Tori interrupted. "Not yet. You need to hear us out before you make that demand because once you do, things get messy, and they will get worse for you, *significantly* worse."

"I have my rights."

"One of which is the right to remain silent. Exercise it. We're not going to ask you any questions. We are going to explain the reality of your predicament. It isn't good but maybe we can make it better."

"Right, sweetheart," Bianchi replied derisively. "You want to help me?"

Tori smirked wickedly back.

Braddock shook his head. "The fact of the matter is, we've got you for as long as we want you. But, here's the thing, we want the bigger fishes and you're going to deliver them to us."

Bianchi snorted. "I don't think so."

Tori laid down several photos on the table of the van, Bianchi in black delivery uniform, packages under his arms, opening and closing the lockboxes, locking the cabinet in the back of the van. "This is you the last few days, delivering drugs and picking up cash payments. That's in Manchester Bay, Holmstrand, Pequot Lakes, Crosslake and then Pine River. And here are a couple photos of the cash paid. It's a handsome amount. And then what you were delivering."

"And we'd be remiss if we didn't include photos of you making deliveries of the cash you picked up to Cullen Crossing Plaza, where greeting you at the door are your friends Jimmy Mileski and Paul Marrone." Tori picked out one particular photo. "Look at this one. You're handing that very package to Mileski. There's money in there. And we know that that money is being laundered through the strip mall. In fact, we suspect the Chicago Mob's money is being run through that place, as well as all the places Rudick owned."

"It's funny what you find," Braddock said, "when you know what you're looking for."

Bianchi leaned forward and slowly started sifting through the photos. The slump of his shoulders and grimace of his expression confirmed to her that they were right about the drug trail. Braddock next dropped a one-inch-thick binder clipped with a stack of papers on the table. "That's your criminal record. It's never good when it needs that big a binder clip to hold it together. Lots of activity back in the day down in Chicago."

Tori made a show of thumbing through the pages she'd already committed to memory. "There's like four or five arrests that don't lead anywhere. In one case a witness disappeared. In others, witnesses declined to testify which led to a dropping of charges. They were probably intimidated or paid off, being Chicago and all. Through it all, you were developing a rep. Then you popped your cherry doing five years for assault and trafficking in stolen property and then you went big time and did eight years for drug trafficking. That made you a two-time loser."

"And now at age fifty-three, you have your third strike," Braddock said. "And with what we have—"

"You'll never breathe free air again," Tori finished.

"Pfft." Bianchi laughed, defiant. "I'll be out in ten years, if that. You maybe got something, but it ain't all that."

Braddock's eyes shifted to Tori. They expected defiance. And while they had him dead to rights, that didn't mean he would go to prison for as long as they were posturing. That would be in the judge's hands and if they couldn't prove his involvement in the murders, or if he didn't give them what they were looking for, he might gut out another lengthy prison stretch. It was par for the course in his line of work. Physically and mentally, he could make it through.

Tori met his defiance head-on, leaning back in her chair, laughing. "You think we're jacking you around? You think we're just going to put this out there without knowing what we can get? *Exactly* what we can get? Do you think this is the first time we've done this? That we're just some local yokels who can't put together a case against some eff'n mook like you? That this was our only play?"

"Steak?" Braddock called, smirking at Bianchi.

"This isn't just about you," Tori asserted.

Steak stepped to the table and put a laptop in front of Bianchi and turned the screen around.

"You fuckers," Stevie muttered quietly.

It was his brother Joe. He was being held upstairs, sitting in a room with Nolan, handcuffed, terrified.

Braddock laid out more photos. "Here's you and your brother at the warehouse earlier. Here's you leaving the warehouse in the van. It's as if you're smiling at us."

"And then what did we find inside the warehouse?"

He set out more photos. "Coke, heroin, opioids, weed, meth among others. It was all there and in your brother's possession. He's running a drug distribution center out of that warehouse."

She reached for another clipped set of documents and set them down in front of Stevie. "This is your little brother's prison record. Unlike you, he's only had one tour, but it was a pretty bad one." She selected a photo of Joe Bianchi with two black eyes and bruises on his body. "You're a big dude, but Joe isn't. He doesn't have the ability to defend himself and it shows." Tori held up a photo. "The beatings he took. And the assaults."

"I'd hate to think what would happen now? Being that much older, fragile and vulnerable," Braddock said. "This kind of drug charge, that's hard time. In Minnesota, first-degree felony possession of a controlled substance with intent to distribute. That's thirty years on a first offense. He has a record. You have a worse record. And," he paused, dropping his voice, "we haven't even gotten to the murders yet."

"Murders?"

"All the murders tied to the drugs. Reardon Banz, the drive-by in Holmstrand. Gresh and Gill, the list goes on."

"Take Banz for starters," Tori said, standing up, starting to pace around. For all their own calculated bluster, this was where they were bluffing. They were certain that Bianchi knew the details of the murders. The question was whether they had the leverage to make him give it up. "We know he was killed at Gresh's apartment. We know he was wrapped up in a rug." Now the risk. She leaned in and looked him in the eye. "We know you and Marrone were there that night checking on things, pulling all the strings."

Stevie looked down, slowly shaking his head. They were on the right track.

She looked to Braddock who stood up and sat on the edge of the table to Bianchi's right.

"That makes you an accomplice to murder," Braddock noted confidently. "At best for you, it would be after the fact, but add that to all the drug business. And, that isn't all. This case is like a Ginsu commercial."

"And there's even more!" Tori exclaimed, offering a toothy grin.

"The drive-by shooting. Now, you may not have been there when it happened," Braddock continued. "But you sure as hell know what went down. You were at Rudick's house later that night with Marrone talking about it. We have a witness that puts you there just hours after the shooting. You know who pulled the trigger. You know who gave the order and why. It was because of Banz. Because two of those kids saw Ron Gresh and others remove his body from that apartment building."

"And you know that Mileski and Marrone sent killers to take out our witness, a little nine-year-old girl. Nine, Stevie! She was nine! That's attempted murder. But Marta Dudek thwarted that."

Stevie snapped his head to Tori at the mention of her name.

"She's been hunting you guys down. Picking you off one by one. Hell, you're so spooked about it you thought our detective was Marta today. Tell me your phone calls to Marrone in the half-hour before we got you today weren't to say Marta was on you."

Stevie closed his eyes and shook his head.

"You need to think about starting to help yourself," Braddock said quietly. "Holmstrand. We don't think you were there, but you know who was and more importantly—"

"Who gave the order and why."

Stevie Bianchi sat back and closed his eyes. He looked to Braddock. "What are you offering?"

"All depends on what you have. The more you got, the more I got."

Stevie looked to the table, to the picture of his brother. "If I tell you, he goes free."

They had anticipated this. Braddock shook his head. "That's an awfully big ask with what we have. An awfully big ask."

"He can't go back to prison and do that kind of time. He'll never make it," Stevie said matter-of-factly, holding up a photo of his brother. "He was nothing but a caretaker, a record keeper at that warehouse. He spent more time sweeping than anything else. He wasn't running shit."

It was a lie, a respectable one, but it didn't fly. "That's not what a reasonable review of the evidence says," Tori said evenly.

"I know, but he's a pawn in all this. If you know all you claim to know, then you know that," Stevie replied. "I'll play along, but only if Joe goes free with a new identity, relocated. You get me that and I'll tell you everything you want to know. The drugs, Banz, Ron Gresh and Holmstrand."

"It'll be your word against theirs though," Tori prodded.

Stevie offered a wane smile. "Yeah, well, I have some receipts."

They had him.

"You got a criminal lawyer you trust?" Braddock asked.

"Not up here. I call Jimmy, he'll get me one."

"That he's paying for. He won't do it out of generosity. The plug will get pulled quick if you play ball with us."

Bianchi nodded. "You guys know a good one?"

"I do," Braddock said. "She was a prosecutor in Hennepin County. Now she does white-collar crime defense. You want us to get her up here?"

Stevie Bianchi snorted a laugh, understanding that Braddock and Tori were ready for this. "You guys have thought of everything." He said it as if he was impressed. "I'll give her a listen."

"Sit tight," Braddock said.

He and Tori went upstairs. Boe and George Backstrom, the County Attorney and his top assistant, Anne Wilson, were waiting in the kitchen, having watched.

"What do you think?" Braddock asked.

"As you said, it's a lot," Wilson said. "He needs to provide what he has, and now."

"If he does, we can give him what he wants?" Tori asked. "The feds are probably going to get in on this. They can't screw it up, can they?"

"You're the retired fed, you tell us," Braddock said, both needling and asking a question.

"I'm worried they could. Us feds always think we know better. They might come in and try to run roughshod on our case."

"For these two, I'm confident the feds would honor whatever deal we strike if the Bianchis cooperate with the U.S. Attorney's Office and any subsequent investigation," Backstrom said. "If he cooperates there his deal might improve, although I wouldn't tell him that right now."

Braddock looked to Wilson. "Do you have the lawyer teed up?"

"She can be up here in a couple of hours."

"Get her on the road."

Wilson stepped away to make the call. Boe looked to them. "Mileski and Marrone are reacting."

"Yeah?" Tori asked. "Justin?"

"He got a call. It was from a number he didn't recognize. We think it was a burner phone, but he was asked if he got his delivery today. As instructed, he said no and did a little bitching about it," Boe said. "At the strip mall, they closed everything tonight, even the convenience store. Nobody has been outside the building since."

"And the Bianchis' vehicles? Stevie's van, Joe's pickup truck?" Tori asked Braddock.

"Let's let word seep out on that."

THIRTY-FIVE

"I'VE SEEN ENOUGH."

It was after 11:00 p.m. when Vince and his men parked behind the strip mall and slipped inside. He found Mileski and Marrone in the office behind the bar.

"What's the update?"

"There isn't one," Marrone said. "I made a couple of calls, but I haven't heard anything yet."

"Alright. Pauly, you're with me. Let's go."

"Where are we going?"

"To see if we can figure out what happened to Stevie and Joe."

The county road was dark, with no other vehicles as they slowly passed the small warehouse on the left. The only illumination was the singular small light under the canopy for the front door. Parked to the right of the front door was a black SUV.

"That's Stevie's Escalade," Marrone murmured from the backseat.

Vince pulled to the side of the road, checked his rearview mirror. "Did you check if his deliveries were made?"

"He made all but one. He said he made the delivery in Crosslake when he called. He didn't make it to Pine River."

Vince made a U-turn. "Did you talk to the guy in Pine River?"

"Yeah. He said he never got his delivery."

"How was he when you called?"

"Pissed. Justin was his name. He bitched he paid, where's my shit. Blah, blah, blah."

They passed by the warehouse again. "What about the other guy's pickup truck?" Vince asked.

"Joe's truck isn't there."

The Bianchis lived on the northern edge of town, not far from Rudick's house. Vince made a slow drive-by of the one-story ranch house set back from the road. The house was dark. No vehicles were parked in the driveway. "Is their house on a lake?"

"Yes, a small one. They fish it."

He drove further along the road to another house that was dark, a pontoon still shrink-wrapped parked in the driveway. He pulled up into the driveway and killed the lights. "Sit tight."

Vince made his way back east behind the back of the cabins, the small lake down to his left. At the Bianchi house he took the steps up onto the back deck and peered in the windows. In the kitchen he saw a few dishes in the sink, two newspapers spread out on a round table and random boots by the back door that led to the attached garage. The garage had a back window. He peered inside the garage and there were no vehicles inside. He made his way back, gone all of five minutes. When he got into the truck, Marrone was on the phone.

"Anything?" Marrone asked, pulling his phone away from his ears.

"No. No truck. House is quiet. Nobody inside."

Marrone hung up his phone.

"Who was that?"

"A source in the Sheriff's Department. A black panel van was found abandoned south of Pine River, just off County Road 15 at the end of a gravel road earlier tonight. A few hours later, a red pickup was also found abandoned four miles from here. Driver's side door was left open, window was smashed, and keys left in the ignition. No witnesses. No blood. The Sheriff's Department is investigating but my guy says they don't have anything to go on. Joe drives such a truck."

"Anything else?"

"After that, the source says the Sheriff's Department's entire investigative unit, Braddock, Hunter, all of them, is out in the field tonight."

"And Hunter is back you said?"

"Yes. Why?"

"Because she was down in Chicago over the weekend," Vince replied. "Poking around the Polish Palace and asking questions about Marta. I'm pretty sure Hunter knows she's Marta Dudek."

"Marta knows things, about you, me, Jimmy, Bobby, Chicago," Marrone urged.

"That's why we're going to find her first."

"You know where she is?"

Vince shook his head. "I know where to start."

* * *

The digital clock said it was 11:48 p.m. Maggie lay on her side, part asleep, part awake, Rob snoozing behind her. Falling asleep and staying there had proven more difficult as of late, although she felt herself starting to finally drift off, her eyes slowly closing, her mind calming.

Her phone screen lit up. She craned her neck to see she had a text notification, from the other cell phone. She slowly slipped out of bed, careful not to disturb Rob and tiptoed out of the bedroom, slowly closing the door and then light on her feet, made her way downstairs, through the kitchen and into the salon. She sat down at her desk and opened the side compartment and took out the cell phone.

There was a text message: *Call me. ASAP.*

She hit the preset number.

A woman's voice answered.

"Sorry," Maggie said, checking the number on the phone. "Wrong num—"

"No, no, don't hang up. It's the right number. I'm calling for Jeff."

"Who are you?"

"My name is Cordelia. Jeff is my boyfriend."

"How do I know that? How can I know that?"

"I work as a bartender at Dudek's Polish Palace, your dad's old place. Jeff and I have been together for three years. He's told me about you, about your... friendship, about how the two of you dated way back when."

"That was years ago."

"That's not why I'm calling."

"How did you even get this phone?"

"Jeff told me where it was. Where it was hidden in his apartment. After the FBI and this detective showed up, he showed me where the phone was in case one of us had to call you."

"Where is he?"

"He's missing."

"Tell me why you think that," Maggie asked, closing her eyes, balling her right fist.

"I didn't work last night so I stayed at my apartment, but I was supposed to open today. His car was there when I arrived, but he wasn't. The place was all locked up, the security system still activated. He didn't show and he's there every day. That place is his life. I called him all day and he never answered. I'm here at his apartment now. I don't see his wallet or keys. He hasn't been here. That's why I took out this phone. I don't know what to do."

Maggie stood up and started walking around the house, peering through the curtains and into the backyard. "Listen to me. If he isn't responding, hasn't come home, he is in danger." She went back to the desk and checked the closed-circuit camera system. She worked her way through the four camera angles. They were running and recording. No activity.

"How much? How much danger."

"Cordelia... I'm worried for him. Really worried." She was in fact certain Jeff was dead.

"Oh God."

"Cordelia. Jeff called me late Saturday night. He told me the FBI and maybe a detective from Minnesota showed up at the bar."

"Yes. Twice actually."

"Who did they talk to besides Jeff?"

"Well, me, some. And Anna Symanski because she worked here back when DeEsposito and even your father owned the place. I don't think anyone else, at least here."

"I remember Anna."

"She and Jeff gave them all the history of this place. The woman detective from Minnesota, she was sharp. Jeff thought she figured out who you were."

"Besides, Jeff, Anna and you, did they talk to anyone else there?"

"I don't think so," Cordelia said. "What do I do?"

"Three things. First, call the police. In fact, call the FBI agent who came to the bar. Do it the minute you get off the phone. Second, check into a hotel. Don't stay at your apartment and get the hell away from Jeff's. Third, we never talked, you and I, understand? Jeff was the only person I was in contact with. Someone figured that out."

"It wasn't me, I swear. I'm just doing what Jeff told me to. He said if for any reason something happened where he needed to warn you and he couldn't, I was to call you."

Cordelia was telling the truth. Maggie could hear the abject fear in her voice. "Cordelia, don't call this number again. Once I hang up, deactivate that phone, throw it away. This phone will be no more once I hang up. After that, call the FBI. Do it for Jeff. He wouldn't want you in danger. Do you understand?"

"Y-y-yes. I'll do it."

"Promise me you'll do that. Promise me."

"Yes. I will. I promise."

Maggie hung up. She looked at her schedule for tomorrow. She had two appointments in the afternoon. She sent messages to cancel them.

She retrieved two guns from the compartment, quick checked the magazines and then chambered rounds in each. She placed one in one of her sliding drawers for her desk, underneath a notepad. The next one she stuffed into the pouch of her hoodie, turned off the overhead salon light and with the main floor of the house dark, she peered out each of the windows that were front facing and scanned up and down the street. While her view was partially obstructed by the lower hanging branches of the big trees in their front yard, she didn't see any vehicles along the street watching the house or further to the left, Cathy's house.

Given what she had told Jeff, she knew it wouldn't be long before they showed up. She went to a side window and looked over to Cathy's house. The light was on in her master bedroom. She called her.

"Maggie. It's late for you to call. Is everything alright?"

"No. I need to come over."

"Now?"

"Just for minute. I'll come to the back door."

"Okay."

Maggie retrieved an envelope from the compartment behind her desk and closed the door. She pulled on a light black coat and her dark-gray tennis shoes and scooted out the back of the house and around to the back of Cathy's place.

"Hey there," Cathy said, opening the front door and letting her inside.

There was no preamble. "Cathy. Do you trust me?"

"Uh... Yes, why wouldn't I?"

"Because I need you to do something. Cath, I'm not who you think I am."

"You're not? What... are you talking about?"

"I'm your neighbor, your hair stylist, your friend, your good, good friend. You're my best friend. As good a one as I've ever had."

"Maggie? What are you saying?"

"A long time ago I was someone else and I did some pretty bad things, Cath. I was in a life that I escaped. I met Rob, I moved here, I left it all behind."

Cathy looked at her warily. "Why... are you telling me this?"

"Leo's death was the responsibility of some men I knew in that former life. Now, I didn't know they were here until well after Leo was shot. But once I knew they were here, once I realized that they were responsible for Leo's death, and Cameron and Grace too, well, I started—" her voice turned dark as she pulled her gun out so Cathy could see she had one "—hunting for them."

Cathy's eyes went wide. "Hunting? These other shootings since?"

"Like I said. I had a former life."

"Oh my God, Maggie. I can't believe—"

"I thought I could do this without... revealing it was me. I failed. They know I'm here. They're coming for me."

"Who is they?"

"It's a long story. It involves the Chicago Mob. They know who I was, but not yet who I am now. They killed someone I still communicated with from my old life. They somehow figured out that he was in communication with me and knew generally where I was. He didn't know my new name or my address or what I look like now. But after Leo's shooting he got me some information and I told him why I wanted it. He knew I wanted that information because of what happened to Leo."

"And what about the kids? And Rob? Does he know this?"

"No, Rob knows nothing and I'm keeping it that way. And I'm protecting them, by first protecting you." She took a deep breath, letting it all sink in for Cathy who was wide-eyed in disbelief at what she was hearing. "They want me. They're going to kill me when they find me unless I get them first. The only way they can find me right now, is through you, Cath. They're going to come looking for you."

"Oh my God," Cathy blurted, her hand to her mouth.

"I'm betting they're coming, if not tonight, tomorrow. You need to go until I tell you it's safe to come back."

"Go where?"

"The Twin Cities, Duluth, Fargo, maybe Des Moines. Check into a hotel." She took out the envelope and handed it to Cathy. There was $5,000 dollars inside. "Pay cash just to be safe. Keep your phone with you."

Cathy looked at the envelope while Maggie went to the front picture window and looked outside, scanning the street. "Go pack a bag. Two days clothes at least. Do it now."

"And what are you going to do?"

Maggie looked back to her. "I'm going to end it."

* * *

It was well after midnight when the defense attorney finally arrived from Minneapolis. She spent an hour conferencing with her new clients and then spent another half-hour with Anne Wilson. The good news for Braddock, Tori and Steak was they were able to grab naps for a few hours while they all waited. By 3:00 a.m. the i's were dotted and the t's were crossed on a contingent deal. What were the receipts that Bianchi alluded to?

Coffee was brewed and everyone moved to the dining room table. The session would be videotaped. Wilson and the defense attorney made statements for the recording outlining the deal. Wilson turned it over to Braddock and Tori.

Braddock wasted no time. "Did the murder of Reardon Banz lead to the drive-by shooting in Holmstrand?"

"Yes."

"Why? Explain."

"Waltripp, Sweeney, Gill and Gresh were trying to convince Banz to keep working for us."

"He had worked for you?"

"Yes, then he went back to his old supplier and wasn't coming back into the fold, despite Ron Gresh's efforts. Jimmy and Pauly sent Gresh back, but this time with Tripp, Nico and Gill. They weren't to take no for an answer. Banz was stubborn and refused and got in Nico's and Gresh's faces. Tripp, who could run hot, snapped, and strangled him in Gresh's apartment. That had not been the plan, to kill him there if he refused. Too many people around. Normally, we would have just followed him for a day or two and found the right time when he was alone, out late at night, snatch him and that would be that but Tripp snapped. It was a problem. I got the call."

"What to do with the body?"

Stevie nodded. "We put together a plan to wait until later in the night, wrap him in the rug and move him out. Pauly, Jimmy and I drove over there and observed from a distance. Once our guys had Banz's body in the back of the SUV, they drove away. And then, that's when Pauly screwed up."

"By Pauly, you mean Marrone, correct?" Braddock said.

Stevie nodded. "He wanted to talk with Gresh, so he has me pull up. That's when those kids maybe saw us."

"They did."

"I figured. Did they come to you?"

Braddock shook his head. "But we know what they saw. What happens next?"

"Gresh reports to Rudick after we left that he saw his old girlfriend drive away with her boyfriend, plus they had been there earlier. He doesn't know why they were there or what for sure they saw, but he tells Rudick that he saw them driving away. Rudick calls Jimmy and Pauly and they say they have to go."

"You heard Jimmy and Pauly give the order?"

"They gave *me* the order and I gave it to Rudick and Waltripp. Waltripp takes Gill and Sweeney with him. They followed them all day and the first chance they had was up in Holmstrand. They took it."

"Just like that?" Tori asked, shaking her head.

"Yeah. It was a problem. It had to be dealt with."

"It had to be dealt with. They were college kids," Tori railed. "They had their whole lives in front of them."

Stevie shrugged. "What can I say, wrong place, wrong time. It was them or us was how Jimmy and Pauly looked at it."

"Gresh wasn't involved in the shooting in Holmstrand?"

"No."

"Then why kill him? And Gill?" Braddock asked.

Stevie raised his eyes. "You know about that?"

"It didn't look right."

Stevie closed his eyes, shaking his head. "Gresh was set-up to take the fall for Holmstrand. He was dumbass to begin with. And it was his old girlfriend who saw us, and we'd heard he didn't take it well when she broke things off with him. Waltripp saw the shrine to her in his bedroom. It was messed up. Guys like that can be unpredictable. We hid him for a few days to see what shook out. You were hunting for him, so we told Rudick to stage it to look like he and Gill fought over drugs and money. Like I said. Gresh was a dumbass."

"He was disposable."

"Something like that. We figured leave the gun there, along with drugs and money, your investigation would end with Gresh's death." He sighed. "Clearly, it didn't."

"How does Marta Dudek fit into this?" Tori asked.

"How'd you identify her?" Stevie asked.

"We just have."

"We had no idea she was up here. I was in prison when Lamberto had Angie DeEsposito killed and when she smoked Philly a couple of weeks later. When her father was alive, Marta would come with Stan when he delivered envelopes to Philly for Angie. Everyone liked Stan. He was a good neighborhood guy. When he was killed, it was because Kranz's guys mistook him for Angie. It wasn't supposed to be Stan. That was a royal fuckup."

"When did you realize she was here?"

"Nico called Marrone when she was chasing him. His description got Jimmy and Pauly wondering. I got into Rudick's house before you all did. I saw Rudick and Waltripp, how they were shot. It was a pro job, no doubt. When she killed Carlo and Max last week when they went after that girl, then we knew for sure. It had to be her."

"Have they found her up here?"

"Not yet."

"But they're looking?"

Stevie nodded. "They know it's Marta. They haven't been able to really work on finding her yet. They haven't known where to look."

They worked through the drug operation, Stevie laying out his role and that of his brother, explaining the drugs came from

Chicago twice a week. "It came here, and we got it out to our network."

"How long have you been making deliveries?" Braddock asked.

"Ever since we lost Waltripp and Nico and the others. Gresh was actually the runner for a number of months."

"The cash. Marrone and Mileski are running it through the strip mall, right?"

"Jimmy is a numbers guru. That's why they sent him up here to build the mall. It was all set up to run money through. Money from Chicago comes up here, all cash, and is run through there. There are two safes down in the basement under the bar with stacks of cash in them. Jimmy, and some banker he works with, runs it through all the businesses."

"Who drove the van they put Banz's body into?"

Stevie looked away, shaking his head.

"Might that have been your brother?" Braddock asked.

Bianchi sighed and nodded. "He didn't have anything to do with killing Banz."

"Until it came time to dispose of the body. Where did you do that?"

"We drove it out to the woods."

"We? You know where Banz's body is?"

"Him and a few others."

"You don't say?" Tori said with a grin.

"Like I said, sweetheart. I have some receipts."

As the sun worked its way up in the east, the morning was overcast, a light patchy fog filtered its way through the thick forested area as Stevie Bianchi directed them along a tight winding gravel road into a dense area of woods. As Tori examined the mapping app on her phone, she remarked that they weren't but a few miles from the location of the Airstream trailer.

Mentioning that to Stevie Bianchi, he said, "To a certain degree that's why we came out here. Gill said it was isolated, quiet, nobody around. He wasn't wrong. Walk back in far enough and nobody would see us, especially at night. All you needed was a lantern and shovels."

He directed them to park. Braddock, Tori, Steak, Boe, Anne Wilson, two deputies, Ann Jennison from the BCA and two of her forensic scientists followed along. A whole team. Stevie walked them back into the woods on a tight, winding trail until they came to a tree with a small crude x carved into the bark at knee height. "To the right here, about thirty feet," he said, walking to a small clearing. The canopy of leafless branches overhead provided cover. The ground was damp and soft, the clutter thick and natural.

"How many here?"

"Banz is this one," Stevie said. "Three others are buried a little further in that way."

He walked back over to the tree with the x carved in it. "The three times I was out here, I marked the spots like this just in case we had to come back out here for some reason and move them. Find something like this and you're on the body."

While the BCA set up their ground penetrating radar, a subdued and defeated Stevie walked them deeper into the woods to find the other trees with x's carved in them. Deputies pounded small stakes in the ground and tied tape around them to mark off the gravesites.

As they walked back to the first site, the BCA had marked the area off and the dig commenced. It took twenty minutes of organized digging until they reached the body, which was wrapped in thick plastic. Two deputies lowered themselves down into the grave and heaved the body out. The seam of the plastic had been secured by three pieces of gray duct tape.

Jennison cut the tape and peeled the plastic back. The body was well preserved.

"That's Banz," Steak murmured.

Sheriff Boe shook her head and then turned to Anne Wilson. "What else do you need?"

"I've seen enough," the County Attorney said. "Let's take the whole thing down."

THIRTY-SIX

"MAKE A BIG PROBLEM A SERIES OF SMALL ONES."

Crack! Crack! Crack!

Maggie dropped the last of the eight eggs onto the center island's cooktop griddle, the eggs slowly sizzling. To her left, the strawberries were cut. In the oven was the rest.

"Wow!" Rob said when he came into the kitchen. "Ellen said she smelled bacon."

"In the oven. The kids coming?"

"On their way," he said, kissing her on the cheek. "Big breakfast. What's the occasion?"

"No reason. I woke up early and thought I'd make everyone a big breakfast is all."

Brian and Ellen bounded into the kitchen a minute later, ready for school. Everyone grabbed a plate and they sat at the kitchen table and had a breakfast of bacon, eggs, toast, and fruit. The kids eagerly wolfed down their breakfasts while they needled one another and surfed the latest texts, Instagrams and TikToks. Rob devoured his food while Maggie took deliberate bites of hers, sipping her coffee, soaking in her family.

A few minutes later, Rob peeked at his watch. "We better hustle gang."

Brian and Ellen immediately scrambled up from the table, taking their plates and dutifully putting them in the sink.

"Thanks," Brian said, giving her a quick hug before he hustled out the door. Ellen did the same. "Remember, I won't be home until later tonight. I'm going shopping with the girls for prom."

"I'm late too," Brian said. "I'm hanging with the guys, watching Game 1 of the playoffs."

"Okay. Have fun. Both of you."

Rob leaned in and kissed her. She pulled him in close and held the kiss for an extra second.

"What was that for?"

"I love you is all," she said, hugging him.

He pulled back and looked her in the eyes. "Everything okay?"

She smiled. "I tell you I love you and you wonder if I'm alright."

Rob laughed. "How foolish of me." He kissed her gently on the forehead. "I love you too. I'll see you tonight." She watched as Rob backed out of the garage with the kids, and away they went.

She quick cleaned the kitchen, rinsed, and put all the breakfast pans and dishes in the dishwasher. Upstairs, she changed into black clothes, jeans, turtleneck, jacket and boots. Her last stop was the salon. She retrieved her iPad, guns and spare magazines and stuffed them in a backpack. Before going to the garage, she scanned the neighborhood one last time, but the streets were empty.

A half-hour later she drove into Cullen Crossing from the west, motoring through the stoplight and glancing to her left to the second story of the house. The curtains were closed except for the same small gap. She drove ahead and pulled into the parking lot of the church. She took out her spotting scope and checked the second floor of the house. If you knew what to look for you could spot the video camera, the black tripod legs just visible, some motion in the background that she suspected was a cop.

But that only gave them a view of the front. There was another small grouping of modest one-story rambler houses to the southeast of the strip mall. She scanned those that had a clear view of the rear of the strip mall.

There you are.

The sixth house. Back corner window. The shades open just a crack. Through the scope she picked up movement and the lens of a fixed camera.

The police were still watching. Mileski and Marrone were dirty as the day was long and they knew it now. They were just waiting for the dirt to arrive. In fact, given how long they'd been watching already, she suspected they already had some.

But how much? And how long would it be before they acted on it?

Would they act on it? Would they find enough to arrest, charge, and prosecute?

And most importantly, would it be in time?

That was the kicker. She did not have the luxury of time. The issue had to be forced. Jeff was the last person she cared about that would die at the hands of these guys.

Pulling down the driver side sunshade to obscure her, she scanned the building with her scope, as well as the location of the surveillance. While she couldn't know for sure, she doubted the police had someone inside. Maybe from time to time someone went inside to look around as she had, but they weren't there permanently.

She snapped her head right at a door opening out the front of the bar.

"There you pricks are," she murmured.

Mileski stepped out onto the front sidewalk from the bar and walked down to the hardware store where Marrone was waiting. Marrone lit up a cigar and smoke billowed around them while Mileski drank from a tumbler. A third man stood nearby, peering around. He was muscle. She knew the look, the way he carried himself, the way he looked around, not to mention the slight bulge in his back underneath his coat, his gun. She suspected there were a few others of the type around. While they hunted for her, they were circling the wagons. She hadn't been watching them daily, but familiar with how these guys thought, she suspected they'd been largely hunkered down at the strip mall since she killed the two men last week.

A debate percolated in her mind. There was Jimmy Mileski and Paul Marrone. And then Vince Smith was here. She'd seen him last week and wouldn't be surprised that he was the one who did Jeff. And Smith himself would have others around. He was no lone wolf. He always ran with a pack. She took out two of his men last week but there were always more hired guns to be found, as evidenced by the man now with Mileski and Marrone. She had to account for five, six, perhaps a few more.

It was a lot to handle.

Was it doable? She snorted a whimsical laugh. At this point, it didn't matter if it was.

She sat back and closed her eyes, breathing slowly through her nose, calming her mind.

Angie DeEsposito had been fat, slow, and would waddle about, but his mind was agile, methodical, patient. He'd been wise in the world in which he operated. He had one particular pearl of wisdom for her when she first started out. With her eyes closed she could remember it clear as day.

"Marta, do you eat a whole pie in one sitting? No. You eat it one slice at a time."

"What's your point, Ang?"

"Big problems are hard to solve. Small ones are not."

"Meaning?"

"See the playing field, see the opponent, kid. Build a plan by

making a big problem a series of small ones. Bite off one piece at a time until you have a sequence and then execute it one piece, one step at a time. Do that and a big difficult problem is simply a series of small easy ones."

Identify your target. Next determine where they are vulnerable. Then, either lure them there or get there yourself first and wait. Solve one problem, then another, then another. Don't act until you have a solution for each problem. Without realizing it, she applied the concept all the time at home or cutting hair. It's all a sequence, you just have to visualize it, understand it then do it.

She opened her eyes and looked at Mileski and Marrone. *You know right where they are. They're worried you're coming, but they don't know what you look like.*

She still had some advantages.

A small smile crept across her face and one name floated into her mind.

Philly Lamberto.

To do it, she needed a few things. She motored away and started making a mental list. The first thing she needed was the kids' car. Second, was a stop at the storage locker.

THIRTY-SEVEN

"NOT TO BE RECOGNIZED IN THIS LIFETIME."

"They're still at the strip mall?" Braddock asked Eggleston, who dropped into a seat in front of his desk.

"They haven't moved in days. They've just been holed up inside. They go from the hardware store to the bar and restaurant, occasionally step out front for a smoke, or for a short drive somewhere, but that's it. They've gone home once in the last week. And they don't step outside or go anywhere else without a guy or two going with them."

"We know why now," Tori said, explaining their fear of Marta Dudek. "Those two are hunkered down until they find her."

"Are we moving on these guys?" Eggs asked.

"We're working on the warrants right now," Boe said. "We're arresting them for the whole smash, the drugs, the murders of Banz and others and the drive-by shooting in Holmstrand."

"Holy smokes. Big day."

"Yeah," Braddock said. "Steak could use some help on the write-up."

"On it."

Tori's phone buzzed and she grinned.

"What?" Boe said.

"It's Special Agent Bahn of the Chicago Field Office."

"No way they know what we're doing already."

"The Bureau works in mysterious ways," Tori said, smiling, putting the call on speaker as Braddock closed his office door. "Special Agent Bahn, to what do I owe the pleasure?"

"Tori, Jeff Tommasoni is missing?"

"Oh God, no." The bar owner from the Polish place. She'd liked him.

"Cordelia went to the Chicago Police. They called me. I'm calling you."

"Have you spoken with her?"

"Yes. Tommasoni has not been seen or heard from since the restaurant closed Sunday night."

"He's been talking to her, to Marta, hasn't he?"

"Recently, yes," Bahn said. "That's what Cordelia said. He told her that Saturday night, after we'd been through there. She told me Jeff dated her back when they were freshmen in college."

"That was right about the time her father was killed," Tori said. "And he never mentioned that."

"They stopped seeing one another not long after, according to Cordelia."

"When she became what she became."

"Why?" Braddock said. "Why were they talking now?"

Tori narrowed her look and then to Bahn said, "Would Tommasoni have been hooked into the Outfit down there? Is he associated with them? Is the restaurant part of the operation?"

"That's not it, Tori. His brother Corey works in the Cook County Sheriff's Office. He ran a license plate search for Jeff."

"And it was for what?"

"According to the brother, the license plate was for a vehicle that had been destroyed two years ago at Petrovic Salvage. Tori,

George Petrovic is Ernie Rudick's brother-in-law. And you can see where it leads from there."

Tori looked to Braddock. "That's how she got involved in all this. Rudick is Petrovic's brother-in-law. She recognizes the name from her Chicago days and does a little investigating and I'm betting she sees that Rudick is working with Mileski and Marrone."

"I'm sorry you're dealing with this up there. Is there anything I can do to help?"

Tori thought for a minute. "Remember the guy who survived being shot at Lamberto's club?"

"Yes, Vince Smith."

"I think he's been up here. Our surveillance crews think he left here Sunday morning. Run a check on him."

"We already know he's not a good guy, Tori."

"No, the last few days. See if he took a flight from Minneapolis to Chicago on Saturday or Sunday. See if he flew back here. If he did—"

"He's the one who did Tommasoni. It's relevant, albeit circumstantial."

"Before the day is over, I may be able to make it more than circumstantial."

"Oh yeah?" Bahn replied.

"I'll have news for you later." Tori hung up and looked to Braddock. "Is Nolan around here?"

"Yeah, I think so."

"Get her." Tori turned, bolted out of her chair and rushed down the hallway. Boe followed, as did Braddock, who hollered down the hallway. "Nolan! I need you."

"I should have got going on this right away when I got back," Tori started, sifting through files on the table, perturbed with herself for not having gotten right to the search for Marta when she returned from Chicago. "I should have been right here, not at Devers house sitting on my fucking ass."

"Hey, this is not on you," Braddock said. "Tommasoni knew things. He didn't tell you those things when he had the chance. Had he? He'd be alive. He didn't."

"Maybe, but this has to be the outcome? You know he's dead. That was the price he had to pay?" She grabbed a coffee cup off the table and whipped it at the wall, the ceramic shattering in a million pieces. "Dammit!"

"Hey, Tori," Boe started. "This is not your fault."

"The hell it isn't."

"It's not. I won't have you carry that," Braddock asserted. "Jeff Tommasoni knew who and what she was. He knew what would happen in giving Rudick's name to her. It isn't hard to foresee this outcome. You play in the dirt, you get dirty."

"And there's only so many hours in the day," Boe replied reasonably. "We've been on the Bianchis."

"That took priority," Braddock added.

"Well, how about now?"

"Who are we looking for, Tori?" Nolan said. "How can I help?"

"Her name was Marta Dudek," Tori said, handing Nolan a picture of her. "That photo is twelve years old, maybe a little older but that's her. There are two questions, who is she now? And where does she live? And I think the latter can answer the former."

"The license plate."

"Right."

"We culled every bit of surveillance video we could find up there," Nolan said.

"Maybe we missed something or, maybe she had it from something we didn't find," Tori said. "She has some technical ability. She placed a tracker on two different vehicles. It's been twelve years, but doing what she did and then disappearing, she had to have some remaining level of paranoia."

"Paranoia?" Boe asked.

"Surveillance system, maybe," Tori said.

"Really?" Nolan said.

"Why not?" Braddock muttered. "No big thing to set up a few cameras. She was using trackers. Why not cameras."

"Right," Tori said as she rolled open an enlarged satellite print of the Randalls' neighborhood. "We know that shooters followed Jensen and Horn from Manchester Bay to the Randall house. To do that, once in Holmstrand, they made this horseshoe like loop through the neighborhood. I'm thinking Marta lives somewhere on that loop. Because she must have seen the vehicle, seen it more than we did, enough to track it."

"Physical characteristics we're looking for," Braddock said.

"She is thirty-seven years old, but I'm betting under her new identity she's not that age, although probably within that general range. Say thirty-three to forty-three. She could pass anywhere in that age range I would think. She had black hair back then. I'm guessing blonde or very light colored now."

"Why not a redhead, brunette or black?" Braddock said. "She had a bit of an Italian look to her, the pale skin, dark eyes, and hair. Dudek is Polish but her mother's last name was Mastriani, Italian. Northern Minnesota isn't without either its Italians or Poles."

"Yeah, we're a melting pot, except if I were to profile, I'd say the Italian demographics are more common up on the Iron Range, although there are plenty of folks of Polish descent in these parts. And it could be any hair color, but she had black hair. She used a red wig when she killed Lamberto. Not that she was seen many times but when she was, one thing she wasn't was blonde."

"I'm with Tori," Boe said. "If she wanted to change her look and blend, truly blend in Minnesota, I'd go blonde. There are Norwegians, Finns, and Swedes, not just here, but everywhere in the state. And pick a common last name. There are Andersons, Johnsons, Hendersons, Nelsons, Christiansens, Olsons galore."

"That's what I'm thinking," Tori said.

Tori opened a folder and took out photos. "The FBI came up with these possibilities of what she might look like now based on her look twelve years ago. They aged her, played with her hair and facial features. It gives you an idea anyway. I can't imagine she didn't have work done on her nose as it was very... prominent. I'd be surprised she didn't have dental work done too. She had an overbite."

"All that costs money."

"She'd have had it," Braddock said. "Nineteen kills that we know of. She didn't work for free and took out some well-connected Mafia types in other cities. That type of work has high risk and a steep price."

"And she would have protected the money in case she had to run."

"Which ultimately, she did," Braddock said. "She completely disappeared."

"That's right!" Tori gestured, suddenly excited, jabbing Braddock in the chest.

"Ow! What was that for?"

"Sometimes you're brilliant, you know."

"Not to be recognized in this lifetime."

"We talked about this once, but we didn't have any context. Marta doesn't emerge and put it all at risk for some random person. What happened mattered to her. It impacted her. It called her to act. You do that for—"

"A friend," Braddock replied. "Someone who means something to you."

"Right, a good friend," Tori said, looking at the street grid again. "And we interviewed the neighbors. You and I."

"Our notebooks." Braddock hustled back to his office, Tori to her cubicle to retrieve the steno spiral notebooks.

"Evelyn Watson," Braddock said as he came into the room and pointed to the map. "She lived right across the street. This house."

Nolan checked the address and found Evelyn's driver's license. "Evelyn, age forty-nine. Five-foot-two. Black hair. Brown eyes."

"Too short," Tori said. "Try, Terry Lee. She lived three houses down, same side of the street. How about her?"

Nolan tapped at her computer. "Hmm. Maybe. She's five-foot-five. Reddish hair. Green eyes." She picked up the photo of Dudek. "Marta has green eyes."

Tori examined the DMV photo. "What's her age?"

Nolan scrolled down. "Forty-six."

"I don't think so. Try..." Tori flipped a page. "Here, Jenny Christiansen. She was there when it happened, and Cathy Randall stayed at her house down the street after the shooting. That's where Braddock and I first spoke with her. How about her? If I remember right, she had blondish hair."

Nolan did the search and pulled up the photo. "Long blonde hair in this photo."

"I think her hair was shorter though," Tori said and then looked to Braddock and snapped her fingers. "That's right. She'd been at the neighbor's salon... getting her... hair trimmed. The neighbor, her name was... Maggie, Maggie something."

"We talked to her in her living room," Braddock said. "She still had the blood on her clothes and hands."

"I talked to her a second time the next day." Tori frantically flipped through the pages of her notebook. "She told me all about Cathy Randall's divorce. How tough it had been. She was... angry about the behavior of the ex-husband, how he handled it. She and her husband had vacationed with the Randalls. She was a friend. A sister. The hairstylist next door."

"Was she tall?" Braddock asked.

"Yes! When you and I talked to her she was sitting down.

Her husband let us in the house. But when I talked to her a day or two later, we were standing. Everybody is tall to me, but she was tall. Long legs, a layered bob blonde haircut that I thought was really cute."

"Maggie, I assume Margaret Duncan," Nolan said, tapping the computer. "Let's check her out."

* * *

Maggie drove the kids aged black Toyota 4Runner to the strip mall and parked in front of the liquor store. She had a white baseball cap on and her dark framed glasses.

She strolled casually into the hardware store, her purse over her shoulder. Inside the store, she made a point of slowly walking the perimeter aisles, her hat pulled low, perusing the merchandise while also getting a sense of the interior. There were two surveillance cameras in the ceiling. One covered the checkout counter in the front of the store and the other the rear, near the office. As she walked the back hallway of the store, she let her eyes drift left to see Marrone sitting at a desk in the office. His neck was crooked to the right to hold the phone receiver while he tapped at his keyboard and looked at the computer screen, paying her no attention as she slowly shuffled by. While she didn't look at him directly, she also caught a glimpse of a security guy, leaning against the wall in the hall-way, his back to her, looking at his phone, his gun tucked in the waistband of his pants.

She glanced to the tight aisle that ran to the front door and then the next aisle, three times as wide with merchandise on tables in the middle, which ran down the center of the store. Then she glanced back, seeing the back door open as another man walked through. There was definitely a back hallway. *Interesting.*

She walked the remainder of the store, grabbing two rolls of duct tape off a hook in the last aisle and purchasing them at the checkout register. She put her purchase in the 4Runner and then went to the restaurant. She'd been here a few weeks ago, when she first saw Rudick and then Mileski and Marrone having lunch.

As with her last visit, she took a seat at the bar counter and ordered a bowl of soup for an early lunch, which came quickly. It was quiet, just as before with only a few patrons inside. As she ate deliberately, she let her eyes drift around the interior. Turning her head almost imperceptibly left, she caught a glimpse of Mileski reading documents, a cup of coffee and half-eaten sandwich in front of him. It was the same table she'd seen him, Marrone and Rudick eat at. The corner booth. It allowed him to see the entirety of the restaurant. At the table he had stacks of paper and a laptop computer. As if that was where he usually did his work. Lying underneath a sheet of paper was a handgun. Glancing left, another goon sat at the next table, keeping a somewhat wary eye out but paying her no particular attention.

Then he came through the back door.

Vince Smith.

Security was three men that she'd seen now. She was mildly surprised to see Smith here instead of out looking for her. If only he knew.

She dropped a ten-dollar bill on the bar. There was only one thing left to do.

* * *

"Take a look at that," Nolan said, sitting back, looking at the DMV photo. "Margaret Duncan is her married name. Peterson is her maiden name. Margaret Katherine Peterson, as anodyne a Minnesota name as you could possibly come up with, but I'm not finding any history of her that's more than—"

"Twelve years old?" Tori said.

"Right," Nolan said. "No DMV record that matches that birthdate or license number prior to then. And not just here, anywhere. I find no record of her in any other state. I've found some Margaret Katherine Petersons but they're not her."

"She's thirty-five according to her license, so within the window we're looking for," Braddock added. "And blonde hair."

"Although you can see the hint of darker roots," Tori observed. "And green eyes. And tall, five foot nine inches. The weight is a little different. Marta Dudek was one hundred twenty-five pounds. Maggie Duncan is one hundred fifty now although having seen her, I don't buy that."

"Nobody tells the truth on their license," Nolan snarked. "Everyone lies by fifteen, twenty pounds."

"I meant she was skinnier."

"Oh."

Tori examined the DMV photo and compared it to pictures of Marta. The nose was different, made thinner and the jawline had been softened, but the eyes were right, not just the color but they looked the same. How better to constantly change your appearance than as a hair stylist? And she had a rudimentary set of security cameras on the outside of her house for the salon. She'd given them all the footage. But if she were a professional, maybe she had something better besides what she gave them.

"What do you think?" Braddock asked her.

"I think she heard her good friend's son shot and killed. She had the blood of Leo Randall on her clothes, her hands, having tried to give first aid. That could trigger someone with her abilities to act."

"It could at that."

"Does she have an Instagram or Facebook page?" Tori asked Nolan.

"Not that I can find. But I look at the photos we do have of her, and this DMV photo and I can see the similarity. She had the nose done. But the eyes, the shape of her mouth, even her ears, you notice her earlobes, the almost circular shape."

"I do now," Tori said.

"It's her," Braddock said.

Boe and Steak stuck their heads in the conference room. "We're good to go," Boe said. "Everyone is assembled."

"Plenty of backup," Steak added with a wry smile. "We're storming the beaches."

"Let's go then," Braddock said, looking to Tori and then the file spread on the conference room table. "I assume you're coming?"

"Is the Pope Catholic?"

"Did you identify her?" Boe asked as they all walked down the hall.

"Maggie Duncan. Cathy Randall's neighbor."

"As soon as we have Mileski and Marrone in custody, we go get her."

THIRTY-EIGHT

"WHAT'S THIS WE STUFF?"

Taking a calculated risk, Maggie drove the Acadia back to Cullen Crossing and circled the small town twice, making one stop behind the volunteer fire station. She had four small devices. She placed one inside the first dumpster. Two inside the second dumpster, keeping one in reserve in her left side pocket.

She parked along the small side street just northeast of the strip mall and scanned the area one more time with her small scope.

It was time.

Getting out she walked across the parking lot on the back-side of the mall, carrying a cardboard coffee cup, a backpack over her shoulder, with a baseball cap pulled down low over the short grayish wig she let cover her face, along with her large, framed glasses.

She walked along the north side of the building, turned the corner, took the two steps up onto the front sidewalk. She glanced to her left through the windows into the restaurant. Mileski was, as she'd hoped, still sitting in the back corner booth. Even better, Smith was sitting with him.

Past the liquor store, she stepped into the hardware store. Inside, she turned to the left and walked down the second to last aisle and stopped two-thirds of the way down. She took a green plastic container of grass seed off the shelf, pretending to read the label, letting her eyes drift to Marrone's office while her hand right slipped into her side pocket and took out the burner phone. She hit a preset number.

* * *

He finished the last of the entries in his ledger, closed the book and turned around. He then entered the combination for the safe and placed it on its shelf inside, stacks of cash on the shelf directly underneath. That work complete, he took a drink of his soda and then opened his humidor and pulled out a cigar.

"Hah," Frank burped from the hallway, leaning against the wall.

"What?" Marrone replied with a wry smile as he opened his desk drawer and took out his cigar cutter. "It's time."

BOOM!

"What was that?"

* * *

BOOM!

"That was an explosion," Jimmy said, looking up from his computer, the building shuddering.

"And close," Vince murmured, getting up from his chair.

* * *

"We'll go lights and sirens when we get to the parking lot," Braddock instructed as he turned the corner into town, Steak and Eggleston, as well as Boe behind him, along with Frewer and several more deputies following. Another sheriff's deputy was coming in from the east along with a patrol officer from Crosslake. The deputies in Eunice and Harold's houses were on standby.

He halted at the stoplight.

Tori chuckled. "You know, you could just run—"

BOOM!

"Whoa!" Braddock muttered.

A fireball mushroomed in the sky behind the fire station.

"Will, no way that's not just random."

"No, it's not." Braddock flipped on his light and siren and accelerated through the light.

KABOOM!

"Holy shit!" Tori exclaimed, ducking down as Braddock jerked the wheel right into the parking lot.

* * *

BOOM!

Everyone in the hardware store ducked but then went to look out the windows. She quickly slipped off her backpack, dropped to a knee and pulled her gun, silencer attached and counted... *one... two... three.*

She darted from the aisle... *four...* covering fifteen feet... *five...* her gun up.

KABOOM!

It was the second, bigger explosion, shaking the building.

She turned the corner.

Pop! Pop! Pop!

The goon outside Marrone's office instantly crumpled. She spun right, Marrone staring at her in shock.

Pop! Pop! Pop!

She hit him three times in the chest, sending him back against his credenza. She set her feet.

Pop!

One last one between the eyes.

She turned around.

Pop!

One more finished the man on the floor. She turned right and pushed open the rear door into the hallway. She turned left, ejected the magazine, jamming in another full one and sprinted down the hall.

* * *

"We've got the restaurant!" Braddock exclaimed and pointed Steak to the hardware store, while he ran to the front door. "Move! Move!" he exclaimed to the people milling on the sidewalk, watching the inferno behind them.

"On it!" Steak replied as he and Eggleston made their way down the sidewalk, deputies in tow.

Pop!

The sound was suppressed but unmistakable.

Pop!

"Those were gunshots," Tori said, her gun out.

"Everyone on the mall now!" Boe ordered into her radio, her gun drawn. "Get out of here! Move!" she yelled to the civilians milling around. "Move! Move! Now!" She gestured for Braddock to go.

Braddock rushed to the front door and opened it and Tori, gun up, pushed inside.

* * *

He'd watched the police vehicles rush in. Braddock and Hunter got out of a Tahoe and were running their way. He spun around to Jimmy. The back door to the restaurant opened.

"Jimmy, down!" Vince yelled as he reached around his back.

* * *

Maggie yanked open the back door to the restaurant. She saw Smith reaching his right arm back. She didn't hesitate on him this time.

Pop! Pop! Pop! Pop! Pop!

She caught the flash of light, police lights at the front door.

* * *

Tori burst inside the restaurant and saw a blondish man, his back to her, collapsing, a gun falling out of his right hand.

She glanced back right. It was a gray-haired woman, with a gun, pivoting right at her.

"Get down!" Braddock yelled, pushing Tori to the right and then rolling left, grabbing, and tipping a table on its side for cover.

Maggie Duncan fired.

Pop! Pop! Pop!

Tori rolled onto her stomach, and between the tables glimpsed Maggie, who was backing down the hallway. Tori fired.

Crack! Crack! Crack!

She thought she saw Maggie buckle as she rolled right behind a downed table.

Boom! Boom! Boom! Boom!

Tori glanced back to see Boe and Braddock covering her, firing. She looked to the back hallway. Maggie pushed through the back door.

"She went out the back!" Tori said as she pushed herself up and ran down the back hallway.

"Careful, now," Braddock said. He looked back and Boe was coming forward.

* * *

Maggie scrambled into the back hallway. Straight ahead a man was coming up the stairway, a gun in his hand. He saw her but it was too late.

Pop! Pop! Pop! Pop! Pop!

He collapsed backwards down the steps.

She rushed past the steps, her left side burning as she pushed her way through a back door on the left. Stumbling down three steps she hobble-jogged into the parking lot. Marrone's Escalade was parked right ahead. She had one last small device in reserve. She set the timer manually and set it on the rear bumper as she ran by, grabbing at her left side. The Acadia was fifty yards ahead.

* * *

Tori moved ahead to the right of the back door, Braddock to the left, his gun up. Boe was fifteen feet back, covering. Tori pushed the door open.

"It's a back hallway," he said, scanning it in both directions. Another door finished closing further down the hallway to their left.

A man came up the stairs with a gun.

"Drop it!" Tori ordered. "Now!"

The man dropped the gun and put his hands up.

Tori moved past him and made it to the exterior door, Braddock right behind her, followed by Boe.

Pushing the door open, she saw a gray-haired woman running. "I see her—"

BOOM!

The blast threw her back into Braddock and then the two of them into the cinder block wall of the hallway.

"Ah... Ah... Ah..." Tori moaned, grabbing at her chest, trying to get air.

"Tori!" Boe exclaimed. "Is she hit?"

"I think she got the wind knocked out of her," Braddock said, rolling to her.

Tori grimaced, nodding, struggling for air. "Ahh, damn, that hurts."

Boe had her radio. "Out the back! Look for a woman running out the back!"

"Gray hair," Tori gasped. "She had gray hair, it's a wig."

"Gray hair. Look for gray hair!" Boe exclaimed and then cautiously moved forward.

Steak and Eggleston came out the rear door for the hardware store door and ran to them. "You guys alright?" Steak asked.

"Yeah," Braddock said. "You?"

"Marrone is dead and another guy. Shot multiple times, executed."

"That was Marta or Maggie or whatever the hell her name is," Braddock said. "That was what all the explosions were about. A distraction. It sure as hell worked."

"What about Mileski?"

"In cuffs, lying face down on the floor in the restaurant, two deputies with him," Nolan said, stepping into the hallway. "He was hiding like a coward in the corner."

Braddock and Steak lifted Tori up. "How you doing?" Steak asked.

She sighed, leaning over, trying to catch her breath. "Singed," she said, standing up and stretching her jaw. "My ears are ringing."

All five of them stepped outside and around the burning

hulk of the Escalade. The deputy from Harold's house came running.

"Did you see a gray-haired woman running?" Boe asked.

"Just for a brief second, Sheriff," the deputy replied. "I saw her come out the back. I ran to Harold's sliding deck door to run over here and then—"

"The explosion."

The deputy nodded. "I lost sight of her after that."

Braddock looked to Steak. "What do you think?"

"There are three ways out of here. We need roadblocks east and west of Cullen Crossing on County 16. We need a block at the junction of County 39 south at the junction with County 106. Those are the main ones."

Boe raised her radio. "This is Boe. I need roadblocks..."

"And the Duncan house," Tori said. "We need someone watching there."

* * *

Mileski was sitting on a barstool, handcuffed under the watchful eye of Frewer when they all came back into the bar. "James Mileski. I'm Will Braddock, Chief Detective for Shepard County. This is Sheriff Boe and Tori Hunter. You've met Detective Nolan."

"What is this bullshit?" Jimmy Mileski hissed at the two of them. "Someone shoots up my place and I'm the one in cuffs?"

"It's not bullshit. It's some serious shit," Boe said. "For starters, you're being arrested for drug distribution. You and your boys have been running drugs in my county."

"But that's not your biggest problem here, Jimmy," Tori needled, her breathing now normal.

"No, she's right," Braddock continued. "Your biggest problem is you're also under arrest for the attempted murder of Alisha Sweeney, the murder of Reardon Banz as well as the murders of Grace Horn, Cameron Jensen, and Leo Randall in Holmstrand. And my guess is that in time, we'll pin a few more on you for giving the orders."

Mileski looked from Braddock to Boe to Tori and then back. "You ain't got shit."

"I don't?" Braddock replied. He looked to Tori and Boe, smiling. "Actually, Jimmy, I think I do. You see, I have the Bianchi Brothers in custody, so I have the whole operation. I've seen it with my own eyes the past couple of weeks. And a few hours ago, we dug up the body of Banz out northwest of Manchester Bay in the woods. I hear it was your dumping ground. More bodies will be found." He leaned forward and poked Mileski in the chest, "And we're going to pin them all on you."

Mileski sat back and shook his head. "We ain't got anything to say."

"We?" Boe said, eyebrows raised. "What's this *we* stuff?"

"There is no *we* anymore there, Jimmy," Tori said. "Your buddy Marrone is dead in his office courtesy of Marta Dudek. She got to him before we could. You're, as they say, the last rat standing. You're going to take the fall for all this and there ain't shit big brother Bobby can do for you."

"Hell, Jimmy," Braddock added. "Before this is all over, with all we got, we might nail his ass too."

* * *

"It is kind of ironic, the volunteer fire department called in to put out a fire... at the volunteer fire station," Tori remarked, watching a group of firemen douse the blazes in the dumpsters behind the station.

"At least they didn't have to go far," Braddock remarked as he watched Boe place Mileski in the backseat of her Tahoe. He half suspected media would be at the government center when she triumphantly arrived. Tori and he walked back into the hardware store and to the back offices.

"Roadblocks?" Braddock asked Steak as he returned.

"They're up. Traffic is stopped cold on 16 east and west and 39 south at 106. Problem is we don't know what we're looking for beyond a blonde or gray-haired woman. Nobody saw where she went or what vehicle she had in all the chaos."

"She might have been shot," Tori said, pointing to a small blood smear on the door frame from the restaurant into the back hallway. In the hallway, she saw another blood smear and then a couple of drops on the floor. Neither her nor Braddock were hit or cut. She knelt by the last drop before the back door she'd used. "She was hit. Maybe not bad but—"

"Add it to the alert."

"On it."

Tori looked to Braddock. "Holmstrand."

"Let's go."

THIRTY-NINE

"I COULDN'T LET IT GO."

Maggie raced around the outskirts of the town and then south on County Road 39. She powered down the window and threw out her gray wig and then looked to the GPS map system on the dashboard screen. She didn't have long on this road. Roadblocks would go up. She was coming up to a left turn onto County 106 ahead when she saw flashing lights come around a corner in the distance.

No choice.

She turned hard left and zoomed ahead. In her rearview mirror she saw the flashing lights stop at the turn. A roadblock. Where did this road go? As she tweezed the map ahead, this road would take her all the way to the southern end of Crosslake, which she guessed was four to five miles ahead. She accelerated, pushing the speedometer past eighty, covering the distance in just a few minutes. There was no roadblock at the intersection with Highway 6 and she made a right turn.

A half-hour later, she reached the storage garage, pulled the Acadia inside and then closed the door. Under the workbench light she examined the wound. It was three or four inches long, under her rib cage. She retrieved her old first-aid kit, then poured alcohol on the wound.

"Argh!"

The wound had to be closed, the blood oozing. From the kit she retrieved a needle, poured more alcohol on it and then threaded it.

She'd done this one other time, fifteen years ago. "I wish I had a local," she murmured as she plunged the needle in. "Ahh." She pulled the needle through, layered it over and did it again. She closed the wound with six stitches and then placed two large bandages over it. She sat back against the workbench, breathing heavy, the wound closed but the pain and sting from it still coursing through her body.

Now what?

With the wound, she had to assume she had left blood at the scene. If they had blood, they would have DNA. And here she was now with six stitches on her rib cage. They would be hunting for her. Marrone was dead. Smith too. At least there was that. With Braddock and Hunter there, Mileski would be in custody. Those responsible for Leo's murder were punished or would be.

That was the good, but there was the cost.

The hunt would be fully on for her now and not just from Tori Hunter. The Bureau, the U.S. Marshals Service, every law enforcement agency would be hunting for Marta Dudek, aka Margaret Katherine Duncan.

She walked over to the Acadia, holding her side and retrieved her backpack from the Acadia. In the very back pocket was the iPad. She tapped on the screen and pulled up the surveillance system for the house. She checked all four of the cameras, the two covering the front, the one over the salon and the one covering the backyard. They were all clear.

She tapped to rewind the footage for the past hour.

"Oh, no."

* * *

Tori rang the doorbell, Braddock behind her. Steak went to the right and Eggleston to the left, swinging around to the back. Four uniformed deputies and two Holmstrand patrol officers provided support.

The front door opened. It was Rob Duncan. "Hello, can I help—"

"We have to come inside," Braddock said, brushing past Duncan. Tori followed and they had their guns out and cleared the main level. Two deputies joined them and worked their way upstairs. At the back door, Tori let Steak and Eggleston inside. They immediately went about clearing the basement.

"What the hell is going on?" Rob Duncan demanded.

"Where is your wife, Mr. Duncan?" Braddock asked.

"I've been wondering about... that. She's not here. Has something happened to her?"

"Have you tried to call her?"

"Yes. She's not answering. Her SUV is here but the kids' 4Runner is not."

"The basement is clear," Steak reported.

"Upstairs as well," a deputy reported.

Braddock nodded and raised his radio. "This is Braddock, set up back two blocks. We'll be inside the house. If she appears it will be in a Toyota 4Runner."

"Dammit, what the hell is going on!" Rob Duncan demanded.

"Mr. Duncan, what do you know about your wife's past?" Braddock asked.

* * *

Maggie sniffed again, wiping her nose with the back of her hand and then the tears from her cheeks. Hunter had identified her.

There was no choice now.

Gingerly, she pushed herself up and over to the safe. Inside, she had a hundred thousand dollars in emergency cash that she stuffed in a black nylon duffel bag. From the old travel trunk, she retrieved a clean gray T-shirt, a brown leather jacket and old pair of black jeans that would do until she bought others. She retrieved the last two Berettas from the safe and the spare magazines and stuffed them in the backpack. The last thing she did was change the license plates on the Acadia from Iowa to Wisconsin plates.

* * *

"My wife was, is a professional killer," Rob Duncan said in almost a whisper, shaking his head, in shock. "That can't be. It just…"

"I'm sorry. But she was," Tori said and took out her cell phone and opened a photo. "This is what your wife looked like before you met her. Her name was Marta Dudek. She was from the south side of Chicago. She was a contract killer for the Mob."

Rob Duncan took a look at the photo, and Tori could see the recognition in his eyes, and he nodded. "Her nose is quite different."

"And I suspect a few other minor changes," Braddock said, standing near a bookshelf full of family photos, holding one of Maggie in his hands. "The others were perhaps more subtle."

"You never wondered about her past?" Tori asked.

"Oh, I did. She was… vague about it."

"What did she tell you about her life before you met her?"

"Her mother died when she was young. She had no brothers or sisters. That she had left home in Chicago after high school to escape an abusive father. She feared what would happen if her father found her so she said that we could never go to Chicago. So, we never did."

"And you believed that?"

"Yeah," Rob Duncan answered. "I did. I tried asking about it, more than once, but when I did, she got agitated and would shut down. I thought it real, the... pain of it. Perhaps she was a good actress."

"She was perhaps that," Tori said gently, seeing his pain too. "I think the pain might have also been real too. Her father was murdered by the Mob. Her surrogate father, a Mob capo named Angelo DeEsposito, was murdered by a rival Mob crew. She killed to avenge her father and then for the Mob. They tried to kill her. It's not hard to imagine why she wouldn't have wanted to talk about it with you."

"Plus, she was wanted by the FBI and the Mob," Braddock said. "She couldn't tell you the truth, for your own protection."

"Especially once you two fell in love and got married." Tori's phone buzzed. It was a number she didn't recognize and was going to drop the call and then stopped. She knew who it was. "Hello?"

"I want to talk to my husband?"

"I don't think I can allow that, Maggie," Tori replied, looking to Braddock. "You need to turn yourself in."

"We both know that's not going to happen. This is a burner. You can try tracing it if you want but it's going out the window the minute I hang up. Let me talk to him one last time. You owe me that for Alisha."

Tori nodded and put the phone on speaker and handed it to Rob Duncan.

"Maggie?"

"Has Tori told you that my real name is Marta Dudek and that I was a contract killer?"

"Yes."

"It's all true. Every last bit of it. I was that person."

Rob Duncan sighed, looking to the floor. Hearing it from her had just made it real.

"I'm sorry, Rob," Maggie said, breaking down on the phone, her voice trembling. "I'm so, so, sorry."

Rob sat back on the couch, "Mags, was any of it real. Or was I just—"

* * *

"No. No," Maggie said, wiping tears from her eyes, the road dark, no other cars within sight. "It was all real. I love you. I love Ellen and Brian. They will always be my children. I will always love you and the kids, always."

"Why, Mags? Weren't you happy?"

"Oh yes. I was happy, very happy."

"Why do this?"

She let out a big sigh. "I fought it. I tried not to. But what happened to Leo and Cathy. I had Leo's blood on my hands, my clothes and then finding out who was responsible. Tori Hunter can tell you all about them but... I should have let it go, I just couldn't. I thought I could do this and... not have to have it cost us... everything." Maggie sniffed and sighed. "I'm sorry. I'm so sorry. I love you, Rob. Goodbye."

She threw the phone out the window, put both hands on the wheel and let the tears stream down her face.

* * *

Jimmy Mileski was arrested, denied bail, and charged a week later with eight murders including those of Leo Randall, Cameron Jensen and Grace Horn, along with numerous drug trafficking charges. Additional counts for money laundering and tax evasion would be added in the following weeks as the business operations at Cullen Crossing Plaza were further investigated. The FBI and United States Attorney joined in the case and, in time, turned their gaze to Chicago and Bobby Mileski.

Jeff Tommasoni remained missing and was presumed murdered.

Alisha Sweeney found a safe and happy home with Paul and Trish Adams, who took her in, giving her a home and new start on life, while the process of their adoption ground along. Paul and Trish's older children doted on Alisha in their ever more frequent visits to check on their new little sister. Aunt Tori's sign language fluency returned through her frequent visits to the Adams' house to check on Alisha, usually arriving with a new outfit for her to try on and wear to her new school in Manchester Bay.

Cathy Randall had done as Maggie instructed her to do and drove to Madison, Wisconsin, and paid cash for a hotel. Braddock reached her and told her it was safe to return home.

Three days after the shooting in Cullen Crossing, the owner of a storage facility near Deerwood found blood smears on the garage door for one of the back storage units. Inside more blood was found at a small workbench, along with bandage wrappers, a bloody needle and thread. An open but empty safe and an unlocked trunk full of black leather clothes was also found.

The unit had been rented for the past nine-years by a Margaret Peterson, all rental payments in cash. The blood was subsequently DNA matched to hair from Maggie Duncan's hairbrush.

Despite a week's long manhunt, Maggie Duncan was not found.

FORTY

"YOU AND I ARE A LOT ALIKE, YOU KNOW."

July 1st

"When you arrive next Saturday, get your rental car and then plug our address into the GPS. It's an easy two-hour, maybe a little more drive up here," Tori said to Tracy. "We set up the guest bed just this morning. The expansion looks great. You'll be our first guests. We can't wait for you to get here."

"We can't wait either," Tracy replied excitedly. "I do have a piece of bad news though."

"What's that?"

"I won't be able to drink martinis with you."

"Why no— Oh wait, no, really? You're pregnant? Are you?"

"Two months. I visited the doctor yesterday."

"What do you mean bad news? Congratulations. Sam knocked you up, girl."

"That he did."

"Oh, Trace, I'm so happy for you both," Tori exclaimed happily. They talked for a few more minutes, promising to connect again later in the week.

"How many baby outfits are you going to buy for her this week?" Braddock asked.

"Depends on how many I can find," Tori replied, grinning. "Aunt Tori will be spoiling Baby Sheets, that is for sure."

The sky was cloudless, a hazy humid blue with the mid-afternoon temperature in the mid-eighties. Tori sat in her favorite Adirondack chair out on the end of the dock, a cold seltzer in her hand, her tanned, sun-lotioned skin soaking up the sun. Braddock sat to her right, leaning back, a cold Kona Big Wave beer in his hand, the small cooler between them stocked. Multiple footsteps bounded down the dock behind her. She turned to see Quinn and Peter in swimsuits, holding towels.

"Where are you two off to?"

"Surfing," Quinn said. "Carson's family is picking us up."

"And I'm sure Isabella too."

"I told you, we broke up," Quinn replied.

"Yeah, they seem real broken up, don't they," Braddock said to Tori with a wry grin, before taking a drink of his beer.

"Whatever, Dad."

A black Malibu surf boat approached, Sam Farner behind the wheel, expertly drifting the twenty-four-foot boat gently parallel to the dock's side.

Braddock grabbed hold of the overhead rack, steadying the boat while the boys jumped in. "Hiya, Sam. Luciana, how are you guys?"

"Great," Luciana replied, with a big smile from under her large sunhat.

"Will, Tori," Sam greeted with a smile. "You two look set."

"We are," Tori replied, holding up her cocktail, smiling.

"Hi, Peter," Izzy Farner greeted. "Hi, Quinn."

"Hey, Izz," Quinn said and then high-fived Carson and two other friends. Izzy had a friend along as well.

"Full crew in there," Braddock said, counting ten bodies in the boat.

"We'll see if we can wear them out a little," Sam said. "We're going to head up the lake a bit, do a little surfing and swimming. Might beach up a little bit out on the sandbar."

"How's the remodel coming?" Luciana asked.

"It's done," Braddock said. "Let us know if you want to stop back here later. We can give you a tour and then I can throw some burgers and brats on the grill."

"We have baked beans and salad too," Tori added.

Sam looked to Luciana who nodded and smiled. "Sounds great."

They watched the group float away before Sam hit the gas and the big boat zoomed off. Tori sat back down in her chair and took a sip of seltzer, completely relaxed.

"I could go for a snack," Braddock said. "Does a meat and cheeseboard sound good?"

"I'd like that."

"Coming up," Braddock replied and walked up to the house.

Tori slid her sunglasses back down and eased back into her chair. Her phone buzzed. She looked at the screen. It was a foreign call. Country Code 61. That was odd, a call from what she thought was Australia. It was probably fraud. She ignored it and took a drink of her seltzer.

Her phone beeped again. It was a text. *When I call this time, answer.*

She'd wondered if this call would come at some point. A few seconds later, the call came again from Australia. "Hello?"

"Tori, how are you?" Maggie greeted. "Are you sitting out on the dock on this fine summer day, enjoying the sun?"

"Are you watching me?" Tori said, bolting up out of her chair, peering around.

"I'll take that as a yes," Maggie replied with a mild laugh. "I looked up the forecast before I called. It looks like a beautiful day, kind of like the one I'm experiencing. The ocean waters a gorgeous aqua blue. There is something about the rhythm of the waves, the sound of the ocean, the crash against the shore, that just eases the mind, right?"

Tori nodded. "The beautiful waters of the South Pacific no doubt. In Australia. Would that be the Coral or Tasman Sea?"

"You know your geography," Maggie replied with a chuckle.

"I traveled to Sydney once. I would love to go back someday."

"Tell me, Tori. Are you still looking for me?"

"I'm sure the Bureau is. They always will be. You killed an agent."

"I asked about you?"

"Me?" Tori let out a breath, relaxed and reached for her seltzer. "I'm happy sitting on my dock on this fine summer day, enjoying the sun and drinking a High Noon."

"Good to know."

"What do you want, Maggie? Or is it, Marta? Or something else now?"

"All depends on the passport," Maggie replied. "I read Jimmy Mileski was indicted. Will he go down for it all?"

Tori thought for a moment. "I think so. When you add up all the charges between drugs, money laundering and murder he's looking at like two hundred years."

"Yes. But will he pay? I need him to go to prison. Will he?"

"Yes," Tori said but sensed Jimmy Mileski's ultimate fate wasn't what the call was really about. She could read all of that online. There had been plenty of reporting. "Why did you really call me?"

"Rob. How is he?"

"Don't you know?"

"I have no way of knowing."

"I thought maybe you might have called him. It's been months now. I don't think anyone is still monitoring his phone or watching his house. Lord knows we're not."

It was Maggie's turn to let out a long breath. "I can't call him. I can't do that to him. He suffered the loss. I don't need to make him keep suffering it."

"Why call me?"

"I want *you* to check in on him from time to time. Make sure he's okay, moves on, starts over, lives his life. Braddock too. You both know loss."

"That's a big ask."

"Is it?"

"Why would I do that for you?" Tori asserted. "After all you've—"

"Done. After all the people I killed. Tori, I'm not asking you to do it for me. I'm asking you to do it for him. He's a victim in all this. He did nothing wrong other than foolishly pursue me years ago."

Tori closed her eyes for a moment and stood still, looking out to the lake. "I don't know—"

"You and I are a lot alike, you know."

"Now hold on a second—"

"We're similar age. We both suffered loss of those we loved the most as teens to murder."

Tori froze at the comparison.

"One of us lost our sister and our sheriff father when they were a teenager and went on to become one of the most highly decorated women special agents in the history of the FBI. The other lost her father at nineteen to a Mafia hit and became a professional killer because she wanted revenge. An eye for an eye. You had your influences in your life. Cal Lund, good friends, Boston College, the FBI. I had mine. Angie DeEsposito. Tell me. Did you not want vengeance on the man who killed your sister?"

"You know I did."

"And you got it, twenty years later, right?"

"Yes."

"I wanted the same for my dad. He was no saint, but he wasn't a big sinner either. I knew the people he dealt with weren't the... best. But to be murdered the way he... was. Even if it was a hit intended for Angie, I couldn't let it pass."

"I get it. But then to become—"

"What I became? Yeah. Angie made the mistake of telling me who killed Stan. He had plans for those men, but I told him I was going to kill them. He laughed until he realized I was serious. Try as he repeatedly did, he couldn't talk me out of it. So, in his mind I'm sure, he did the next best thing to protect me, he... counseled me. Helped me plan it and succeed. I killed the men who killed my father. Just like you killed the man who killed your sister."

"And how did it feel?"

"That was the part I didn't expect."

"It didn't cure everything did it?"

"No. I thought I would feel satisfied. I killed them all. I'd had my vengeance on them. But I felt... no satisfaction, and worse, no remorse. It was like my heart had gone cold in doing it."

"You could do it again."

"I shouldn't have, I knew rationally it was... wrong, but my dad was dead. I had no family. I was angry at the world, at the Mob world, so I killed a lot of people and made a lot of money until Lamberto had Angie killed."

"Was that like losing your father all over again."

"Well," Maggie started, offering a sarcastic laugh, "Angie was no real father. That wasn't his way, but he looked out for me. He was the only kind of family I did have. Then they killed him. They had an ambush waiting for me in Cleveland. I didn't know that man was a special agent. Believe me or not, but if I'd known one of those men was an FBI special agent, I'd have never taken the job. If Angie knew, he wouldn't have contracted me for it. I only killed people who were in the game. I got

Lamberto, Johnny Marrone, wish I would have finished off Smith, but there just wasn't time that night," Maggie said and exhaled a breath. "Do you love Braddock?"

"I'm hardly going to discuss my personal life with you."

"I think you lost your sister, your father, you were a FBI special agent for a long time and never married. You're still not married."

"That's none of your—"

"You come back here two years ago and solve Jessie's murder and you couldn't have done it without Braddock. The news accounts don't frame it that way, but you read between the lines, that's the true story of it all. In a way, he saved you. He gave you a life you didn't think you would ever have. Look at you now? Back in Manchester Bay, living with him, helping raise his son."

Tori shook her head. Maggie was working her.

"Rob saved me. I'd disappeared, had become Maggie Peterson, hair stylist at a Great Cuts in a dingy strip mall in South Minneapolis, keeping my head down, trying not to draw any attention, not sure if I could even stay in Minneapolis or have to be on the move. He came into the salon as a walk-in, still in his black basketball coaching sweats, his black hair swept back, four days of rugged stubble. I was done for the day, but I took one look at him—"

"And you weren't done for the day."

"I thought he was gorgeous, Tori," Maggie said wistfully. "I cut his hair, we flirted a bit, but I didn't think anything of it after he left."

"Oh, you thought about it. You know you thought about it."

"Sure did. And then he came back a week later and then kept coming back. I sensed he was going to ask me out and I knew I would have to say no. I was on the run, hiding, a target of the FBI and Mob. I wasn't out of the woods. I couldn't, shouldn't put someone at risk. Especially someone with two young children at the time. Then he asked."

"And you said yes."

"It just came out. My heart overruled my head. I hadn't felt anything in so long. He made me feel something again." Maggie paused. "I didn't deserve the life he gave me. And he deserved so much better. Now, ten years later, he has lost a second wife. His children have lost a second mom. Killing all those men? That doesn't keep me up at night. What I did to Rob, Ellen, and Brian? That... guts me." Maggie paused, letting out a sigh. "You understand loss, Tori. You and Braddock. You both understand what it means to have someone there for you one minute and they're gone forever the next."

Tori shook her head. "At least you got to say goodbye. I never got to do that."

"Trust me when I tell you, it's small consolation. The person you loved is still gone and you can never get them back. The pain is the same."

Tori looked out to the lake, the waves rolling along, thinking of how long it took her to put what happened to Jessie and her father behind her. It took nearly twenty years to learn a hard truth. "I had to go on living. Because that's what Jessie and my dad would have wanted."

"That's what I want Rob to do. What happened is my fault, Tori. Mine and mine alone. You owe me nothing. I'm asking for Rob, and Ellen and Brian too. Behind all the tough façade you put up, you're a very kind soul, Tori. You and Braddock could help Rob."

"And tell him you asked me to."

"Don't ever mention my name or that we spoke," Maggie insisted. "I don't want him to even think about me being out there. I want him and the kids to let me go, purge me from their memory, and move on. I think it would help them if you looked in and encouraged them to do that."

Tori sighed. "I'll think about it."

"That's all I ask. Goodbye, Tori."

Maggie clicked off.

Tori looked down at her phone. "Huh."

"What?" Braddock asked, returning with a charcuterie tray. "Who was that on the call?"

"Would you believe Maggie Duncan?"

"You're kidding."

"Yeah," Tori replied, shaking her head. "Will you do something with me?"

* * *

Tuesday morning.

Knock! Knock! Knock!

Rob Duncan opened the front door, holding a coffee cup. "Special Agent Hunter, Detective Braddock, good morning. To what do I owe the visit?"

"Social visit," Braddock said easily.

"We wanted to stop by and see how you were doing," Tori added. "Do you have any more coffee?"

Rob Duncan looked to his cup and then to them. "Sure do. Why don't you come on in?"

"We'd like that."

A LETTER FROM ROGER

I'm thankful that you've taken the time to read *The Snow Graves*. If you did enjoy it and want to keep up to date with all my latest releases, just sign up at the following link. Your email address will never be shared, and you can unsubscribe at any time.

www.bookouture.com/roger-stelljes

The great joy of writing a series is that I'm provided the opportunity to continually expand on the canvas of the world of Tori, Braddock, and Manchester Bay. It allows me to get inside their minds and see and write the world as they're seeing and experiencing it. Even more, I get to take northern Minnesota and the lakes area I've visited all my life and turn it into my own little world, taking all the pieces I love and adding to it. And, in this book, I was even able to go beyond Minnesota to another favorite place of mine, Chicago, and bring you a little flavor of that. In a word, it's all just *fun*. Every day I wake up thinking about this world I've created for Tori, Braddock, and the gang, and I hope you enjoy reading their adventures every bit as much as I do writing them.

One of the best parts of writing is seeing the reaction from readers, both those who have read all my books and those new to the scene. My goal every time I write is to give you, the reader, what I always look for in a book myself. A story that excites you, puts you on edge, makes you think, pulls at the heartstrings on occasion, and always makes you want to read just one more page, one more chapter, because you just couldn't put it down.

If you enjoyed the story, I would greatly appreciate it if you could leave a short review. Receiving feedback from readers is important to me in developing and writing my stories but is also vital in helping to persuade others to pick up one of my books for the first time.

If you enjoyed *The Snow Graves*, and it's your first time with Tori, Braddock, and their friends, they can also be found in *Silenced Girls*, *The Winter Girls*, *The Hidden Girl*, *Missing Angel* and in more stories to come.

All the best,

Roger

www.RogerStelljes.com

f facebook.com/rogerstelljesbooks

🐦 twitter.com/RogerStelljes

📷 instagram.com/rogerstelljes

ACKNOWLEDGMENTS

A book doesn't come to publication without the help of many others. Many thanks to Ellen Gleeson and the ever-growing team at Bookouture. I truly appreciate the chance to work with all of you as we bring these stories to life. And, as always, I wish to thank my wife, Sue, for her support and willingness to continually and bravely stand in the line of fire when her author husband gets cranky about her very on-point story critiques. They always make the story better, honey.

Made in the USA
Middletown, DE
01 May 2023

29793059R00248